Season's Sacrifice

Jack Taylor Cases:
Season's Sacrifice

by C. N. Wynn

CNWynn Publications
P.O. Box 328, Cheswold, DE 19936

Special thanks to these teachers: Mrs. McDougal and Mrs. Cauf-White, who taught me just how much numbers influence life. English teachers Mr. Rowland and Ms. Beck, who guided me into new literature and how to analyze it. And Mr. Knight and Mr. Rinker, who gave me the appreciation of art in music. Without your teachings, I would never have made it to page one.

For my parents, whose constant encouragement and pride drive me to fulfill even the most difficult challenges, no matter the giant obstacles standing in the way.

Evidence

Season's Sacrifice

Chapter 1
Trials & Error

"You'll have to move faster than that to survive this, son," called out the exhausted-looking Spirit of Father's Day, with far too many striped and obscure-looking neckties around his collar. "Use their strengths against them. Be aware of your surroundings!"

Jack barely listened to the spirit's advice. Instead, he scanned the fenced-in training area before quickly ducking behind a blockade, lost in thought about a single number. *Four…* It was the one number Jack couldn't get out of his head as he squatted, panting. He wiped the sweat from his forehead with his shoulder of his shirt. *Four…* The number of hours he trained in both combat then survival methods each day. *Four…* The number of people motivating him to fight.

His mother, his lost father, the unintended partner Sonny, and lastly, Teddy. Four was the number of pounds the short spear he clutched during training each day weighed and the number of months that had passed since he'd healed from the bruises, sprains, wounds, and training after the Sandman was struck by lightning. It seemed he'd become taller and stronger quickly in those four months coming into his growth spurt, much like a particular sprout enhanced by magic matured into a beanstalk. Four judges would be deciding his fate sometime very soon.

The Spirit of Saint Patrick's Day had expanded his excellent fortune to providing a useful training area to aid in Jack's preparation for the upcoming challenges. The yard was similar to an outdoor martial arts dojo, with soft mats placed around a spacious field of peaceful grass. Wooden practice dummies and obstacles like metal trees, climbing ropes, and deep sandpits were laid out around a stone fountain. Donations from some supportive spirits, like the garden patch from Dr. de Luca, the Spirit of Valentine's Day, had grown taller by the day into a small forest.

Jack dodged glowing balls of red, green, and blue shot from small cannons throughout the terrain. Despite the cloud-covered open sky above him and the warm summer breeze, the fences surrounding the courtyard of Cloud Three simply reminded him of the cell he'd been returning to daily.

Jack's dark curly mop of hair clung to his face stubbornly as he gripped the splintering wood spear, thinking about what was coming. The challenges set by the Four Seasons were known to be a fitting punishment to dreamers. Dozens of wandering kids had experienced the challenges, yet few had escaped and eventually turned to a handful of stories. Each had been altered so many times over the years that only the basic plots of their adventures were really accurate once they returned home. And after he rescued his father, getting home was precisely what Jack planned to do.

Glowing balls continued to whiz by his ear as he used his spear to dig a buried shield out of the sandpit. He used it to move farther into the open, but the cannons pelted him immediately. The Spirit of Father's Day shouted something, but Jack couldn't hear him with the constant dings of balls bouncing off the shield. He still hadn't spoken to Father about the message from Luminista he received on a birthday card during his first day in Cloud City. It was a clear warning for him not to trust Father, but he didn't understand why. The spirit had helped and protected him since his time in the Holiday Hotel. He couldn't be sure if she was referring to Father or someone Jack hadn't met yet. It kept him up some nights, but lately, that wasn't the only reason he had difficulty sleeping.

"You can't hide forever there, Jacky-boy." The gruff voice of the eclipse player, Tour Guide Morris, projected over the courtyard. Jack remained hidden behind the shield as balls hit it again and again.

Over the period, Jack had occasionally been visited and trained by other spirits. Each had provided tips to survive the challenge: military techniques from Redd Rocket, survival skills from Nina, and prayer and meditation from Ana and Amani. Even the April Fool's Spirit had come to cheer Jack on, although his lack of a functional funny bone left his jokes relatively flat and quite depressing, but Jack appreciated his effort all the same.

Jack's partner, Sonny, skipped into the area daily. He wondered if she continued to visit him out of guilt over their encounter with the Sandman and his symbol. At times, Jack grew resentful of her freedom, but each day she returned, he

~ 3 ~

could tell how bad she felt and how much she wished their positions were switched. Jack was sure she would eventually stop visiting altogether, but he hoped he was wrong.

Jack watched glowing, spiked balls of ice and flame fly overhead, and footsteps approached. It was the last day of his training—not only had he not seen Sonny once, but Father seemed colder and more distant than ever. It had grown easier for Jack to no longer see his own father accidentally whenever he glanced at the spirit. However, as June sixteenth came closer, the urge to look twice became stronger. Father's Day was already a natural struggle for Jack, who felt abandoned by his own dad, but that day, it seemed to push him harder—or due to his holiday coming, Father was less emotionally protective. Imagining his mother waiting for him in his world, his own father lost somewhere in this world, didn't help. *And now Sonny's missing training…*

"Keep your head in the game, son!" Father yelled from the side. "You're almost fourteen now. I'm sure the beasts and monsters the Four Seasons have created for you won't treat you like a child—and neither can we."

Jack was suddenly surrounded by all three Morris brothers he had met during his travel of the city. They were just as strong and agile off the field as they were on, and most days, Jack wished he had a bottle of Fiz to boost himself. Butler Morris aimed the larger cannons at a distance, spraying the field with red flaming balls that singed the grass as they ricocheted off the deteriorating blockade. Tour Guide Morris and Banker Morris attacked Jack from different angles, swinging large clubs. With Father's constant instructions in his ear, Jack tilted the shield up and sidestepped Tour Guide Morris's swing, fighting back.

Dodging the swing, Jack struck the tour guide hard in his chest just before a second swing came. Rolling between the two brothers, Jack hid from a string of burning red shots. Smoke trailed him as he dove, grabbing onto a climbing rope. Jack climbed higher, struggling with the short spear as he maneuvered the line, rotating around it so the continued cannon fire would miss him.

"Watch his trajectory, TGM," Banker Morris warned.

"Might as well come down, kid!" the tour guide barked. "Only a matter of time before that rope catches fire. Only place to go is down!"

"Or you could be nice and just give up?" Jack suggested. "Just brainstorming ideas."

Sure enough, one of the balls landed just below the rope, and a flame began crawling up toward Jack like a blazing snake. Using his legs, he swung the line until he was near the fence. Clumps of burning rope fell to the ground as the fire spread farther up. Jack could feel the heat on his heels through his shoes, warming his ankles as he tried to concentrate. With a strong swing of his legs, he was able to reach the chain-link fence surrounding the courtyard. Pushing off hard, Jack leaped from the rope and kicked Tour Guide Morris, who stumbled back toward the garden patch. Vines snipped at him as he regained his footing. Jack was amazed by just how agile the Morris brother was as he landed softly on the ground.

Jack went right to the tour guide's legs, attacking repeatedly while sidestepping swinging clubs. Ducking and spinning behind the tallest Morris brother, he used the tour guide's massive height against him by striking behind his knees with both hands.

Tour Guide Morris began falling back, flailing for anything to keep his balance. He found a hanging vine of the garden patch just before dropping in. "Almost had me for—"

Three monstrous thorny vines lashed out from the garden's darkness, wrapping around the Morris brother's body. It pulled him in instantly.

Banker Morris struck Jack from behind with the strength of a sledgehammer, almost knocking him into the garden patch, as well. Tumbling onto the ground, he quickly scurried up before a large orange flower with petals bigger than his head was able to reach him. He could feel the pain in his back but tried to gain as much distance from the banker as possible.

Butler Morris switched his ammunition to the green balls. Each created a spinning gust of wind around Jack as he rushed around the yard. Holding tightly to his spear, he moved in and out of the metal trees. More than a few times, the wind gusts were so strong, he had to hang on to a metal tree for support. Banker Morris, as the brother with the most girth, seemed to have no trouble taking a slow pace toward Jack, stalking him like a hunter. Jack knew he needed to use his speed and agility, rather than force, against the banker.

"There's no logical reason to run away at this point, Jack. I could go at this pace and withstand these effects far longer than you in this condition. I'm sure you've realized I've taken away many of your options with that last hit."

Jack slumped against the metal tree as shots bounced off the branches.

On the sidelines, the Spirit of Father's Day shook his head. "Don't look at me, son. You got yourself into this—figure a way out. Step into the battle. Don't run."

The glowing green balls continued to blow Jack away from the tree and closer to the sandpit, spreading sand all around as Butler Morris reloaded again. Banker Morris advanced on Jack, gaining speed like a rhino. Jack tried to think quickly as ice balls began freezing the tree. Frost spread across the tree's silvery finish, forming a cold, glossy finish and leaving pointed icicles on the branches. As the ice balls hit the ground, patches froze instantly, giving Jack an idea.

With his spear, he began hacking at the tree like a lumberjack, swinging with all the strength he had left. The spear vibrated in his hands, but he held tightly. Banker Morris charged faster with his massive club dragging on the ground just a few feet away from Jack. With a yell, Jack swung his spear at the tree one last time, causing the vibration to ripple through the metal and ice until an icicle fell to the ground. He kicked the icicle, causing it to glide across the frosted path toward Banker Morris just as he took his next step. The slick area threw the banker's massive size off balance, giving Jack the perfect large target.

With one hand, Jack swung the butt of his spear up like a golf club in an arc, hitting Banker Morris's chin and flipping him into the sandpit. After a moment, he was buried up to his waist, dazed and stuck in the sand.

"Just one more left." Jack eyed Butler Morris as he continued to aim at Jack. Rapid shots of frosty balls sprayed around him repeatedly as he strode closer to the last Morris brother. The balls of ice splattered the ground faster than ever, chilling large patches of the grass until Jack was finally hit in the leg. He stumbled, feeling the stinging frostbite paralyze him, beginning at his knee and spreading toward his ankle until he was dragging his foot.

"Poor organization and planning on your part, it seems!" Butler Morris called out, focusing his shots on his weakened opponent.

Jack leaned on the short spear, using it as a cane, edging closer to the side of the field. When the next shot was fired, it sailed toward Jack, and he tossed the spear up, caught it near its point, gripped it tightly like a baseball bat, and swung.

With a single strong swing, he hit the ball back at Butler Morris's cannon, where it froze the muzzle. The final Morris brother backed away from the gun as it began to vibrate violently. The components sparked and smoked, jammed with pressure. Jack hobbled to his right, taking aim. A few steps forward, he launched his spear as hard as he could. It struck the nose of the cannon, turning it back toward its controller. Butler Morris attempted to get up, but it was too late. The balls inside broke free from the corked muzzle and sprayed him against the wall until his entire body was an ice sculpture.

As the machine powered down, Jack breathed heavily yet smirked triumphantly.

"Jack!" Sonny called from outside the fence.

He turned to see the young journalist waving as she left a group of women draped in white cloths covering all but their faces, with the image of the sun patched on their arms. He was distracted for only a moment before his leg was swept from beneath him. He fell to the ground hard, and the Spirit of Father's Day stood above him, holding a dotted tie in one hand with the other end wrapped around Jack's leg.

"Didn't I warn you to watch your surroundings?" the holiday spirit asked.

"I was focused." Frustrated, Jack brushed himself off. "You just caught me off guard. I wasn't planning on *you* attacking me."

Father stroked his tie. "Sometimes you have to think with your heart, son, not your head. That's where your bravery lives. You'll be alone in the challenge, and outthinking people may not work all the time."

Jack slowly got to his feet. The Morris brothers assisted each other out of their predicaments. The Spirit of Father's Day waited as all the players walked out of the fenced area, clutching various parts of their bodies, shaking apart ice, sand, and plucking thorns as they went.

"Let me go again. I can get it right," Jack pleaded.

Father whipped his dotted tie around Jack's short spear still stuck in the cannon above. With a sharp tug, he retrieved the wooden practice weapon and handed it back to Jack. "No, your combat skills will suffice as is. With the limited amount of time we have, we need to wait for Nina to continue your survival training as soon as possible before—"

A side gate of the tall spiked fence burst open. Cloud Keeper Matthews, one of Jack's least favorite of Cloud City's law enforcement officers, known as J.A.C.K.s, stood beside another cloud keeper in the doorway. He, of course, would be one betting against Jack. "The four judges are ready to present their challenges tomorrow. The investigating detective is being briefed and has to prepare the prisoner."

The other cloud keeper remained silent with a blank expression, much like a robot, as Jack protested. "No, I'm not ready yet. I need more time to train. I still have to do survival studies and today's mind games with Dr. de Luca—"

"Too bad, kid. Your four months are up, and Old Man Winter decided to push the trial to today. Come on now."

Jack slammed his practice spear down harshly. "No, I can't go yet!"

Cloud Keeper Matthews made a movement toward the pouches on his belt. "Are we going to have a problem?"

Father turned to Jack, grasping him by the shoulders firmly. "Calm down, son. What have I told you about controlling yourself? You need to focus."

Breathing deeply through clenched teeth, Jack looked around the courtyard, caught Sonny's gaze, and held his fury back.

The spirit looked Jack over, and his demeanor changed. "The moment you step into the challenge, you will be ready, because you must be. You have been trained by the strongest spirits, and you will have an advisor watching over to aid you and offer advice."

"An advisor? You'll be my advisor?" Jack asked, hopefully.

The spirit returned a disappointing look. "I'm afraid not. With my holiday approaching, I won't even be in the city. I've arranged for another spirit to volunteer in my place. Redd is more than capable of advising you and is knowledgeable in all of your pieces of training and skills. His holiday is nearly a month away, and I don't expect the challenge to last that long. As your advisor, he will be able to send you advice in a way, to help you through. As long as you remain focused on your task, you will be fine. My best advice for you is not to get caught up in that world. Several dreamers remain there, unable to escape… or unwilling to."

Cloud Keeper Matthews cleared his throat. "Are we doing this the easy way or not?"

Jack nodded stubbornly in the J.A.C.K.'s direction. "Yeah, I'm ready."

Jack was escorted to his holding cell on Cloud Nine to change and clean up before being taken to the courtroom. He was marched down the same hall he'd been forced to walk through every day — one lined with the portraits of past dreamers who'd been subjected to the same fate he was approaching. Yet the young detective felt a new connection to the dreamers in each picture as if each one had a silent message of inspiration, wisdom, and warning. The stories and challenges he knew well were all more current than the ones near the hall's intersection.

The first portrait, which he usually never gave much thought to, depicted an older boy holding a golden hen and a quill of red and silver feathers, writing in a book as a monster and shadow fought behind him. Jack was sure the fading picture was thousands of years old. As he stepped closer to the J.A.C.K.s' headquarters, the portraits became newer and more recognizable. One portrayed a young man riding a magic carpet out of a cave. Another picture was of a younger boy pulling a large sword from a boulder, and in another, four brothers and sisters climbed into a closet. This continued until Jack reached the latest one—a portrait that should never have existed. The dreamer had cheated the system he'd deemed unjust.

Jack's sight lingered on Teddy longer than any of the others. He hadn't seen his flashlight the entire time he was locked away, as it had been collected and retained for evidence. The smug look on Teddy's face made Jack more aware of the challenge he would be entering, driving him to be better than the boy he was glaring at. Not for pride or admiration, but to know that he could be better than him, so when they did finally meet, Jack would be able to beat him for all the headaches he'd produced.

"So, Lach, did you hear?" Cloud Keeper Matthews asked the other officer. "The Investigator found a code in that instruction manual the kid dropped."

Jack's ears were buzzing for answers, but he knew there was no point in asking. There were only three people the cloud keepers would refer to as "kids," and if they weren't talking about him or Sonny, it had to be Teddy.

"Yup, and led him into a room of Phoenix's mansion," the other officer continued as Jack listened intently. "The others said it was a trap, though. The door closed and locked, and he was trapped somewhere for three days. When the J.A.C.K.s went in, it was empty, like he vanished. Some trapdoor or something."

"Yup, but somehow, he made it out, and not only that. He found the—"

"Hey, not in front of the dreamer." The other cloud keeper stopped him. "Still a case going on, and questioning to be done."

He always idolized the lead detective because of the stories he'd heard about not only him but also the training he'd put himself through to sharpen his mind and skill to find the less-obvious clues. Apparently, the cases he'd solved were incredible, although there weren't very many evil spirits in this world.

After a typical full day of training in combat, survival, and puzzles, he found it hard to sleep when he returned to his cell. The room held very few items. A few books were piled in a corner. They contained information on landscapes, first-aid healing methods, and enemies from past challenges, including cave monsters, wars between warlocks, and elemental beings. One book detailed the history of Cloud City, including the Sandman. Yet, learning the history of the holidays and the spirits he'd been trained by was more interesting than nearly anything else.

He would study the history of Valentine's Day as a warrior priest performing secret marriages against the wishes of an empire. The Spirit of Mother's Day had fostered unwanted children when she was alive, and the devoted weatherman turned Spirit of Groundhog's Day had died alerting a small town with no communication about an impending meteor strike. Phoenix was ignited with a unique spiritual life source every new year, not only giving him a new appearance but also a new personality with only fragments of memories from his other afterlives.

Jack had found very little information on Mr. Shadow, except that he'd served in the Navy and traveled for several years in his youth. Unlike the other spirits, Mr. Shadow did not have a history that seemed to match his holiday. One book did notate that Mr. Shadow had spent over half of his life in the dark, but even that was unhelpful.

It was strange for Jack to find his own name listed among a chapter of notable citizens. At first glance, he was sure the book was referring to his father, until reading the details of his profile notes.

Jackson Eli Taylor, Jr. For aiding in the arrest of the political terrorist, the Sandman, and shortly after (according to the opinion of several citizens, then wrongly) arrested for conspiracy and currently awaiting trial in the challenge.

At times, Jack would wake up in a cold sweat, unsure if he was still stuck in a never-ending dream, unable to wake up. The effects of the Sandman's dream sand had been so strong that both Dr. de Luca and the witch doctor from Cloud One were forced to work together to cleanse the city. For the first month, lines of people entered Dr. de Luca's small therapy center to be checked for sleepwalking. Some were more difficult than others, and a unique dream catcher device was eventually made to detect those still affected.

Once the doors to his cell were locked, Jack was usually left to himself for an hour. He changed into his usual pair of jeans and leather jacket over a T-shirt. He couldn't stop counting the time, no matter how hard he tried not to think about it. It wasn't until he noticed a pair of sneakers near his cell door that he looked up from his bed.

"Wasn't expecting you to show up." Jack sat up.

"Well, you are normally stuck on a puzzle at this point during the day, aren't you?" Sonny responded. "Are you all right? You look exhausted."

Sonny usually visited daily, playfully teasing Jack as she documented his progress. She would spend part of her day following Nina, the Spirit of Thanksgiving, as she presided over the Cloud City News, or finding new information about the city from books and the Sisters of the Sun. In the afternoon, she would visit Jack until he was forced to return to his jail cell in the J.A.C.K.s headquarters, and at night, before she went to stay in Lucky's penthouse, she would tell him stories. They were always absurd tales her grandfather had told her growing up as if they actually happened: stories of a vain man in search of a perfect rose, seven brothers taking seven different paths, and witches posing as beggars.

"Haven't been sleeping a lot lately," Jack admitted.

"I understand that too well," Sonny responded mournfully. Lately, she hadn't seemed as annoyingly optimistic as usual. The one noticeable change was what the aspiring journalist didn't talk about. At any mention of the Sandman's control of her, she would instantly change the conversation or find a reason to leave. With the challenge just around the corner, Jack felt a greater need to know what scars she was carrying in her thoughts that she refused to share.

"Why haven't you told me about it? I figure it's like being hypnotized, but you won't tell me."

Sonny started to turn but stopped herself. "I don't sleep well anymore, either. It was like a nudge. I thought I was making my own decisions, but something was making suggestions, pushing me in a direction, like leaving the dream catcher or the moment in Holly Woods when we nearly—"

She cleared her throat, and Jack knew the moment she was talking about.

"What else?" he asked, hoping she'd continue.

"Then there were moments I would be listening to someone who wasn't really there give me direction. It sounds insane now, but I could've sworn holiday spirits or someone on our side was helping us and speaking to me directly when you weren't around, but they gave me compelling reasons not to speak of them. Yet, that wasn't the worst case."

"What was that?"

"Sleepwalking," she admitted. "It was as if I could see myself doing things I couldn't control. I knew it was wrong, but I was pushed to keep doing it as if I really wanted to. Sometimes I would black out completely, and moments later, I would come back, and minutes were gone. It was like a skip in my memory, but it would be filled with things I would normally do… I never want to be used that way again."

Jack instantly felt terrible for never recognizing how different she was behaving before. Sonny studied him, meeting his eye. "Why do you ask? You don't feel as if—"

"No, I'm fine." Jack shook his head. "Only my life on the line, not too long from now. What's that you got?"

"I wanted to show you a book I found when I left the Sisters of the Sun. But they wouldn't let me keep the book. Apparently, it's ancient, but I was able to take a page out."

Jack raised an eyebrow in question as Sonny pulled out her book. "Are those the women who walk around in white bedsheets?"

"They're not bedsheets," Sonny argued. "They're ceremonial clothes of light, and you know that's where I've been getting all the books I've found. They seem to like me. The Sisters keep telling me I have a very old spirit. Do you remember I told you they follow the Being of Light and prepare for her return?"

"Right, the statues." Jack rolled his eyes. "You know, I'm working with a short time frame here."

"Well, I finally found a book about what we've been discussing. This might be what you've been looking for about your father. There's a chapter here about the being of darkness, death, and something about the… about the Sandman." She cringed. "I found a page that could help."

Jack stared at her for several moments as she slipped a folded page to him through the bars. He took the yellowing paper. "I haven't heard anything about the cloud keepers finding him yet. There may not be a point anymore, but if there's even a possibility to bring my dad back home with me—"

"Don't let Father know I gave this to you." She took Jack's hand. "You know he'd be furious if he knew you were still looking."

Jack realized her hand was still on his through the bars when a cloud keeper called out. "Are you the other dreamer? Sonny?"

"Yes…" she responded.

"The judges will need you to witness," the cloud keeper said. "The officers will escort you to the new courtroom."

Sonny looked at Jack. "No worries. You'll be brilliant and brave. Just think, what would Sonny do?" She smiled.

"You be brave," Jack said to her. "I'll just be logical."

Jack waited until no one was near his cell before unfolding the page, being sure no one was watching him. He expanded it so quickly that he nearly ripped through Sonny's crisp edges of the page. He skimmed through it quickly, catching a few words about the dreams fading in and out from one plane to this one, death's relation to sleep, and reanimating life using power from the Sandman. His eyes darted across the page, reading the lines when the lead detective stepped in front of his cell.

"Good news, I hope." The lead investigator removed his dark glasses, and a small smile curled on his dark-brown skin. "I'm sure you could use some good news before this event."

"I could probably use a flamethrower, too, if you have one to spare, Detective Young."

"I see the snide remarks and games continue, Mr. Taylor. I do happen to have news for you, as well as some information you may find interesting."

Jack grasped the bars. "I'm listening."

"Before my death, I was a soldier and then a Texas Ranger. I've remade the officers in this city and created a program to ready officers in other areas. My disciplinary practice has been tough but effective. This practice has led to some new discoveries about the other dreamer."

Jack's head popped up. "Sonny?"

"No, the other one," Detective Young said. "We may have discovered evidence that he has been maneuvering in and out of the rooms of the New Year's Spirit's estate. As he'd been hiding there for so long before and with so many rooms available, he knows it very well, but we are getting much closer. Your enemies may try to manipulate this challenge, and I intend to see that does not happen."

"Why are you telling me all this?" Jack asked.

The detective unlocked his cell. "Information is a powerful tool, Mr. Taylor. And I was told you want to be a detective."

A few officers stepped through the main door, helmets, and visors on and shields ready, looking at Jack and surrounding his cell.

"I do," Jack said timidly.

"If you complete your challenge and I believe it is something you truly want, and if you're not a caped superhero with a grudge, then I will train you once you return." The detective put his enhanced sunglasses back on. "In the meantime, show me what you're capable of while you're inside."

He stopped and tilted his head before looking at Jack a little harder as if examining his movement until an officer tapped his shoulder. "Sir, the judges will be arriving in the courtroom soon."

Jack recognized the voice as Cloud Keeper Matthews's.

The detective hesitated then turned and continued out. The two shielded officers escorted Jack out, with one cloud keeper remaining in front and one behind him. Several J.A.C.K.s they passed were discussing matters privately and exchanging looks between each other then at Jack. Just before being marched out of earshot, he heard various whispers of "Father" and "Old Man Winter." Some compared him with other dreamers, including Teddy, Alice, Robin, and Arthur.

As Jack and his escorts neared the portal to the courtroom, Father joined them, wearing a suit not quite as tattered as his others, several formal ties around his neck… and a look of disapproval. "You're still looking, aren't you, Jack?"

"What are you talking about?" Although Jack figured he knew what the spirit meant.

"Books on bringing someone back from the afterlife? Sending Sonny out to different places for research that she wouldn't normally need to do. And you've been talking in your sleep lately. Sometimes, while you're awake."

"Sonny told you?" Jack guessed, bitterly.

The Father's Day Spirit removed his wallet from his back pocket. It was empty of any money, but hundreds and hundreds of wallet-sized photos unfurled from it, going on and on and continuing to change. "The children I've come in contact with. A parent always knows when something is wrong with their kids. I've warned you how dangerous it would be to tamper with these things. It would be a terrible mistake to dive any farther into these pages. Trust me, son. You don't want that trouble. We do have other pressing matters to go over now, of course."

He explained what would happen next and offered some last-minute encouragement. "Your verdict has already been decided, so there isn't much to be worried about in that aspect. That is why you've been trained, but you should still remain respectful. The judges pride themselves with creating these imaginative and difficult challenges, usually trying to outdo one another, and it's been half a century since the last one. I wouldn't be surprised if several spirits come to witness it. The one season you should be worried about is Winter, but luckily, each challenge is chosen at random from one of the four."

"Why should I be worried about him?" Jack asked, remembering what Spring had once said about fearing an old man, yet that was before he'd known she was a judge.

"Each season has developed a preference for certain challenges," Father explained. "Spring has an affection for nature, so her challenges are more landscape friendly and full of fantasy, and although very broad in scope, they're not quite as difficult to escape. Summer… well, he prefers a mix of freewill and extreme adventure under much warmer climates. He usually creates island and aquatic challenges and the occasional pirate ships or underwater ventures."

They turned a corner to the barred green portal that would transport them to the hidden courtroom, and Father continued hastily, "Autumn has always been the *fairest* of the four judges, so to speak. She rewards patience, kindness, and goodwill while punishing what she sees as mean, disrespectful, impatient dreamers, usually in a manner suiting the crime. To this day, I believe there's still an ungrateful and over-confident young girl belching blueberry juice lost in a forgotten challenge somewhere."

Jack hesitated. "And Winter?"

A frown spread across the spirit's face as if his optimism had suddenly been removed by an eraser. "Like the season he represents, Winter's challenges are always just as harsh and cold as he has been, and I'm afraid it will be even worse for you."

"Why worse for me? What did I ever do to him?"

"I believe it's not you, as much as your namesake," Father continued. "Winter is probably the oldest of the judges. He is the last remaining judge chosen by the Two Beings. The others were picked after the previous judges' retirement. As such, he can be extremely short-tempered with the untraditional. And with so much ancient power, he does not like being refused."

It took a moment, but Jack realized who the dispute was really about. "This is about my father again, isn't it?"

The Spirit of Father's Day nodded. "Your father is a gifted architect, both in his life and after. Each season has a palace somewhere hidden that was made specifically for them. The courtroom serves the public as needed for judgment. However, Winter was driven to create a legacy prison that would be unmatched, to keep the criminals and dangerous items away from the public. The perfect prison system would be remembered for both its ability and design—the ability to hold prisoners so well that even with a small group of guards posted, no one could discover an escape. Yet, only your father could create it properly."

"And my dad refused to help him."

"Your father felt differently about building this prison than he did with other buildings he'd designed," the spirit explained. "He did not want to be a part of something that would simply feed an old man's ego, and creating a place of negative confinement on a distant island was not something he would be proud of."

"But the prison was created, wasn't it?" Jack said. "That's where Trick and the Sandman are being held, isn't it?"

"Yes, but without your father's designs. This is only my best conclusion, but I believe these are the reasons Winter is no friend of yours. The architect who designed it did an incredible job of creating a maze inside the prison that is well hidden. However, it still depends on a larger group of people, and to Winter, there is a way to escape because of that error."

They stopped in front of the portal and waited for the protection bars to be lowered before they could step through.

"What error?" Jack asked. "Can the Sandman and others escape? Is it possible?"

"Yes, unfortunately, it is for one reason."

The bars of the portal slid across, and the investigating detective walked out. As he walked by, his glasses gleamed, and he adjusted the baton on his waist.

"People…" Father continued. "Not only to guard it but to predict prisoner movements. If there is a flaw or an error in the system, it would be emotional, irrational, or the slightest moment of poor judgment. Simply put, the only crack in the system is it depends on us."

The detective made his way over to Jack and Father. "The judges will be ready to present the challenges in a moment. Winter was in a rush to get your sentencing done today. You were lucky he waited this long. If it wasn't for one of my officers temporarily misplacing your paperwork, you'd have entered the challenge at midnight without rest."

He nodded to Father, walking by them, heading back toward the hall. "Any final advice you have for him, this may be your last chance before we take him in."

Father nodded. "Thank you, Detective."

"So what kind of challenges should I expect from him?" Jack asked.

Father looked down. "His challenges are made for warriors. For the type of dreamers who can outlast the harshest environments, tough wars, brutal animals, and nearly impossible puzzles. But I do have some good news."

"Good news?" Jack asked.

"It's a weapon of sorts that you'll be familiar with. Something to help you in the challenge."

"Like a tank?" Jack asked, hopefully. "Because I'm sure that would really be helpful."

"Not quite." Father removed a handkerchief from his suit pocket and handed it to Jack. He unwrapped a box with a small wooden cuboid inside, a bit wider than a roll of quarters and the length of a ruler. "Very little about the challenge has been revealed. As you know, I've created totems that create a bridge between both worlds for every challenge since I've been a holiday. Every totem has been based on the original created by the two beings to offer the dreamers a fair chance at redemption."

Chatter funneled in from beyond the portal, where the people inside the courtroom waited for the sentencing to begin, but Father ignored it. "I was given the basic objective of your challenge that all four seasons agreed to include. You will be tasked with locating the heart of a mountain separating the thin veil between science and magic, and enabling your return to Cloud City. At the moment, this is all I know, but it was enough to create this."

Jack examined the wooden piece as if it were a toy. It had six sides like a cube or die, but it was long enough that he could fully grip it in his hand. The top held the image of a leaf, while a mechanical cog had been engraved in the bottom. Several notches circled the entirety of its length. He swung it curiously. "I think I'd prefer the tank. I mean, what kind of weapon is it? I don't think it'll do much damage to hit over the head with?"

"It's a totem. *Your* totem, actually. This is what will allow you into the challenge. Just press the gear on the bottom firmly with your thumb, and you'll begin to see what it can do."

Jack did as he was instructed, and instantly, the wood began separating within the notches, revealing tiny gears and thin metal plates expanding the wood to longer and slightly thicker lengths before becoming one solid piece again. When it was finished, it was nearly the length of Jack himself.

The holiday spirit presented it proudly as if it were the most exquisite piece he'd ever made. "This is Nucalibur. It's a fishing rod, like those made for hundreds of years before fishing poles with spools of wire were invented. This has been perfectly carved from a strong ancient wood usually used to make battle staffs, and the recycled metal of a legendary sword was used for the metal. Lightweight and capable of beneficial magic. Once I present it to the judges, it will be provided for you in the challenge and belong to you when you return."

Jack had never been fishing before. He and his father had always planned on taking a trip for just the two of them, where he would finally learn. After his father had broken the promise of a trip to a nearby lake in Pennsylvania for the third time because of work obligations, Jack had given up hope. He didn't miss the irony of it at all, though.

"It feels familiar." Jack struck the air, somehow already adapting to the weight and size. "Like I've used it before."

Father smiled. "It should. This is why I've been training you on the spear. Twist the notch of the cog to the left and then to the right."

He turned the bottom notch, and a long, wiry string with a metal hook at the end unraveled. As he bobbed it up and down, the line pulsed and became longer and longer. When he turned the bottom notch to the right, the string retracted fully, and a sharp metal point sprung from the end, identical to his practice spear, although much sharper and clearly not for practice purposes. Jack spun it effortlessly as if the sole purpose of his hands were to hold it, like his flashlight.

The cloud keeper in front of Jack appeared oblivious. Yet Cloud Keeper Matthews glared at Jack's new totem as if he were about to lose a bet.

Father pointed along the fishing rod, offering his final bit of advice. "The button located atop the rod with the leaf will enable the magic of the holiday spirits who have blessed it. Several of whom you have trained with. You'll only need to twist the notch of the holiday."

Jack pressed the leaf, and the pointed end retracted. The length of the rod began to glow, emblazoned with ten illuminated symbols, including a heart, a wishbone, a green clover, and a striped candy cane.

"When you enter, learn the ways of the people, stay focused, and be patient," the Father's Day Spirit added. "Your advisor will be able to see your actions, similar to any highlighted moments you have. The days that pass here will be a small fraction of what you experience there, and when you return, not much time should have gone at all."

Jack's eyebrow rose. "Kinda like my time in this world?"

Father checked the portal nervously. "Similar. Their ways could be primal or much older in tradition, but these periods are always an important time of possibilities, and you could influence the people you interact with greatly. If you recall, Teddy had an issue with trusting others to help. While you've been dependent on it to make decisions or gather your confidence, your mind will not be enough there. You will need courage, as well — and plenty of it."

"Great pep talk." Jack sighed. "It's all right, though. Once I get out, it'll be like none of this ever happened, right? I'll wake up back here, and it'll be fine. That is why dreamers have stories afterward, right? They survive, but it's not real."

Father turned and looked at Jack thoughtfully. "Son, if you learn nothing else from me, remember this: just because you can't prove something did happen, doesn't mean it didn't."

Jack thought about that, wondering what effect this challenge would have on him. He felt strong and ready physically, but mentally, he was less confident. He hoped the Independence Day Spirit would be prepared to help him when the time came.

"I'd wager you've been well prepared for what's to come." A man stepped out of the portal; Jack felt his ancient aura right away. He wore a shimmering silver robe with crimson red trimming. His face was familiar, like someone Jack had known when he was much younger. However, the man was at the very least, thirty. The man was tall and muscular, much like Redd Rocket. It wasn't until he adjusted his robe, revealing a necklace of a small hourglass, that Jack connected the dots.

"Phoenix?" Jack asked, handing the totem back to Father.

"Yes." The New Year Spirit smiled politely. "I rarely get to witness such a reaction as I don't often leave my throne for my unnecessarily increased protection, you see. I apologize I have not been able to visit our young hero during the training, but I did want to wish you a safe return today. After all, you've done for this city, and myself, so many times, I believe I owe you at least that."

Jack was at a loss to see just how much the spirit had changed from the first night at his father's hotel. No one had even recognized the spirit because he was only ever seen on the night of New Year's Eve and on New Year's Day, when his holiday was celebrated, never throughout the year. However, Jack was able to see him just three weeks after his birth, when Phoenix appeared as a young boy. With a thin scruffy beard and slicked-back platinum blond hair, he was nearly unrecognizable from the boy.

Jack was only able to mutter, "Thanks," as he continued to stare at the city's oldest holiday.

"I dearly wanted to help in the creation of your totem, but I was unable to be away from my throne for so long." Phoenix examined the rod. "It seems you've gained quite a bit of magic from other powerful members of the union, and… perhaps one other is missing?" His eyes narrowed—counting the symbols, Jack assumed.

"Mr. Shadow, for one," Father answered. "He claimed he would not be eligible to assist, although I can't understand why, and to be honest, he is not exactly a big supporter of dreamers… or of Jack."

"Or of anyone, it seems, since those Y2K accusations thirteen years ago," Phoenix added.

"He's a heartless old man. I'm not surprised," Jack said flatly. "Makes me wonder if he and Winter have a members-only club yet."

Jack thought back to a few months ago when he'd spotted a picture of his neighbor, Mrs. Johnson, and a young girl on Mr. Shadow's mantelpiece before he'd struggled with Dr. de Luca over a jar. He still didn't know what any of that meant.

"Well, I am confident this holiday hero will be perfectly capable with the tools and skills he already has without my, or Shadow's, assistance." Phoenix withdrew a black metallic wristwatch from his pocket. "However, I did bring you something. I've had another brilliant inventor modernize an old pocket watch into a watch undetectable by the judges when you face your challenge. It's been in my lifeline for nearly a millennium, and I've kept it safe in my personal vault."

Jack looked deeply into the watch face as the luminescent green second hand ticked away. He could see the spirit's face reflected in it and immediately felt awkward. "I can't take this from you. What if it gets broken or I lose it?"

"I'm positive you will keep it safe, and it will keep you safe." Phoenix smiled. "It has a touch of power from daylight savings, and it may come in handy. This city owes you a debt of gratitude, not a trial. As do I. Honestly, I would not be here now as I am, if it were not for you, Jack. This will help you keep time and perhaps aid you in a speedy return."

Jack took the watch gingerly, wrapped it around his left wrist, and clasped it securely. It fit snugly without being tight. He muttered a small thank you before the spirit nodded at him.

"I know our traditions, and the events here may seem unusual to you, but I trust when your journey ends, it will all make sense to you and you will be better for it." Phoenix took a deep breath. "Well, I should return. I wish I could attend your proceedings. I am mildly surprised Shadow has decided to attend."

"Mr. Shadow's here?" Jack asked. "Probably hoping to see me eaten by a dragon."

The portal pulsed and the murmuring inside quieted quickly.

"All right, kid, it's time to go in." Cloud Keeper Matthews pushed Jack forward.

Phoenix put a hand on Jack's shoulder. "I must be getting back to my throne. I know you've learned this for yourself, but try to remember that every cloud has a silver lining."

Jack nodded. He knew immediately what Phoenix was referring to. Just four months ago, Jack and Sonny had both made it out of an impossible situation with the Sandman thanks to a silver lining in the clouds and the luck that it had been Sonny's birthday. At the time, he'd had no idea why everyone in Cloud City used that phrase so often or that it was true, but it didn't seem to annoy him nearly as much as it once had.

"The rewards waiting for you when you return will help you maintain motivation in the challenge." The spirit continued walking down the hall, but this comment caused Jack to stop everyone at once.

"Wait—what do you mean my 'rewards'?" he asked, looking at Father.

The spirit closed his eyes tightly then exchanged a short look with Phoenix. Jack noticed it instantly and became defensive. "What haven't you told me?"

"I didn't want you to be distracted when you enter the challenge," Father said.

"I apologize. I didn't realize the boy didn't know," the New Year's Spirit said before he departed.

"What don't I know?" Jack asked again.

"Dreamers are given a reward if they return from the challenge," Father explained. "Something you desperately want. Until recently, I assumed it would be your flashlight, but that is now part of the evidence. I'm not exactly sure of your reward for escaping, yet I have a theory. But, Jack, you have to understand these challenges are meant to test your limits. You may have to choose whether to save one life of someone important to you or the lives of many. Possibly sacrifice your own well-being by diving into the mouth of a beast and fighting for your survival. Or possibly something crueler: deciding the destiny of innocent people."

"No, there's always another way if you look hard enough," Jack said.

Father sighed. "A coin only has two sides, Jack. Just two options. You could argue a third option would be not to flip the coin, but then we would not be moving forward, would we? Sometimes you have to make that difficult choice, son — no matter how hard it is — or you may lose everything."

Jack felt there was something else left unsaid as the cloud keepers began pushing him through the portal. "Is that all? Nothing about this reward? That's what you didn't want to tell me?"

"No." The spirit followed as Jack was guided in, struggling to listen. "Your father was found by the cloud keepers today. I believe he will be in the courtroom."

Chapter 2
Sentencing

Chatter began the moment Jack stepped into the courtroom. Spirits filled the benches and even more lined the back walls to watch the proceedings. They all turned their heads as if he were a species they'd never witnessed.

He continued following Cloud Keeper Matthews up the aisle, passing more familiar spirits. Nina, Mother, Dr. de Luca, and Anna, the Spirit of Hanukah, along with several others, gave him encouraging smiles.

Redd Rocket, the Spirit of Independence Day, stood, giving Jack an encouraging salute. He whispered encouragement to Jack before he got too far away. "Remember what I taught you about fighting. You hit them, and hit them hard to keep them down."

"What if that doesn't work?" Jack whispered back.

"Then you hit them again. And if that doesn't work, then keep hitting them until they *do* stay down."

Confused, Jack shook his head. "What if they never stay down?"

The spirit chuckled. "Then you better think of something, because you've got yourself a soldier."

Mr. Shadow sat near the end of a front bench alone, merely glancing at Jack sideways. His cold eyes were barely visible beneath his dark hood before he returned his attention to the center podium. Oddly enough, it was the first time Jack didn't sense that familiar chill from him, as if someone else were beneath the hood.

Jack thought of his father, who had been found and would be waiting for him when he returned. He was thrilled and worried all at once and with good reason. Jack began wondering where Teddy was. Walking beside the cloud keepers, he looked around the courtroom. To his far right, a silver cylinder like a large chute angled upward held a white shuttle large enough to fit a person and ready to launch like a cannon.

"They use it to transport prisoners to the island," Father said. "Sandman's hourglass is headed there, thanks to you. Nothing for you to worry about, son. Your challenge is your only obstacle."

"What about Teddy?" Jack asked bitterly. "Where has he been hiding all of this time with my dad?"

"Apparently, one of the few places he knows well in Cloud City," Father whispered. "He hid within Phoenix's estate, changing rooms daily. After so long hiding there as a chauffeur, he's had enough time to know the grounds well. He was able to decode the security system, slip by guards and staff, and was nearly impossible to find. No one took notice of his stay until a recent trail of the dream sand from his escape surfaced that led the J.A.C.K.s to his whereabouts."

"Why didn't you tell me or let me see him?"

"It only just happened, but you have to understand I wanted to keep your focus on the challenge," Father whispered before sitting at a bench.

Jack took in just how crowded the courtroom was. Several spirits from clouds one through nine had come to watch the challenge. He recognized Madelyn from the Candy Labyrinth. Smudged with chocolate, she wore punk-rock purple and black clothes and her usual sweet demeanor. The Morris brothers and the April Fool, whom he'd proven innocent for another crime the year before, were also there. J.A.C.K.s stood guard around the room in full protective gear, with pouches and badges ready. Sonny, however, was nowhere to be found, and Jack wondered with frustration if he would ever see her again.

The courtroom wasn't nearly as dark as he remembered but just as intimidating. Its grand cathedral had the familiarity of cold stone, with a semi-circle of four alcoves high above. Jack remembered the alcoves were where the judges had entered before. He spotted something hanging on the wall beyond the podium but was unable to make out the figure protruding from the tarp. It hung in the center, below and between the second and third alcove. Beneath it was a table with a card marked "evidence." Laid about the table were all the objects he had possessed when he was arrested for a crime he hadn't known he was committing.

The flesh-colored mask that changed his face given to him by the Spirit of Mother's Day was next to the sack Holly had sent. The hand buzzer that vanished when he wore it sat on the other side of the bag. His gold coin from Lucky, which was now mostly silver, rested beside the item he wanted back most of all—the green detective's flashlight with the magnifying glass lens handle left to him by his father. Although it was in its flashlight form, the J.A.C.K.s had been careful enough to lock it inside a small cage to prevent it from transforming into Jack's faithful pup, Rocho. He was reasonably sure the cage wouldn't hold Rocho if he really wanted out. Strangely enough, Sonny's red-and-silver pen and yellow notepad were also next to the cage, but because she wasn't the one on trial, Jack was confused why her belongings were there.

Just as it had been four months prior, a mass of rocks remained chained inside the large pit just at the foot of the podium Jack stood at. Every few seconds, something beneath or inside the rock pulsed under the chains like a slow breath, but it looked as if only the four colored stones made any change at all as they glowed. Jack had been told of the two beings who'd stopped the elemental rock centuries ago. Like a moth circling a light bulb, Jack couldn't tear his eyes away from the formation of those four patches of the rocky mound. They were the only part that still had power. One by one, these four sections lit, beginning with blue. The second was green, another red, and the fourth an orange-yellow.

Cloud Keeper Matthews caught Jack's eye and snickered. "The rock should be the least of your worries. Not even alive anymore."

Jack finally looked away and addressed the cloud keeper. "Is that why it's chained down?"

A moment later, the courtroom fell deathly silent.

"All rise for the four respected judges," Cloud Keeper Matthews announced to the courtroom. "The honorable four seasons, designated by the two beings, are presiding. May we all be bound and blessed by their collective justice and rulings."

The four judges entered the courtroom from their individual alcoves, draped in their seasonal robes and radiating with the power of all four seasons. The scent of rainforest, beach sand, evergreen trees, and dried leaves mixed together, filling the room like a dozen scented candles. Jack recognized Spring, a small girl, as she entered on the left. The red strip of her black hair was prominent beneath her fluttering green robe, and the scent of flower petals and grass mixed with warm rain fell throughout the court. Summer rode in like a surfer coming onto the beach, riding a wave of pure heat. For several seconds, the courtroom felt like a sauna. The hood of his red robe was down and showed his ocean-washed hair. He looked physically strong and youthful, like a college student on spring break.

Autumn was much more reserved with a classically styled beauty and shoulder-length dark hair. A fair expression marked her firm brow and flawless bronze skin. She held a more mature and calmer nature than Summer. A few orange, yellow, and brown leaves fell above her with a slight tremor strong enough to shake the court as she approached the lip of the rocky alcove. Lastly, Old Man Winter glided in slowly, and the benches rapidly turned white and cold, frosting the dark area he walked through. Snowflakes fell near him as if afraid to touch something even icier than themselves.

"Be seated." Autumn surveyed the room, then her gaze struck Jack. "Over the last few months, the other judges and I have been developing challenges to allow you an opportunity — to earn your freedom, among other items that may be important to you. How have you utilized these few months?"

"I've been training." Jack stuttered slightly. "Every day."

Winter snickered, and a cold wind fluttered his beard. "I am highly doubtful."

"I have!" Jack objected. "I could use a little more time to be fully ready, though. Maybe today isn't the best day for this? Stars aren't aligned. Mercury is in someone's orbit. I think my allergies are irritated. We should probably wait until next year."

"Be that as it may, things do not work that way for dreamers," Autumn stated sternly, clearly unamused. "When the challenge comes, that is the time. No one can simply bargain for more. Do you understand why we have these challenges?"

"Nothing good on TV?" Jack whispered.

The Spirit of Father's Day gave him an intense look of warning, shaking his head.

"The Elemental Rock," she began, "is the last remnant of the stone-demon ruler Emperor Onyx. Before the two beings were able to contain the core in this tower of justice, Emperor Onyx was known as the Absorber. His four children who ruled beneath him destroyed the world, shaping it into their own. They flooded the world for forty days, causing an age of ice, drying entire seas with heat, and ripping the ground apart. They were the first to be defeated. When the emperor discovered his children destroyed, he absorbed the power they left behind to get his revenge. When the two beings defeated the king, it left the world in a state of constant chaotic change with no one to control it."

"The fallen emperor is gone, but his core remains powered," Old Man Winter finished. "The challenges of dreamers are the sacrifices we must make, as this is the activity that powers them. Your activity inside is what keeps it going. This is what keeps the Four Seasons powered and what continues the change in the world. Fortunately for us, it makes no difference if you survive or not."

"Do you understand now why this is a fair and just punishment for dreamers, as it aids in the world as a whole?"

"I should hope he does." The whiskers around Old Man Winter's mouth spread slightly for the tiniest grin. "I have quite a few surprises in store that will surely adjust that attitude. Not that I have any reason to believe you'd survive it."

"I will… I have to." Jack stared at the judge stubbornly then looked at his new watch.

"And why is that exactly?" Judge Winter's eyes grew colder and large. "Oh, that is correct—your ungrateful father has been found. A pity he is being cared for at the moment and unable to watch you fail as surely as he would've had he privileged to build the prison I requested."

"My dad is not a failure!" Jack shouted.

Old Man Winter's head rose slightly, so he looked down at Jack as if he were an insect he hadn't bothered to step on yet. "Do you see the defiance today's youth offers? Is this what your renewal of seasons has led us to now, Spring?"

The youngest-looking judge appeared too timid to speak until her rainbow-colored eyes settled on Jack's frustrated face. "Yes," she said with a tiny voice. "This is why a seed grows into flowers even during unpredictable weather or when left alone. The strongest tree survives in the harshest conditions, and I think he is like that tree."

Summer put his palms down on the alcove's lip and looked at Jack, tapping his chin with his finger and thinking carefully. "Heck yeah, bruh! He's got some fire in him. I wanna see what the little dude can do in there. Let's get this thing goin'."

Judge Autumn cleared her throat. "We must display proper order, Summer."

"Umm, hello?" Summer revealed his shoulder and arm beneath his cloak. "Check out the new tribal tattoo. Says right here, *Max Heat*. Respect the new name and the art, dude. Life and the afterlife are too beautiful to be reduced to a name I've never liked. I'm like the ocean, washing up the things I don't like and leaving them ashore."

Autumn continued speaking, gesturing to the items on the table. "As I was saying, we have the evidence of the crime you were found guilty of displayed on the table."

Jack's gaze lingered on Sonny's pen, and he became more concerned. "Actually, the pen—"

"Are we prepared to present the challenges or not!" Winter interrupted.

Autumn sighed as if she were ultimately used to, yet still annoyed by, the frosty season's lack of patience. "So be it. Cloud Keeper Matthews, fellow judges… if you would please."

The four judges pointed their palms toward the elemental rock. It pulsed once, and a portal appeared for each season across from them, just beyond the large rock mass. Spring lowered her hand first, followed by the others, and the cloud keeper gathered a clipboard. After flipping through two pages, he began reading from it.

"From the very first challenge created by the two beings to create a justified solution to handle exposure to the other plane by dreamers and to power the seasons, ensuring the existence of the world, we honor both light and dark, positive and negative, and the balance of justice today.

"Following the traditional proceedings, I will now read over the events of the origin. This new system began centuries ago with a country village and a massive mountain that echoed with cries. A large hen with the ability to lay one golden egg daily was found by a cottager and his wife near their home. Under the influence of greedy ambition, they believed the hen must contain a great source of gold inside. To gather the large sum, they sliced the hen open and, to their shock, found it to be no different than any other hen. The pair of fools who'd hoped to become wealthy at once instead lost the daily income they once had. This was the setting for the first challenge."

The J.A.C.K. flipped the page and read on. "The dreamer who was sent through this challenge was a young storyteller who found it difficult to finish his stories, with his limited patience and lack of focus. The two beings challenged him with this task to see if he would be able to remain silent about everything he'd seen in our world. The dreamer was sent in, tasked to locate a single feather of the golden-egg-laying hen. He was instructed to create a nest for it and protect the feather from all harm. The following day, a goose egg would appear in its place. The dreamer would only be able to return to his world if he was able to climb the village's famed crying mountain while protecting the egg and place it inside a cave quietly without waking its inhabitants."

Cloud Keeper Matthews flipped to the final page. "Unknown to the dreamer, however, the cave dweller inside who had inspired the mountain's name was a slumbering baby giant who would wake and cry for months at any noise at all. Through patience and determination, the dreamer remained quiet and placed the goose egg near the baby's sleeping area. For his true challenge was to learn patience and remain calm. After escaping the cave, he was transported back to the city, where he was rewarded with a red-and-silver quill made from the feather of the goose that would later lay golden eggs for a fully grown giant atop a beanstalk. Armed with this quill, he began telling new stories of a dream world, and this was the challenges' first victor." Finished with the origin story, the J.A.C.K. looked up at the court.

"Prepare the challenges to be chosen to be sacrificed by the seasons," Judge Winter ordered.

Each portal swelled, and Jack could see a whole world inside. Spring's portal had green edges, revealing a friendly-looking neighborhood with pleasant weather. Near the neighborhood's border, however, was a crater. As if an explosion had just occurred, debris fell from the sky. Parts of an impressive laboratory were scattered about, including a two-person rocket shuttle, a shrink ray attached to a powerful microscope, a metal chamber labeled "time machine," a spastic robot with exposed sparking wires, and a transporter plate among broken vials. Near the smoking lab, debris was a white-haired scientist wearing dark gloves and goggles atop his head. With wild eyes, he invited Jack to enter.

The portals began spinning slowly like a top around the elemental rock, and Jack was able to peek inside Summer's red portal. A town featured various summer activities twisted with strange circumstances. A moving truck spun out of control in a hurricane, which had demolished a summer camp and flooded a school haunted by a dead janitor. Elsewhere, a smoke monster was destroying a beachside burger stand near a car that had come to life. Finally, a crinkled letter floated in the wind toward him, just out of reach, with his future scribbled on it.

As each portal settled to be chosen, he could feel Winter's fierce anticipation as if he were willing his to be selected next. Jack was almost sure he heard Lucky closing bets on which portal Jack would get. He attempted to focus only on the eldest judge's portal and spot what lay in wait for him if fate should be so cruel. His eyes narrowed, and he blocked out all the others, concentrating on Winter's blue outline.

It was an academic institution or some sort of prestigious school, yet it was not typical in any way. Hidden by trees and intertwining trails, it was much like a prison protected by matters of harsh weather, including snowstorms and hurricanes. Students were training in various forms of combat, both armed and unarmed like a military school. However, the instructors and students seemed more like hired hit men or assassins. On an impossibly dangerous obstacle course leading into a prison, students were conditioned so they wouldn't feel pain. A short distance away, several others were learning to pick locks. Near the back, vehicles built with cannons and blades raced on a track. Sprinting toward the school were mutated beasts tearing down the gates and ripping guards apart as students and teachers used high-tech gadgets to repel them. And in the school's large stadium, three students, their weapons at the ready, waited to fight. After seeing inside this portal, he knew Winter had designed it as a place that would be impossible to escape.

Jack watched each one as the spinning slowed. The courtroom was silent. Each portal challenge spun like a horrible game of roulette. Then, finally, his fate was chosen. Spring's portal moved on, followed by Summer's twisted vacation challenge. Jack barely looked at Autumn's as Winter's edged closer and closer. The wheel of portals teetered between the two. Those watching in the stands leaned in, not daring to breathe until it finally stopped — and fell back onto Autumn's challenge. Her portal collapsed over the elemental rock and pulsed as the others vanished.

"No, this is impossible!" Old Man Winter stormed. An icy film fell over the room, and icicles protruded from his body sharply like armor. "My challenge was to be chosen! You were meant to be *my* sacrifice! What did you do, boy! How did you manipulate it?"

"I haven't done anything!" Jack shouted, and the cage on the display table shook suddenly.

"Lies! You have brought nothing but trouble since the moment you stepped into our existence, and this shows just how far the ripples of your selfish insolence will go."

"I had nothing to do with your prison, and you can't blame my dad for not wanting part in it!"

The icy spikes that had formed along Winter's shoulders, spine, and hands subsided slightly. "You believe *that* is why I judge you so harshly? Not the trouble you carried in with you when you stepped into our world. It was never just a flashlight that ended up in your possession from a thoughtful father. He was more careless and thoughtless than anything, and you really are nothing more than a simple thirteen-year-old boy who will never see the full picture, aren't you?"

Whether because of patience or curiosity, Jack fought back the urge to yell again. He looked at the spirits behind him, spotting the Spirit of Father's Day, who seemed just as curious about what the judge meant as Jack was.

"How would my flashlight cause more trouble here?" Jack asked, biting his lip.

Old Man Winter pointed a pale bony finger at him. "You have no idea the trouble you have brought with you, the inevitable destruction that would occur from the moment you returned that item. That totem was cast out years ago for a purpose: to shield the defiant dreamer Theodore from retrieving it. Totems could allow someone to walk right into this world if the right doorway were found, or it could let something very dangerous escape. Ever since you entered your father's hotel, we have had to endure a malicious symbol in hiding, followed by an escaped ex-holiday terrorist, and you always seem to be in the center of it all. You and your father should both be arrested for conspiracy to destroy this city. However—"

"However, this is not the place for personal opinions, only justifiable ones," Autumn interrupted. "And the sentencing is for this trial only."

Winter continued to breathe slowly while muttering to himself. "Justice first, among and above all."

The court became quiet. Jack looked into the portal in front of him. Deep inside the yellow glow of her portal, he saw a vast amount of land parted in sections, with a town of machinery and cogs in a broad valley. Near it, a mining area of rock and rubble led into several tunnels. After a stretch of plains and a lake was an area of dry sand, where strange birds preyed from above. A mile or so beyond the desert, on a mountain surrounded by a vast forest with the most enormous and vibrant trees Jack had ever seen, two groups of people were scrambling up the mountain's peaks. They approached each other as if going to war.

Neither group seemed fully human. One group was abnormally pale as if they'd remained inside all their lives. They were tall, muscular, and lean, wielding magic in their long fingers. Using blasters and large metal suits with attached weapons, a shorter, brutish race of people with orange skin attacked from the opposite side. The blasters and suits made up for their short stature, but their massive arms and legs were nothing to snort at, either.

Jack assumed he would be entering this challenge in the middle of a war. Whatever they were fighting over, he hoped to avoid it and find his task, although he was already sure that would not be the case. Turning to Redd, he was thankful the spirit had trained him in similar combat and had volunteered to aid him.

Suddenly, a motion from the tarp on the wall caught his eye. It made him feel uncomfortable, although he didn't understand why since he didn't know what hid behind it, yet the situation felt familiar. Memories of Dr. de Luca chained up beside his cell when the Sandman's sleepwalkers and Teddy had captured him suddenly sprang up, and he couldn't dismiss it until the judges prepared his departure.

"Father!" Judge Winter called. "The boy's totem. Is it prepared and ready to be inspected?"

"Yes, I have completed Nucalibur as requested." The Spirit of Father's Day stood up slowly and presented the fishing rod in its compact form. Cloud Keeper Matthews inspected it thoroughly, expanding it to its full length and surveying the multiple symbols from the holiday spirits who'd blessed it. A moment later, he nodded to the judges and handed it to Jack.

"A fishing rod?" Autumn inquired with an amused expression. "I sense the old sword in its core. A marvelous totem, as well, designed and matched as the silver slippers and golden tickets of the past. It should suit you well in my challenge and remain inconspicuous."

Holding the totem securely in his hand, Jack glanced at his flashlight. A part of him felt like a traitor, and for a moment, he was ready to grab Rocho. But the young detective quickly thought better of it. A small hesitation seized him when he thought he saw the flashlight roll toward him inside the cage, but he quickly looked away. He could feel the seconds counting down to his eventual step into the challenge as if each tick from his new wristwatch weighed his hand down more and more.

Autumn looked at Jack. "You will use the totem to locate a great power source that will allow you to return here. You will need an item from each group to unlock it. A moonleaf made of stone and an ancient cog that can fix any machine. Doing this will require you to choose a side that you believe is right and just in their cause. Helping them save themselves will help you, as well. You will need to find your own way of completing this, dreamer. Assist an honorable king with the love of his life or aid a fearless war chief in protecting his people and villages. Now is the time, Winter. You may reveal his reward."

Winter grinned and raised his thin, spiny hand. The cuff of his robe slid down slightly as he waved. A gust of cold wind rose from nowhere, just as chilly as ever. Jack's leather jacket and shirt were blown sideways, and he was forced to shield his eyes. Moments later, the drape clinging to the wall fell, revealing a person shackled onto a platform on the wall, barely moving at all.

"Sonny!" Jack yelled. "Why is she chained up? Let her go!" He ignored a murmur behind him, and from the corner of his eye, he was almost sure he noticed Mr. Shadow begin to stand. The cage on the table banged against the wall, but no one seemed to notice. Sonny's blond hair covered her face as she hung from the wall by reinforced chains clasping her wrists. Her head remained tilted down, and the only movement came from the slow rise and fall of her chest. She appeared unharmed, and several people snickered when she snored suddenly and loudly.

"She is merely in a very deep sleep," Judge Winter said smugly. "I'm sure by now she should be used to it. You will gain both your freedoms *if* you return. She did have a part in the Sandman's escape. Seems fitting that the people you care for will be waiting for your return. Besides, we cannot use your cherished flashlight as it is evidence and technically doesn't belong to you anyway, and your father is already in his afterlife, so there is not much to lose, is there? So let's see if you can place your priorities now."

Spring continued to look down as if she were ashamed of taking part in the trial. The eldest-looking judge, however, appeared to delight in it. "It's time. Send the boy in."

"Wait!" Spring shouted. "He is entitled to an advisor."

Winter rolled his eyes. "Don't be such a child. Who would volunteer for this degenerate?"

"She is right," Autumn interjected. "I offer no favoritism, but this proceeding *will* remain fair. Does anyone volunteer to be the advisor of this dreamer in the challenge that awaits him? Will anyone be volunteering to aid in his journey, watch over his actions, and offer assistance according to the laws?"

"I volunteer," came a cold yet smoothly familiar voice.

It was difficult for Jack to look away from Sonny, but the voice he heard broke his trance. He'd already been told that Redd would be stepping in for Father, yet as he turned to look at the holiday spirit who'd volunteered, he could clearly see the Independence Day Spirit slowly sitting back down. A stunned and confused expression spread across his usually fearless face as the spirit lowered his hand, and his eyes focused on another. Jack's heart skipped a beat as he glared at the skeletal hand still raised in the air.

"No…" Jack shook his head. "Not him," he pleaded.

Mr. Shadow lowered his hand slowly and returned to his seat on the bench. He never looked at Jack, but instead at Sonny chained to the wall across from him.

Judge Autumn opened her arms. "You have your advisor. The challenge is ready."

"No worries, brah. You got this." Summer added. "Gonna be a gnarly event, dude, and an epic story! You know… if you survive."

"Prepare to enter, dreamer." Old Man Winter's eyes were frigid. "And may the two beings have mercy on you in this world or whichever one you shall remain in."

All four judges raised their arms wide, and the core of the rock began shimmering in all its colors. Autumn's portal grew, and the yellow glow brightened the courtroom. Jack was so stunned that he realized too late that he was slipping into the portal below the podium. His foot slid around, then he fell flat on his face as if someone had pulled a rug from beneath him. He scrambled to gather Nucalibur before being propelled up in the air. The portal swirled like a cyclone, and in an instant, he was pushed up to the ceiling.

From above, he could see all four judges at eye level while he twisted in the air. The spirits below remained watching, and he spotted Father nodding at him reassuringly. Sonny's body was pulled in the cyclone's direction but remained attached to the wall. There was a short pause then the loud sound of snapping metal, like a wire hanger being broken and bent. A flash of gold shot across the room with the speed of a lightning bolt. It sprinted around the circular walls with incredible agility. Faster and faster, it climbed in a short blur of green, leaving a trail of gold that Jack could only glimpse between leaps.

Sparks flew, and shouts rose from below. J.A.C.K.s aimed their badges up, attempting to locate the speeding bolt. They threw pouches that expanded into nets, but the green blur quickly slipped by them. Another gold flash whipped by and then pounced directly at Jack so he could see Rocho's green fur, glossy eyes, and gold strip. Jack remained pinned against the ceiling. He reached out with his free hand to catch the loyal pup, its tiny paws outstretched. Another pouch exploded nearby, and an instant later, Jack was hurtling from the courtroom's ceiling and swallowed by the portal of his challenge.

Chapter 3
The Challenge

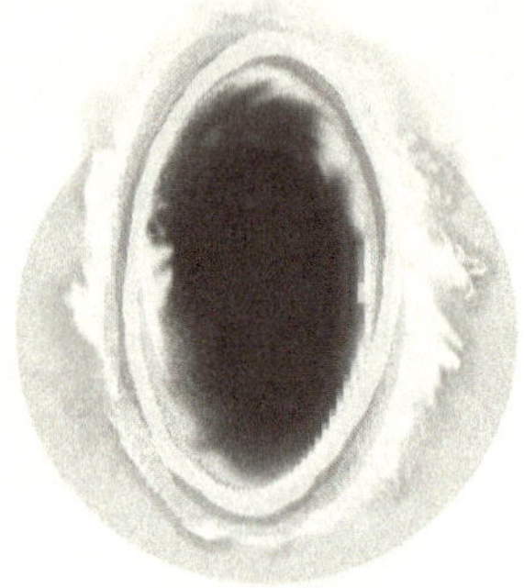

He couldn't tell how much time had passed since he'd been pulled into the challenge, still clutching the fishing rod as if hoping it would deploy a parachute any minute. He checked his other hand. Somehow, either by good fortune or skill, he'd been able to catch Rocho just before being taken by the cyclone. The pup had returned to flashlight form the moment Jack grazed his fur. Jack stuffed the flashlight into his pocket to keep it safe. It did cross his mind that light would be beneficial at the moment since he continued falling blindly.

It was eerily dark in the strange vortex, but the quiet and peacefulness frightened Jack the most. No sound other than the pounding of his heart. Nothing to see. The only thing he could feel was the cool air rushing between his fingers as if he'd put his arm through the car window during a road trip. That, however, lasted only until the lightning struck.

A flash streaked several yards away from him and lit up the portal like the first preview in a dark theater. He was in the eye of the cyclone, which was much bigger than it had been when he'd entered. He kept his arms stretched out, hoping to grab onto something to slow his spinning before hitting the ground. Yet even the ground seemed nonexistent. The only visible thing below him was a tiny pinhole amount of light that never seemed to get closer.

The cyclone continued to twist around him, but he could tell that only because of the debris that suddenly rose up. He had to look carefully before recognizing they were broken pieces of a house. Cracked window panes, wooden panels, and a shutter flew around him, and soon after, an entire farmhouse whizzed by. Seconds later, an eerie cackling followed.

Lightning flashed again, and the illumination lingered much longer. The green skin, hooked nose, and black pointed hat shot by him so fast that Jack was sure he'd imagined it. Then the cackling came closer, and a witch appeared in front of him on a mangled broom, laughing maniacally before flying off.

As he continued to fall past them, the cyclone changed, funneling into a hole with walls made of dirt. The pinhole-sized light grew a bit bigger, and the wind of the cyclone ended. He fell through the large dirt hole just as a cat vanished, leaving only a broad human-like smile. He soared over a blue caterpillar atop a mushroom, blowing smoke from his mouth into the shape of a question mark. A well-dressed white rabbit checked his pocket watch before scampering through the hole Jack fell closer to.

Once again, the scenery altered. The walls of dirt and large hole changed into a hallway of someone's home. Jack was bounced between the coats of an open wardrobe closet. He tumbled through the closet and entered a forest blanketed in snow. In the distance, he spotted a friendly-looking faun, a powerful white witch in a sled, and what almost seemed undoubtedly to be Santa as he hurtled toward a hole in a frozen lake. Jack braced himself for the icy water, but it never came. He fell into the hole as if the water were unable to slow him, traveling by mermaids and hidden treasures. It continued on like that for some time. He fell from one hole to the next as the light at the end grew only slightly larger.

After what seemed like an eternity, Jack found it—the end was close. The light was much larger and came much faster. He plummeted through a new sky full of fairies, flying children, pirates in the distance, and an enormous crocodile in the water. The light was in the center of a cloud, and as he went through, he felt a cool rush followed by a warm, sunny embrace. He blinked, and the image from the portal in the courtroom came into view. The mechanical town in the valley lay to the left, where a few animals grazed. The tall forest stretched through the valley was far to his right, and the mountain lay just beyond it. A lake, a sandpit, and a murky swamp were all getting closer. He fell toward the plains and sandpit below him, where a man and woman stood in an embrace as they watched him fall.

Panicking, Jack realized he wasn't slowing. He turned in midair to see the pit of lightly reddish sand waiting to envelop him.

"Not more sand!" he yelled, clutching his totems tightly. He thought of his father, his mother, and Sonny as he closed his eyes. His heart beating rapidly, he took a deep breath and waited for the sand to swallow him.

It was an unusual sensation, to have the wind knocked out of him and suddenly feel the need to sleep. The sand was much warmer and inviting than he'd expected, like a blanket. Everything suddenly felt like a dream, as if he were watching someone else control his actions. The fishing rod totem was out of reach as he tried groggily to grab it while covered in sand up to his armpits. His head fell back, and he was able to see two suns in the sky, one much larger than the other. As the first reached its highest point, the other was just beginning to set, blinking itself out of view. He felt a strong urge to sleep. If it weren't for a tickling sensation around his legs, he might have. Slow-moving clouds in the sky hypnotized him as he sank deeper until he realized they weren't clouds that were moving above him.

A reflective glimmer twitched against the sun's rays. One of more than a dozen birds with feathers of mirrored glass, long vulture-like necks, and pelican-sized twisting beaks similar to drills swooped down in his direction. It sped toward Jack, and as he raised his arms to protect his face, it dove into the sand just in front of him. Its beak was barely visible as it dug deeper and deeper into the sand with its talons before finally pulling up the biggest worm Jack had ever seen. Flat like a ruler, but the length of Jack's forearm, it wiggled wildly in the bird's beak.

Sand had flown up, and Jack yawned, coming to a realization. "Dream sand… it's mixed into the pit," he said to himself, noticing grains of red sleeping sand. In an instant, the sky suddenly seemed to change direction. The entire flock of birds began circling each other where the first bird had landed. Sand drifted up as if lifted by a vacuum, freeing more of Jack's body. He tried tossing sand at the birds, but they quickly blew it away with their wings. He stretched his hand out for Nucalibur as it rose into the air, too.

"Come on, just a little closer—ouch!" He pulled his hands back as one of the strange birds pecked at him. "They're fingers, not worms! Ouch! Quit it!" he yelled.

A few more birds dipped lower, searching for their morning meal and attacking Jack in their haste. He attempted to time his next attempt so the birds would not be able to peck him away, scooting himself forward. He lunged for it, and the birds fought back.

He shooed them away the best he could, waving the rod back and forth, swinging it like a bat. He accidentally pressed a button, and a long line of luminescent fishing wire reeled out of the rod. The line bobbed out and lay along the shimmering sand. Jack had an idea. Hoping it would be strong enough, he whipped it over his head. More of the line reeled out and eventually reached the edge of the pit, several yards away.

Unfortunately, the hungry birds continued to nip at him as he tried to pull himself out. The birds became vicious, and Jack grew desperate. Jack dug a hand deep into the sand while the birds pecked his face. He sank deeper into the sand, fighting the overwhelming sleepiness and ignoring the pain of the flock as he rummaged for another worm. Feeling it around his knees, he yanked out a plump one and held it up just as the flock's leader came soaring back.

A large bark roared throughout the area with the power of the first crack of lightning in a storm. It startled both the birds and Jack. A second bark, louder than the first, rippled the sand like a reverberating drumbeat, dispersing a dozen birds at once. Taking advantage of the distraction, Jack yanked out the fat worm and hurled it away from him. The moment their attention was drawn away, he used his Nucalibur to gather as much anchor as possible and began the difficult task of digging himself out.

The pit seemed unwilling to let him go, but he inched closer to the outer edge. His muscles ached, and every part of his body screamed for him to simply stop and sink. But at that moment, the sand began easing away from him. It drifted past his waist as he was dragged along. A tall, slender young woman with long ivory hair, a lean athletic build, flawless pale skin, and thin leather clothing made from some sort of animal hide stood over him. A green ball of fur tugged on the line behind her—Jack assumed it was Rocho. Once he reached the edge of the green field, Jack felt the line go slack; however, he retained a firm grip on his totem.

He continued to breathe slowly, hearing the fluttering and grinding wings of the birds flying away in the distance, but the damage was done. He could have drawn a constellation in the numerous pockmarks denting his face and arms. Rocho licked the back of Jack's head and face sympathetically as Jack attempted to stand.

Jack gawked at the young woman, taking in her lean muscle and the belt around her waist, holding an array of knives and daggers. She could obviously take care of herself and showed no fear at all.

Standing, leaning woozily on Nucalibur, Jack felt a short poke in his chest. "Hey, I don't squeak… why are you poking me?"

"You… speak their language? You fell from the sky and lived? What are you?" She eyed Jack.

Jack debated thanking her or asking her the same question before he noticed another reflection of sunlight headed toward him. He wasn't quite sure what to call them, but they looked remarkably like pumas with metallic armored bodies. They were spread out in hunting formation—and closing in. Their joints expelled steam as they gained speed. Rocho began growling in their direction, and to Jack's surprise, the pumas' ears detached from their heads and rotated as if focusing on a sound. Moments later, the mechanical creatures were sprinting.

"What are those?" Jack pointed.

The white-haired woman turned and instantly withdrew two daggers from her belt. "Masasi pakas… hunters." She backed away. "We should run, Sky Boy."

Jack struggled to keep up with the woman's pace. She was agile and knew the plains well, hurdling over boulders and tree stumps. Rocho trailed behind Jack in his pup form as the metal pumas chased them. They seemed to never lose momentum as they closed in. Jack could hear the gears and cogs that made up their joints working rapidly.

One of the mechanical hunters opened its muzzle wide, and a wire net shot out. Once landed, it shocked the ground, sparking wildly before snapping the points together just as Jack leaped over it. The other three sprinted forward, preparing to pounce as the woman split a single dagger into four thin knives and tossed them over his head. Jack ducked as they hit the mechanical cats' eyes, causing them to stumble and crash, shaking uncontrollably.

She pulled two long daggers from her belt and dove onto one of the machines. She wrestled with it, one blade stuck in its head, the other on the side of its neck. It rolled and fought back as she dodged its claws. After a few twists, she kicked the head of the machine off. The body buzzed and sparked, clawing blindly until finally falling to the ground, and she rejoined Jack.

The woman led Jack and Rocho closer to a cliff high above jagged rocks poking from the sides over a vast body of water. The remaining hunting machines came within a few short yards. Jack fumbled with Nucalibur, turning a random notch. Without warning, a green mist expelled from the rod's base, spraying a long strip of the prairie land. Vibrant green three-leafed shamrocks sprouted from the ground like bed springs in the hunters' path. The moment they made contact, the shamrocks' vivid-green color hardened into a dull-gray stone, clutching one of the mechanical puma's legs. It happened so quickly, the limbs were ripped apart from the body mid-run. Its lifeless torso and head continued sliding forward, broken tubes and gears steaming like a train just after a wreck. The woman stepped back in surprise, holding a dagger defensively, edging closer to the cliff as the final hunter dodged the path of shamrocks. But it wasn't the puma she was backing away from.

"What magic do you hide?" Her eyes narrowed. She held her dagger as if prepared to stab Jack right then. "Are you a shaman?"

"Shaman? No." Jack backed away from the stalking beast.

With the cliff at their heels, he made every attempt to use Nucalibur again; however, the shamrock symbol had gone dull, and the other notches were slowly re-illuminating. As the machine paced in front of them, he pinpointed a strange marking on its forehead—a carving of a gear that matched the one on the totem.

Rocho growled at the beast, which seemed to be debating which to devour first. As the woman prepared a curved dagger in each of her hands, Rocho's fur sparked. His growl became deeper, his mouth foamed, and gold electricity circled his body.

In a snap, the metal puma pounced, claws ready to mangle just as Rocho grew into the bear-sized dog. The transformation was faster than the first time Jack had watched Rocho change only four months prior. With a swift jump, Rocho met the puma midair, hitting its side and vaulting it over the cliff. Its impact with the water below was similar to a car in a trash compactor until it finally sank into the water and powered down.

Jack heard a small grunt behind him. With so much going on, he didn't realize Rocho's rapid growth had scared the woman right off the cliff. She struggled to hang on to the rocky ledge but was losing her grip. Jack hurried to pick up his fishing rod.

"Quick, grab on to it!" he yelled to her. She grabbed the end while Jack used his weight to leverage her up, lying on it entirely until it was level. Rocho began to growl again behind him.

"Oh, what now?" Jack tried his best to survey the area while the white-haired woman took his hand. A group of people sped through the plains on three-wheeled motorbikes with bronze plating. Their engines roared, belching steam from their pipes.

"Are they with you?" Jack asked, hopefully.

"No, they are of *mflame*," she stated as Jack continued to pull her up. "King Aurum's soldiers and his general. They sent the hunters, and if we are found, they will kill us — or worse."

"Worse?" Jack struggled to hold Nucalibur steady; the woman was considerably taller and broader than he was. "Death isn't bad enough?"

"We must leave before we are seen."

Jack was unsure if Rocho understood the conversation or simply knew danger was coming, but he instantly sprinted toward the squad with impressive speed, even in his bear-sized form. Jack called out for the pup to return, but he was already near the soldiers, barking at them. Jack hurried to pull the woman up, nearly ripping the bracelet dangling from her wrist, continuously calling for Rocho to return.

From his vantage point, Jack could see the pup fighting the group back. His barking was forceful, and he easily knocked two of them off their bikes. A few approached from different angles, but Rocho growled to charge himself. His fur stood on end, electricity danced down his gold stripe, and a surge of energy shocked those soldiers, dropping them to the ground, unable to move.

Another soldier rode in from behind the others on a two-wheeled motorbike sporting silver plates and dual guns on the sides. Before the rest of the group could regain their footing, the silver-armored leader pulled up, stepped away from his vehicle, and walked up to Rocho fearlessly. Jack assumed he was the general. The pup swiped at him, chasing the rider like a play toy, but he calmly dodged Rocho's attacks, with surprising agility in his armor. He removed a trident bonded to his back, pointing the prongs at Rocho. As the pup jumped, the general flipped him closer to the bike using the trident's handle. He then slammed his armored shoulder into Rocho with impressive force and pressed a button on his arm. The dual guns of his bike rotated to fire two nets over Jack's companion.

"Let him go!" Jack started after him, but the woman held him back.

"You should not chase them. The animal is safer away from us. We must go from this area to another place. The forest will embrace us."

Jack fought her, but she was just as strong as Jack had assumed. He was left with very few options as he witnessed Rocho struggle for freedom, howling and shocking through the net, but the trap material was unaffected. Chains hooked to the bike kept him from moving as a surge of red energy soared through them. The leader climbed smugly onto the bike and pointed in Jack's direction. The poor pup's golden eyes saddened as the bike dragged him away.

Jack was pulled away and led into the forest. His guilt was nearly intolerable as he gave in, following the woman through the trees and into the shaded forest that easily outstretched Holly Woods. They brushed by large tree leaves of radiant green and purple. A blue hue outlined the trees when sunlight struck momentarily, and the leaves shuddered as if bracing for an attack. Jack could hear an ominous howl coming deep from within the woods, or perhaps beneath it.

The woman held her hand out for Jack to stop, then pressed her finger to her lips and pointed behind them. "Wait here," she whispered. They stood behind the leafiest parts of a tree as the soldiers approached.

"Sir, what are your orders?" one of the men asked. A new member of their group, not dressed quite like the others, approached the forest. He'd caught up to them on a bike similar to the general's but with a gold emblem of the gear. Up close, Jack could see how different the soldiers were from the woman who'd saved him. They were all much shorter, barely taller than Jack, but with a much wider build and bulky muscle. Their skin was a deep tan-orange color, and their faces held a rougher expression and wild facial hair.

This new man, however, appeared almost scrawny compared to his men, though nearly a foot taller than Jack. The tall soldier had an air of royalty and a kinder face as he peered into the forest. With black shoulder-length hair, he was built more like an underwear model than a bodybuilder. Sporting a gray vest with gold buttons, he wore twin pistols holstered on his hips, each with three long barrels and a gleaming gold grip.

He stood at the forest's edge, staring past the leaves and directly at Jack. He was sure they'd been spotted. The soldier and the tall, white-haired woman were practically following each other's movements. Because of the way they mimicked one another, Jack would have sworn they belonged together. Another growl came from the forest, and the squad took guard instantly. Two held nets similar to the one used to drag Rocho away. A few others were armed with short staffs that sparked.

"Men, circle around to the sides," the new soldier ordered. "She's trying to lose us with a false trail. Check the outlying areas then return to the town if you don't find anything. Spread out—quick!"

The squad hesitated before dispersing, and their leader's gaze lingered on the forest before he rode away. Jack took his first breath since stopping, afraid they would hear him. He panicked for a moment before realizing he'd managed to hang on to his totem—it was his only way to return home. Relief was followed by a new dread. His father's flashlight had been taken, and even if he did make it out of the challenge, he'd already lost the one item that still tied them together.

The woman walked deeper into the forest, and Jack had to hurry not to lose her. "Who… who are you?" Jack asked, stepping over thick vines and twisting roots. "What do they want with us?"

"Branches," she answered.

"What?"

"They are branches from a much larger tree root. Their king is who threatens us, and he wants what all men of great power desire."

Jack thought for a moment but had no answer. "What's that?"

"The power of every other great man. The green animal that protected you, the machines that will follow his command—all of these are weapons for him to use to gain power. The king is cruel. People fight in his arena, and many die for his entertainment. Capturing me would bring one of two ends. The surrender of my people into slaves… or war."

They stepped between trees and muddy waters, passing oversized mushrooms and glowing insects that brightened the ground shortly before dimming. Furry magenta creatures resembling rabbits with ears that were twice the length of their bodies and trailed on the ground behind them stared up at Jack with big soft eyes. They had curved shells like armadillos and tails that appeared to wag in delight before they playfully rolled away. Gray baboons half Jack's size, with four arms and tails so long, they coiled around branches nine times, swung from tree to tree with ease. Houseflies with scaly skin and snouts like dragons buzzed by. It took him by surprise when one puffed a tiny flame at him then flew away.

Two creatures like overstuffed teddy bears with black-and-white fur and fluffy fox tails searched for fish with their paws. Color-changing toads that blended with surrounding trees leapt away from birds with tiger-striped feathers and long talons. He stared awkwardly at an overgrown orange flower bud that blossomed to release dozens of tiny insects that resembled floating jellyfish trailing their tentacles through the air.

The woman would occasionally brush her hand over a tree stump, look up, turn, and continue on. Jack couldn't understand how she knew where to go or where they were headed. Every tree looked identical, each with a trunk thicker than any he'd ever seen before. More than once, he was positive they were being followed by several pairs of glowing green eyes.

"What will they do to my pup?" Jack asked, unable to shake the stinging guilt.

She continued traveling swiftly with nervous steps. "If your friend is unique enough, the Zookeeper will study it. The kingdom will experiment."

Standing in his spot for a moment, Jack thought about what experiments they would do before Jack rescued him. "The Zookeeper?"

She seemed to have caught his misstep as she paused to look at him. "Yes, an animal collector living in the kingdom. I have only heard stories. I'm sorry your friend was taken. He will be prodded, tested, and sampled, most likely for his attributes in difficult scenarios. What is wrong with your face?"

Jack looked at her uncertainly, wiping away a tear that had trickled down his face. "What do you mean? I'm fine."

"I've seen this from people outside of the village. Sensitive to emotions… you are afraid?"

"What, you've never been afraid?"

Her face remained expressionless. "My people don't believe in fear. Our traditions train us out of it as a child. I care for my animals, my village, the people close to me, and the Usiku Forest, but we do not allow emotion. I don't remember being afraid. Just the danger we have to face."

"Well, you're missing out on some rocking uplifting happiness, too," Jack added before changing the conversation. "So it wasn't me they were after, really, but why are you so important?" He watched her brush a hand onto another tree and move forward. "I mean, how does taking you start a war? Who are you to them?"

At first, she looked offended, and Jack realized he'd made her presence seem unimportant without meaning to.

"I am Celeste, the daughter of my peoples' highest war chief."

"There's a chief?" Jack looked over the woman, noticing the glistening jewels in her bracelet. "So you're like a princess or something?"

Celeste smiled politely, ducking beneath a tall branch. "I would prefer not to be. I am forbidden to do many things because of my blood."

"Because of your father? What can't you do?"

She moved around another tree, navigating the woods as if she were part of the forest itself. "My family must remain in the village to be safe. We are strongest near the Great Tree. My father is very protective of what is important to him. We are all trained in fighting and hunting, but my father will not risk me leaving, because I am so very delicate." She balanced the tip of a knife on the end of another for several seconds before launching it at a piece of hanging fruit, pegging it to a tree."

Jack had to look at her to see she was joking. "Have you always been this good?"

"I am more talented with a dagger and knife than any warrior in our village. Illness is the real reason my father chooses for me to stay in the forest. He believes the forest magic protects me from the illness's full infection—especially now, it seems. Days ago, thieves followed our warriors into the village and stole something important from my father. He has very little trust for outsiders."

"How does your mother feel about it?" Jack asked. "And is that why the soldier at the forest's edge wouldn't walk in? He was looking at you like he knew you."

She paused for a moment. The look in her eyes told him she was done talking, and she continued through the forest silently.

Jack thought back to the moments leading up to his dive into the sandpit. He remembered seeing two people hugging below as he sailed by. Now he wondered if that was the person she thought about in her silence and if that person was the scrawny soldier.

They journeyed on for nearly an hour with a dozen thoughts running through Jack's head of Rocho, Celeste, Sonny, the soldier, and his father. Other than the shamrock, the emblems on his fishing rod had re-illuminated. The glowing notches let him see well enough as the area became darker and colder. He assumed it was from being so well shaded by the trees from the sun, but there was a strangely familiar sense to it Jack couldn't shake off.

After so much time in silence—except for eerie howls and the suction of his shoe stuck in the mud—he finally asked Celeste a new question that had been plaguing him for the last several minutes. "Where are you taking me?"

"To my village, where you can rest if my father allows it. Not much longer now."

"I don't think I'd ever leave if it took me this long to get there." Jack breathed heavily. "How can you even see where you're going? It's so dark."

She rubbed her arm, gingerly shaking her bracelet. "My people have been living in the shade of the trees for many years. We are a people of the night and have adapted to the shade. This entrance is used for outsiders, usually trading goods or bringing messages, but only when blessed by magic. Or else the forest will swallow you and never let go. If I took you through the entrance my people have grown adapted to, your muscles would ache, your mind would become dizzy, and you would become blind."

Jack's eyes widened, and he stumbled. "So, I probably should have written these directions down on the way in?"

"The protected magic is from outsiders only. A special marking applied to my people protects us. You may earn yours soon, as well."

He brushed his curly mop of hair out of his eyes, shaking loose grains of sand. A few of the branches waved as he noticed the four-armed monkeys swing by. Then the long-eared rabbits scampered ahead of them, wearing frightened looks. Although it was curious, Jack ignored it for the moment. "Is that why that soldier didn't follow us?"

Celeste stopped mid-step as if he'd spoken another language. Jack debated whether to continue then decided knowing was better than not. "He just seemed to look right at us but didn't follow. Do you know him?"

Her head drooped, and her eyes narrowed, following from Jack's shoes then behind him as if just noticing his tracks. The plants and trees behind them had turned a beautiful snowy white. Frost covered the ground, the plants, and the leaves leading up to them. He quickly felt the bitter cold settle in with the same tingle he'd felt earlier, like a chill from Mr. Shadow.

"Does it always get cold this fast?"

Her eyes shifted from curious to suspicious. She shook her head slowly, studying the white substance.

"Have you ever seen this happen before I came here?"

She shook her head slowly again, drawing a dagger from her belt.

Jack backed away as he heard something shatter off in the distant trail. Frozen leaves, grass blades, and branches shattered from the simplest breeze, causing a chain reaction.

"Sky Boy, run." Celeste warned.

Jack turned, confused. "What?"

"Fast now!" she yelled.

Jack pressed the button on Nucalibur, collapsing it to its smallest size, making it easier to carry. He sprinted behind her as the frosty path slithered toward them faster, chasing them. It twisted through the forest like a thick white fog with a purpose, freezing the ground and plants within seconds. The repeated sound of shattering followed each step.

Celeste brushed by trees, glancing up and changing directions sharply, but the frost was bitterly persistent. Jack continued to struggle, unknowing where they were going and stepping past turns. "We are close, Sky Boy."

The entrapping cold froze the air, making it difficult for him to breathe, piercing his lungs with every heavy gasp. They raced through the forest, ducking branches, and leapt over a steady stream as the frost grew closer, nipping his heels until Jack slipped. The water had frozen too quickly, and his jump didn't quite carry him over the stream. His head hit the ice and slid him to the edge. Celeste stopped at the bank, studying the foggy frost as it closed in. Daggers ready, she was obviously unsure what good they would do against such an attack.

Jack was stunned but lifted his head just in time to feel the frost crawl up his shoes. He hastily expanded his totem, holding it threateningly, but without knowing what each symbol would do, he had no clue as to what notch to twist. Feeling a snapping pain in his toes, the young detective gripped the rod tightly and chose the egg symbol. Prepared to release its abilities, he stopped at the sound of a stretching bow.

"Mashambulizi!"

A dusty red haze trailed through the air as a few dozen arrows struck the ground. From the arrows' points, a red mist spread onto the ground like melted candle wax. The frozen ground continued to approach Jack, but as it met the substance from the arrows, it was forced to back away. Eventually, the frost evaporated into mist like dry ice. The plants, trees, and leaves became lively again, dripping water like a simple soft rain.

Jack looked up, brandishing his fishing rod, pressing the gear symbol, causing a sharp point to eject out. Above him, archers were perched in trees. Warriors with pale skin like Celeste's but covered in dry mud stood battle ready in the trees, draped in leather armor and leaves. They reminded Jack of the elves he'd met at the Holiday Hotel inside Holly's Villa, except they were much taller, even compared to Celeste, and had red-hued eyes that glowed in the dark like ultraviolet. Each one was armed with a crossbow, loaded with a new arrow, flickering in red mist and targeted at Jack. A large lump swelled in his throat as he peered up at the nearly one thousand sharp points circled around him. His thumb slid down the length of the rod, but once again, he stopped before twisting a new notch.

"*Kuacha!*" Celeste pleaded. "*Kuokolewa yangu. Tafadhali. Si adui!*"

Jack had no idea what she was saying to them, but her eyes had locked on to one warrior in particular marked with several indigo tribal symbols on his face and arms. He wore little armor compared to the others. The warrior held up his hand, staring between Celeste and Jack. He glared at Jack for a moment before focusing on the totem. His expression changed from suspicious to angry rather quickly as his hand sliced through the air.

"*Mashambulizi!*" he roared.

All at once, nearly a thousand arrows flew through the tree branches.

"No!" Celeste screamed. Though he could barely hear her and did not know the language the warriors spoke, somehow Jack understood. In that instant, he felt death's greeting. It was such a quick action, the only things he could see were the red flakes flying toward him like a trail of fireworks just before impact, and he was the target for every last one.

Chapter 4
The Great Tree

For a moment, Jack thought it would be the last breath he ever took. Everything seemed to slow down all at once. The arrows rained down on him with a promise of pain. He could see the surrounding warriors balanced on branches continue to look down at him as if he were another animal being hunted for food. Celeste's eyes were closed as she turned her face, and the lead warrior looked on silently, still pointing at Jack. Yet it wasn't until Jack felt an odd wave over his skin that he noticed the misty red trail still sailing through the air. And he was able to poke at the flakes with his finger.

It was another experience of déjà vu. The moment Phoenix had been in his old age at the Holiday Hotel and hastily seated onto his throne, time had slowed down and nearly stopped permanently. His body felt the same, tightening his muscles into a statue-like pose, and his surroundings did almost the same. The arrows lingered in the air, still trailing the glittering flaming tips. The warriors, escaping animals, and even the insects fluttering their wings were all moving much more slowly.

Gathering himself up, he backed away, closer to Celeste, avoiding the arrows that inched closer. The branches the warriors stood on bowed slightly under the weight, bouncing gradually in place with the archers' movements. Searching along Nucalibur, he saw each symbol, with the exception of the shamrock, gleaming back at him.

As the arrows came closer to impacting the ground, his joints, legs, and arms began to cramp. Crippling pain surged through his body. In his reflection in the stream, his curly black hair had aged to gray, his eyes were sunken, and his pupils had turned white. As his hands touched his face, he could feel his youthful skin start to wrinkle. The reflection of his hand against his face also showed the wristwatch.

Jack quickly realized his wristwatch had stopped ticking as rapidly and had slowed to match the pace of the world around him. The dials and second hands had each turned red and were pulsing. He cringed again, feeling his body leap forward in years painfully. Pressing the buttons around the watch's face, he felt his muscles relax, and the pain vanished instantly. He could see his hair and skin return to normal. A second later, he was stunned by the arrows striking the ground all at once as he looked on from a safer distance. Looking up at the warriors searching the woods for him, he could tell they were just as confused.

Celeste jumped at Jack's presence beside her, alerting the warriors to his movement. The archers prepared to shoot again as new arrows appeared from nothing, loaded in their crossbows.

Then the leader stopped them. *"Kushikilia!"*

Celeste made a motion, blocking Jack from their shots and making what sounded to Jack as a new plea. *"Kubwa uchawi. Yeye aliniokoa. Angeweza kuwa jibu letu!"*

The lead warrior glared at Jack intensely before leaping from the branch and joining him on the ground. He appeared even taller and more alien-like up close. He looked over Jack as if judging his worthiness to live. After another glance at his totem, Jack understood the warrior must have noticed the gear symbol and recognized it as the symbol of the kingdom.

"What exactly did you say to them?" Jack asked.

Celeste continued looking at the warriors but spoke to Jack quietly as if they didn't know she knew how to speak another language. "I told them you held powerful magic that could aid our cause, and you saved me from the hunters. Both metal and the king's science is forbidden in the forest, so I warn you to move slowly with your weapons."

Without a word spoken to Celeste, the warrior leader pointed to two warriors. *"Kumpeleka mkuu!"*

The two warriors jumped down and stepped over to Jack, roughly taking his totem and jacket.

"Hey! What are you—" He quickly gave up fighting as they lifted him like a doll.

They tried to collect his watch, as well. However, Phoenix's magic seemed to overpower their strength, and it remained bonded to his wrist. After a few attempts, one of the warriors threatened to use a knife to either remove it or remove Jack's hand—he wasn't sure which, but he doubted they cared. Luckily, the tallest warrior directed them to escort him farther into the woods.

The trip to the village center was much shorter than the trek through the forest. Jack assumed the warriors had been stationed there to protect their home from intruders. The walk felt reminiscent of marching into the courtroom of Cloud City, with a warrior guarding him on each side. He didn't see Celeste anywhere near them, but he doubted she was in any danger. He only hoped someone would be more inclined to listen to him than the warriors — and able to understand.

He heard drums as he traipsed through the thickest parts of the rainforest lit by torches with blue flames. He no longer heard the swift steps of animals or buzzing of insects, as if they knew better than to follow. Celeste ran by him and through a doorway of cleverly grown branches. He was guided into a camp area, where a large dancing fire cast sparks of green, yellow, purple, and blue into the air. Crackling with every visible color in the rainbow, it was reminiscent of the fountain in his father's hotel.

Thousands of huts had been built around the fire pit, not only on the ground but also in the branches of the trees as high as Jack could see. The trees themselves had even been hollowed out to make room for more. The tree homes extended for miles and miles as a light illuminated inside of each with a soft green glow like hovering lanterns. It was less like a village and more like a city of native people coming and going from tree to tree. Though they varied in age and height from children to the elderly, they shared the same lean build. Many had indigo markings that Jack assumed identified families. Everyone seemed to be looking out from the huts at once, as if they knew a stranger had entered their land.

The drums grew louder. Like the heartbeat of the earth itself, they vibrated through Jack's body. His guards pushed him into the camp area, where the fire roared several feet into the air with each beat and lowered instantly as the drums came to a sudden stop. Only the crackling embers refused to remain silent.

Across the fire pit, opposite Jack, stood a man draped in an animal hide and feathers of a strange bird Jack was glad he hadn't seen yet. He was shorter and much thinner than the other warriors. A twisted beak circled with a crown of feathers hung over the villager's head, pointing toward his hooked nose. A gruesome scar twisted the stern expression on his face. His injury showed a portion of the inside of his mouth and eye socket.

Leaning heavily on his staff, he limped toward Jack, glaring as if he were a new subject to experiment on. *"Ni kitu gani?"*

The warriors forced Jack to his knees as the man used his gnarled staff to gesture at the warriors. They dropped Jack's totem and held up his wrist, displaying the watch. Jack noticed the warriors seemed to look at him in both disgust and fear, and wondered if the scarred man was Celeste's father, the chief.

"Uchawi mpya." The lead warrior sneered, pointing at Jack. The strange native looked at Jack's items before revealing a pouch beneath the animal hide on his waist. He grinned sinisterly, unraveling the knot, before a loud voice rang out like a loudspeaker.

"Kuacha! Binti yangu maombi uwepo wake." A massive warrior stepped out of the largest hut beyond the fire pit. He had a strong build, wider than most of the warriors, yet it was covered in a beautiful white crystalized skin from his left shoulder to his waist, displaying the head of a massive dragon-like animal with three horns around its head and long whiskers. Tiger-striped feathers Jack recognized from the bird he'd seen earlier had been tied around his waist and shoulders. His skin

was pale white like the moon, with markings of the darkest midnight violet that matched his hair, which hung in several long braids down his back. Despite the wrinkles on his face, his eyes seemed youthful and animalistic, ready to pounce at any moment. Just behind him, Celeste poked her head out of the hut, and both the villagers surrounding them and the warriors began speaking in hushed tones Jack still was unable to understand.

"*Kutoa hotuba.*" The massive warrior pointed at the limping villager. Jack assumed the larger warrior was the real chief. Looking disappointed, the wounded native revealed another pouch as if he were losing his new favorite toy. After removing a handful of blue powder, he gripped Jack by the throat, throttling his neck and shoving him onto the ground with his one good hand.

"Get… off!" Jack choked, fighting off the villager. The leather cloth made to cover his arms shook wildly as Jack fought him off, revealing only a shoulder, where he was missing most of his arm. Jack felt his throat and ears pinching shut and a fiery pain all at once. Seconds later, he was released, and the pain drifted into his chest then left altogether. The murmuring of the people around him became fluid as he was able to understand the chattering, catching a few words here or there. The longer he lay on the ground, the more he understood. Although it seemed he would be able to communicate, Jack already didn't like where things were headed from the crowd's accusations.

"Is it a spy?" one villager asked.

"It must be. Look how tan it is."

"It must be from the Siku Kingdom. I don't trust it."

"We should have destroyed it." A warrior spat. "It must be a new breed from the gray outbreak. He uses magic from the kingdom!"

"*Silence!*" the elder warrior ordered in a deep voice, stepping down from his hut. He addressed all of the villagers within listening distance. "We are *not* the animals the Sikupess think we are. My daughter has asked that we listen to the creature, and so we will."

Celeste's father raised his hand, gesturing for Jack to tell his story, and Jack was fairly sure his life depended on how well it went. Jack stood, still rubbing his throat, glaring at the strange villager who had attacked him. The village chief took a deep breath, making his tall stature even more titan-like. "Talk, Sky Boy. Tell us how you came to this land, and so we may understand you."

Jack studied the villagers then looked up at the chief, regarding the wrinkles of wisdom but lack of patience already forming. "Well, it's sort of a long and confusing story," he mumbled. "My name's Jack, and this is all a part of my challenge to… well, the important thing is that I'm not a threat. My, um… dog was taken from me when I landed in all that sand. I was sent from another world to find a source to power this totem, along with two tokens or keys? Once I find them and unlock the power source, I can go home."

Jack realized how odd the story sounded and held Nucalibur, displaying it as innocently as possible, although several villagers stepped away. "I'm not your enemy. I don't even know who those soldiers are. I just want to find my friend, find these keys, the source, and go home."

"He wields magic with *their* symbol, Chief Mizzi." The lead warrior approached. "It is magic we have never witnessed. It is my burden and privilege to protect our people. He is strange to us and a potential threat. I doubt even the shaman has seen such things. It is an unnecessary risk."

The one-handed man sneered at the warrior intently before walking by the fire pit.

"Are you to tell me our greatest warrior is afraid of a boy with a stick?" the chief asked before addressing Jack. "Our village is buried deep within the Usiku Forest, where my people, the Usikupess—Night People—have lived since the beginning. Thieves have entered our den and stolen secrets handed down from our ancestors' great chiefs. I will not have their lives threatened. You may have precious little time. Choose these final words wisely. Why should we trust that you are not a thief who has been caught?"

His voice was stern and ferocious yet calm. Jack noticed the wounded villager he guessed was the shaman the lead warrior spoke of prepare something in his pouch. Warriors stepped toward him with daggers more lethal looking than Celeste's, and that was when Jack had an answer.

"Because she trusts me." He pointed. "Celeste, your daughter, trusts me to be here, so I would ask her," Jack said carefully. "I'm not here to steal or hurt anyone… your, um, chiefly-ness?"

The chief studied Jack before turning to his daughter. "Tell me of his arrival. What makes you believe in this *boy*?"

Celeste took in a deep breath and began with something Jack hadn't expected. "I believe in him because of the mystics."

Gasps followed, but Jack remained confused.

The shaman appeared to be angry. "What does he have to do with the ancient ones?"

"The signs," she answered. "He fell from the sky clutching an enchanted beacon that changed before my eyes into an *mbwa* pup and then into a great beast! His magic is different than we've ever seen. Ten years have passed since the fall of the smallest sun, and I believe he is here as foretold by the mystics."

The buzz of murmurs began again, and Jack couldn't tell if he was already losing his ability to understand them or if everyone was talking about him at once. The chief studied Jack carefully as if they were playing a card game that would cost the loser much more than money.

"*Mystics?*" Jack asked. "A mystic what?"

The chief raised his chin, looking down at Jack, debating his worthiness. Sighing deeply, he seemed to come to a conclusion. "My daughter… join me at the ancestral path… and bring your *Jack*. We will test his worthiness and allow *them* to decide."

Jack's eyes darted to Celeste's, where he hoped to find reassurance. He could feel her attempts to not appear worried, but she was doing poorly. She looked similar to how Spring had when sentencing him to face the challenges. He had no idea who the chief was referring to as *them*, but he had learned quickly that surprises in Cloud City were rarely pleasant.

She guided Jack up a path covered by smooth stones and patches of freshly fallen leaves. He could tell the trail hadn't been walked along in quite some time. The leaves alone covered his sneakers as he proceeded, kicking up bunches of the debris as though it were soft snow. Eventually, Celeste led him to the far end of the village, where long vines and mangled shrubs hid a small cavern. A young white tiger cub with purple stripes followed her to the outside of an entrance before curling up just outside the cavern.

Black scorch marks scarred the opening, curving out as if something had broken out many years ago. Crystalized rocks inside all held the same ominous pale-red illumination, humming with trapped energy. Hieroglyphs had been carved and burned into the surrounding walls, and a phrase atop read: *Nchi Kubwa Analala.*

"Earth Giant Sleeps?" Jack finally asked. "What is this place?"

"This is where the mystics first made the predictions shortly after connecting with the essence of life nearly a century ago." She held her arms tightly as if afraid to be inside the cave. "They experienced visions and marked them here to permanently maintain the message throughout generations."

She pointed at the rough drawings around the cavern from one side to the other, stopping in the middle each time. "Three mystics each scribed their messages separately. The one to your left, another to your right, and the one in the center. Two stories concluding into one."

To the left, a long-haired figure running followed a crown. The drawings depicted an animal, a tall tree, a crescent moon, a person falling from something high, and a mountain. On the other side, carved similarly, was the same long-haired figure wearing the crown, then a picture of a gear, a fallen tree, then a person falling from a high point again. The second set of drawings also ended with the mountain.

"Beginning, middle, and end?" Jack guessed.

The chief's daughter shook her head. "No. The left is one story, the right is another, and the mountain in the middle is an ending that completes them both equally."

"I don't understand," Jack admitted. "How can they both have the same ending?"

"Only one story will come true, and it will end the war between the Night People of the village, and the Day People in the kingdom." She pointed to the figure in the middle, with its crude illustration of a glowing heart. He struggled to understand the stories the simple drawings were telling.

"Has someone figured out what they mean yet?"

"Mostly theories until this day, but with your arrival, the story became a reality we cannot allow." The chief walked in, towering in the small amount of space. He guided Jack around the left side of the wall, deciphering the crude drawings in his low, beastly voice.

"The three Mystics returned from a powerful source of ancient magic as old as the earth beneath you. They were guided from the source to these woods, where we have built this village that provides food, shelter, and shade from the suns' dangers. The first great mystic's vision tells the story of a young king and his army chasing a woman into the forest. A dangerous beast would arrive, with antlers the size of tree branches, hooves that shook the ground for miles, and the strength to strike fear into both man and animal alike. No one survived an encounter with this ruthless animal, and it never showed mercy. A long-haired woman with unmatched beauty escaped from the king and was attacked by the beast. It seemed she, too, was destined to share the fate others had, until a rescuer came." The chief pointed to the image of a tree.

"A warrior's strength and magic-blessed from the forest, he maneuvered around the forest, confusing the beast, then uprooted a tree to fall on the beast's head and remove part of its antler. From that moment, they were to be married and give birth to a child. She passed away, birthing their daughter. The false king hasn't stopped hunting for her. Nearly twenty years elapsed before the next part of the prophecy came." The chief pointed to the falling figure diving toward wavy lines.

"Is that supposed to be *me*?" Jack stared at the falling figure next to the crescent moon and tree. "The tree is the great warrior. And the crescent… the daughter moon was Celeste? This is about *your* family."

The chief's daughter nodded slowly as if ashamed; however, her father touched his fingertips to the long-haired woman on the wall as if the drawing were a shrine.

"Your arrival could mean a more dangerous path for my people." The chief gestured to the marks on Jack's right. "Her mother held a terrible sickness caused by the king's fallen sun. I must keep what she has left me safe. My daughter and my people have been through enough tragedy with my wife's passing and the dangers since. There are many more of us, but we are weakened in the daylight. Your presence could cause more suffering if the wrong prediction comes true."

A familiar lump of fear and worry formed in Jack's throat. He found it harder to swallow than a large pill as he asked the obvious. "So what does that mean for me?"

The chief stepped closer to Jack, fully displaying his stature, making Jack feel like a houseplant next to a tree. "We are a people of pride and respect. My daughter means more to me than the war stirring with the golden king, but I will not have my people enslaved by those tiny people. You are a threat to the future, much like the gray ones. We must handle threats for the good of our people."

He then glanced into his daughter's eyes, and Jack saw the weight of the battle within him. "But you also saved my daughter. My people believe in balance, and that includes a debt of life. For that, I will let fate and your strength decide your destiny. If you survive, you will have earned your place among the village and be welcomed."

"If I survive?" Jack asked.

"In our village, we understand that every life comes with a cost." Celeste unfolded her arms. "Including the ones you save. You'll have to go where the gray ones wander."

Jack brushed his hand on the mountain, feeling a heart shape in the center of it. "What are you talking about? What gray ones?"

"There are just two suns and one moon left now," the chief continued. "Years ago, there were three suns that shared the sky. The first sun was the mega sun and began the day. Once it nearly set, it was followed by a smaller sun half its size. Then finally, the smallest sun came. Once the suns fell, night began, and we were able to leave the forest freely in the moonlight. This was the cycle before the last sun burst."

Jack leaned against the cave. "One of the suns burst?"

"Yes," Celeste confirmed. "It was blinding for anyone who was caught outside when it happened. The king's people were able to escape inside their homes, and my people were protected by the forest. Those between our village and the kingdom either ran to the forbidden swamps or were branded by the sun streaks. The embers burned parts of the land, created the sandpit you landed in, and covered the people caught outside in gray ash after blinding them."

"Most became wild, unable to see anything at all suddenly," the chief explained. "Those people started attacking like animals, using their other senses, hunting anything that smelled or sounded like food. But many of these people lost more senses from the gray ash covering them. A sickness spread, and they were drawn to the shade of the forest, as they are sensitive to light and heat. A few wandered into the forest's valley."

"That's horrible," Jack muttered, yet a part of him was strangely intrigued by the story.

"We were born of night, and only my daughter, most likely due to her mother, can walk in the sun without being weakened or without magic. But with the smallest sun gone, there is now a new part of the night, called 'the gray.' Where there is no sunlight and no moonlight. No visible stars for a period each day. It is the darkest part of the night, when nothing can be seen. If you can survive during this time, you will be an honored guest of the village, and I will show you the way to your friend. If the forest deems you worthy, it will help you."

Jack thought about the spirit of Father's Day and his warning of the challenge. He looked down at the marking of the tree then the cog. "I'll also need a moonleaf made of stone. What do I have to do to get one of those?"

The warriors took Jack deeper into the village as the second sun was setting. He soon understood the chief's hut wasn't his home but more of a welcome area that was merely the forefront of just one section of the village. The village expanded nearly the length of the forest itself, and Chief Mizzi led them all.

Villagers began following the moment Jack returned from the cave, and even more gathered along the way. A few dozen quickly became hundreds, and before long, a few thousand people—all with dark-purplish or green hair and pale skin—watched as Jack was ushered by. Whispers of the Sky Boy spread like the fire ignited from torch to torch. They followed Jack, the chief, his daughter, and the scarred villager to the lip of a valley.

"This is where all of us have been tested!" Chief Mizzi announced near a veil of vines and branches. Villagers both young and old encircled them, watching patiently. "This is where each of us became part of the night and has proven our right to be more than a part of a village, but a part of this noble tribe working as one. And this is where the visitor will be tested to judge his will and his nature! For you to survive, Jack the Sky Boy, you must trust in the balance of nature."

The native with the scarred face limped forward. Waving his hand beneath the vines, he chanted, repeating a command that caused the vines to unravel. They released each other, snaking away as the branches rustled and bent, unfolding like paper fans. A well-traveled dirt path stretched down into a deep valley of trees, circling down into a funnel. One tree stood out like a skyscraper, rising above all the other trees and glistening with fresh dew in the moonlight. It was grander than any other, shadowing them all like a protective parent.

The lead warrior tossed Jack's totem at his sneakers. "Take your magic. Use what the world offers you to reach the tree at the bottom of the valley and return a single leaf touched by moonlight to me before the first sunrise. The great tree holds roots tapped into the great power source touched by the mystics. If you can survive the time of the gray and the night, you will be welcomed back as our brother."

"It's there?" Jack pointed at the large tree. "Is this where the power source is?"

"Fool…" the limping villager spat. "The source has an *end* here. Even powering the Great Tree, its weakest point is down in this valley. The true source is much, much stronger, and well hidden in the heart of the mountain, but it won't be long before I discover how to utilize the roots."

"If you can return, we will aid your preparation to enter the kingdom and rescue your pet," the chief finished. "Our shaman will be able to turn the moonleaf into stone once you return. It will hold as your mark of the village."

"Maybe I could take a written test instead?" Jack requested. "There are a lot of trees around. Has anyone heard of mystic paper and pencil, possibly?"

Thousands of eyes watched Jack as he picked up his totem. Celeste reached down to pat his shoulder, leaning in to whisper, "This is tradition. Only the ones closest to the moonlight will hold its shimmer long enough for you to return with it. Follow nature, and you will survive, but be careful. The animals beneath the Great Tree were born in the shade, and the ash-covered people who wandered there are just as dangerous. Listen to the visions and remember: men who run away from fear bring back the most noise." A breeze rushed by, rustling the leaves as Jack began his first steps onto the dirt path.

The trees were merciless, providing neither warmth from the last sun setting, nor comfort from poor sight. The branches scratched and fought back with Jack's every step forward. The looming shadow of the Great Tree supplied an unsettling darkness that hid nearly everything left of the sun within a few yards of him. Yet the worst part of his journey was caused by his own thoughts of what might be hiding or watching him. Images flashed through his mind as he listened to the sounds of an animal running by or calling out. At least he assumed it was an animal. Then, just as suddenly, it would stop with a quick snap, followed by the sound of chewing.

Jack held Nucalibur tightly. The totem's glowing emblems, along with his watch, offered him little illumination. He missed his flashlight. Not only for its light, but a companion he felt safe with. For the first time since arriving at the hotel, he felt truly alone. He hated not knowing what was happening to Rocho—or to Sonny while she waited for him.

His thoughts drifted, but the sounds grew steadily closer. The cruel sound of gnawing forced him to look over his shoulder repeatedly, but he continued forward. His heart thumped harder, fueling his adrenaline. His hands shook, squeezing the totem harder. He convinced himself to continue on, though he wanted to run away. Jack pushed away branch after branch, muttering the same list repeatedly to carry on. "Grab the leaf, magic cog, Rocho, get to the heart of the mountain, save Sonny, then Dad."

Before he realized it, the sun had set, and the darkness settled into the woods. Closing his eyes left the same amount of visibility. He swung his totem out, only hitting the occasional tree before stumbling over a vine. In the light from the totem, he noticed footprints on the ground, heading away from the Great Tree. The totem's illumination lit only the area around his face when he was not holding it near the ground. Before long, he couldn't tell if he was actually seeing figures or if his mind was creating things in the dark.

Sounds of chewing were soon replaced by silence, then running footsteps. Something rustled through the branches then rushed by Jack. He stood utterly still, careful not to breathe loudly. Something soft brushed his neck, and he hoped it was just a breeze. Soft panting near his ear caused him to turn slowly, and what he found would be burned into his memory whenever he closed his eyes. It was a woman—at least he thought it was. Clumps of her hair had been torn out, leaving patches, and her skin clung to her frail body like leather covered in tattered clothing and gray ash. Jack took a few steps back.

The woman let out a bloodcurdling screech, baring her teeth and widening her cloudy eyes. Jack extended his totem, the sharp point ejected out, and he struck her in the leg before sprinting. More screeching followed on either side of him. He still couldn't see as something scratched his face, then one of the gray people tackled another before something new came into view.

A soft shimmer of light poked out of the branches farther down the valley. Jack could see the gray people outside the trail getting closer as he hurried down. One clawed at his back, and he rolled down the remaining part of the hill until he finally landed near a pond drenched in the light radiating from somewhere deep down within, like an aura. The gray people shielded their eyes and ran off as if the soft light were eating away at their skin. Jack crawled closer to the lip of the water, hoping he wouldn't have to go inside because he wasn't the best swimmer. Mist shrouded the pond, obscuring his vision, but he stared at it as figures danced into his sight.

A deck of cards as tall as Jack patrolled around the brim. Eventually, the joker marched forward, flipping itself and tumbling until a black magician's hat appeared. Every card leapt into the hat before vanishing completely. Then a giant walked through an ocean, wearing a crown and swinging a tree like a baseball bat. The giant was suddenly struck by a shadow, and the vision changed as it fell. His body transformed into an island covered by a sizeable crumbling stone. As it fell apart, a single playing card rose from the rubble. The king of spades with the head of a skull stared at Jack with empty sockets, then the images faded.

Jack prepared to crawl away but heard the brushing of leaves and the snapping of twigs. As he turned toward the sound, he spotted white scaly skin glimmering in the water's light just as he was propelled backward through the air and into the pond. He was walloped in the chest with what felt like a massive club as a tail whipped out of sight.

Though stunned, Jack regained his balance. "That wasn't a gray…" He searched for the animal. His totem was ready, spearhead ejected and pointed. Holding it threateningly, he panted heavily, waiting for movement, scanning the area. The scurrying sound came from every direction. He backed up to the edge of the water, where the most light was visible, and waited. Without warning, the creature leapt from a tree limb, landing on top of him. Jack held the spear in place, fending it off. The lizard's rubbery skin changed to blue, and piercing red eyes followed Jack through the darkness. It snarled within inches of Jack's face. The snout dripped onto his shirt, and it continued to bite and lash at him. The beast was strong, and its claws were digging into Jack's shoulder. He held the spear between them, barely holding the creature's weight, keeping himself out of the pond, and yelling in pain until he was able to get his legs up to kick the animal off.

The lizard was stunned as it landed in the pond, but that didn't last long. It quickly maneuvered out of the water and was changing its color into a sickly green. Lurching back, it spewed a dripping green ball at Jack like a cannon. He was barely able to roll away, but it caught the edge of his leg. The burning sensation was the worst he'd felt since the mask Mother had given him and Sonny. The skin on his leg bubbled, leaving it raw and red as he limped away onto the other side of the pond. He made sure to keep the lizard within view. Its tongue slipped out like a serpent's as it waited across the shimmering water. It continued to just stand there, snout in the air and red eyes watching. It wasn't until Jack scurried to stand that it began chasing again.

He wanted to run farther into the woods, but he would lose any advantage in the darkness. He thought about using the watch, but the aging effect was too unpredictable. The lizard creature continued to lob acid at him but missed by a wider and wider gap. Whenever Jack stopped, the lizard would attack again and again, firing dripping green blobs that burned away trees and portions of the ground and caused a few branches to fall. He backed up, ducking another ball that struck just above his head, and a glimmer of hope shined through.

Moonlight peeked through the forest. The lizard raised his tail, turning a bright-orange color, and closed its eyes. From head to tail, a long flame ignited, dancing brightly down its spine. The heat radiated from across the pool. It began sniffing the air, searching for Jack—and that was when Jack stopped.

"It can't see me unless it's dark," he whispered to himself. "His eyes… they've evolved in the darkness beneath the tree's shadow."

The lizard paused, looking in Jack's direction, then began sprinting after Jack with its back ablaze. Jack ran his hand down the totem, feeling the notches, unsure what the next twist would do. His bleeding shoulder made it difficult to hold onto, but he stood firm. The lizard lunged at him, its body engulfed in flames, mouth open wide with those dangerous fangs.

Then Jack braced himself for what would happen next.

The lizard landed atop Jack, pinning him against a tree. The embers around its body seared Jack's face and hands. The creature wriggled from head to tail, and it shook and scratched until the fire dimmed. Finally, with great relief, Jack pushed the beast off. His spear was stuck in its chest. Jack released a line, collapsed his spear, and rolled behind the tree, throwing the small totem over a branch. The moment the lizard lurched toward him, Jack pulled the totem, leaning back with all his weight and making it impossible for the animal to reach him. It scratched and clawed inches from his face, but Jack held tightly, hauling the animal higher into the air. The biting and snapping of its jaw slowed, and as the claws went limp, its flaming back burned out, and its head bobbled slightly then stilled.

He released the totem, and the lizard fell to the ground with a thump. A foul-smelling liquid bubbled from its skin. Scratches crossed his face and back, and he could still feel the burns. The shoulder wound was the worst. It made the task of crawling over to the water that much more difficult.

Jack cupped water in his hands, poured it over his face and head, then collapsed. A few moments passed. He was unsure how long, but he lay near the pond, sensing the calm water near him and feeling very relaxed, when he heard a familiar voice. "How do you keep going from bad to worse, son?"

Jack's eyes fluttered to fix his vision. "Dad? What are you doing here?"

"You know what I'm doing here, son. I'm here for you."

Jack lay still, confused. "You can't be. You're still trapped in the city. It's the whole reason I'm here. To rescue you and…"

"And me?" The voice of a hopeful girl rang behind Jack.

Jack turned his head quickly. "Sonny, what's going on? How are you both here?"

"You know why we're here."

Before he could form a response, Rocho appeared as the tiny loyal pup he'd grown fond of, followed by the Spirit of Father's Day, Christmas, and finally, Jack's mother. Their sudden appearance around him was dizzying, to say the least. Spots dazzled his vision as he looked at each of them around the pond.

"This isn't possible. None of you are really here." Jack repeated the words again and again. "I'm here to save you. Sonny, you were chained to a wall. Mom, you're supposed to be back home."

"That's where you should be, sweetie," his mother replied. "Come back to me. You have to come back. You need to snap out of it."

"I can't. I have to help Dad. I have to save them," Jack pleaded. "That's why I'm here. I have to save them."

"How will you do that, son?" his father asked. "I've already passed away. You can't bring me with you. What are you here to do?"

Jack shook his head. "Get the heart of the mountain to save you. I need to save you from this place and make sure you're all right."

"Why?" His father stepped closer, his outline blurrier. "Tell me why, son."

"Teddy took you!" Jack argued. "And I have to make sure…"

"Why are you really here?"

"Because… because I can't let you go," Jack admitted. The blurred images of his mother and the holiday spirits faded away, leaving Sonny, Rocho, and his father. "Now ask me again, son."

"Why are you here?" Jack asked sternly.

Sonny vanished, followed by Rocho.

"You know why I'm here, son. I know you know. Your mother and I have taught you how to be strong, be smart, and be a decent person," his father said slowly.

Reaching out to his father, Jack's hand traveled through him. "To remind me why I keep going because… you're not really here."

The image of his father vanished, and Jack stayed on his knees near the water. He was staring into the pond, which continued to shimmer, and his legs felt weaker than ever as he stood as if he'd been standing endlessly. He was dangerously close to the pond, as if he would like nothing else but to dive in and stay under for eternity. Checking his watch, he became more confused. A few hours had gone, and he hadn't noticed.

When he regained his footing, he quickly maneuvered around the water. His shoulder was still hurting but not as much. He was able to remove his totem from the motionless lizard with a single pull. The smell had become horrible by the time he limped away. He paused, hearing another swish just beyond the pond. More tails rustled through the woods. And he spotted four more of those lizards, each sniffing the air as it edged around the water.

Jack looked down at the spearhead of Nucalibur, where he could still smell the dead lizard. Before the others had a chance to surround him, he picked up the dead animal and threw it into the pond. He backed away slowly as the others turned toward the loud splash. One by one, possibly confused by the shimmering light or following the spoiling smell, they all followed it into the pond, flailing as they hit the water. Jack backed away, and when he was far enough to barely see the light, he turned and didn't look back.

Echoes from the woods no longer followed him, and his eyesight had finally adjusted to the darkness. Occasionally, he would come to a divided path, but he made quick decisions as if he could feel the Great Tree near. The moon was out, brighter and closer than he'd ever seen, and he spotted glowing leaves in the distance. After a bit more walking, he finally felt it. His entire body thumped with the sensation as if it were a part of his own heartbeat. A slow pulse rippled through the woods and faded every minute or so. It led him a few hundred yards farther into the valley until he found its end.

He ran into a hard, rough wall stretching farther and farther from either side of him. The edges were rough and jagged, and upon touching it, he realized he was able to chip it away like tree bark. He used the glow of his totem's symbols to search for any weaknesses or a doorway, but none appeared. Jack pushed on the bark then traveled around the surface, wondering if the wall was a border or meant to block him, but it remained firm. His head turned quickly as he heard snapping from a distance, but he continued searching. A pulse rumbled through the bark, and his heart beat excitedly.

"It's the tree," he said astonished. Up close, it was much, much bigger than he could've imagined. The wall was the trunk of a tree so extensive that it created a wall of unmovable bark. Vines and moss hung from the tree branches. Its leaves were identical to the leaves of the treetop, yet they were missing the glow of the moonlight that he desperately needed. As he prepared himself for a devastating climb, he heard another snap, almost like a resounding clap. Jack stretched up to reach the vine but came down hard after missing it altogether. His totem rolled away. Nucalibur's glow flashed with every roll against the bark.

Jack squinted at the symbols: a heart, an Easter egg, a candy cane, a star, a hammer, a candle, a firecracker, and a wishbone. The shamrock remained dull, but the brightly lit crescent moon of his totem drew his eye. He looked up into the distance as the rays of the first sun broke over the plain. He was quickly running out of time and wondered how he could possibly grab a leaf touched by moonlight without climbing.

"I wish Rocho was here." Jack sighed. "All he eats is moonlight. One quick flash might've gotten me…" That was when it struck him—both an idea and what felt like a razor across his cheek. He wobbled, grabbing his cheek where it began to bleed, then scrambled to his totem. He continued hearing what sounded like rubber bands stretching and that same snap before seeing them wriggle around him. Plants from all around the Great Tree's trunk began stirring. Flytraps more sickeningly ferocious, dripping with nectar and hungrier than Jack had ever seen, lurched forward like cobras. Vines covered in thorns slithered toward him like living barbed wire.

"Definitely brings back unpleasant memories of the doctor's garden." Jack took two steps back, and it all began. Half a dozen vines snaked their way toward him while plants with rows and rows of teeth waited for him to be dragged back. He retreated as quickly as possible while they snipped at his heels.

Swinging around a tree, most of the vines were forced to stop short. Yet one was able to wrap around Jack's ankle just before he drew out of reach. He fell to the ground with a loud thud, and it began pulling him back like a winch. Clawing the ground, he reached out for anything that would slow him down, but everything was just out of reach as he was dragged closer to the waiting plants. Nearly missing his totem, he pressed the gear, lifted it as high as he could, and plunged it down onto the vine. It spewed nectar then released a painfully high-pitched squeal that rang out from the biting flower bud, sending more vines after Jack.

Scrambling to his feet, he pressed the leaf symbol and waited for Nucalibur to change. His thumb slid down the base, resting on the crescent moon. He waited until the vines were a few feet away. They raced toward him, slithering among the withered fallen leaves on the ground. Their thorns shredded everything in their path, carving through the forest. Springing up from the ground, they lashed at Jack with stabbing precision just as he lifted the totem.

The vines filled with light, radiating with an ominous blue before shrinking back like dried worms in the sun. Jack had to shield his eyes but forced himself to look at it a moment later. A second moon floated above him, powerful with lunar energy burning away at his surroundings. Tree branches, grass blades, and the leaves on the ground began to fade as if burning beneath the new moon. The blue glow traveled through the vines like electricity through power lines back to the source. A moment later, they, too, were shriveling back to the tree.

Jack chased them through the woods while nursing his bad leg. Whether it was following him or the totem, he didn't know, but the moon hovered just above him. He hobbled over burnt leaves and twigs, feeling the crunch with each step as the vines raveled themselves and the blue glow faded away. Just before they were able to slink back up the tree, Jack leapt forward and clutched the thorny vine.

It pricked his already-burned hands, stinging him without restraint, but he held on. It pulled him between the remaining trees and finally lifted his body so that he was dangling by one arm like an ape. His moon began to flicker, but the plants still shriveled away, igniting the mauling flowers along with the Great Tree's bottom leaves in a soft glow. Once he had reached a proper height, he took his chance. Ejecting the spearhead out of Nucalibur, he swung his spear, cutting down several leaves along with the vine holding him.

The moon faded, and for the second time, he fell through the air. Gripping the totem in his crossed arms, he clenched his eyes tightly, waiting for the impact. The fall knocked the breath from his lungs, but he maneuvered quickly in case the plants returned. He rolled over, watching most of the plants still burning away. A few retained the blue glow he desperately needed. Aching with new bruises and fresh wounds, he grinned. Three leaves floated to the ground, beaming with new moonlight, and landed in his lap like a gift, which he accepted gratefully.

He could still hear the plants shrieking in pain as he stomped through the woods, avoiding the pond where the lizard bodies still floated and ignoring the misty visions attempting to materialize. The sunlight peeked out over the horizon, guiding him back as he slumped forward. A calm reserve washed over him as he felt surprising confidence. While he trekked up the valley, the last thing on his mind was the sun bringing on the morning. Clutching the glowing moonleaves, Jack realized today was only the first day.

Chapter 5
Travelers

Three weeks had passed since Jack's return. His legs had given in near the final part of his climb, forcing him to claw his way up, yet he'd made it. Celeste had waited all night for his return and wrapped her arms around him the moment he arrived. Most of the villagers continued to treat him like an outsider, yet the chief's acceptance was most welcomed. Jack was sure it was due to the mystics' vision and what his triumphant return might mean for his people.

The leaves glowing in moonlight were being used to make Jack the moonleaf stone. After the first week, his wounds were healed and his scars were barely visible. The healers were teaching him how to blend specific plants for medicine, while the warriors reluctantly showed him tracking techniques and how to attack from above. Day after day, Jack healed and prepared for when he would leave to find Rocho then head toward the mountain. He felt stronger and more confident than ever after his trial to the Great Tree, and he took pride in his adopted tribal name of Sky Boy.

He still couldn't get over their many traditions, though: a ceremonial dance to praise the moon before meals, their practice to thank animals for their lives as they hunted, the strange headdresses, digging holes to hide from the highest sun… and the list continued. Jack considered his trek for the moonleaf to be the most concerning tradition. Children half his age were expected to survive the same events. Jack thought that seemed impossible and cruel, but he was told it was meant to erase fear, so he didn't bring it up to anyone.

The last few days, Jack learned about the animals, techniques to fight, and the moon-worshipping culture of the village. He learned how the warriors moved in the darkness like the animals of the area. Some nights, they would ride over-sized iguanas with puffed ruffled necks all around the prairie after the gray period ended and night came. However, he was most excited when the chief finally gave him permission to learn magic from the shaman. The leader walked with him, explaining the history of their village and why they were protective of their magic. After being surveyed and approved by Celeste, he was allowed access to some of the sacred practices of their people.

Chief Mizzi accompanied Jack to the shaman's area while providing details of the village's beginning. "Our village has survived in the valley of this land for centuries, dependent on nature and independent because of it. The war between the Sikupess and Usikupess has stretched and built since the beginning of our existence. They survive during the day, while we do at night. The moon survives, as the suns seem to be dying. We greatly outnumber the kingdom; however, they have manipulated dark magic to create new creatures and increase their army. Our warriors practice natural magic against those who would cause harm to both us and nature."

The chief placed his hand on the ground. "But the first battle began over the earth itself. Our ancestors all knew the earth was alive and must be taken care of, while the Sikupess believed it is a resource. Something to use, to be manipulated and remade in their vision. That is where our war started."

"Why haven't they attacked the forest?" Jack asked. "Burned it down or come in and just fought?"

"Our forest is larger than the hills of the golden king," Chief Mizzi answered. "Burning the forest would cause another period of gray and further destroy the map he's been after. Magic protects the forest from soldiers entering. The sound of the great beast I defeated years ago echoes around it. None of the outsiders can enter because of it."

"What about—"

"Our warriors attacking at night?" the chief guessed Jack's next question. "The day kingdom has found a way to create stone creatures that come to life at night, protecting the borders. Many scouts were lost."

They made their way toward a clearing, where flashes of purple beams streaked out along with the sound of gurgling from a cauldron. "Do you know why I've told you all of this, Sky Boy?"

Jack thought about the lessons he'd learned recently and the stories he'd been told. He shook his head.

"Our magic is sacred and an important part of our heritage. Days ago, thieves discovered a way into our village and stole a map left to me by the mystics who've been to the same source you look for. I believe they've discovered how to use magic to access our village. We are all capable of producing strong magic because the source of our magic has roots everywhere, but our shaman knows more than any other. He serves as my right hand as my warriors are my left, and together, they cannot be stopped. What he shares with you is entrusted to only you and must never be shared with those outside these woods. Is this understood?"

Jack nodded slowly. Then the chief left Jack alone, squinting through the branches at his new teacher. Jack moved toward the clearing as quietly as possible. Stepping between the curtains of dangling leafy vines, Jack spotted him. He hadn't seen the scarred villager in weeks. The marks on his face and back were worse than Jack had realized. They looked like deep claw marks made by an animal or possibly the people covered in ash.

The villager stood over a cauldron, mixing plants with a silver liquid from a vial, shimmering water Jack recognized from the pond near the Great Tree. Different ingredients Jack had never seen were piled on a table beside him. The shaman studied a sheet with diagrams of parts and equations Jack recognized as a much older version of blueprints. Then the sound came.

"Ahhhhh!" The shaman grunted, attempting to stifle a yell, gritting his teeth. It looked like the cauldron had somehow bit or pulled him in up to his armpit. When he raised his arm into the air, Jack noticed the man's missing arm had become a gleaming lustrous gold dripping with a green substance. He watched in astonishment as the shaman flexed his newly formed metallic fingers and folded them into a fist. He was breathing heavily but grinning with accomplishment.

Horrified, Jack stepped forward, but a bubbling sound followed by an alarming smell stopped him. Burning meat.

"No, no, nooo!" The shaman watched as his newly formed arm disintegrated into a puddle of liquid metals. He pounded his strong hand onto blueprints before tossing over the table, startling Jack and making his presence known.

"What are you doing here, boy?" he shouted, waving a hand over the papers, causing them to vanish.

"It's my last day," Jack stuttered. "Chief Mizzi said you would teach me how to use magic, but…" He wanted to mention how the shaman's "magic" seemed more like science—and ask why the arm had fallen apart.

"It appears magic can't fix everything, without the right materials." The shaman's face screwed into a bored, cruel smirk. "Whatever the chief wants, I will supply."

Jack took notice of his sarcastic tone. "I'm guessing this was a waste of time? You think the chief was wrong to let me stay?"

"Chief Mizzi saved my life and gave me a great purpose." The shaman looked at the empty space below his shoulder, where his arm should've been. "I took a trip into the swamps for a powerful ingredient. It cost me a limb and earned a few other permanent marks, but I would do anything for him and my people."

"An animal took your arm?"

The shaman's gaze drifted off. "There are some things much worse than beasts, but they hunt you just the same."

Puzzled, Jack continued into the clearing. "What were you looking for?"

"The source," the shaman answered in an annoyed tone. "The one thing I cannot seem to find a way around."

"Isn't that supposed to be in the mountain?"

The shaman stared at the puddle of his arm soaking into the ground. "There's a beginning and end to everything, and it is not always in the same area. The Great Tree has roots from the source, but even it is not pure enough. Some great magics are larger than you could ever imagine and grander than your mind can understand. I found an end easier to locate, but much more dangerous to get to. Teaching you our ways is just as dangerous. But I would never go against our rightful leader."

"What makes you think I'm so dangerous to—"

"Because you were and are a threat, Sky Boy! A new threat to this village and someone with magic I've not seen."

Jack studied his new instructor's workspace. A few metal bolts lay among the smoking cauldron that had caught his attention. "I thought metal wasn't allowed in the village?"

"It wouldn't be if I were an outsider," the shaman explained, holding up a vial of thick black liquid. "This is a very powerful ink gathered from spibs found underwater. Permanent when written with but will paralyze you in seconds unless dry. It can be deadly if swallowed unless weakened with water, and it is the basis of much magic we use. Burning it allows us to send messages from one part of the forest to another. Those who walk into the village are all capable of magic. It is our closeness to the source that allows us this ability and our will that makes us strong enough to wield it. The red roots from the source stretch deep into the ground, deeper than any of us can access. I am able to control it better than any other since the mystics."

Walking through the entrance, Jack was able to survey the materials and area. Some vials and a tree stump used as a table reminded Jack of Dr. de Luca's laboratory. "This looks more like science than magic."

"Magic of the foolish king. Do you understand how our magic and the king's science are different?" the shaman asked, producing a proud blue ball of flames in his palm. "Magic cannot be explained simply. It cannot be proven to work the same way. It must be willed by someone who can. It is a belief in yourself and the earth. It is an ability that must be felt through your spirit and aided by real power!"

He glanced at his missing arm and wounded shoulder beneath his leather tribal wear before clutching his fist and extinguishing the flame with a snap. "And one day, my magic will have no limitations. Let us begin."

Jack dripped in sweat, grunting, his palms on his knees, while the shaman levitated his totem effortlessly. "You're not trying hard enough. The little ones in our village master this in their sleep by accident. Connect with everything around you and feel it breathe."

"I'm trying!" Jack panted. "Can't you teach me how to make a fireball or something instead? Turn people into sheep?"

"I don't know how you found a way to get the moonleaves here, and for some reason, the chief's daughter believes in you, but you are not one of us! Making it go away is not possible. You must conceal it. Bend the natural colors to blend with its surroundings and hide it. Use every emotion of love, hate, and passion pulling into your stomach and then release it. That is where your magic will build. If you do not believe that this magic tool can do more, you will never succeed." The shaman waved his arm, and Nucalibur was gone. Then he produced a ball of fire in his palm that grew larger. "If you cannot hide something that is already here, you will not create something that is not. Now find your magic!"

Jack continued trying for hours but had little success. He eventually was able to change the totem's color, though nothing more. The shaman demonstrated some of his abilities to produce phantom daggers and the arrows the warriors used.

Mixing a few rare ingredients, he changed himself into the weird color-changing lizard that had attacked Jack near the pond. For a moment, he wondered if the shaman had followed him into the woods then pushed the thought out of his mind.

After the session wore down his will, the shaman let Jack sit and used the spib ink on parchment paper to make a map leading to the kingdom where he would find Rocho. Shortly after, Celeste gathered Jack for his final night in the village, and Chief Mizzi provided a feast in his honor. He tried to remain spirited but needed rest. The day had been his most exhausting mental workout yet. The moment his eyes were closed, he fell asleep.

The next morning, he prepared himself. He'd been up for hours studying the map. The villagers gathered around him near the village's entrance, as they had the night he'd arrived. During a warrior ceremony, the tip of Jack's totem was dipped into a red powder. Celeste made a travel pack of food and water for him. The chief gave him a blessing of protection before his final departure.

"With this blessing, nature will make your arm strong, your heart pure, and your weapon swift. As you protect this village, it will protect you," the chief announced. "If you wish to use the source to travel home, you will need to find the stolen map. It is protected by magic so only I can read it. I suspect the kingdom may already have it."

"An encoded map?" Jack asked. "And you'll read it for me?"

The chief scowled. "I fear my daughter may carry the same illness as my wife. She can survive the daylight, but if she leaves this forest, this sickness could kill her in a day or so. If you can save her, I will help you get to the source."

"Do you understand, Jack?" Celeste pleaded. "I may be cured if you help us, and we will do all we can to help you."

Jack didn't hesitate before agreeing. "Whatever I have to do to get us back home and help you, I will."

Celeste bowed gratefully. "You will need to find an old medicine man who survived the kingdom's illness. It is said he created a cure and lived. If the map is held by the gold king, we will need to give something of value to aid him."

Jack looked between the chief and his daughter. "What are you giving the kingdom?"

"The end of the war," the chief answered.

Celeste continued. "My father will agree to give King Aurum access to the source once he returns the map, as long as the source remains in the earth and we can get a cure for the illness. There will be no need to fight any longer, as we will use and preserve the earth."

Chief Mizzi took Jack by the shoulders. "Return with your friend before the moon devours the sun. Our shaman has predicted this is when war must come. It will be our only chance to defeat them during daylight. We will be celebrating the moon's triumph at that time. If they have not agreed to these terms by then, we must use this advantage to attack."

"So get to the kingdom, find the Zookeeper to get Rocho, the Medicine Man for a cure, bring back the map, and I still need an enchanted cog," Jack summarized. "Any milk from the corner store, or is that all?"

Celeste hugged Jack, pressing into his wrist while whispering in his ear, "I thank you for your bravery and for saving me. You *are* the savior we've been waiting for. The moonleaf stone will guide you through the forest. The earth will help you find your way."

The journey out of the forest didn't feel nearly as long as his chase in. None of the animals seemed to notice him, and none of the strange frost returned. Besides the purple rolling rabbits, which the villagers called "cross-hares," they were not followed. As the silent warriors guided him out, Jack began wondering what other surprises he would need to watch out for.

Finally, he spotted the natural daylight in the distance. He'd reached the outline of trees bordering the plains, careful not to be seen if the king's guards patrolled. None of the mechanical animals that'd chased him into Night Forest were around, and neither were the guards.

"It appears they have abandoned their watch," the warrior said. "Be safe, Sky Boy."

Jack paused for a moment before he took a careful look out. The transparent birds he'd encountered over a week prior were already diving into the sandpit for their breakfast. Memories of their pecking flooded back in a wave, and Jack found himself rubbing his arm absentmindedly. After some time, he was confident the area was clear, so he hoisted his pack and Nucalibur then made his way out.

If he weren't pressed for time, he might've been able to enjoy the serene view. It was a beautiful cloudless day with a soft breeze. Wild blue-and-black-spotted horses with tightly spiraled horns and manes and tails long enough to brush the ground grazed a short distance from the sandpit. Jack had learned to ride the swollen iguana-like reptiles with ruffled necks while in the forest, and Redd Rocket had taught him to ride horses. It didn't take Jack long to mount the animal and begin his ride across the prairie.

"Around the pit, through the plains, follow the river to the lake, head through the town, over the mines, and into the kingdom." Jack read the map carefully. "Only a few days, Rocho. Hold on, buddy."

Jack rode through the plains for most of the day, until the second sun rose. He followed the river, doing anything he could to pass the time. The young detective practiced the magic the shaman had taught him to hide his totem, but that began to tire him out quickly. He used the rod to catch fish with fins the color of fire. He'd always imagined he would go fishing with his father, and he got a chill from a breeze just after. Later, he spotted white doves with reptilian bodies and flippers like turtles flying above him headed toward the same lake he rode toward coming into view. He remained guarded, checking his surroundings for anyone or anything that might approach him.

He was determined not to stop, hoping to get as close as possible before the gray period. The natives from the village had warned the zookeeper's treatment would be torturous to Rocho, to say the least. They told Jack often of the king's experiments using animals to create steam-powered mechanical versions. He had unfortunately experienced the results firsthand. He was afraid of what they would do to someone as unique as Rocho. Jack was even more afraid he might be too late to stop it. After a few hours, however, he had no choice but to rest.

Not far from the lake, he ate from the small pack he'd brought. Studying his totem, he bobbed it up and down until the spool of wire and hook reeled out. He was tempted to fish again, but those old promises from his father steered him away, and eventually, he pressed on.

He approached the lake just as the second sunset began. Its shore stretched a few miles to his left and right and was at least a mile wide. Luckily, a bridge divided the lake in half, so he could cross to the town on the other side, but he immediately noticed the risk. The bridge was old and rickety, made of wooden planks suspended by frayed ropes. Celeste had advised him that tradesmen who used it when traveling to the kingdom for supplies often weighed too much upon returning. They would be forced to go around the lake, but Jack's time was limited. When the second sun set, the ash-covered people would roam wildly without the worry of being burned by the light. So Jack climbed off the odd horse, allowing it to run free as he pressed forward.

The bridge was much worse than he'd realized. The wooden planks were very well worn, and a few were missing entirely. With each step he took, the creaks seemed to get louder. He held the ropes securely while balancing his totem. After just a few yards, he noticed ripples in the water below. Going against the breeze, it sent an identical ripple up his spine as he spotted a fin swim toward him then dive beneath the bridge. Minutes later, another sailed by, followed by a third. Before long, the fins began circling him.

"It's okay," Jack reminded himself. "As long as they're in the water and I'm up here, I should be fine. Others take this route all the time."

He continued watching the fins follow him as if waiting for him to be lowered for feeding, but Jack remained careful. He stepped cautiously on each plank, testing it before putting his full weight on it. Unfortunately, he was taken off guard when the wind shifted.

The bridge swayed, and Jack did his best to brace himself, but the ropes waved uncontrollably. His foot slipped, and the plank below him broke, making him stumble. Two more planks fell into the water as he regained his balance, lifting himself into place—then the waters turned angry.

When the wooden planks hit the water, the surface began to thrash. The water bubbled furiously, splashing and soaking both the bridge and Jack. He scanned the lake, but the waves started to settle. It was quiet. The fins vanished below as he leaped forward over the missing planks, sure of what was about to happen.

Teeth… rows and rows of teeth rose from the water, tearing through the bridge. Like a hybrid animal, it had a flat feline face with whiskers like a prehistoric cat. The bulging body was scaly and striped in black and orange. Three fins ran down its back to its tail. The term *tiger shark* came to his mind instantly.

Jack got a closer look than he could ever have wanted as one sprang out of the water, chomping the planks near his shoes into splinters. As another sailed over him, Jack turned on the spot and ran across the bridge as quickly and as lightly as possible.

"Make it to the shore," he said to himself. He moved as fast as his sneakers would carry him, refusing to look back. The fins sank beneath the water, but he was sure they weren't too far away. He'd crossed three-quarters of the bridge, and the shore was within sight when they attacked again.

This time, they came as a group from shore. Teeth tore through planks Jack had to leap over to avoid being mauled. He landed hard on the next few, clinging to the rope to dodge them. A tiger shark wedged between the broken pieces shook its tail violently, making the bridge quake. Jack had nearly made it ashore—and the town was in view across the horizon—when the rope stabilizing the bridge jerked from his hand and went limp. Looking behind him, he spotted the tiger shark ripping the line with its clenched jaws, freeing itself. And for a second, Jack thought he caught it smile.

The rope snapped suddenly, and the bridge twisted sideways. Jack fell into the lake like a stone before swimming up to get air. Saltwater filled his nose and mouth. He gasped, swinging his arms when he witnessed the terrifying scene. Nine large fins were headed toward him and gaining speed.

Clutching his totem tightly, he realized the odds against him were weak at best, yet he turned to swim, hoping for some luck. His arms and hands stabbed the water like daggers as he swam. The shore was still a few dozen yards away. He didn't want to look back but knew they would catch up to him no matter how fast he moved.

He turned to see them approaching, close enough to smell rotting fish from their last meal. All of Nucalibur's notches were illuminated, excluding the moon and shamrock. Before he could make a decision, he was forced to turn sideways as the lead tiger shark opened its jaws.

It ripped through his shirt as he spun to its side.

"You wanna fish? Fine!" Jack yelled, producing the spear end of his totem. Driving it down into the water, he caught the second tiger shark in its eye. The third one, however, dove onto Jack and grabbed the spear's other end with its teeth. Thinking swiftly, Jack let the fishing line to unravel as the one-eyed tiger shark swam away. Its friend tugged on the other end, and their leader was quickly circling back. Jack took the moment to make his decision.

"Why couldn't someone give instructions with this thing?" As he twisted the star notch, stars appeared above him just as the moon had. He felt a tingle, followed by a sense of heaviness. Seconds later, the star faded. Nucalibur lost its glow, and nothing new happened.

"Lame." Jack yanked the totem free. "Really, really lame!" Two of the tiger sharks still chased him relentlessly. He knew he wouldn't be able to outrun them, so he prepared himself to fight. They whipped around a few yards away and together came at him like twin missiles. Jack lifted his spear over his head as he bobbed above the water, but felt something unusual. His arms had reached a ceiling he couldn't see. The dreamer kicked, but the motion also had no effect against the water. No matter how much he swung his limbs, he was in a protective bubble. Even his voice sounded muffled when he took in a deep breath.

Panic flushed his face as he searched the area. Waving his hands to stay afloat, he remembered the watch clasped to his wrist. He squeezed the watch's crown firmly, preparing for time to slow the tiger sharks down, but their pace remained the same. Again and again, he pressed the button, but their hungry jaws continued to race forward until they finally caught their prey.

They bit down with full force onto Jack, gnawing and chewing with enthusiasm, tearing through his pack. He could feel every row of teeth bite down on him from the first tiger shark and hear the rubbery squeaks. He remained unharmed through it all. The sounds coming from its mouth was like chewing on plastic or gum. The second tiger shark collided into Jack, and he instantly went flying forward beneath the water, completely protected in the bubble. Even with his head below water, he was able to breathe.

He sailed within a few feet of the shore as water began suddenly flooding over him. The temporary stun wore off from the tiger sharks, and their chase resumed. Jack swam with every muscle he could muster, feeling his body getting wet all over again. The shore was in reach, but the tiger sharks were gaining on him quickly. Water crashed over him as the star's bubble wore off. The sharks were nearly close enough to bite down on his ankles, with their jaws open wide enough to chomp a small boat. Jaws snapped shut like a bear trap as he was pulled onto the shore.

He kept rolling, just to be sure of his distance, panting on the grass. Looking out into the lake, he watched the sharks circle for a moment before diving back into the water. Part of him was relieved, while another was worried that they would be able to jump onto land.

"Someone up there is looking out for me… all right, Autumn, what's next?" He suddenly felt a small boot on his face.

"Oh, don't worry, they won't be back," said a small voice just above him. Jack's eyes focused around the boot to the little orange-skinned girl with brown hair and a cute piggish face staring down at him, holding a large gun nearly as big as she was.

"Did you pull me out?" He panted with a squished face. "Can you understand me?"

The girl nodded, appearing annoyed. Pointing at the lake with her gun, she let Jack get up. "No one stays out after the second sun sets, not even the animals. I had to pull you in to shut them up. All that noise will tell them where we're at."

Picking himself up from the soft grass, he dropped his soaked pack to check the contents. All of it was drenched, mostly ruined and useless. Only his map and the moonleaf stone seemed undamaged. He gathered them and his totem, securing it all before Jack shook his soppy hair and face like a dog. "Them?"

"The gray people covered in ash," she stated, getting a better look at Jack. "Where are you from? You're all thin like the natives, but *different*. Tell me what you want, or I'll blast you."

"I'm just trying to get to the kingdom."

She pointed the gun threateningly. "What business do you have in the kingdom? Natives ain't allowed there. Don't try to fool me with that magic you got. I heard all about how they send little kids to fight off gray ones and lizards alone to learn magic. Just mean is all that is. My momma told me all about y'all, and my daddy taught me how to use this gun, so spill it."

Jack had thought about it, and it did seem harsh, the way she put it. "I'm not from the village. I came from somewhere else. I promise, I'm not here to hurt you. I just need to get my friend back from the kingdom and find the Medicine Man."

She lowered her gun slightly. "The Medicine Man? Momma told me about him. Haven't heard nothin' since he won in the arena."

"The arena?" Jack asked.

"Oh no… the second sun's almost set." She looked out into the distance. "Gotta hide. Oh no, oh no. Should've been back home by now."

Jack stood, confused, as the girl gathered small trinkets lying around into her pockets. "Hide… where?"

"Middletown's not too far away. Help me carry these there, and I'll get you that far before the darkness settles."

Agreeing, Jack helped her gather her small colorful stones and trinkets before she stopped him. "Try to steal from me, and the only thing you'll walk away with is two halves of yourself. Got me?"

Jack stared down at the gun barrel and nodded again. "You got it."

It was another hike to Middletown. Jack hauled the stones and trinkets as he was told while she followed from behind, toting her gun and checking for ash-covered people. His damp clothes clung to his skin, and he could feel the air getting colder. He shook off the feeling and continued forward.

"So what's your name?" Jack asked.

"Keep your voice down." She poked him. "You want all them wild ash people to come running in for us?"

"Okay," Jack whispered.

The girl rolled her eyes. "Opal. My name's Opal."

"All right, Opal," he whispered. "What makes this town so safe to hide?"

"A lot of the people caught when the sun blew used to live here. The town was hard to hit because it's in a ditch to protect from animals. It's hard for the people who made it to find their way back without falling in."

"And what about this arena?" Jack asked. "You mentioned the Medicine Man winning."

"Now don't go telling me you don't know about the arena? My daddy's volunteering for the next games to take care of my mother. You can ask for anything you like, and the king will make it happen. If you live."

"So you're against the natives' rituals, but you don't mind the king forcing people to fight in an arena?" Jack smiled.

"For sun's sake, you're stupid. No one is forced to fight in the arena—they choose to. Everyone loves the king and his son. They protected us from the gray, let people right in even when the guards said he may be infected. Checked the town himself for survivors. The prince even saved me from that lake when I was a little kid."

"A little kid?" Jack asked. "You can't be much older now, can you?"

"Hey, I'm almost nine years old, but that's plenty tough for my people, so don't get any ideas. Now move, stick boy." She shoved the gun in Jack's back, and he moved along quietly.

By the time the last few rays of sunlight were barely visible, he was overlooking the ditch the town was hidden in. It was long like the lake but strangely narrow for a town, dividing the regions of where the village ended and the kingdom began. It held only one dirt road down the middle, with stores and homes on either side. Jack instantly thought of the Old West when he looked down—shabby wooden buildings, desert sand, several prickly cacti, and frail broken wagon wheels.

"Only thing missing is tumbleweed," Jack said to himself. "Oh no, there it is."

Near the rolling dried-out weeds, he spotted a path leading down into the town and up a short distance through the other side to cross it. "All right, let's get this one out of the way."

It was a complete ghost town. Every building appeared to have been abandoned for decades. The wood was worn down, and the letters on the signs were barely visible. A few wagons near the old shops were tipped over, their metal wheel bracings rusted and weak. Doors randomly creaked as he stepped by. Several windows had been broken, yet others remained boarded-up by wood planks.

"All right, that's enough," Opal said, taking her things from Jack. "You head that way, and I'm heading this way. Hide in any building you like until nightfall and stay quiet."

"Shouldn't we stay together?" Jack asked.

"And get me caught with you not knowing nothin'?" she whispered. "You're too big and loud to follow me. Besides, I don't trust those cloudy eyes of yours. You look like you could be infected." She took off on her own, ducking into an alley between two buildings.

Cloudy eyes? Jack thought to himself, assuming the cloudiness was caused by the water, before walking carefully through the town. He followed the road to where he saw the exit path, occasionally stopping when a noise funneled from down the road. Vultures nested atop the highest buildings, watching Jack with hungry eyes. Large bulging eyes protruded from craning necks, along with large beaks. The black feathers reflected the final light's rays more like leather, and they buzzed instead of squawking.

A door slam caused Jack to turn on the spot. He heard multiple voices followed by footsteps, and they were headed in his direction. Jack stepped quickly to his left, where a house with busted shutters offered a decent hiding area. The door was closed, but with a good shove, he was able to push himself in.

The house, along with the room itself, wasn't very big at all. A few chairs surrounded a cold fireplace. Two other rooms sat to the side with a few empty beds that no one had slept in for ages. Everything was covered in dust as if it had been neglected for many years. He checked each room to be sure it was empty, and when he returned to the living room, he was sure he was alone.

Through an open window, he could hear people headed his way. They weren't the gray ones, but there were four of them, with red masks covering their faces like bandits. They dressed similar to the people of the kingdom, with vests and stiff slacks, and they carried odd guns, with a sketchy appearance. Their greasy hair, dust-covered clothes, and orange skin were smudged with dirt. They were all Jack's height, yet stocky with muscle. Only the one who seemed to lead them appeared thinner and more agile with a black mask.

"Think I heard him go this way, Brock!" one of them yelled.

The four of them split into pairs and began checking houses left and right. The loud bangs were swallowed by the street as they kicked in every door.

Jack went from room to room, looking for a better place to hide, as the bandits grew closer. The beds were too low, and the closets were tiny. With no back door, he had no other exit. He did his best to sneak around the shabby house searching for somewhere to hide. Then another loud bang came.

He fell through the floor with a noisy crash, landing on a lower level. Dust filled the air instantly as he found himself in a hidden basement. He coughed violently before rolling over to find some old crates and chests he'd fallen through along with sleeping cots and a ladder in a corner.

Sitting up, he discovered more old trinkets like the ones Opal had found, along with a few pieces of jewelry and some photo albums spilling out of the box. It was all just as ancient as the town itself, covered in layers of dust. The albums showed a whole family who'd once lived at the house. Someone's parents, grandparents, and a few kids were all displayed. It was difficult to tell much about them from the faded photos, but what did stick out was their matching ivory-white hair.

Above him, he heard another loud bang next door. They were making their way to the house he was hiding in, and he was running out of time. "Doubt they'll miss the gaping hole in the floor," he said, staring up at the ceiling. Pushing the crates out of the way, Jack used the ladder to find a hidden opening beneath the bed above. Sneaking up to the window, he spotted a bandit heading toward his door.

"Hey, I got him over here!" one yelled.

Jack watched the bandit leave the house, and they all met in the center of the road. They'd found a weasely-looking man with slumped shoulders hiding in the house across the street. He looked weak and tired as they pushed him, guns pointed threateningly until he was in the center of the road. The sun was almost gone completely, and they were barely visible.

"All right, where is it, you little weasel?" the leader of the bandits demanded.

The man struggled as he was pushed to his knees onto the ground. "I don't know what you're talking about."

"Oh, don't play that!" another bandit argued. "We know you got it hidden somewhere. Don't make us get personal now, runt. Give Brock what he's askin' ya for, and we can be done with this."

"We know you have the map—now give it up before things get all unpleasant." Their leader, Brock, pointed the barrel of his gun at the man's nose.

Trembling with fear, the weasely man looked down at the barrel then back at the man's eyes. His hands up, he whispered, stuttering, "I t-traded it away to a stranger. I don't have it."

Brock snickered, holstering his gun. "So be it. Shoot him, and let the buzzards have what's left."

The three bandits raised their weapons, preparing to shoot. Jack assumed they were the ones who'd stolen the map from Chief Mizzi. He hesitated, not knowing whether he should risk leaving his hiding spot. Then before he realized it, he was out the door and walking toward them on the darkening narrow road.

"Wait!" Jack yelled. "Don't shoot him."

The four bandits glared at Jack with both curiosity and confusion.

"Who or what are you?" Brock asked, squinting.

"My name's Jack. I was brought here from… the sky." He tried to seem mysterious, keeping their attention away from the weakened man. Enough time hadn't passed for Nucalibur to be repowered, and fighting all four of them with just his spear and surviving seemed unlikely. Even a move to his wristwatch would be problematic if they all shot at once.

The bandits exchanged looks, and even the scrawny man seemed puzzled at Jack's presence.

One of the bandits snickered. "And why do you care wha' we do with him?"

"I don't, but I thought you should know he's telling the truth." Jack continued a bit closer.

"Is that so, my tan friend?" Brock stepped between his men. "And how were you able to figure this?"

"Because… I have it." Jack patted his pockets and pulled out a folded piece of paper. It was the undamaged map to the kingdom. He hoped that, if nothing else, it would offer a delay.

Brock's gun pointed at Jack, who raised his hands in the air: one clutched the fake map, and the other Nucalibur. "Bring it to me."

"What about him?" Jack asked. "Will you let him go?"

The group of bandits laughed maniacally, and even the buzzards seemed to caw with their laughter, causing a cruel shrill to wave through the old town. "Sure, kid. Bring me the map, and I'll let you both leave with all your parts."

"Not that I don't trust you won't still shoot us," Jack said lightheartedly, "but how about I leave the map here on the ground, and you let us both go while you get it?"

Brock took two more steps in Jack's direction, his grin disappearing along with his relaxed demeanor. "Hmmm. I could do that. *Or…* I can shoot you both now and get my map when yer both too dead to run anywhere. How's that sound, falling stone?"

Jack paused. "Painful and unpleasant… option one, I think, is better. I'll just bring it to you, then." He moved toward the bandits. His mind spun, thinking of what to do when they realized he didn't have what they wanted. His gaze wandered from the folded paper to his watch, then the idea sparked into his mind.

Holding his pistol steady on Jack, Brock snatched the folded paper from his grasp. Jack made a move to his wristwatch, hoping it would work outside of the protective bubble. "Eh! Don't you move even a bit, or I'll blast you away right now!" the bandit spat.

Defeated, Jack separated his hands and kept them high as the bandit leader unfolded the map and chuckled. "You tryin' to trick me? This just leads back to where we were. Last place I'd go to now that the games are near."

Jack searched for something to say or do to stop them, but he was at a loss. His training hadn't prepared him to be in this position without any tricks. Then it came to him. "Yes! It is a trick. Magic I learned traveling with the natives, to conceal it. It changes so no one else would know that it's the right map. It won't get wet, either. It's special."

The bandits exchanged looks as Brock studied Jack carefully. "Then show me," he demanded.

He looked out at the last rays of light fading. "I... can't, yet."

"I'm through with his games, Brock," the bandit holding the man hostage bellowed. "Let me throw him in the lake with them tiger sharks and be done with 'im."

The two other bandits nodded.

"You're pushing it, kid." Brock fired his gun, causing the buzzards atop the building to jump. A shrill noise came from above, and Jack recognized it as a few ash-covered wild people. "Show it to me, or you and the weasel here will be talking to Rocky, and the conversation will be very brief."

"My fishing rod!" Jack lied. "It can show the real map but not until after the sun has set fully. It has to be fully dark. If I turn the notch when it glows, the picture disappears, and the real map will show."

For the second time, the bandits exchanged looks. Brock squinted at Jack and took his totem. "What is this? A magic wand from the animals in the village?"

"No, it's a fishing rod." Jack held out his hand, watching their leader survey his totem. "But the natives changed it to show maps. Only after sunset, of course, since they're night people… yup, that makes total sense."

The bandits waited impatiently for their leader's answer. "The way you're staring at it seems like this is important to you. Brave kid to wanna be out in the gray period. You'll wait here next to him, and when the darkness settles in, I'll twist it myself."

When the sun vanished completely, only the glow of the totem's symbols remained. To his relief, the timer had reset. The bandits bounced to their feet when it was ready. Jack still didn't know what to expect from the totem or if it would work while Brock held it.

"This better work, kid," Brock whispered. "If you wasted our time, I'll make sure every ash-covered wild person from here to the lake finds you."

Placing the map on the ground, he waved the fishing rod over it then twisted a notch. As Jack expected, the remaining symbols stopped glowing. Jack sat next to the tiny man he'd hoped to save, plotting his next move.

Then something moved in the darkness behind the bandits—a figure holding a gun. Jack was sure it was Opal, at first.

A belt unexpectedly appeared around Brock's waist as they studied the unchanging map. Twelve Easter eggs in assorted colors of blue, pink, green, yellow, and red were holstered onto the belt like grenades, but Brock hadn't noticed.

"What's taking so long?" Rocky whispered harshly.

The other bandits began chiming in. Suddenly, a gunshot rang out in the distance, and Rocky's gun flew from his hands. Instead of Opal, Jack noticed a thin, dark-haired person running away.

Without hesitating, Jack quickly snatched four eggs, kicked Brock in the chest, and rolled backward. He hurled the pink egg at two of the bandits, and their legs were instantly bonded in pink gummy foam. Brock and the last bandit recovered quickly, but Jack tossed the green egg in their direction. A horrible smell erupted from it, and they both wheezed, holding their noses, coughing and gasping for air.

"Come on, let's go!" Jack called for the weasel-faced man to follow. He grabbed Nucalibur from the ground, leaving the map as he turned. The man was already on his way up the hill to the woods as the fumes began to waft away from the bandits. Brock was up, waving his pistol in the darkness, following the totem's glow. Jack released the last egg.

It burst in a ring of fire around the bandits, dancing at the perfect height to obscure their vision. Jack could hear the loud shrieks of the ash-covered people in the distance and spotted at least eight shielding their eyes and skin from the fire but waiting patiently. Jack raced up the hill. The sound of gunshots and yelling reverberated up to the inky sky.

For a while, he wandered the wooded area, blindly feeling the trees. "There's no way I'll find my way out of here." He sighed. With his ruined pack still by the lake, he had no supplies to camp with. Other than the last egg remaining in his pocket and his recharging fishing rod, he had nothing at all. He didn't know how he had ever made it through the natives' ritual. He decided to head in a straight line to put as much distance between himself and the bandits as possible.

Finally, he spotted a white glow in a clearing and heard clanging metal. Jack stopped walking. Before he could inspect the new sounds, he was crashed into.

"Oh good, it's you and that fantastic stick." It was the weasel-man Jack helped escape. In the dark, it was difficult for Jack to see anything but the man's large eyes, which examined Jack. The man gestured into the clearing. "Please, come with me. Don't worry; the gray ones won't come near here."

He guided Jack into the clearing and lit a small fire using a tool from his pocket. In the firelight, Jack saw a wagon with several chunks of raw metal, a few dozen scrolls of paper, a small lantern with a decent glow imitating the moon, and some other gadgets connected by gears and levers. A small cart was attached to the end, and a horse-like animal like the one Jack had ridden before stood grazing nearby. Along the ground was a tripwire attached to pots and cups.

Jack sat near the fire to warm himself up. "So, do you stay here a lot?"

"You could say that." The man sat across from Jack. "I'm a tradesman. I find things from all over and make deals with those in need. Everyone calls me Peddlin' Pete, and you're Jack, from the sky?"

Jack nodded as a group of those magenta rabbits with shells rolled in like armadillos from the woods. They got closer to the fire and began playing with each other, then with Jack's foot.

"Polymoos," Pete answered before Jack could ask. "Natives call 'em cross-hares, I think. They're supposed to be lucky. They run from danger, so if they're near you, it must be somewhat safe. Very playful. Speaking of safe, how did you make it through the lake? I noticed the bridge was torn apart—thank you, by the way. It'll be the long way around the lake from now on."

"Oh right, the bridge," Jack said remorsefully. "Sorry, those tiger sharks were pretty bad."

"No, don't apologize." He gathered two teacups and began brewing something in a kettle. "You saved my life tonight. I'm still not sure why, but I'm thankful."

Jack thought about it but couldn't come up with a reason. "Just seemed like the right thing to do, I think. So what's so special about that map?"

Pete poured two cups and offered one to Jack before rolling up a piece of paper and stuffing it into his pocket. "What makes that stick you have so special?"

They exchanged glances and came to a silent understanding that neither was ready to reveal answers. Jack watched the polymoos roam around as he sipped the hot beverage, wondering what he would need to do to see the map for himself. If it was the same map from the village, he had to get it.

The brew tasted very bitter at first but warmed him promptly. His fingers had begun to become numb in the cold but were tingling with the warmth.

Pete watched the magenta critters roll around, bumping into each other playfully, and he smiled. "Sorry I don't have any food to go with this. I haven't had any other good company besides the back end of that graceful creature there."

Jack shifted his gaze from the polymoos to his totem. His stomach growled loudly, causing even the playful rabbits to pause. The symbols had just re-illuminated, and one, in particular, glowed like an answer. Raising Nucalibur, he twisted the notch of the wishbone. "I can't guarantee what this will do, but I have a hunch…"

Peddlin' Pete sat back as a feast appeared all around them. Roasted turkey, potatoes, steamed vegetables, pies, cakes, stuffing, and a dozen other delicious dishes appeared on plates. If possible, Pete's eyes grew even more prominent, and the polymoos began nibbling on the steamed carrots.

"That is one impressive tool, my friend." In his excitement to get food for himself, Pete knocked over a vial of black liquid. Jack assumed it was what Pete had made the tea with. He refilled Jack's teacup before taking his first bite of roasted turkey. "If I was a lesser man, I'd want that for myself. Least I can do is keep you warm after all this."

"Being warm right now is a huge plus." Jack sipped thankfully from the cup. "But there is something I'm looking for that you might help me with. Do you know where I can find an enchanted cog?"

Pete paused with the drumstick in his hand, "*Enchanted…* not that I know of. Heard rumors of the kingdom's scientists using charged cogs to power their advanced machines. "

Jack took another sip of his tea before continuing. "I helped fight off those metal hunter-pumas. Are these advanced machines like those?"

"Oh no, these things are monstrous, and the scientists get more creative every year. If those red cogs are worth it to you, then be my guest. But they only display those machines for the volunteers to tackle. I wouldn't bet on you making it through that fight alive, even with your special pole there."

For the next few minutes, they ate together. Jack devoured everything he could until he was both full and warm.

After placing his plate down, he was overwhelmed with a feeling of calm and peace.

"I'll tell you, today has been much better than expected," Pete began as Jack felt numbness wash over his fingers. "Those fellas you found me with were once my crew, by the way. I stole the map from right under their noses. I was fresh on my way to find out where this map leads, but your stunt on the bridge took my shortcut. They would have been far too heavy to follow me across, you see. Guess I can find a buyer simple enough. Suppose you saving me and providing this magic *thing* makes us even."

The polymoos scuttled off just as the moon peeked out. A crash of thunder shook the skies as the clouds became stormy gray over the rising moon. The wind picked up swiftly, brushing through the blades of grass, and more of the area became visible. The polymoos disappeared into a hole they had dug in the ground nearby just as a streak of lightning ripped through the sky.

Pete picked up Jack's totem and tossed it into his cart. Jack tried to stand and argue but discovered he felt frozen all over. All he could do was blink and breathe as he watched the weasely little man gather his things.

"I would leave you here, too, but my crew — pardon me, my *ex*-crew — may find you here soaked in this rain. And you could be of some value to me. So I'll do you a favor. Since I won't be headed to the lake anytime soon, I'll see what you and this map are worth in the kingdom."

He rolled Jack into the cage attached to his cart. Jack remained frozen, only able to stare at the empty vial he knew he should've remembered but couldn't see well enough before. The tradesman must have caught his gaze because he picked up the bottle just as the rain began to fall.

"Slipped it into our brew," he said, tossing the empty vial into the fire. "Made from spib ink. Useful in my trade for making permanent agreements, and has the useful benefit of paralyzing you in just a few breaths after enough sips. Traded an old woman I met near the forbidden swamps for an antidote, which I keep elsewhere. Looks like ordinary water to most, but frees me from any frozen state, you see. You should've taken a sip of it yourself. Of course, you shouldn't trust a random traveler now, either. Never know what kind of lesser person they might be."

Jack remained stiff, sitting in the cage. The black ink still dripped from his lips and onto his shirt, but he always felt the rain when it began coming through the bars.

Pete freed a few rocks from the corner of a tree and brought out a folded piece of paper. Patting the animal harnessed to his cart, he said, "My deerbra is quite strong. She'll get us to the mines by first sun. Won't be safe to travel these parts during the day, so I'd advise you to get comfy. It'll be a bumpy ride to the kingdom."

<h1 style="text-align:center">Chapter 6
The Zookeeper</h1>

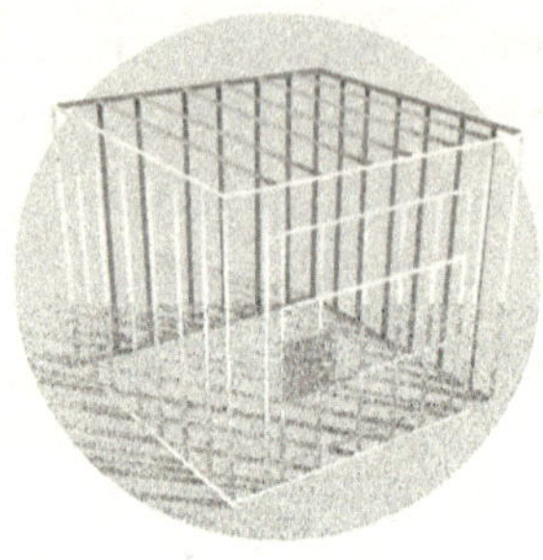

It was dawn of the first sun when Jack awoke, although he hadn't really slept much in the cramped cage. The rain dripped through the bars and onto his face all night, rolling off paper scrolls and onto the ground. As he remained unable to move, all he could do was close his eyes and think. He thought about how much he wanted to reach through the cage and attack the tradesman, but he was never so violent before. Counting the droplets helped ease him, but pouring rain had flooded the area, so the wheels of the wagon squished, making a sound like stepping on a particularly plump slug. The tradesman kept looking around worriedly as if he'd never seen so much rain before. Jack recalled Celeste's reaction to the ice.

Besides the anger swelling inside his chest when he thought of how easily he'd been tricked, Jack wondered where his fate was leading him. He debated with himself silently if he was learning a lesson not to help strangers, but he also knew Celeste had been a stranger when she'd saved him from the sandpit. The blue Easter egg weighed heavily in his pocket, but his body was still too stiff to gather it. Although the effects of the spib ink were beginning to wear off in his fingers, he was forced to stare at a new vial, which was repeatedly rolling into his forehead as if taunting him. He remembered what the tradesman had said about an antidote that looked like water. Hoping the vial held the remedy, he waited for the right moment.

The complaints from Peddlin' Pete about the rain slowing his travel plans put an invisible smile on Jack's face. Through the bars, he watched the weasely man direct his blue-and-black-striped deerbra. The wheels were caked with mud — Jack knew they would be forced to stop soon. His fingers were feeling less numb, but his arms were still immovable.

The terrain turned rough as they approached a new area of caves and mines. Rocks littered the ground and shook the wheels violently as they were pulled along. The cages were jolted so much that the items in the cart shifted. The vial slipped between the bars, threatening to fall through the bottom of the cage and into the mud. Luckily, Jack's nimble fingers caught the cork.

It was only half filled, but the clear liquid flowed like syrup in the vial. Forcing himself to control his breathing, Jack brought it up through the bars. Then he witnessed something strange: the bottle magnified anything seen through it, including a dingy white envelope among the tradesman's goods. Jack blinked rain from his eyes, unable to stop staring at the words scribbled on the envelope, begging to be recognized.

He continued holding the vial with his gaze fixed on the letter as the rain began to trickle. Finally, he could feel the first sun's rays against his face. It was just as inviting as the fire had been the night before. After a long night of rain, it was a welcome change when the gray clouds began to separate. When the rain no longer blurred his eyes and he could read the name clearly, he saw that the envelope was addressed to… *Jackson Taylor Jr.*

"You all right back there?" Pete called over his shoulder while riding atop an unusually large boulder. "Hated having to put you in the cart. Don't like small spaces none myself. Hope the ride isn't too bumpy for ya! Headin' past the king's mines now. I planned for that spib ink to wear off just in time to meet whoever's gonna pay the highest price for ya!" He laughed, clearly amused with himself.

Jack quickly emptied the vial as best he could before letting it fill halfway with the remaining rain dripping from the cage bars. After pressing the cork against the bars to seal it, he allowed it to roll to the side naturally. He remained seated in the cart, his head bobbing like his fishing rod. As they moved forward, Jack caught only occasional glimpses of Nucalibur, which was lying next to the driver.

Vast mining caverns surrounded the wagon, tunneling in far beneath them in every direction. The sounds of chisels, mining picks striking, and the squeal of rolling carts on rails echoed along miles of tunnel. Through the bars, Jack saw several dozen stout orange people covered in soot heaving rocks and shouting at one another.

The only name Jack could come up with to describe them was dwarves, but they were a bit too tall to claim that title. The miners were nearly the same height as the bandits and the soldiers he'd first encountered. Empty carts were pushed into tunnels, carried down by elevator shafts, then rolled out and filled with raw silver and gold ore, a few jewels, and other metals from rocks he'd never seen before.

As he was dragged by inside the cage, he heard a miner yell out, "Boss, I found one! I gotta vein o'er here. Need containment quick!"

A man with a clipboard turned, pointing. "I need two of you with gloves on, double time! Move it!"

Two miners with thick gloves covered in mesh wiring ran over to that particular mine, escorted by the man with the clipboard. He carried a lockbox storage container with the lid open. A rumble vibrated the tunnels as if something inside were alive. Three people ran out just before a loud pop followed a plume of smoke. The more protected men ran out with the box sparking and radiating red from what looked like a plant's root.

Once Pete's deerbra pulled them past the cavern, Jack saw farmland on either side of a narrow path. Plump orange children played in the yards, while their parents tended to the animals. It was a small town of country houses and barnyards, and Jack wondered if Opal had gotten back home yet. After the cart had traveled a few miles down the narrow path, Jack gained the full function of his arms. Peddlin' Pete steered his cart toward large gates as Jack hoisted himself up quietly, his head still lolling to the side.

Stone walls rose into sight like the first sun after Jack's journey from the Great Tree. Guards patrolled two sets of tall gates. Creatures with horribly carved faces and mangled wings looked on silently from the tops of pillars along the wall. Jack stared, assuming they were the gargoyles the chief described.

Dark smoky clouds hovered over the city like an omen. The inner metal gate was emblazoned with the same golden cog insignia worn by the soldiers who'd taken Rocho. It reminded

Jack of his first time seeing the gates of Cloud City. The guards stood just behind the bars, suited in the same metal armor they'd worn when Jack has first encountered them.

"There she is!" Pete pointed as Jack lowered himself and became still. "The gleaming City of Sun and where I plan to get my small fortune. This wooden rod of yours should fetch a pretty pocketful alone. And I bet I know someone who'd be mighty interested in you."

As the cart approached the gates, the effects of the spib substance faded faster and faster.

"What business do you have here?" a guard asked.

"Got a few items to barter with the good people of the city," Pete replied.

"No one needs more of the junk you've stolen from the old town," the other guard responded.

He smiled slyly in response. "It's not stolen, just recovered. And some of it's from the swamps everyone is afraid to go near. But I also have something the Zookeeper might want. And something special King Aurum will be interested in."

The two guards exchanged skeptical looks as Jack inched his arm beneath the pile of items in the cage and toward the totem. His hand was nearly to the seat when the guard yelled to another, "Let him in and inform the general!"

Jack fell against the cage bars as Pete trotted the cart forward, grinning at the guards and nodding. The gates opened to a city of sandy ground, sturdy stone, and gleaming metal. Jack instantly thought of Rome, with the exception of the people and machines. The men and women walking the streets were all stocky and muscular. Their peachy-orange skin was complemented by Victorian-era clothing with various gadgets as they walked along the streets, either shopping or managing the stores in the market.

Machines reminiscent of the Industrial Revolution created clothing, managed food prep, and spurted steam into the air. The people sported goggles with adjustable lenses. Bakers wore attachments on their arms, which produced a reasonably accurate flame. Self-propelled bins on tracks carried equipment, and the city folk used cooking chambers and handheld machines, all powered by steam. It was like nothing Jack had ever seen, as crude older machinery was a part of everything they used.

As Jack was carted through the market, people spotted him moving in the cage and took notice. Pete sold and traded items from his cart to the merchants on the streets. Some would ask about the strange *child* in the cage, and the tradesman would tell them he'd brought Jack especially for the Zookeeper.

Jack grew anxious under the onlookers' stares. Whispers of him being a criminal gained more and more traction as the day went on. Jack wanted to argue but thought it better if the tradesman still believed he couldn't move. If he could reach his totem, he could prove the weasel had stolen it from him, and he could find out what they did with Rocho.

He inched his hand closer to Nucalibur while Pete was occupied with a sale. Jack's fingers had barely brushed it when a figure blocked the sun, casting a shadow over his cage.

"This better not be a waste of my time, runt!" said a cold, unforgiving voice. An especially muscular man picked his way through the crowd. Silver armor covered his broad chest and shins, each engraved in gold with the kingdom's symbol. Several people walked away while Jack stared with a bewildered expression at the soldier's face.

"Oh no, sir!" Pete explained. "I have a spunky little criminal who tried to steal my map. Think he'll be perfect for the zoo. Got something special for the king, too."

When Pete reached beside him for the totem, Jack sprang up in his cage and objected. "Hey, that's mine! And I didn't steal anything from him. I saved his life, and he took my fishing rod."

"You're supposed to be stiff." Pete turned. "Ignore him; he's not one of us anyway. What's important is you get a new specimen for that special zoo of yours. King Aurum will be happy with some very unique magic I found, and I've finally got the map, for the right price, of course."

The man held out a hand, accepting a folded paper and Jack's totem. "What makes you think I consider *you* one of us, swindler? You've been imprisoned for theft more than anyone I buy from. But this map, will it really get us what we need?"

Eyes wide, the tradesman sneered. "It's what he's been looking for."

The soldier looked over the totem next, then at Jack before questioning it. "Do I look like a native? What am I to do with a cheap piece of wood?"

Jack was moments away from reaching into his pocket and hurling the final Easter egg when he realized who the soldier was, and his eyes grew as big as Peddlin' Pete's when scamming someone out of money. "The general near the sandpit? You're the Zookeeper? You took my dog from me. What did you do with Rocho? *Where is he?*"

"Dog?" The soldier looked at the cage then at Jack himself. "Is that what you call that green beast with root power? That's interesting… animals are a hobby of mine. I capture the unpredictable wild, find the most ferocious of them, and put them to good use for the kingdom. Sometimes we simply observe; other times, we test or attempt to recreate. You'd be surprised how a simple study can unlock many benefits." He surveyed Jack for a moment as if he were checking a horse's pedigree.

"I don't care. He's mine, and I want him back!" Jack argued.

"Not that you have many options, but your *dog* is a truly unique specimen. It's being researched by our most intelligent people, but if you cooperate, there are ways you may see it again."

Jack glared at the general then at the tradesman as his temper grew, and he gripped the bars of his cage. "Before I leave this place, you'll lose something valuable to you before I leave you locked in a cage like an animal, thief."

Pete pressed his crooked nose closer to the cage and grinned. "I prefer the title of tradesman or provider of documents, if you don't mind. Feisty, ain't he?"

The general smiled with amusement before tossing a heavy pouch into Pete's hand. "That should be enough not to see you for a while. Leave the cage. I'll have him placed with the others." Bending down to get eye level with Jack, he tapped on the bars. "We can discuss just how badly you want your friend back."

Jack was brought in by a few of the general's soldiers through the crowded markets, down narrow stone paths, and beneath a bridge to a whole new area. A large patch of land confined several animals. Prison cells were stacked atop each other in the form of a coliseum overlooking an open yard. Green grass, a few trees, and a few boulders had been placed here and there to feel more natural, but Jack knew better. A prison was a prison no matter who or what was behind the bars.

"Home sweet home," he remarked, being pulled past elephant-sized animals resembling brown boars while many more wild animals clawed and growled behind bars, snarling and biting. Some, strangely enough, laughed with foaming snouts and watched Jack with an unmistakable hunger in their eyes. After Jack's recent victory in the village, he barely flinched. He felt light-headed, but otherwise, he was simply looking for a means of escape.

"Whatever it is you may think of me, I'm actually doing you a favor," the general said, directing his men to an empty cell. "Anyone not branded as a citizen of the kingdom is considered an outsider spy from the villages of the northeast forest, and must be treated as criminals. However, in our marvelous kingdom, we have opportunities to prove good intentions to stay here. Travelers are either imprisoned or given the option to compete if deemed entertaining enough for the public. The prison would keep you for years until your sentence is completed, but win in the arena, and you'll be allowed to leave whenever you like… in your case, with your *dog*."

Jack slumped against the cage's bars. "Why does this all sound so familiar?"

The soldiers set the cage down and detached the lock confining him. The gate swung open, and the general stepped in front of him.

He struck the cage lock with a mining hammer. "One of the tools my people are well versed with. Are you ready for this?" He removed a vial of brown liquid from his coat.

Jack watched the vial being held over his head. "Do I have a choice?"

"Not if you want your beast back. He is quite extraordinary, and there is a possibility that the power it generates could solve several issues if we can reproduce it.

Losing that animal will cost you. Question is, are you willing to pay the price?" He poured the substance over Jack and gestured him out to the open field.

"Wait, I also need to find the Medicine Man," Jack added. "I need the cure for some kind of smoke sickness, too."

"Smoke sickness? No one's been affected by that illness in years. Only the king knows where the Medicine Man has retired to, and the only way you'll get to him is if he agrees to it. For that, you'll need a favor from the lawyer, and his price is far too high for you. Your only option would be the main event of the arena, where you could ask for virtually anything. But you should be more worried about the task at hand. It won't take long for the change." The general stepped away. "I can see it in your eyes: the fearless spirit of a fighter waiting for you to let it out. Prove your worth, and I'll sign the documents and walk you out myself. You could make an entertaining entry."

Jack felt his pants loosen, and his skin became itchy. His scalp burned as the chemicals spread over him. Brown fur sprouted all over his body, and pain shot from his back as he felt his spine twisting. His body was changing rapidly, and a moment later, his clothes were too big for him.

Staring at his hands, he found brown patches of hair covering all but the palms. His fingers felt strangely stronger. His hearing suddenly became more sensitive. His limbs felt more powerful, as if he could jump twice the usual distance. Feeling for his lower back, he found a long, curling tail. He tried to yell, but a shriek peculiarly similar to a monkey's came out.

The Zookeeper made his way up a twisting metal staircase to an overlook connected to the bridge. It held a control console with a table of buttons and a large lever. He watched Jack survey the grassy area of larger animals. Jack tightened the belt around his falling pants, wondering why he was standing on their feeding patches.

Looking down and removing his helmet, the general displayed a weathered face aged by war and a burn mark just over his forehead. "Animals are not always as intelligent as we would prefer them to be. They react on instinct passed down through generations, but that is what ultimately had them captured. Science has provided a way to unleash your inner animal, allowing us to deeply research an animal."

The Zookeeper's gloved hand grazed over the buttons on the console. "Survive, and I'll give you a chance to get your friend. Lose, and you become a part of my newest attractions from another world." With that, he pressed a few buttons and pulled the lever.

The large piggish animals grazing stopped mid-chew. Their ears perked up as the gates jerked away from the ground. The gears controlling the gates screeched with age as the bars rose. The grazing animals retreated to a corner as the gates halted.

Two of the most vicious animals Jack had ever witnessed stood in the open gateway. They weren't quite wolves, but some terribly mixed breed of a rhino and wolf. A piercing horn pointed out from their foreheads while a pair of sharp curved fangs hung from their foaming snouts. Growling, they stepped forward. Matted fur, as black as night, covered enormous muscular bodies. Their eyes were a shocking caution-light yellow as they barked at Jack, daring him to run.

"Survive long enough against my two zanos, and tap the key above their cell, and I'll walk you out of the zoo myself. It's survival of the fittest, boy. Let's see what you can do. Game on!"

A bright-red button lit above each cell as the beasts took chase, and Jack ran off. He followed the trail of the larger animals to the opposite side until they dispersed. In his monkey form, he stumbled but quickly learned to control his movement with better agility than ever. Soon, he was moving past the stampeding boars. He scooped up the mining hammer left on the ground as he sprinted through the field on all fours, leaping over boulders and diving over rocky peaks. The zanos were horribly ferocious and insanely strong, digging up the ground with each step, continually growing nearer with every attempt he made to lose them.

As he reached the other side of the zoo, he gripped the bars of a cage and began climbing to the second level. The horned wolves leapt for him. Their paws slashed at him from below, but he was just out of reach. Jack made his way higher, occasionally looking down. Steam jetted from their necks randomly, heating the fur on his legs. He realized they were each wearing collars around their thick, scruffy necks. He nearly fell into their barking mouths as he grasped a cell firmly only to be startled by the screech of animals hiding inside. A spider monkey like the one he'd seen in the forest sprang forward, banging the bars and screaming wildly. Collars around their necks spit steam, too. Other animals appeared in their cells, joining in. They howled and roared, spraying spit and scratching for the zanos to get away. Jack carefully made his way over, noticing the dull-red buttons above the cage doors.

He had to figure a way to get past them, onto the other side, and smash the button to end this hunt. Outrunning them wouldn't be possible, and fighting seemed hopeless. He could feel something bobbing in his oversized jean pocket and remembered the blue Easter egg waiting to be used. Taking the hammer to hang from the bars, he shoved his hand into his pocket, only for it to be jolted out.

"I won't let you hide up there, swinging on those bars all day," the general shouted.

The gates Jack clung to jerked up, forcing him to climb before he had nothing left to grasp onto. With the zanos below him, there was only one place left to go. He climbed higher and higher until reaching the lip of the stone prison, then atop the cells themselves.

More animals began escaping their prisons. Flying serpents with forked tongues and orange scales dove at him from above, while the zanos followed below. Jack swung his hammer, stunning two of them, and smacked another with his tail then three more with the hammer as they clawed at him. He stabbed one with the hammer's pointed end and swung it away like a baseball bat until the serpent went sailing. He ran onto the bridge, where a broken section made a gap just above the dirt road. Seconds later, the flying serpents pushed him in.

He fell with a crash, temporarily dazed. Luckily, the ground was still soft from the rain the night before. The zanos bounded toward him, half-running, half-fighting each other, slipping, as well. Jack fumbled in his pocket nervously, searching for the Easter egg as he neared the cage Pete had used to drag him into the zoo. He pulled it out and noticed that it was cracked. His heart raced as quickly as the attacking horned wolves. They pounced, pinning him down. Their paws were as big as his head, pushing into his ribs and forcing the breath out of him. Drool dripped from their teeth onto Jack's fur. He swung his hammer, hitting the one on his left sharply in the nose and again in the snout, knocking out a fang. He quickly rolled sideways, clutching the hammer, as the other pierced Jack's tail with its horn and flung him toward the center of the field.

Jack crashed against a stack of boulders. He winced in pain from his wounded tail. Searching for the egg, he realized he'd dropped it. As it rolled by the cage, he scrambled over several boulders. The zanos began their chase toward him again as Jack ran, but they cut him off.

They watched, shaking off Jack's previous attacks and waiting for his next move. From the corner of his eye, he could see the other animals returning to their holding cells. Jack thought it was abnormally organized, then he noticed the general pressing several keys on his console. "He's controlling them through their collars."

The zanos chased him between trees and through the grass until they reached the stack of boulders, where Jack turned to face them.

"Come on, you unicorn rejects!" he yelled, unsure what actually came out of him.

Just as they leapt after him, Jack dove to the right. One zanos went head first into the massive boulders, and its horn was plunged deep inside. The other crashed into the first and was pinned beneath the crumbling stack. Growling, the first struggled to free itself, but the horn was wedged too tightly.

Jack took advantage of the situation, climbing onto its back. Using the pointed end of his mining hammer, he struck the collar repeatedly. Hammering it down over and over, he finally got through the metal casing. Sparks flew as he made his final strike, shorting out the circuitry. Smoke replaced the steam, and the zanos fell unconscious.

He wasn't as lucky with the second one as it shook its body and boulders off in a rage. Jack rolled off and sprinted for the egg, scooping it up just before the horned wolf tackled him into the cage. The zanos thrashed as part of his massive head was stuck inside. Jack moved to the far end. Finally, he smashed the hammer against the zanos like a rock, tossed the egg at its head, and leapt over.

A blue substance oozed out like pudding. Once it made contact with the ground, grass shot up twenty feet high, entangling the cage and growing wildly, hiding everything except the sky. Jack could hear the zanos jumping and running from place to place, searching for him in the wild grass.

"What did you do?" the Zookeeper shouted out. "Where are you?"

Jack remained perfectly quiet, remembering what Celeste told him before finding the Great Tree. He allowed the last zanos to gain some distance from him. Once the rustling grass grew out of earshot, Jack made a run for it.

He had a good head start, but the zanos turned to charge after him right away. Jack ran through the grass, toward the red buzzer. He could feel the zanos close to him and sense its snapping jaws at his back. Suddenly, a clearing opened like curtains where the grass was an average height, but he didn't stop running. He jumped for the bars, but the zanos had caught up. Jack kicked his leg to push the animal away, but the beast was stubbornly strong. Twice, it almost clutched Jack's leg before he kicked again, swinging sideways.

Though he'd reached the buzzer, his attacker was relentless. The zanos rattled the cell, and Jack lost both his grip and his footing as he stretched out to press the buzzer.

Just like that, he fell. With its jaws opened wide, the zanos waited for Jack to fall into its fanged mouth. Jack brought the hammer across his shoulder and flung it up like a Frisbee at his target. It spun in the air just as the playing cards had during his fight with Trick in his father's hotel. With a firm thump, the button pressed in, and it illuminated like a stoplight. Jack tumbled down, landing on the zanos, but he felt no biting or mauling at all. The animal had become calm. Its eyes drooped as if it were sleepwalking, and as if hypnotized, it slumped into its cell then waited for the door to close.

"Well, I suppose I should've searched your pockets before this began." The general scribbled on a piece of parchment then handed it to one of his soldiers. "However, you'll be fitting entertainment enough for King Aurum, where you'll have your chance to win your friend."

He descended the spiral staircase, scribbling another note, then lit it on fire. Jack watched curiously as it burned quickly to a puff of smoke. The general stood over the panting monkey, where he poured a warm orange liquid over him. Jack's body began the transformation instantly, twisting his bones, irritating his skin, and burning his spine. Moments later, his fur was gone, as was his tail, and his hands had returned to normal. He was still gasping as the other soldier threw him the rest of his clothes before shackling him in chains.

Once he was restrained, he called out to the Zookeeper, "What happened to me being free? You said you would walk me out of here yourself if I survived!"

The general turned to address him. "And that I will do. Your pet has already been given to the king, but you can win him back. Today is the final day to accept new competitors and your only option to leave here with your green beast. Or you can leave without it? If not, this is your only option. This could be an opportunity to do whatever you came to this world for. There must be something else you need?"

Just then, a lean, muscular man with jet-black hair stepped up to the general, who bowed. "Ah, Prince Orblanc. I have something of value to present. It is a gift of untold abilities discovered in the ruins of Middletown."

The prince was still for a moment, his eyes glued to Jack.

"You have always been fascinated with objects found in Middletown, have you not, Prince Orblanc?" The general's eyes darted between the prince and Jack as he held out a gloved hand containing Jack's totem.

The prince tilted his head slightly, glaring at Jack with an inquisitive squint. Jack remained in deep thought before lifting his head, curious at the silence from the newcomer. With his first glance at the prince, he realized he'd seen him before.

Jack stared bewildered at the black hair, gray vest, and twin holstered three-barreled guns. It was the man who'd saved him from the bandits and the same one he'd witnessed just outside the borders of the forest. "Hey, I remember seeing…"

The prince's eyes grew as large as Peddlin' Pete's when money was mentioned before he held up a hand to Jack and began speaking quickly to the general. "Release him. I pardon him for any crime he's committed. Let him go."

The general was taken aback. "Sir, I can't."

"What do you mean you can't? He… rescued a member of the royal family, and we owe him a debt that will be repaid. A life for a life. Now please release him. I want him out as soon as possible."

Jack glanced between the two of them in silence, wondering why the prince was saving him for the second time. And more importantly, why he was lying about who had saved whom, when he was sure it was the prince who'd saved his life just the night before.

"I am sorry, Prince Orblanc." The general bowed. "It's a command I have no control over now. The soldier has already sent the agreement papers to have this traveler sent to the arena as a competitor. The boy is in search of something important to him, and I only intended to give him the chance to win it back.

The contract is completed. The only one with the authority to cancel a contract is—"

"The king himself," the prince finished. "And my father has never released anyone from the annual competitions. They are the only tradition my father does not forget."

He looked at Jack with a mournful look as if he had never resented anything he was about to say more. Finally, the prince said, "I'm sorry. You'll have to fight in the arena."

"Wait?" Jack looked between the two of them. Even the Zookeeper looked apologetic as Jack spoke. "Why wouldn't the king let us go? Maybe if he hears what I have to say—"

"No," the prince interrupted. "It won't matter what you have to say when it comes to contracts. He considers it binding by the sun itself. That's our laws. It is one of the only traditions my father will not alter."

Jack shook his head. "I don't understand. Why?"

"The arena games are to honor the queen who left us too soon, and he will never let my mother's memory die even if she has. The final day of the games was her birthday. That was before Chief Mizzi and the natives took her and had her killed. I must go prepare my demonstration for my tribute." With that, the prince walked away, leaving both Jack and the general in silence.

Chapter 7
The Gem Arena

For the third time, Jack found himself trapped behind bars and bound by chains. His prison was cold and dark. Lit by a few torches placed yards apart, the place smelled of iron, sand, and blood. The ground was rough and unforgiving, but it was much better than Peddlin' Pete's cart. He'd been forced to put on an oversized blue jumpsuit but was lucky he was able to just pull it over his own clothes. The moonleaf stone remained safely in his inner pocket.

Across from him was another cell, dark and empty. Sitting beside him were several chained people, also wearing the blue jumpsuits. Some were average big brutes of the kingdom, with far too much muscle. The ones that stuck out strangely were a small boy with an emerald necklace and a frail woman wearing a single orange fuzzy slipper and bathrobe. A man with a bad burn on his arm stared curiously at it as if he didn't recognize his own limb. Two of the prisoners were forest natives. They didn't seem to recognize Jack, so he was sure they'd been imprisoned before his arrival. One or two were more like what Jack imagined the ash-covered people looked like out of the darkness, but much less wild. They were similar to the people in the photo Jack had found — white hair, eyes as large as goggles, and slightly webbed fingers. They were fidgety, shaking their hands as if hiding that they'd consumed a ton of coffee. They spoke only to each other, and their language sounded like one he'd heard before but didn't understand, like French.

He could hear another group of prisoners on his other side, but their conversation was muffled. A thick wall of stone separated the two groups, so only the occasional argument from the other end was audible.

His thoughts racing, Jack kept to himself. He wondered how long he had before his luck ran out and if Rocho would forgive him. He must've been concentrating hard, because he didn't hear the first time the men beside him asked a question.

"You gonna tell us or not?" the man asked. Like the bandits', his smug face was covered in dark smudges. He was definitely a citizen of the kingdom. He had the same skin tone, short stature, and bulky muscle of the citizens, but there was an air of confidence to him.

Confused, still distracted by thoughts of Rocho, Jack asked, "Tell you what?"

The man rolled his eyes. "I said, why are you in here, boy?

Jack looked down, frustrated. "I was caught and traded to the Zookeeper by this little weasel man…"

"Peddlin' Pete? Ha, tell me you didn't fall for his victim stunt? You must be new here. Thought you looked scrawny."

Jack didn't want to comment, but his curiosity got the best of him. "So why are you here?"

"Me? I'm here for the scenery."

The other prisoners shook the chains as they all laughed, with the exception of the two villagers who seemed unable to understand any of them.

The man stopped laughing when he saw the serious look on Jack's face then pointed at another man. "Well, don't get all frowned up. The two guys there are here for stealing one of the king's deerbra and fighting in the street over it. One over there accidentally set the labs on fire."

"Weren't no accident." The burned man rubbed his neck gruffly. "Just don't remember doin' it, then woke up with a pain in my neck, but I know I planned it! I think I planned it…"

"So you keep telling us." The first man rolled his eyes. "The kid over there, wearing the necklace, huddled by his mum… they came here together, but no clue what they were arrested for. Could be volunteers. They won't speak to no one else."

"And what about the gray people and the two from the forest?" Jack nodded in their direction.

"Most gray ones are too wild, but I think they were experimented on by the scientists. Somehow got them to behave slightly normal, but they have their moments. None of them can speak to no one else, 'cause we can't understand 'em." He barked a laugh. "Only the translator comes around to let them know what's going on. Anyone not from here is considered a spy, so we all get the same treatment. They were probably caught by the gargoyles."

"You still haven't told me about you," Jack said. "Why are you really in here?"

The man studied Jack for a moment before answering. "I told you already — the scenery… and to make it to King Aurum."

At once, thoughts of Opal with her large gun came to mind, and he knew he'd discovered the truth about the cruel tyrant king the villagers had warned him of. "What did he do to you?"

He laughed much harder at this than anything else prior, as did most of the other prisoners. "Nothing yet, but I hope a great deal soon."

"Kid, what have you heard about the king?" the burned man asked.

Jack shrugged and shook his head, realizing there wasn't necessarily a lot he *had* heard of the king except for the drawings in the cave and the arena. "He's power hungry and… well, not a lot more really, besides this arena he forces on everyone for entertainment."

"Look, my name's Stoney. And the king might be obsessed with power and the future of the kingdom, but since his rule, none of us have gone hungry in town or been mistreated. The gargoyles protect us. Might not be best for travelers, but what should he do to possible spies, eh? Just let everyone leave or…" Stoney drew a line across his neck. "Even this prison is better. He likes to keep the entertainment happy, I've heard."

Jack snickered just as a few guards walked in.

"Breakfast!" they yelled, walking in mugs of water along with plates of eggs, toasted bread, and sausages from an animal Jack didn't want to know about. It smelled delightful.

Jack took one look at the others, who were already eating, and began eating it himself. When he noticed the smile on Stoney's face, he paused.

Stoney continued smiling, food falling from his mouth as he spoke. "Told you he ain't so bad. Even the guards are nicer. It's that chief that's twisted. You know that village over there sends kids though survival tests. That's insane. It's dangerous in those woods. Least here we have a choice. Serve time in prison or head to the arena, and the perks ain't bad, either."

"So what do you want, boy?" the burned man asked Jack.

"What do you mean?" Jack asked.

"The reason why you chose the arena?" Stoney asked, belching. "That's why I'm here. No crime. But if I make it all the way through, I get whatever I want. One reward, one request. And between you and me, I know I can get past the first event easy."

"And they keep you here?" Jack pointed his fork to the ground.

The burned man waved his empty plate. "We all get treated the same, and once we're in, there's no leaving. I worked the mines for years collecting precious metals for the kingdom. Figure this is better than rotting in prison, and when I win, I'll have some of that gold back to live on."

"So what is it you want?" Stoney asked again, but before Jack could answer, the soldiers returned.

"All right, you lot, the people have gathered, and the king is waiting," a soldier stated to both sides of prisoners, opening the locked doors. "Finish your meals quick. Let's see what you're made of."

The group in the cell to his left were marched by first. Several were just more citizens of the kingdom followed by another lone native villager. Then Jack spotted a pair of eyes staring at him. He was sure he should recognize them, but something was off. Then it happened again with another behind him. Then another and another, until there were four men staring at Jack, each with a sly grin as they nudged one another jokingly.

"What's the matter, boy?" one said. "Map sent you in the wrong direction? Or don't you recognize my beautiful face without my mask?"

"Brock." Jack instantly remembered. "The bandits."

"Can you believe the guts he has?" one of them said. "*Calls us* bandits after helping that weasel steal from us?"

"I didn't know *he'd* stolen the map from—"

"Hey, quiet in there, people!" the soldier interrupted.

The bandits gave Jack a sly look of resentment before being walked out. Seconds later, Jack's cell was opened. Chained to his cellmates, he was directed out of the cell, and they followed the first group out.

Two more soldiers met them and led the group down a long staircase, to two large metal doors.

"So how does all this work?" he whispered. "Is it like a footrace, all of us fighting a few zanos? Or something harder, like a joke-telling contest?"

"Could be anything," Stoney whispered back. "That's why I try to be friendly. Case we all need to work together. O' course, in the end, we may need to fight each other, and if that be the case, watch your back. There's no mercy in the Gem Arena."

They waited as a loud boom of cheers pounded through the doors. The sand vibrated from the stomping above. Dust rained down as the eager crowd yelled. The bandits looked back at Jack just before a loud bang rang out from the other side.

"That's it. Remember what you're fighting for, people." The soldier pushed the doors open, and Jack felt like he was entering the Eclipse Tournament of Cloud City all over again.

In the stadium, rows and rows of benches were filled with people. Stone walls encircled them, reminding Jack of a Roman coliseum. They stretched up high, separating the arena from the spectators, and the ground was covered in a fresh blanket of untouched sand. A dozen targets were being carted out of the field pocked with blasts all in the center. They still seemed to be smoking, so Jack assumed they were just recently shot at.

Both groups were led to the center. Fans pointed and called out, commenting on how small Jack was and how frail the boy and woman were. Others shouted encouragement to fighters they were sure would win, like the two large men who'd stolen the deerbra. Talks of strategy and fighting styles stirred.

Jack looked out into a section of the stadium blanketed in gold cloth and plush seats. He saw Prince Orblanc sitting to the right of a grand throne and another like his to its left. Horns blew, calling for everyone's attention, and a wave of silence washed over them all.

The man who stood at the throne was one of the muscular people Jack had ever witnessed. He certainly wasn't the tallest, just barely Jack's height, but he was broad, more muscular than even Chief Mizzi. Gold armor covered his massive chest and legs, and a long blue cape trailed behind him, sporting the cog symbol of the kingdom. A gleaming crown, which he wore proudly, covered his black hair. His beard was long and full, neatly managed into two gold rings. As he sat in the middle chair, he opened his arms wide, welcoming his people.

"By the blessing of the two suns and in my darling queen's memory of this great kingdom, let the Gem Arena open and the games begin!" King Aurum announced in a powerfully cheerful voice.

He was greeted with loud applause and cheers. Prince Orblanc sat beside him clapping, focused on Jack.

"And now for the contestants, who have volunteered," the king continued. "If it is meant for you to win in these games, you will be freed to do as you please with one gift and one request of your choice. And if it is achievable, the victor who survives the main event battle will also be rewarded with the kingdom's highest honor, so the world may know of your triumph. We all thank you for your strength and powerful will. Now for the choosing of the three events!"

The four bandits looked at Jack with greed in their eyes as if the announcement would hand them the weapons they wanted. Stoney seemed optimistic enough as he leaned toward Jack's ear. "This is how we find out what games we'll be competing in."

Jack balled his chained hands into fists of frustration. "This all seems really familiar."

"Not as many of us as last year," Stoney stated flatly. "Guess no one wants to fight Fusion this year if it comes up?"

Jack already knew it didn't sound good, but he asked anyway. "Fusion?"

"Just hope you don't get paired against it in the main event, kid."

"Any chance there's a good behavior, automatic-win option?" Jack said.

A servant approached the king with a bowl of etched gemstones. After shuffling through the gemstones, King Aurum chose three before dismissing the servant. Next, he held up a gem sporting a picture of a spiral to the stadium. "For the first event, the obstacle course has been selected. Those who make it to the end will continue to… the deadly puzzle box," he announced, holding a stone with a cube marked on it.

Finally, he held up the last stone: two crossing swords. "The final event will be the well-known classic, Battle of Colossus! For all things new and the empowerment of science, let us prepare the first event!"

The crowd cheered loudly as the king gestured for the soldiers to take the volunteering prisoners back in. As they were all escorted back into their cells, Jack caught a glimpse of spiked floors rising from the arena grounds, steam-powered roadsters being pushed through the rear gates, and a large grate sliding open to a rocky tunnel beneath the ground.

An hour passed before the first group was collected. As they paraded past, the bandits promised they would be back for Jack soon enough. Jack waited for a sign or a message, but nothing came. Only the empty walls of the prison and the people who occupied it with him remained. Stoney sat beside him, discussing what he intended to do in the first event, but Jack once again was lost in his own thoughts before he heard the mines mentioned.

"What was that about the mines?"

"Just before we left—you didn't see it?" A smirk spread across Stoney's face. "The tunnel that opened up on the floor. It leads to a mining area. I shouldn't have any problem navigating it long as I get that far. Don't know what the king's inventors will come up with."

Just then, a soldier entered, followed by the surviving prisoners. Only four remained. One was shaken up with fright, while the native from the village walked in as if she were simply coming home from a long day at work. The last two, Jack was surprised to see were Brock and one of his bandits. Only Brock looked in Jack's direction. He gave Jack a very nasty glare before turning his head, and Jack could guess why. He obviously blamed Jack for the loss of his two friends.

"All right, you lot are next." The soldier opened the door and pointed back to the hall.

It was one of the longest walks Jack had taken. The cheering crowd was drowned out by his panicked heartbeat pulsing in his ears. They were each released from their cuffs and taken into birdcages just tall enough for him to stand in. As the cages rose, the spiked floors of the pit below them were revealed, and the stadium's cheers suddenly waved into his consciousness.

"Group Two!" A servant stood, shouting, "There are currently eleven of you locked in these cages. Your goal is to cross the spiked floors, navigate through the tunnels, and find the keys to unlock the doors, where you will race around the outside track. Each of the steam-powered roadsters will overheat and blow if it is not one of the first four to cross the finish line. Those final four will move onto the second event. Each part is timed. You will lower over sixty seconds until the cages are released into the pit."

The king stood, looking around at his subjects, his arms wide, while his son looked on timidly. "Group Two may begin!"

Jack stared down at the spikes waiting below like a dozen bear traps he couldn't avoid. From the corner of his eye, he spotted the kid of their group hammering away at the cage with his tiny fists, trying to break the latch. Others tried pulling or twisting the lock, pulled on the bars, or watched the rope nervously. One of the gray ones started foaming at the mouth and looking at Jack hungrily. The small elderly woman waited patiently as if a bus would be picking her up shortly.

Jack looked over at Stoney just as his cage jolted. Every cage dropped suddenly at once. Through the bars, the ropes were being burned away near the top. Each cage swung back and forth before becoming still again. The crowd grew louder at the suspense of each cage falling a bit more. The banging of metal continued. Then, with a snap, a big guy built like a mountain—Jack had missed him somehow—swung around his cage, leaping to the frail woman, and ripped open her cage door. He clung to the outside of her cage with an open arm to greet her.

Jack's cage jolted and dropped again. It swung before becoming still again, giving Jack an idea. Running to the far end, Jack rocked his cage back and forth repeatedly until it began to swing. The fire continued to burn away several more strands, and the cage dropped again before his momentum grew. Before long, his cage was swinging in a long arc as far back as the stands.

The hungry flames ate away at the fiber faster and faster under the extra stress, but Jack continued. He couldn't see much more than blurs, but the cheers from the crowd told Jack at least one other person had made it down or had fallen. Stoney and some others began following Jack's motion, flying over the pit like a pendulum. Jack's rope finally snapped, and he went sailing against the arena wall. With his cage bent, he kicked and kicked until the door finally swung open.

Above, the big guy was preparing to jump over the pit with the tiny old woman beneath one of his massive arms like a doll. The man landed just inside, gripping the edge of the pit wall with one hand. The woman dangled in his other, just over the spikes.

Jack rushed over quickly. "Pull her up to me!" he yelled. The bulky guy looked down at the woman, who smiled and nodded simply as if going along for the ride. He lifted her, and Jack took her hands, pulling her to safety. Seconds later, the mountain-sized man had pulled himself up, too. An emerald necklace dangled from his neck. The frail woman lingered for a moment, smiling at Jack, then took the man's hand. A moment later, they were off into the mines, and Jack watched them disappear.

Stoney wasn't as lucky with his final swing as his momentum hadn't grown enough. His rope snapped, and the cage fell toward the outer edge of the pit. It hit the side hard before tilting in. Jack sprinted over as Stoney held his arms out, falling helplessly. Jack slid through the sand, extending his arms out over the pit just as Stoney tumbled in. He was barely able to grasp the other man's fingers, but it was enough to catch him. Jack pulled with every muscle, bending the cage up over the lip, but the man was heavy. Jack's fingers slipped, and he was left gripping the bars.

"Come on kid. Help me up here, and I'll get you through the mines. Pull harder."

"I'm trying, but you're like lifting a car!" Jack used his legs to push against the lip—and finally rolled the cage out. The metal cut his hands, but otherwise, he was all right.

Together, Jack and Stoney worked the bars open using the other broken cage parts as leverage. Just as Stoney was freed, they ran toward the tunnel. Piercing through the cheers and applause, Jack heard a wild scream just before the remaining cages hit the spikes. Then there was nothing.

Stoney stopped just inside the mines. "You could've been long gone. Why'd you stay to help me?"

"Like you said before," Jack panted, "we could help each other."

Stoney seemed to ponder that while looking down the long stretch of intertwining tunnels. "It's gonna be dark down here, so stay close," he told Jack, who followed his new partner.

The tunnels were just as dark as he was warned. Jack followed Stoney through the twisting tunnels, spotting the occasional glowing crystals that would light their path for a moment. He could feel the sweltering heat of the sun bearing down on them even below the earth. He began sweating more than ever, but somehow, he felt at ease in the dark. Whenever they made a turn, something in his stomach told him to keep going or occasionally offered a feeling of uncertainty.

"The crystals absorb daylight, so the closer we are to an exit, the brighter they should be."

That made sense, but Jack still had a funny feeling about the area they were in. A rock would occasionally flash red only for a moment, but he brushed it off as the darkness playing tricks on him. Then it happened, again and again, the farther they went. Finally, he saw a light in the distance. Jack felt a warm sensation in his pocket, like the moonleaf was heating up. When he understood why, it was a moment too late.

"Stop!" he yelled, just as Stoney stepped onto a rocky platform. Jack pulled him back, but it caused rocks to thunder down, blocking their path.

"What's that about, mate?"

Jack patted his pocket. "The Usiku Village. They gave me something before I left them. I think it helps me see in the dark because they're people of night."

The tunnel began to shake violently. Rock and rubble fell down on them, and the crystals flickered with light.

Stoney scanned the mine with an expression full of dread. "Oh no. They're causing a cave-in. We need to get to the keys and get out now."

They sprinted through the mines, with Jack leading. Green rocks flashed, alerting him of the right paths. He found himself making turns like Celeste had through the forest. The rubble had closed off portions of the mine, but before long, they found themselves at a row of doors. Seven total doors were once available, but some were barred over where Jack assumed other volunteers had made it through. A few, luckily, were still open.

Unfortunately, the doors were still locked, and there were no keys to be found. Jack looked around but found only the rocky walls staring back at him and a few crystals, broken and dim. "How do we open them?"

Stoney slammed his shoulder against the thick metal door before shaking his head. "Won't budge." He squinted around at the wall, moving slowly toward the broken crystals. His rough hands rubbed over the jagged edges gingerly as if he recognized every lump. "These weren't broken naturally. Someone did it on purpose."

He grabbed a rock lying to the side and smashed another crystal until it burst open. The light dulled, but inside he found a key to the door. He smiled at Jack, who quickly grabbed another rock and smashed a few other crystals before finding a key himself. He ran to an exit as Stoney made his way through. He could hear the tunnel collapsing behind them. The instant Stoney opened the door and stepped through the threshold, metal bars slid down, blocking him from the mine.

"Hurry up, kid!" Stoney yelled.

Jack turned the key and swung the door open. Sunlight punched him hard in the face, and he dropped his key. The heat was overwhelming, and his body became instantly drenched. Seven cars waited on a wide track surrounded by another stadium full of people to cheer them on. Steam oozed from the drying cracks in the road that was soaked with rain not long ago. A clock ticked away, counting down the time, and Jack remembered he was still a part of the contest and had to hurry. Just as he reached down to grab the key, he stepped through the doorway, and bars slid down. He reached his hand through the bars and snatched the key just as the tunnel filled with rocks following the final countdown.

The crowd counted the seconds together as the sun rose higher into the sky. Jack jumped into a vehicle, using the key to start the engine. The engine emitted a red glow, and a light was centered on the steering wheel. He noticed only six of the seven cars had anyone in them, and he assumed this was all that was left. One of the villagers sat in a vehicle beside him, but the other was empty. He wasn't sure if anyone was lost in the tunnel, but he didn't see the big guy or small woman who'd made it from the cages. A knot of guilt developed in his stomach as he wondered who else he could've saved.

Seconds later, another horn sounded, and his steering wheel light illuminated. Instantly, they were off again. The villager sat there, looking just as confused as Jack was. He'd never driven before, but he knew the basic mechanics of a car. This thing, however, was not really a car.

"Forward to go. Back to stop!" Stoney yelled just before taking off.

Jack found a lever next to him just as the villager sped off. As he slid the bar forward, he heard the engine rev up. Steam jetted from the sides, and the wheels gripped the road aggressively before the vehicle took off. He moved much faster than he'd expected and was pushed back in his seat. Climbing the curved walls, he jerked the wheel to the left before whipping around the corner, maneuvering the lever to slow himself down.

The other racers were having a hard time controlling their vehicles, too. They raced up and down hills and onto the side walls, all while wildly crashing into anything and everything around. Thick fog from the mix of rain and the hot sun made it that much harder to see. There were times it looked like one of the ash-covered prisoners would launch off into the stands. Jack made every second count to catch up.

He was launched from hill to hill until he took the inside of the next left turn. A loud bang in the distance shook the track. One of the vehicles was pushed up on its side. Then another explosion flipped it over completely. Jack spotted two cannon traps across from each other shooting at the track. He made a hard turn to avoid one and was shielded by the turned-over vehicle as he went by the other.

With one roadster destroyed, Jack bounded down on the remaining five racers. "I just have to be top four, and I'll make it to round two." Jack drifted around the next bend. Steam billowed up from vents in the road, levitating the lead roadster as it drove over. Vehicles went flying off course and crashed onto the ground like meteors then swerved wildly.

Jack dodged the first vent smoothly and caught up to the group. Within seconds, he was on the tail of the fourth-place roadster. He tried to overtake the driver a few times but was blocked at every attempt. Maneuvering to the right, he cut quickly to the left just as the driver moved, and Jack caught a vent. He flew several feet up and over the fourth-place racer but landed so hard the wheels nearly buckled. He slammed against the wall. The fourth-place driver went up the wall and blasted past Jack furiously. Jack watched the kid drift around him, and once again, he was behind—but not by far.

The five cars weaved around each other and rounded the final corner. In the distance, an archway marked the finish line. Torches wavered around it in the desert heat. Jack quickly recognized it as the doorway returning into the stadium. Unfortunately, the last length of road held a new surprise.

Sections of the wall ejected out into the racetrack, striking two of the vehicles on their tails and forcing them to collide into each other. Other racers swerved aggressively around them, showing no signs of slowing down. However, being in fifth place meant losing it all. Not only would Jack miss any chance to get Rocho back, but the roadster would explode the moment the fourth roadster crossed the finish.

"Not like this. I won't lose like this." Wind whipped over Jack as he raced forward, watching the first roadster finish, closely followed by the second. The heat was still so brutal, and his wet hair covered his eyes. Wiping the sweat from his forehead, he felt the hot metal of his wristwatch hit his face, burning. His eyes widened instantly. "And I'm not going to lose, either."

Pressing the button on his wristwatch, he forced the hands to light in red just as the third roadster crossed the finish line. They instantly paused there. Both the crowd and the remaining racers had slowed in time while the pain set into Jack's body. He jumped out of his roadster then climbed over the hood and onto the tail end of the next racer. It was happening much quicker this time. His body aged faster, and he could feel his bones straining to move. After only a few seconds, he couldn't take the agony any longer and gripped his wrist tightly.

The fourth-place roadster sailed between the crushing walls, through the doorway, and over the finish line. Jack could hear a chain reaction of explosions as the engines of the other vehicles, including back at the starting line, blow. Behind him, his roadster swerved back and forth, slamming against the walls until it finally exploded, leaving a pile of flames and broken parts.

The four winning cars all stopped just before the spike pit. King Aurum stood looking down at the four vehicles, clearly counting the five competitors, before pointing at Jack, who'd just climbed off the back end of a roadster. "How did you possibly survive the racetrack?"

Jack shrugged. "I was trained in the ancient racing art… of Mario Kart."

"Only four racers are able to survive the track," a soldier called out. "One or two volunteers have already escaped. You will be disqualified from continuing in the Gem Arena."

The crowd remained quiet, but Jack questioned the decision. "Disqualified? That's not right. The rules said only four roadsters would cross before the engine blowing, not four racers. I made it through the event on one of the first four vehicles. It was never announced I had to be one of the first four *drivers*."

The soldier stepped closer to Jack as a murmur of boos stirred from the crowd. "You do not come here and question—"

The king raised his hand before the onlookers could interject. "I am well known in this kingdom as a fair and just ruler, and on the anniversary of my queen's departure from us, this will remain a fair and just arena. The event guidelines were announced, and the competitors were all within the guidelines. As such, the foreigner has argued well. I will allow all five to continue to the second event!"

The crowd leaped out of their seats with apparent agreement. The five volunteers were escorted back to the prison as parts of the obstacle course were moved out of the arena. Jack could hear blades being sharpened behind him as he was shackled and led forward. His eyes lingered on the prince's empty chair beside King Aurum's throne.

Jack's return to his cell was met with both a small amount of satisfaction and sadness. He'd lived through the first event barely, but that was only the first thing that worried him. Rocho was nowhere near the king, and that bothered him more than anything.

"You survive the first event, kid?" Brock called out from the cell on the other side of the wall as his group was locked away. "I sure hope you did, because when you go down, I plan to see it. You hear me, boy? We only got caught because of you, and I lost two of my crew in here. That's all on you!"

Jack tried to tune him out with his own thoughts, but it was difficult. Stoney clapped him on the back with his cuffed hands before taking a seat. The other survivors included one of the gray ones, a native, and the kid. The old woman with the fuzzy slipper was gone, along with the big guy who'd rescued her. Jack knew it was possible they could've been the ones to escape, but his attention was drawn to the sound of a woman sobbing. He realized the ash-covered person was actually a woman. She sat crying to herself over, what Jack assumed, was losing her friend. Thoughts of Sonny snuck into Jack's mind. He wondered if he would lose her after long and be left with no friends and no companion.

"Where are you, Rocho?" he repeated to himself. "Where did they take you?"

Jack looked up as a door creaked open. He hadn't heard anything from the other cellmates he was chained to for some time, and the guards had gone. Someone stood in front of him with a sack and a long-barreled gun.

"Opal?" Jack whispered, rubbing his eyes. "What are you doing in here?"

"Was gonna ask you the same thing," she said quietly. "I saw you in the arena. Figure, they must'a caught you outside. Kingdom's not a big fan of strangers, so I came to get you out. Plan on hittin' the road myself."

"Hitting the road? What about your dad?"

Her eyes dropped to her boots, and Jack instantly recognized it.

"I'm sorry. I didn't realize he was one of the ones…"

"I knew it was impossible." Opal examined the lock, tears and anger swelling her face as she took out a few tools. "Daddy ain't been right since that fire, but I can still get you out before the same happens to you."

"Wait, Opal, I can't leave." Jack stopped her before she could make any noise. "I understand what happened to you was really bad, but I need to win in the arena. I have someone I can't leave without."

She stopped with an annoyed look of confusion. "Are you stupid? If you keep going, you're not gonna make it. You don't know what's waiting out there for you. You're scared and not strong enough to make it through."

Jack checked his cellmates before continuing. "You're probably right, but I can't leave until I finish."

"Fine. Then you're on your own." Opal stopped herself from screaming. She walked a few steps with her gun swaying before turning to Jack one last time. "When you see my daddy, tell him I said I love him." A moment later, she'd snuck out, and once again, it was like she was never there.

Some time had gone by, and Jack wasn't sure if he'd fallen asleep or not, but he was startled when he looked up again. A stranger hidden beneath a hood walked in. He stood at the bars for several seconds, looking over the prisoners. Pistols at his side gleamed, and Jack recognized the bracelet around his wrist. Before Jack could register that it was the prince, an object wrapped in cloth was tossed to him through the bars.

Jack quickly gathered the covered object. Before he removed the wrapping, he knew what it was. The weight and length was too familiar. He promptly ripped off the cloth, which fell to the ground, and there it sat in his hands. It was Nucalibur, just as he'd had it before it was stolen from him. He looked up, but the prince had already gone. As a soldier stomped into the prison, Jack pressed the button to shrink the rod and hid it in his pocket. All that was left was the cloth wrapping, which he noticed had writing on it.

"Sun to sun?" he read aloud. Stepping on the cloth and sliding it beneath his bench, he watched the soldier walk by.

"Keep it down in here. Next event will be ready this evening, and your two groups are going against each other, head-to-head."

Jack kept to himself the rest of the afternoon, still wondering three things. Where was Rocho? Why did the prince want him gone so badly? Why did he have so many visitors?

"The puzzle box will be your next great challenging event," the king's servant announced. "Each box is identical. Four boxes make up the larger outside box. Inside, each box contains a riddle on a door that will dissolve, revealing a puzzle. Solve the puzzle within the time limit, and your team will move on to the next area. Solve all four boxes, and you'll be taken to the safe zone of the fifth box in the center and then released for the final event tomorrow upon completion."

The servant paused, and each volunteer waited for the deadly part that would follow. "Lastly, if your team fails to solve a puzzle before the time limit, a member of your team will be sacrificed."

Jack's team still had five members, while the other group was made of the prisoners beside his cell — four members, including Brock and his last bandit crew member.

Two massive transparent boxes were raised into the arena on platforms. Each side held an engraving of the sun. The stadium was open, allowing the setting sun to shine brilliantly through the transparent walls of the box. Jack noticed the separated box chambers had metal slots, spouts, walls, and buttons. Each of the two boxes was held up by poles like a rotisserie. The crowd cheered loudly as the prisoners were escorted into the first section. A thick metal wall for their first riddle sat before them and appeared unmovable. The clear door closed behind them, shutting them in and muffling the crowds' cheers. The air instantly thinned.

The king, in all of his golden glory, raised his hands again. "This second event taking part on this beautiful evening of the second sun begins… now!"

A click confirmed the door they'd entered was locked while the first riddle sizzled onto the wall like acid in front of them: *Not the beginning and not the end, but only as far as you can walk in.*

Jack read it over and over before the riddle vanished, leaving them in an empty room. The floor marked itself off in sections from one to nine, and a clock on the wall counted down from thirty.

"Anyone got an idea?" Stoney asked.

"Looks like it's a code…" Jack counted the sections. "But they're all the same. Maybe we have to stand in one of these sections before the clock runs out."

"Yeah, but which one?" Stoney took a step forward.

The whole team stood around, staring between the floor segments, the ticking time, and each other.

"Section nine!" Stoney said finally. "It's the farthest we can go in. That must be it."

The kid shook his head. "Too simple."

For the first time, Jack heard the villager speak, and he could still understand him. "Perhaps simple is what they want us to think. I don't trust them after what they did to my brother."

"Well, we're running low on time," Stoney said.

The villager walked to the fifth section in the center, but only Jack noticed. "Do… do you know the answer?"

"Yes," the villager answered. "I could not read the words until I heard you speak them. You've been touched by magic from our shaman. And the item in your pocket holds the blessing of the Great Tree."

The others stared at them both with confused expressions.

"We have an old proverb from the village," the villager continued. "You can only be guided halfway into the forest and into life. Any farther, and you are walking out or not walking for yourself."

The time continued to tick away, and the others grew impatient. "What are you two saying?"

"I think he's saying we should stand in the middle. The riddle says go in as far as you can. That's halfway." Jack nodded to the native. "Any farther, we're walking out."

"Uh, need a decision." Stoney pointed. "We're almost out of time."

Most of the team took to the fifth section, while the woman stayed in the first. "What are you doing?" Jack asked.

"You won them over once," the ash-covered woman replied in a thick French accent. "I don't trust they'll let you again. The kingdom and village have never helped us after the smallest sun crashed. And now the king experiments on us? The love of my life has been taken from me. I'd prefer us both wild and together than knowing I am without him. I will be with my dear Adam."

Time ticked away; Jack wondered if he'd made a wrong decision. The final few seconds were pestering him as he looked at the villager, who remained sure and fearless. The timer buzzed zero, and spouts lowered from above their heads while a clear liquid poured down, forming walls blocking each of the nine sections. Gas billowed into each room, except one—the spot where Jack and the others stood. The section instead held a vent above it that sucked gas out.

The one ash-covered woman in section one began choking, her eyes set on the king, pointing as she smiled, until it was done. The others banged on the door, trying to get to her, but it was too late. When the gas was vacuumed out, the walls retracted. The puzzle box rotated, causing them all to slide forward, and the liquid walls dissolved. The door opened, allowing them inside, then shut abruptly. Soldiers removed the woman's body as the chamber settled.

Jack looked down at her being taken away. "Are they really—"

"I don't know," Stoney answered. "I don't know what that stuff was. Let's assume she's sleeping, but it might not be safe to touch."

Jack took notice of the box of the other team, realizing one of their members was missing, as well. Unfortunately, he couldn't see if the bandits had made it through before the next riddle appeared on the new metal wall and they were sealed in.

I protect you, I destroy you. I stab you, I block.
Heated I mold, and cooled I form more solid than rock.

Jack and his team stood in the chamber containing a wall with five slots. The slots all had tiles with a letter on them that could be cycled through from *A* to *Z*. A timer above began counting down from sixty.

"It's lava!" Stoney suggested. "It molds, it's heated, protective of sorts."

Jack shook his head. "Doesn't stab, and that's not enough letters either?"

"Hmmm… lavas?" Stoney asked.

Jack sighed before trying a few combinations. *Water, knife, stones, earth,* even *bread,* but none of them worked. They were getting short on time, and Jack looked up, wondering what trap would come for them next. He began repeating what he remembered of the riddle to the villager. "Any ideas?"

The villager looked at the wall of letters, shaking his head. "These symbols, I do not know. The riddle does not sound like anything we keep in the village."

"I was afraid you'd say that."

Time ticked away. Jack secretly brought out his totem, preparing for the worst. Searching the notches, he found nothing that would definitely be useful in solving the puzzle or escaping.

"What did he say this time?" Stoney asked.

"He said it's nothing they have in the village, so he doesn't know what—" Jack paused, with only a few seconds to go. Above him, he could see blasters targeting them all. Jack ran to the wall, flipping through the letters hastily. When he was done, he'd formed his word. *Metal.*

The blasters powered down, and the room rotated. A new door lay in front of them, and this time, they'd all made it. "Two more to go!" Stoney cheered as they were rotated through the next door, revealing another riddle.

Only one chance for both left and right.
Two different times matches noon with night.

"Clocks?" Jack stared at two large clocks inlaid on the floor. Each of the hours and minutes were accounted for. Both hands pointed at what Jack assumed was the current time, and they ticked in unison.

The answer was suddenly apparent in an unlikely place. "I think I know this one," Stoney said.

"There's no timer. I think we only have one chance at this one," Jack said. "Are you sure?"

"I'm pretty sure." Stoney slapped Jack and the villager on the back. "Both times have to match. And they gotta be from noon to night."

"Okay?" Jack watched as Stoney moved the clock's hands to the twelve o'clock position. The villager appeared worried Stoney was making all of the moves since Jack hadn't translated much.

"So what's the night version of noon?" Stoney finished.

Jack reluctantly answered, wondering if the answer was really that easy. "Midnight?"

Stoney smiled broadly. "Exactly. Two different times, but they're both the same." As he moved the final hand into the correct position, they stopped ticking. From the side, a dozen spouts appeared with small flames prepared to burn them, and sweat poured from Jack's forehead. But then the door slid open, and the final room emerged.

The box rotated a final time, and they climbed into the next room. The door had a new riddle: *Put me in a box. See me easily make the box lighter.*

"That's all of it?" Jack asked after reading it aloud. He glared at the newest room. Symbols on the floor were etched in what Jack assumed were the sun, stars, and the moon from the various sizes.

Stoney looked down on the ground. "Maybe it'll shut down once we get across?"

The villager pointed behind them, where the wall slid down, revealing spouts that began flooding the room with water quickly.

Stoney stood on one of the star symbols, causing it to light up. He pointed at their newest threat. "Does the water have anything to do with this? Maybe we have to gain some water weight."

"I don't know!" Jack panicked as the water rushed in even faster. "Don't step on the wrong one; it's making us flood faster."

The water was already up to Jack's knees, and he couldn't think fast enough. He knew his watch would be useless if it sped up the aging each time he used it, and the totem would be too random. He would have to save it until he had no choice. "I need more time. Maybe the water is a part of it. If we wait too long for it to fill up and we're wrong… it may have nothing to do with water, and there's nothing I can do to stop it. What did he say last night? Sun to sun? Is that it?"

Surprisingly, the kid with the emerald necklace spoke up. "You said 'lighter' before."

With the water at his stomach, Jack turned, panic running through his whole body. "What do you mean?"

"When you read the riddle, you said it would make the box lighter," the kid explained. "Why are you talking about weight?"

"Lighter?" Jack repeated. "Because maybe we need to weigh less in the water. How else can we make it… lighter?"

Jack stepped onto the sun symbol. The water continued rushing in but not any faster. It had reached Jack's shoulders, but he was gesturing to the others.

"Sun to sun." He remembered the note wrapping his totem from the prince. "Step onto the sun symbols and only the sun symbols. I'll take these two."

They all stood on the sun symbols, expecting the water to stop, but it persisted. The walls on either side of them remained solid, and the water rose considerably. Jack was barely able to communicate with them before taking out his totem.

"That should have been it. I don't know what else to do." He stared at his totem, wondering which symbol would save their lives, when he heard a click. A door swung open from above them into the center box.

Jack stashed his totem and pointed up, choking on the water. They were forced to swim up through the box, but eventually, they all made it up and out. The water ceased to flow once it reached the top of the first box. This smaller room held only control levers, a low seat, and a sun engraving with a small hole.

"Are we still going?" Jack asked.

"What else could be left?" Stoney replied.

The forest native shut the door beneath him. He quickly alerted Jack when he noticed the last riddle.

Only sunshine will set you free.

Jack stared at the riddle for longer than he realized. Time ticked away, but nothing else happened. They stooped down, looking at one another and the seat. Jack could see the other group rotating their box already. Suddenly, it all clicked. "It was a hole… that's what you put in a box to make it lighter. They weren't suns—they were bigger circles. We just got lucky. The sun to sun must be this riddle."

Jack quickly grabbed the levers, pushing and pulling them until the entire box rotated.

"What are you doing?" Stoney asked, watching the chambers rotate.

"The sun has to meet the sun," Jack answered, aligning the sun's rays. "There's a sun in this box, one on the outside, and the real sun. That's all three of the original suns, and if we can align them just right with these holes…"

They were rotated nearly upside down, aligning the hole that would line up with their suns just right. Just as the last setting sun hit the clear puzzle box in the right area and filled the two indented carvings, the next click was a moment of pure relief. The side of the smaller square opened. The crowd's cheers were explosive as the dome above was closed. Jack felt as if he'd been in a hotbox all day. Still dripping with water, he was happy to be crawling out.

Before long, the other team crawled out of their box. Only two of their members had made it out. Brock and a woman stepped out, just as soaked as Jack's team. Brock looked over, and the look on his face was nearly as scary as the last few minutes had been.

"The final volunteers have emerged!" the king's servant announced. "These six will be facing the final event in one-on-one matches beginning tomorrow. Who will they be faced against, and who will be in the final main event? Who will face the new threat specially brought in for the Gem Arena? Who will take on our champion beast? A new experimental threat of advanced metal ferociousness we have birthed from the beast named Green Fang!"

The crowd cheered louder than ever as soldiers began escorting the two teams out. Jack was deep in thought. *Ferocious Green Fang? That has to be Rocho. It must be!*

"I'll do it!" Jack swung his arms, getting the king's attention and pushing the soldier out of his way. "I want the main event!"

A murmur broke out among the crowd, and the king raised his eyebrow in surprise. "You wish to volunteer? That's unheard of. Are you sure about this?"

Jack was so sure, he didn't hesitate for a moment. "Yes, I am."

"Then it's decided," the king said flatly. "Should you survive, you will be given the kingdom's highest honor." Both the crowd and the king proceeded with a respectful clap. However, worry struck Jack as he was again pushed away by the soldier, and he caught a glimpse of Prince Orblanc. Once again, the prince was shaking his head sadly, as if he were seeing Jack for the last time.

Chapter 8
Letters

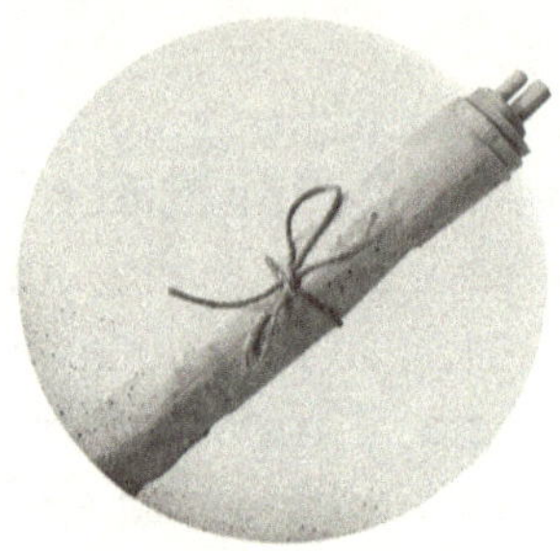

It was a long night, and an even longer morning followed. He questioned his decision over and over again. *Why would the prince look so worried?* Jack wondered. Maybe it wasn't Rocho he would be meeting after all. Both Stoney and the forest native tried to question his choice, but Jack was too focused. He continued to remind himself that he still had his totem and a few things the arena would underestimate about him if the worst was to come. Unfortunately, it appeared he would need them.

"If I do not return…" the villager said while being escorted out for his turn. "Please tell my people the shaman's whispers are true." He walked out proudly, following a soldier to the arena doors.

Jack wasn't sure what to say to reassure him, but he managed to nod, realizing he had never learned the man's name. The natives had helped him so much, and the man's help escaping the puzzle box the day before made Jack feel horrible watching what could be his final walk.

An hour went by, and a woman in the cell beside theirs was marched out next. She looked straight ahead, showing the smallest bit of anger, with her head low. Then the kid younger than Jack practically smiled as he was led out, clutching his medallion. That meant Brock was still there, waiting, and if things went the way they seemed, Stoney would be next since Jack had chosen the main event.

"Well…" Stoney began. "Looks like I'm next, kid. You know, you never did tell me what you want if you win. Must be a person. Probably a girl, right? Can't imagine what else would be this important for a kid to go through all of this."

"I'm almost fourteen!" Jack said. Stoney had asked the same question several times, but Jack still hadn't answered him. Because it could very well be the last moment he would have the chance to, Jack felt he owed it to Stoney. "Short answer: I'm here to save my dog… and my father and, yeah, this girl I met a few months ago."

"So there is a girl?"

Jack turned quickly. "It's not like that. She's just a friend. For me to save them, I have to get my dog, Rocho, and then get to the heart of the mountain with the moonleaf and—"

"The heart of the mountain?" Stoney laughed. "Only the natives know where that is."

"Well, it won't really matter if I can't find this enchanted cog."

Stoney shook his head, "I don't know nothin' bout an *enchanted* cog, but enhanced cogs, you'll see one of those soon enough."

"How's that?"

"Fusion. That thing is the most powerful machine in the kingdom. The scientists use enhanced cogs to power it. See, King Aurum had us looking for years up the mountain for the source. Only thing we managed to get are piles of sand and a few veins if we're lucky, but that's what they use for the enhanced cogs."

"Veins?" Jack asked.

"Yup, from the mountain's source. Probably the most dangerous place in these parts, besides the swamps, are those mountains. Those red veins hold a lot of power if you can stabilize it. We find them occasionally in the tunnels when mining for metals. King's scientists create new machines and use it to power them, but the advanced ones use those cogs."

"That must be what they found the other day when I came from the village," Jack said.

Stoney sat up with a raised eyebrow. "The village? Is that why you can talk to the natives?"

"That's a whole other story. But I had to find the Zookeeper, who didn't have my dog. To find this heart of the mountain, I have to get medicine from the Medicine Man for the chief's daughter, and to get King Aurum to release the Medicine Man to me, I may need to find some lawyer for a contract."

Stoney barked with a new laugh as the soldier re-entered the prison. Stoney's laughter made both Jack and the soldier look at him oddly.

"What's so funny?" Jack asked finally.

"The lawyer," Stoney answered, still chuckling. "You've already met him, kid. You said you came from the villages. I figured you were our inside man getting us new materials to him."

Jack thought for a moment but was sure since he'd left the village that he hadn't met any lawyers. Then a nasty thought crossed his mind. "You don't mean…" Jack pointed next door, to where Brock was being held, but Stoney shook his head.

"Him? No. I don't know what's up his bum over you," Stoney answered while being taken out of the prison. "That weasel tradesman that caught you! Why do you think he has all those scrolls? He makes deals and writes documents. That's all he does. If you want the lawyer's help, you better have something he wants from you! Good luck, kid."

Except for the man who hated him next door, Jack was alone.

"Peddlin' Pete." Jack sat stunned in his locked cell, unable to believe he hadn't seen it before. "The tradesman was the lawyer. How am I supposed to get a contract from him? What else could he want after getting paid off from the general? And what did Stoney mean by an 'inside man'?"

Jack stopped, hearing the laughter of someone else in the prison. Jack tried to ignore it, but soon, Brock was saying a name as he laughed.

"The Medicine Man… ha, ha, ha!" Brock roared.

Jack ran to the bars and gripped them tightly, hating being locked up so much since he'd entered the kingdom. "Why are you laughing? What do you know?"

Brock continued laughing. "I just know you'll never find him. Ha, ha! He hasn't been seen in *almost ten* years. Most think he died off; others think a witch is keeping him alive. Some think he's roaming in the swamp, lost. Either way, you'll never get what you need, even if you do find where he is. And that's the perfect ending to all of this."

He continued laughing, but Jack simply shook his head. He tried to focus on the fight ahead of him and on what to do about Peddlin' Pete. He tossed his totem from hand to hand, thinking. Nucalibur was small in its compact form, making it relatively easy to hide in his hand. Over the next few hours, he attempted to make the totem vanish using the methods the village shaman had taught him. Even when Brock was marched by, still heckling and kicking his bars, Jack persisted, pulling all of his emotions into his stomach. Using Brock's heckling, the drive to get his friends back, and remembering his parents, he felt the strain through his body. After the young detective had struggled for so long, the totem finally vanished, and he couldn't find it at all. He couldn't feel it, either.

Bringing it back was much easier, thankfully. Jack willed it back to existence, picturing the details of the wood and the notches, imagining the feel in his hand—and it reappeared just where he'd left it on the ground. He practiced again and again, getting better each time. By the time the soldier returned for him, he was somewhat rested, and he had a plan. Only the final event of the arena stood in his way.

"And now it begins!" the king's servant announced. "Three of six champions have won valiantly, where nearly two dozen others have failed. And now we bring to you the main event. This young man, who has traveled from beyond unknown places, will face an unimaginable beast to honor the loss of our queen on that sunless day."

The crowd gasped into a hush. A heavy sword at his waist, Jack stood in the arena, looking at the other side, as the gates rose. He hefted his sturdy shield as the steam puffed out and the gears stirred, lifting the heavy metal door.

"The most ferocious and monstrous creation seen in many years," the servant continued. "A fierce being we rescued from the edge of death. Its legs replaced and made stronger with the king's science. Witness the next great wonder of the world that blends life with machine. I present to you the nightmare dreamt by our brightest scientists, Fusion!"

The audience, the prince, and even the king were all more focused than Jack had ever seen them. The only sounds were several metal spikes hitting the ground in the rhythm of a train charging forward and spinning hundreds of gears. A large shadow fell over the walkway. Jack stood steady with his shield and sword raised. He hoped in the end he would be right and Rocho would come bounding out, ready to lick him. What came out of the doorway was covered in green fur, and it was large, with those same gold eyes, but it was definitely not Rocho. Jack shuddered.

Six legs, all mechanical, carried the torso and pierced the ground sharply like the legs of a crab. The top was a combination of machine, green skin, and fur. His chest was massive and plated in armor, and he gripped two mallets the size of truck axles in his fists. Small holes on the side of its head were used as ears, fur covered everything but its face and chest, and its eyes were black, with a gold pupil and red glow. A metal collar ringed its mammoth-sized neck so tightly, Jack thought it would burst if the creature swallowed. Fusion raised his mallets mightily in the air before striking the ground and rumbling the arena.

Jack shook his head. "Why do they just keep getting bigger?"

After a low howl, the monster hurled a mallet at Jack's head—and the fight began. The hammer sailed just over the dreamer's head, striking the wall so fast, he almost couldn't avoid it. Concrete fell over him as the creature charged forward. Jack dodged to the left as it slammed against the wall, swinging the other mallet. Jack ran, rolling between a forest of metal legs. Fusion pried the mallet from the wall and raised both in the air.

Jack was able to escape the first one as it hit the sand. It shook the ground even harder, and several spectators bounced in their seats. The second swing hit Jack's shield, sending him flying. He skipped across the sandy ground just as a pebble would across a pond, then tucked into a roll. The crowd cheered as Fusion roared. Its mouth foaming, and teeth bared, it displayed the weapons proudly, stirring up the crowd.

Panting, Jack scrambled up. "He's too quick for his size."

Those metal legs sprinted across the arena, leaving a trail of steam, as the creature chased Jack. He tried to dodge again, but Fusion struck the ground, blocking his path. Jack swiped with his sword but missed. A mallet soared down from the sky and hammered into Jack. He intercepted it with his shield, but Fusion was relentless.

Fusion swung wildly, pounding Jack's shield, denting the metal with every hit. Jack could only hold on as he was hit repeatedly like a nail sinking farther into the ground. The blows came too fast for Jack to react, and his shield was becoming more and more useless with every strike. Finally, the creature swung down with both mallets at once, and the force was too much for Jack.

He was crushed into the sand, leaving a crack in the ground. He could feel his body being squeezed beneath the weight, and his breaths were short. Fusion batted Jack's shield away. Leaping into the air, Fusion came down for a final blow.

Somehow, Jack's instincts brought him back to watching the fight against the Sandman, when the Spirits of Independence Day and Valentine's Day had fought bravely together. Before he knew it, Jack was on his feet, leaping at the wall.

The arena vibrated when Fusion landed, throwing sand into the air. Jack propelled off the wall, slashing his sword down across the beast's arm. The green skin was tough, but the monster dropped one of its mallets. Jack refused to stop, making every strike count.

"You're the last thing standing in my way." Jack ran between Fusion's legs. "Let's fix that!" He swung at the mechanical legs, but his sword clanged against the sturdy metal. He continued to swing the sword, staying just beneath the monster's center where he couldn't be seen. As the monster brought down the remaining mallet, Jack finally found a tube of fluids.

Fusion howled as Jack sliced open the tube, spilling a tan fluid into the sand. Steam billowed out as though its body were a teapot, whistling as it escaped, and he could hear the legs weakening. The monster recovered quickly, leaping back. Jack charged forward, sliding beneath the mechanical body again, swiping at two more tubes. Now, only half of its legs were fully functioning.

The crowd cheered loudly, but Jack's small victory was short-lived. In the center of the arena, Fusion slammed the mallet down, denting the ground, as Jack continued to run around the slowing monster. He climbed up a steaming leg and onto the beast's back as it flailed, trying to reach him. Jack was forced to grip its fur to stay on but finally dragged his sword across its shoulder.

Fusion lurched back with a mighty roar, snatching Jack and shaking the sword out of his grip. It slammed Jack against the ground. The chanting crowd stirred him awake. He opened his eyes long enough to catch blurry images of Fusion circling the arena with its arms raised. The beast was gathering its favorite weapons.

Jack felt drowsy and struggled to keep his vision straight. His head was pounding, but he did his best to focus. His hands grazed the ground as he sat up, feeling the crumpled shield to his right and jagged exposed metal on the ground to his left. Sand poured through the gap in the metal ground that led to the spike pit from the first game. Moments later, Fusion returned, slamming the mallet down once again.

Fusion hammered the crease again, exposing a larger gap in the surface as Jack scooted away. Jack managed to focus long enough to make his spear reappear as Fusion swung in a large circle. Ducking the mallet, Jack extended his totem and jabbed the monster in its side. The beast roared violently, and although it appeared to weaken it, the creature seemed equally angered, lashing at Jack even faster.

The monster growled harshly. Red bolts generated from within the remaining machine parts. Electricity flowed throughout Fusion's body, surrounding its arms and chest until red sparks seemed to pop from its core. Static filled the air, heat swelled around the torso, and sand rose from the ground. Right away, the monster, reborn and recharged, chased after Jack. He realized instantly what they'd experimented on Rocho for.

This time, when Fusion swung, the hammer didn't need to connect with Jack. A pulse of red bolts sailed over the ground. Sand jetted into the air, separating as if a rocket had gone through the arena. It hit Jack like an ocean wave, throwing him back into the arena wall. His skin burned, and he felt the volts coursing through his body. He twitched wildly as Fusion charged across the arena on three limbs.

Jack made a quick decision as it closed in on him. Choosing the hammer symbol on his totem, he twisted. A new wave of blue light surged through the arena grounds. A rush of dread overcame him as he instantly wished he'd chosen a different symbol. The shield and sword lying on the ground straightened out and flattened until they were gleaming, renewed and re-formed as if they'd just been forged. It also had the unfortunate side effect of fixing Fusion's mechanical limbs. Tubes reconnected, and the new fluid cycled through. The beast stood taller and grander than ever. Only the wounds Jack had left on its flesh remained.

The hammer symbol, along with the others on the totem, went dull. The gap in the arena floor remained. The mechanical hybrid was distracted as it healed, allowing Jack to hurl his spear like a javelin at its head. The spear landed squarely in its eye, just before Fusion swatted Jack away again. Both opponents wailed in pain. Fusion struggled to remove the spear, while Jack clutched his shoulder, unable to move his left arm. What happened next, Jack least expected.

Fusion gripped the end of the spear firmly with its large hands. In a single motion, the beast yanked the totem out along with its eye, snapped the spear in half like a toothpick, and tossed it aside. Jack instantly felt a pain in his chest, as if both his father and Sonny were drifting farther away.

A loud pop rang out over the shouting crowd. Several people were on their feet. Magic spilled from Nucalibur and onto the ground, and all Jack could do was stare. Seven candles appeared in a line, nearly blinding everyone in the arena. Broken candy canes with jagged ends spiked from the ground in a trail, attacking Fusion until it was stuck in a red-and-white-striped prison and tearing apart the arena floor. Fireworks blasted off into the air, streaming trails of red, white, and blue flakes. Hundreds of rockets exploded on various points of the beast's body, breaking through the candy cane prison.

Each hit knocked Fusion farther away from Jack, who watched from the opposite side. He grew angrier the longer he watched it, and then opportunity struck. Clutching his broken arm with his remaining good one, he sprinted over to his fixed shield and scooped it up. Fusion staggered, blinded and battered but sturdy. Panting and tired, Jack rammed it with the shield, pushing it closer to the growing gap in the center. Then he threw his shield like a Frisbee.

Fusion's metal legs slid as it toppled back into the exposed spiked pit. The green machine's weight was enough to collapse the remaining structure. The audience in the stands, Prince Orblanc, and even the king looked shocked as the tides quickly changed. Jack's challenger scrabbled at the sand for something to grip but eventually slid down into the pit.

The crowd exploded with new excitement. Even the king was clapping, and the prince did his best to hide a huge smile. Still nursing his broken shoulder, Jack could only manage to trudge over to the fractured totem and gather the two pieces in his hand. Fusion's eye was still stuck on the pointed end.

"To our victor!" The king clapped. "After finishing a most difficult race, conquering a puzzling box, and defeating a contender of unmatched scientific power in the thrilling main event to close out this celebration, we come to your most deserved rewards. What is the item and wish you would like to obtain? Unfathomed riches, perhaps? Lord over land? Name it, and it is yours."

Jack gripped his broken totem angrily. He could hear the mechanical eye attempting to function, but it was stuck. Removing the eye from Nucalibur's point, Jack noticed the red glow. He broke the casing and pried loose a bright-red cog nearly the size of his palm. It continued to radiate with energy from the source.

The arena continued to wait as Jack shook his head and sighed before looking up at both the king and his son. "Rocho… I want my green dog back. The Zookeeper took him away from me near the forest, and I want him back!"

The prince whispered into his father's ear, and his eyes widened. "Oh, the green animal belongs to you?" He tilted his head, studying the situation. "Your animal was difficult to tame, but as promised, he will be returned to you. Now, as our main event winner, what is it you wish for?"

Jack clutched his broken totem, knowing he had no choice but to hope he could still use it. He chose his next words carefully. "I want you to sign a contract of peace to end the war between you and the people of Usiku village. The chief will agree to decode the stolen map that leads to the mountain's heart if you agree not to remove the power source in the mountain, and have the Medicine Man make his daughter a cure for smoke sickness. Will you agree to this?"

The king looked down at Jack with a curious gaze. "Smoke sickness? That is the smog illness no one has had in many years. How long has she been afflicted?"

"She may not be," Jack replied. "Chief Mizzi worries it may have been passed on to her. I won the main event. I beat the arena and get anything I wish for. Will you agree to a peace contract?"

"This is a very bold request." King Aurum stroked his beard for several seconds with a skeptical look as his citizens waited. "Who exactly are you, champion? What is your name?"

Jack winced, still unable to move his other arm. "My name is Jack Taylor."

"Jack Taylor?" Surprisingly, it was Prince Orblanc who'd spoken. "As in Jackson Taylor?"

The king stood. "Get him bandaged up and ready to meet us out in the court."

Jack backed away a few steps as guards approached him. "What's going on?"

"We've been expecting you," the king stated simply. "A package is waiting for you."

The guards took Jack to a room where one of the royal attendants put his arm in a sling and dressed his wounds. It was the first time since arriving in the kingdom that he'd been in a room and not shut in by bars. Finally able to look from a new viewpoint, he realized how incredible the castle appeared. Walls and floors were made of smooth stone the color of milk chocolate, with gold etchings throughout each hall, and the kingdom's gear symbol was present in each room he stepped through. For now, he was able to relax for a moment and looked forward to seeing Rocho, but he knew that was only one small part to getting back to Cloud City.

Once he was fully bandaged, the attendants provided a meal and guided Jack down to the city streets. There, he was met by Prince Orblanc, who was finding it difficult to hold back his smile.

"I have to admit, I did not think I would be speaking to you right now." The prince smiled, patting his tri-barreled pistols. "I am more than capable with my blasters, but what you did in the arena and against Fusion—that was pretty impressive."

"Thanks." Jack knew he'd gotten lucky a few times but didn't feel the need to relive it. He was curious to find out who else had survived the arena, but fearing Stoney hadn't made it, he couldn't bring himself to ask. "I've been wondering, why did you help me? You brought me the fishing rod, but it seemed like you've been trying to get me out of the city as fast as possible. You could've just let me die."

The prince surveyed his surroundings before gesturing for Jack to follow. "I helped you because you rescued someone very important to me, but I'm sure you already know that."

"You love her?" Jack asked, recognizing the bracelet around the prince's wrist. "That's why you helped me?"

"Well, yes, of course, but it's complicated." He played with the bracelet. "We have a bond I've never known before. We can't understand how it's possible, but we know it's true. Our fathers would never allow us to be near each other. If they knew, things would only get worse, and we don't want to be responsible for the war to hit its peak. But ever since I found those letters in the archive…"

"What letters?"

"In the archives, before the fire," the prince answered. "I was having my new blaster reconditioned. I found an old box covered in dust. It had the same set of gems as my bracelet. I must've been in there a dozen times, reading about the world before the separation. I found stories about a giant being and strange swamp magic while waiting on the scientists. But I'd never seen this before. They were letters from my mother."

"Your mother?"

"Before she died. I was only able to read a few of them before the fire. I didn't want to take them with me, but now I wish I would've. I assumed they were locked away for a reason and taking them would've alerted someone. They didn't seem addressed to anyone, just pages of her thoughts for anyone who might find them. My father doesn't talk about her much anymore. We don't hide our feelings like the villagers. The kingdom uses love, hatred, and fear as a passion to make us stronger, but I believe discussing my mother brings my father too much pain."

Jack knew this feeling from his mother too well. For a moment, he was lost in thought of his parents again. After a moment of silence, Jack realized the prince was waiting for a response. "I don't understand how the letters connect you with the chief's daughter."

"In the letters, she mentioned escaping to a less modern world more like where she came from. I had no idea she wasn't from the kingdom, but after reading her letters, I began to travel toward the village in secret, searching for information. I wondered if maybe the chief hadn't caused her death, after all. I ran into Celeste, weaponless, and running from an animal that turned out to be her companion. She was unlike the other villagers. Not as tall, and the ivory-white hair. She stood out. She understood me."

Jack felt as if he'd heard the story long before: two people destined to be together only to be ripped apart by their families. He thought about how terrible it would be to feel so strongly for someone and have it cause so many problems. "So what do you plan to do?"

"It seems that may be in *your* hands now," the prince said slyly. "My mother disappeared shortly after I was born, and my father believes Chief Mizzi had something to do with it. I don't think it's true, from what Celeste has told me. We were able to meet only a few weeks ago, but it feels like so much longer. She wants freedom more than anything else for herself and her people. I plan to help her with that one day."

"And what do you want?" Jack asked.

"One day, I'll change the arena to a tournament where talents and skill can shine through for honor without all the violence that my father prefers," the prince said nobly before pausing. "And a real family would be nice. Celeste is my greatest friend and closest bond. Your help will give us that chance."

Jack stumbled and almost bumped into a woman walking with her daughter. "Why me?"

Before the prince could answer, a man in a heavy leather apron and goggles spotted them from a doorway and came bouncing over. "Prince Orblanc, we've been expecting you and your guest," he said cheerfully. He was just as muscular as any other of the kingdom's citizens, but his mousy hair and goggles made him look like an excited beetle.

"Yes, this is Jack, the one you've been waiting for. Jack, this is our top scientist and keeper of the archives, Geo."

Jack looked between the two men. "Why have you been waiting for me?"

"A letter arrives here for a stranger no one has ever met or heard of, and it just so happens to be the same person who defeats one of my greatest creations inspired by his own pet!" Geo replied with enthusiasm. "We've made some great leaps in science studying the animal, but I still have so many questions about his energy production and size manipulation."

"Maybe another time." Jack tried to be courteous, but time was never really on his side. Geo appeared disappointed but nodded as Jack went on. "Where is this package, and when do I get Rocho back?"

"Well, about the package…" Geo began. "It appears it was sent somewhere else."

"What do you mean?" Jack's annoyance was rising.

Prince Orblanc interrupted. "It would be easier to understand if you read the letter that came with it first. As for Rocho, my father is having him brought down from the stables. He needs to speak to you before this contract deal is made. If you can get them to sign, this could make several things possible." He gave Jack an encouraging look before walking him into Geo's lab.

Beakers were laid out haphazardly on tables, bubbling and casting off plumes of smoke in green and orange. Other scientists dripped liquid onto rocks, causing them to change color. Another worked on a pistol, using one of the sparking veins Jack witnessed the other day in the mines. Jack was impressed with what they had produced with their limited technology, and he wondered if Dr. de Luca would find it as fascinating.

"This is an invention we've just completed after creating a new blaster for one of the arena's winners." The lead scientist pointed to a metal rod nearly the length of a radio antenna. "It's an instrument that can harness your energy to manipulate matter and change its structure based on your mind's intentions. Isn't that incredible? You just point and concentrate. Of course, it's limited for now."

Jack glared at the rod quizzically. "So it can change things just by pointing at it? Like a magic wand?"

"Magic what?" Geo laughed. "No, this is all science. Like the portal we were able to fit into random objects like this handbag and that top hat. Pulls objects through time and space, and instantly, it's in your hand. It would be a lot to explain to someone unfamiliar with such advanced techniques, but this took a lot of organic manipulation to create."

"Advanced?" Jack whispered, eyeing the top hat as they followed Geo out. "Pretty sure Amazon has an app for that."

"The archive room is just past my latest project, but I think you'll find it remarkable." Geo led them to another area where several items were burned and covered in papers. Jack noticed schematics for something resembling mechanical suits, and he saw one with six legs, which he assumed was used to make Fusion. The room grew darker before Geo lit a torch using rocks as a spark. A trail of fire lit the way into a seemingly empty room. The scientist lifted a white cloth from the floor, revealing a nearly completed mechanized suit.

"I've been working on this for some time now," Geo said. "Our numbers are outmatched by the natives, but with enough of these, we will be better prepared to win any battle. The general somehow obtained a new substance from the natives' forest that will allow us to control the machines much better than the metal hunters we've been using. That's what gave us the power to control Fusion so well. We are very close to the end."

The machined suit was nearly as deadly looking as Fusion had been. Cold metal stretched over a large skeleton as tall as the natives. A blade ejected from one arm, while ammunition was loaded into the other. An enhanced cog was exposed just above the torso. Jack reached down with his good arm to touch the cloth that hid the machine.

"How did you make it disappear with this?" Jack asked, holding the cloth.

"It's a complex chemical compound spread over durable cloth," Geo answered matter-of-factly.

Jack inspected it carefully. "Looks like a magic cloak."

Geo laughed harder. "Again with magic? You were with the forest natives too long. Do you know what the difference is between the natives' magic and our science?"

Jack remembered a similar conversation in the village. "Magic... can't be explained."

"Yet..." The scientist covered his machine. "Everything can be explained in time. What you believe is magic will always be one explanation away from a scientific breakthrough. It's not blind belief. There is a reason for how everything works."

He wasn't sure if he could completely agree or not, but Jack nodded as he was guided into the archive room. Books and papers littered the shelves. Several maps had been tossed aside, while letters were thrown into a pile. Much of the archive room was severely burned.

Jack surveyed the sooty pages. "What happened in here?"

"One of the general's assistants went crazy after losing his job," Geo said, examining the room. "Lost some important document that was sent here apparently, but we were able to salvage most of the books and papers. Fortunately, your letter arrived after the fire."

He sifted through the pile before handing Jack an envelope addressed to him. Jack recognized it as the same one he'd witnessed in Peddlin' Pete's cart. Jack held it for several seconds, wondering who would be sending him a letter. Hoping it wasn't more bad news, he opened it and read from the torn piece of yellow notepad paper.

Jack,

Read carefully, as I will likely not have the displeasure to write you again. Things have become unstable after your departure. I'm sure one way or another, you are entirely to blame, but as your advisor, I must warn you. Someone is tampering with your challenge. It is unclear who exactly, but there are theories based on the attacks I have only discussed with the investigator. The frost chasing you through the forest, the downpour of rain, and the heat drying out the kingdom, causing the fog. They all point to one of the Four Seasons' manipulation. I'm sure your simple mind has already landed on Winter, with his understandable distaste for you, but it is not nearly enough to be certain. After all, if others feel as I do, several people find you annoying. Autumn created the challenge, Summer adores action and thrills, and although Spring may look like an innocent girl, she happens to be the oldest of the Four Seasons, and her origins are cloudy at best.

You have been very lucky, helped by the children of the leaders. I've watched you nearly fail over and over again in this challenge, and you do not seem to be getting any smarter or more skillful as you press on, so I've sent you something to aid your journey: the remains of the pumpkin-handled sword recovered from my mutinous symbol, Trick. My shadow was able to deliver this letter and the sword through the portal, but I don't trust some of the sneakier travelers. So the sword is being held by someone I do trust. You can find her in the swamps. It should still wield abilities useful to you if you're brighter than I believe you are, and I highly doubt anyone with intelligence will venture into that area. Use your flashlight to map your way there.

Many lives depend on you, boy. Do something about it. Do something I would never believe to be possible… impress me.

Mr. Henry Johnson,
Spirit of Halloween

Jack finished reading the letter but continued staring at the name signed at the bottom. "Mr. Henry Johnson…"

He knew the message was from Mr. Shadow from the tone of the first sentence, but he had never known the name the holiday spirit had gone by when he was still alive. Though Jack had never met him before, the name sounded familiar.

Geo cleared his throat. "Well, I'm sure you must have much to think about from that letter. Heading into the swamp has been said to be just as dangerous as the mountains. I'll send for you when the king has arrived with your reward. Prince

Orblanc, I have your monthly item ready to be bottled in the lab."

They both exited the room, leaving Jack alone in the archives. He read the letter a few more times, walking about the room. Again, he wondered why Mr. Shadow, of all people, had volunteered to be his advisor in the first place and what he might be up to. If anyone wanted to set Jack up to fail, the Halloween spirit was near the top of the list. But if one of the seasons wanted him stuck in the challenge, he was in a whole other world of trouble. Mr. Shadow had gotten one thing right about Jack in his letter. He did believe Old Man Winter had something to do with it, and the first frost attack only made more sense.

Jack walked around the archives, kicking up black ash and coughing on the dust. Off balance with his one good arm, he knocked over a stack of books, which landed in a pile of letters. Most were too smudged with soot to make out the words, but one stood out like a beacon, written in a different language and addressed to the king.

Curiosity got the best of him, and a moment later, Jack was reading. "To my king and golden prince. This is the hardest thing I will ever have to do—"

He stopped reading and stuffed the letter into his pocket where he hid the enhanced cog just as the door swung open. Prince Orblanc returned, carrying a vial of what appeared to be spib ink. "My father asks that you meet him outside."

The prince guided him outside the lab, where King Aurum waited with two soldiers just outside the door.

He gave a disapproving look at the vial in his son's hand. "How often have I told you to keep your hair dye hidden?" he whispered harshly. "What if the citizens see you?"

Prince Orblanc discreetly hid the vial in his vest pocket then stepped out of the doorway. After watching his son walk away, King Aurum returned his attention to Jack, a satisfied expression spreading over his chubby face. "Mr. Taylor, the Fusion crusher and tamer of Green Fang. I see you've received your letter. You and my son appear to be bonding. One day, he will be a powerful king when I bulk him up. If he would only listen to me and train more instead of playing with his blasters, I'd nearly be proud of him.

"He's a really good shot, though," Jack said. "That must be worth a lot when fighting, too?"

"It's a useful tool, but the real strength of a person comes from size and power," the king said firmly. "I appreciate our scientists enough, but when the blasters run out, all you have is your own power. Like your animal friend. It's not nearly as dangerous without his flashing energy, but his size helps. I'm sure you are eager to get your animal friend back, and I assure you he will be awaiting your arrival at the city gates. However, there are a few things we must discuss first regarding the wish you requested. It is a nice, sunny day. Please, walk with me."

They walked through the grand city, where the stone streets were clean, the citizens shopped or worked happily, and the children played freely. Several people praised the king as he walked by, and he shook the hands of his people and presented a small sack of coins to a poor family on the street. They all seemed to genuinely like the king, which still surprised Jack after what the natives had said of him.

"I do not often do this," the king said. "I try my best to make sure my first decision is the correct one. Wrong ones can cost so many lives. However, the capture of the green animal that belonged to someone else was a mistake. My people are not thieves, and we earn what we keep. I apologize on behalf of my general."

Jack was taken aback and could only mutter a simple thank you in response. They turned a corner and were headed in the direction of the market as the king continued. "We were able to learn a great deal from it before your arrival. We were blessed by the suns once again. We have been fortunate to embrace the suns' favor. The last person affected by smog sickness was cured just after the last sunless day."

King Aurum paused, looking up at the sun. "The energy your animal can harness is similar to the veins connected to the mountain. Studying it may allow us to complete the vision I've had that began with Fusion, and will continue to replace our armor and introduce a new revolution. Mecha suits, powered by the strongest power source we know. More powerful than our enhanced cogs."

Jack nearly fell over a fruit stand. "Those red sparking parts that lead to the mountain? Why can't you trace it without the map?"

"None of the veins seem to connect where we can follow. It is the most powerful substance in the land, and gathering a few pieces is so unstable, it destroys nodes quickly. With enough of it, the future is limitless… but of course the chief doesn't see it that way. Old men stuck in the past of traditions believing the ground is alive and breathing? Forcing children to trial prove their fearlessness at such a young age? These rites of passage are just savage ways."

Jack couldn't disagree with the king but was also quick to object without meaning to. "You believe what you do is better? People die for entertainment every year. Is it that different?"

King Aurum appeared to take direct offense. "You should be careful with your tongue, boy, especially about matters you do not understand. Having lost a loved one, someone as important to this kingdom as myself, I will not forget her or allow my people to. And unlike the native savages, those who fight are not children — they volunteer. Their sacrifice for a better life is their choice."

"Or rot in a prison just for traveling to the wrong area," Jack whispered.

"We are here to enhance this world, not die with it. Our way — my way — is the way the world should be, and the natives need to accept that. Which brings me to your request. I must ask, what are you getting if a peace agreement is reached?"

"I need to get home," Jack said honestly. "The power source should help me get there."

The king stopped his guards and took a hard look at Jack. His crown shifted and made his face look sterner than before as a shadow draped over his eyes. "Well then, I suppose our goals are aligned. I don't know how you or the natives knew we'd obtained the map even before I had, but I will tell you I sent no one to steal it. If I want something, I fight with honor or buy it as lawfully as I demand my people to be.

"As you have won the right to choose your reward, I must put aside my hatred and will agree to sign this contract of peace if the night folk decode the map. For my part in helping his daughter, I will warn you the Medicine Man was not one for safety. Many of his experiments were more dangerous than any we attempt now. His vision to create a way of immortality drove him more than anything else. As such, he left the kingdom a decade ago. If he is still alive, I would assume he is still in the swamps, searching for a way to live forever."

"So Brock was right," Jack said, defeated. "And Mr. Shadow's sword is supposed to be there, too. Seems like everything is leading me to that place."

"It is a dangerous place to venture to. People enter and are never seen again, but their presence is felt throughout the wetlands. Searching for my lost wife, I've seen tortured expressions carved into the area itself."

Jack's frustration began to rise as he had little hope of getting back home with so many sudden limitations. "I don't understand. What is so dangerous about the swamp and the mountain?"

"Whatever creatures are in there have been changed by the veins of the mountain. Its power is incredible but can manipulate life, as well. The mountains, we've had no chance of getting to. There is only one entrance we've heard rumors about, and the natives guard it heavily. Only stories of monstrous animals and giants are told now. Giants so large they block the suns themselves. At least for now, the people of this kingdom will know the Fusion slayer by this." The king presented Jack with a necklace that resembled an Olympic gold medal, except the medallion bore a cross between the gold gear symbol of the kingdom and a sun nearly the same size as the moonleaf stone.

"There hasn't been another crafted since before the smallest sun fell. The gold is melted using the suns' rays and molded from an ancient symbol. You should wear it proudly."

Jack examined the medallion and instantly felt the warmth it radiated. He had mixed feelings accepting it. "Thank you, King Aurum."

"There is, however, one other issue you must conquer before your journey, young champion."

"And what is that?" Jack asked, depressed.

"I will agree to these terms. However, I cannot force the lawyer to create the contract. We have freedom of will here, just as you did to enter the arena. The items he uses will make both myself and their leader unable to break the agreement. If you would like this to happen, you will need to convince him to write it."

"Oh, don't worry about that." Jack smiled for the first time in a while, holding his totem. "I'll take care of him."

Jack found Peddlin' Pete in the market, packing up his cart for the day as the markets closed. He grinned, delighted with himself while weighing a sack of coins. Jack stepped in closer, trying to go unseen, but the weasely man spotted him immediately.

"I'd say I'm surprised to see you in one piece, but a look at that shoulder tells me that's only technically true." He snickered. "Hope you didn't take it personally, sell'n you to the Zookeeper. Just business, you know, but it all seemed to work out for us both just fine."

"How's that?" Jack asked. "I save your life from those bandits, and you lock me up where I fight for my life against two wolf hybrids, an obstacle course trying to set me on fire over a spike pit, followed by the worst Rubik's Cube ever, and a monster more mutated than comic book villains, all while you got paid! How is that just fine for both of us?"

"Well, you still have your health." Grinning, Pete held up his sack of coins. "And I won a bet for one of the arena winners. Too bad it wasn't on you. I could've retired on those odds. Let me know if you wanna sell that medallion you got around your neck. I'll make you a good deal."

"Well, I do need something from you, and after everything you've caused, I think it's only fair that you do it," Jack said sternly. "I need a peace agreement written up between the king and Chief Mizzi."

Peddlin' Pete stopped packing and glared at Jack. "So you discovered my profession, except I don't think I will be helping you. After all, if the village and the kingdom stop fighting, then they won't need me to trade between them, will they?"

Jack smirked, not taking his eyes off the pouch the lawyer held so securely. "I thought you might say something like that." Concentrating carefully, Jack waved his good hand, and a second later, the pouch vanished.

Pete tightened his grip on the pouch, but his closed hand was empty. "What, where did my — what did you do?"

"Missing something?" Jack replied slyly.

Jack had never seen Peddlin' Pete so frustrated, even with the bandits. "You know what I'm missing. Where's my money pouch?"

"I don't know," Jack lied, pointing to two guards near the corner. "It might be in my pocket, but if you tried to take it from me, it would only take a second to call those guards over and accuse you of being a thief. Who d'you think they'd believe? That I took it from you with one good arm after winning the competition where I could've asked for unlimited wealth, or you, the ultimate liar in the kingdom?"

Pete glared at him with such fury, Jack was forced to hide his amusement. Peddlin' Pete was stumped and outplayed, and Jack could see it in his face. With a long, hate-filled sigh, he opened his half-filled cart then withdrew a roll of parchment paper, a vial of spib ink, and a writing utensil from his pocket. "All right, spit it out, kid. What's the agreement?"

Jack explained what Chief Mizzi had requested, making sure to include a cure for Celeste and the decoding of the map that would allow him access to it, as well. When it was finished, all that remained were the signatures of Chief Mizzi and King Aurum.

"The spib ink makes the agreement impossible to be altered." Pete rolled the paper and sealed it with wax. "That paper there is made from a tree root that's darn near impossible to find and just as hard to rip or burn. And the pen is from Usikupess magic to make each signer bound by the agreement no matter what. Coated in spib ink, so be careful. They each poke their fingers and sign. Anyone breaks it, instantly poisoned. Which is why supplies cost me a fortune! Here, take it."

The lawyer shoved the contract into Jack's hand.

He examined it, pleased with himself. "This is everything I need?"

"Except for their signatures, yes. Now, where is my pouch?" Pete demanded.

Jack waved his hand lightly. "It's right inside the cart."

Pete looked behind him. "I don't see nothin'…"

"It's just a little farther in; you can't miss it." Jack watched the lawyer crawl deeper into the crate in search of his lost pouch.

The lawyer paused and tried to scurry back, but it was too late. Jack shoved him in with his foot and quickly shut the door, locking it securely. The weasely man shook the bars, but everyone around seemed to ignore the situation. Jack assumed they were all just as tired of his shady dealings as Jack was. With a wave of his hand and deep concentration, he caused the pouch to appear in Peddlin' Pete's hand.

"Lucky for you, I keep my word." Jack snatched the vial of spib ink and threw it onto the tradesman. "I told you I'd have you in a cage before I left. I'm sure someone will pity you like I did and let you out sooner or later."

Ink poured over Pete's face and hands, paralyzing his mouth. "You forget I had the cure in here? Won't take me long to swallow this and be out. Where is that thing? Did you hide that, too?" he mumbled, clumsily searching for the vial of clear liquid.

"You mean the one I switched with rainwater?" Jack said, walking away. "I don't think it'll help you much now anyway."

"Wait… you can't leave me… in… here." He struggled to plead as the effects of the ink took hold. "I thought you were… better… than… that, kid?"

Jack hesitated, looking over the cage, thinking of what he'd been through because of this person, what his father or Sonny would think of him. Then he heard a yelp from a distance and spotted something running toward him. The rays of both suns cast a shadow, but Jack noticed reflecting gold. He bent down, watching a small green ball of fur limping toward him, trying to run. It bounced in the breeze, racing toward Jack like a fuzzy ball of lightning until finally, it jumped into his hands.

"Rocho!" Jack hollered, embracing his friend. It felt like forever since he'd seen those gold puppy-dog eyes and felt the licks on his cheek. He smiled more broadly than he had in months. Everything else seemed to disappear, until he heard Peddlin' Pete's voice behind him.

"Just…let … out, kid. No… real harm… right?"

Jack looked from his loyal companion's soft eyes, wagging tail, and drooping tongue to the pathetic figure locked in the crate. Over the cage, he spotted Opal heading into an alley with her shotgun and a small sack of scavenged goods to trade. She shook her head slightly, and it all rushed back to Jack: all of the experiments done to him, the way Rocho was captured and dragged away in a net by the Zookeeper, and what the pup must have felt, wondering if Jack had abandoned him completely.

Placing the pup on the ground, he secured the contract and his letter from Mr. Shadow in his pocket along with the burned letter he'd found in the archive room. He led the pup toward the kingdom's gates, ignoring Pete's muffled begging and kicking.

Chapter 9
The Medicine Man

The letter from Mr. Shadow trembled in Jack's hand. That tingling sensation of holding something dangerous crawled up his neck. He followed a new path to a small opening surrounded by bushes and moss-covered trees. He was lucky to have Rocho back, with his multiple abilities. After seeing Jack's shoulder, Rocho changed to his bear size and practically pulled him onto his back. His limp healed instantly when he changed, as if his larger size were another animal altogether. Jack rode the pup all the way to the swamps, and it appeared just as unforgiving as he'd been warned.

Bog gas wafted through the trees as if wanting to escape, but the perimeter of trees kept it contained. Moss draped branches like curtains, hiding whatever lived deep within. The trees were much more twisted and grotesque than those in the

Usiku Forest. They almost resembled people posed in wild positions of pain and planted into the ground. He could see the river in the east draining into the woods as it slowed to its last journey in the swamp.

Jack took a careful look into the wooded area, wondering how stupid he was to even try after all the warnings. "What do you think?" he asked Rocho.

The pup sniffed the ground near the woods and began to whimper. The danger was obvious, but it wasn't the first time he'd confronted it—and it wouldn't be the last. "I know, boy, but if we don't go in there, we won't get back home. And we won't get back to my dad or Sonny, either."

Rocho switched his gaze from the woods back to Jack before giving an affirmative bark. Jack checked the items still in his pockets: the letter from Mr. Shadow, the smoky letter from the burned archive room, the agreement from Peddlin' Pete, and his broken totem. He hoped the Medicine Man would have an idea of how to fix Nucalibur.

Stepping through the draping moss was like stepping into Mr. Shadow's home on Cloud Nine—eerily quiet, except for the breeze rustling leaves and gurgling of swamp bubbles. Rocho returned to his small puppy size to better travel through the murky land. The ground was soft and moist. Dull-red vines flowed throughout the area, along with fog that seemed to react to his movement.

Jack examined Mr. Shadow's letter. "Use your flashlight to view the map," he read aloud.

Rocho barked at Jack excitedly, creating small beams of light. Jack placed the letter on the ground, allowing Rocho to sniff it. A few seconds later, he began barking again. The light he projected revealed something on the back of the letter. When Jack flipped the page over, orange lines began to fade.

"It's the map."

Rocho sniffed the page and began barking excitedly —
then he was off. His nose stuck to the ground like a high-
powered vacuum, and Jack following closely.

Jack followed his green companion around small areas of
water that separated patches of muddy ground. Large lily pads
floated on the water while horseflies and dozens of tiny
mosquitoes buzzed by. More and more trees were covered by
mushrooms that appeared to get larger farther in the swamp.
The sun, luckily, was more visible there than it was the forest, so
he stepped over thick tree roots without issue. He could hear
hooting nearby and spotted an odd four-eyed owl looking in
four different directions. It hung over them in a branch with one
of its eyes watching them as they lumbered through. The
hooting was soon followed by the mesmerizing sound of
crickets. The crickets seemed to chirp in a soothing melody. Jack
wondered if Rocho was annoyed by it, because he kept stopping
to shake his head.

"Hey, buddy, are you all right?" Jack asked.

Rocho barked, again shaking his head. Jack knew
something was wrong, but he didn't understand what until they
got closer to the source of the sound.

Hundreds of crickets surrounded them, chirping in
unison. The more he heard the rhythmic sounds, the dizzier he
became. His head was pounding, and everything appeared to be
spinning. Hazy images of monsters ready to fight appeared in
front of him. Rocho growled at Jack as if wanting to attack, and
Jack realized the sound must have affected Rocho's sensitive
hearing much more than it had his own. Before he knew it, the
pup took off. Jack only caught a glimpse of him but stumbled in
the direction he'd gone.

Occasionally, Jack spotted green fur running in a circle or the spark of lightning speed behind twisted trees, but he couldn't catch up. As he climbed a hill to a cliff, the noises began to ease away. His vision started to focus as he edged closer to the top. The dreamer's head finally clearing, he could see Rocho at the top as a small pup, slumped on the ground, breathing hard. Jack patted his head.

"Hey, boy." Jack scratched the pup's ears, climbing to the top. "It's over now. Are you all right?"

"No." The voice surprised Jack so much that he almost stumbled back down the hill. "You both won't be when I'm done with you."

Jack turned to find someone he definitely hadn't expected to see.

"Brock?" Jack squinted through the brown fog at the bandit leader, who was sporting a fresh eye patch and an advanced-looking blaster. "What are you doing here?"

"Surprised to see me make it out of the arena? Hurts that you think so little of me. I'm more resourceful than you think. Had to sacrifice some of my crew, and that last fight took a piece of me fair enough, but I always find a way. Just like I heard you somehow won your fight, I knew you'd be on your way here."

"What do you want with me?" Jack asked, surveying the area. Rocho growled loudly, and his sparks began to flare as if he were about to change.

"Don't even try it!" Brock yelled at Rocho, his blaster aimed at Jack. "Lost my map, my gang, and nearly my life 'cause of you. After I won, I had the scientists build me this beauty. A blaster with more attachments and ammo than a mecha suit. Stronger and better than the prince's. So, trust me when I say I'll get to you before it gets to me. Now that I've been pardoned of all my crimes, I can take care of you with a clean slate."

An odd smell began to overwhelm Jack, but he tried to focus on distracting Brock. "I thought I was saving his life. I didn't realize Peddlin' Pete stole the map from you. He tricked me, too, you know."

Brock stepped closer, jerking his weapon threateningly. "I don't even care about the lawyer anymore. Found him locked in the crate. Made sure he paid me back with interest. But *you* owe me a debt. And you're gonna pay up. We'll start with that medallion you won."

The smell had gotten worse, but Jack suddenly thought about how he'd left Peddlin' Pete locked in the crate and wondered if Brock finding him now was justified. Jack tossed over the necklace. "So you're just gonna shoot me?"

Brock laughed, slowly picking up the gold medallion. "Oh, no. That just wouldn't be as much fun. No, the way you'll pay will be slower than that. I've heard the sounds and followed them here. You're going into the center of the swamp's bog. All that water there is waiting for you, and so is something else. You're gonna be my bait for what's waiting. Now move it before—"

Brock stopped mid-sentence, turning to see the brown fog rising. He tried to take a step forward but couldn't move his leg. He panicked, screaming and shooting wildly, forcing Jack and Rocho to duck. "What is this?" Brock yelled. "Get it off! Get it off!"

The brown fog crawled over his ankle and up his leg. He removed a vial of clear liquid from his pocket, uncorking it quickly. Brock chugged it before falling to the ground, and it rolled over to Jack. The brown gas crawled up Brock's back, wrapping his chest and arms. His body hardened with a creaking noise. Rocho dove forward, knocking the blaster out of Brock's hand before the fog covered it, too. Jack recovered the necklace and backed away.

The fog rose over Brock's shoulders, creeping over the back of his head and eyes, turning him to stiff tree bark. His final yell was muffled as the fog covered his mouth. Moss grew from his head and arms, and he remained rooted in the swamp, a part of the swamp forever crawling and reaching out toward the vial at Jack's sneakers.

Jack realized why the trees reminded him of twisted wooden statues. He recognized the vial, too. It was the rainwater Jack had switched with Pete's spib ink cure.

Rocho barked, and Jack looked away from the horrible remains of the bandit. The brown fog had crept closer to them, and the only escape was the long drop behind him. Rocho sparked and growled, but his electricity seemed to have no effect. Jack looked over the sides, but the fall seemed too far to survive. The giant lily pad floating along the water below appeared to be their only safety net.

He hastily removed the contract, fearing it might get lost even if it couldn't be damaged. He folded it carefully and stuffed it into his shoe. As the brown fog inched closer and closer like the icy frost that chased him in the Usiku Forest, Jack grabbed Rocho and took a leap.

The water was warm and thick like syrup, sticking to his skin, refusing to release him. Red veins were everywhere and seemed to center in the area. The brown fog edged over the cliff above them and wafted into the air. Brown bubbles swelled from the water and burst with a loud pop. Jack and Rocho did their best to swim to the edges using the large lily pads to move about. Jack could feel the medallion weighing him down. He stopped as something strange gurgled from below, and he felt a ripple through the murky water.

"What's that sound?" Jack turned to see Rocho dog-paddling out. He followed, only pausing when he heard the sound again. It was like a belch from beneath them. The water sloshed back and forth as a pair of yellow eyes with dark-black pupils the size of bowling balls rose from the water in front of him.

The yellow orbs rested just above the surface, blinking. Jack stayed still, mesmerized by the eyes until a few horseflies flew by. The eyes darted back and forth, sometimes in two different directions, watching them. Then a long tongue stretched out, striking several flies at once. Jack climbed out of the water and onto a muddy mound as Rocho growled and barked at what shot up from the water like a geyser.

Boils covered the creature's slimy red skin. Its eyes stuck to the top of its head, blinking slowly. And a bulging bubble protruded from its neck with every breath. It was repulsive and resembled a bullfrog the size of a van. The front limbs led into red human-like arms and hands.

It jumped from lily pad to lily pad, causing tall waves as it landed. Its long tongue lashed out, sticking to everything, yanking rocks and trees out of its way with ease. Jack fell onto his shoulder hard, dodging the swinging tongue. He was surprised to find the pain he expected didn't come. He ripped the bandages off to discover his arm had miraculously healed. Unfortunately, the red frog's tongue struck him.

It hit his back with the force of Fusion's mallet. Rocho tried his best to bite it, but that didn't seem to affect it. The frog lurched back like a crank, yanking Jack into the water. Fighting through the mud, Jack raised his broken totem. With the mechanical spear portion still working, he drove it into the creature's tongue.

It wiggled free just as Jack pried his totem out to stab again. The red skin brightened, hinting at its anger. The bubble on the frog's neck expanded like a balloon. A gurgling noise expelled from its gaping mouth. Once again, the waters bubbled, and the thing that emerged was just as revolting as the red frog.

It was the darkest indigo, nearly black, with the slimiest skin Jack had ever seen. Dripping tentacles covered in dull-red spots and thousands of hair-like thorns erupted from the swamp. Eight in total, the limbs lingered in the air surrounding Jack and Rocho, pushing aside trees and rocks as if they were toy blocks. The tentacles were all attached to a head shaped like a light bulb. Dozens of insect-like eyes stared back at Jack. Black goo flew from its mouth, hitting Rocho, and the creature's tentacles struck.

Near the water's edge, the pup was dazed but awake, though he was apparently unable to move. The black goo was like mud but hardened over him.

"Spib ink?" Using the broken spear, Jack chipped away at the muddy substance. The frog jumped closer from pad to pad. Jack nearly had all the black goo off Rocho when two more blobs of ink hit him. He hid from the tentacles behind trees, occasionally diving back into the water, but they were everywhere.

Dropping into the water, it hardened over his leg, and the weight caught him off guard. A tentacle hit him in the chest like a whip, flipping him around.

The frog croaked loudly and dove back into the water. It sailed toward Jack like a submarine gaining speed. Those odd red leathery hands reached out to him. Jack struggled to free himself, with Nucalibur just out of reach.

Rocho growled, sparking brightly and biting at both the hardened goo and red roots to free himself. Jack could see him trying to grow, but the mud tightened with his every movement. Jack fought to free himself, but nothing budged. His body bobbed up and down, sinking slowly into the water. The tentacles wrapped around him, squeezing his remaining air. Before he sank beneath the water's surface, the last thing Jack heard was Rocho's sorrowful howl.

Jack opened his eyes under the water tinted in red and green just in time to see the monster frog coming at him. A flash of flaming gold ripped over the surface then dove into the water. Pain shot all over his body, much worse than the red wave of electricity in the arena had been. His body felt hot beneath the water with a surge of volts that wouldn't stop. Next, he felt the cold air as he was pulled out of the water. He could hear Rocho barking in the distance, his fur practically on fire. Lying on the wet terrain, gasping, the weight of the gold medallion on his chest, Jack was startled by a soft voice above.

"Looks like you barely made it, Jackson," came the brittle voice of an old woman. A moment later, Jack's eyes closed, and sleep consumed him.

When Jack awoke, he was surprised to find himself lying on a bed in a poorly lit room with candles, instead of under water or on the damp soil. Sizable holes stretched along the roof in pairs a short distance from each other above him. Rope was woven loosely in and out of the holes, and a nearby window allowed him to look outside. Rusted metal plates and gears were scattered about the yard, and just beyond that was the vast body of water Jack had escaped from. He could see the bubble grow and pop from the brown water, but he still didn't know how he'd gotten to wherever he was.

Jack panicked, remembering Rocho stuck in that black goo, battling the giant red frog. Taking in the room, he didn't see his flashlight or the pup anywhere, only a few books on dusty shelves, his medallion, the moonleaf stone, and the letters he brought from the kingdom. Looking over them, he was relieved to find they were still in decent shape after the dive into the water, including the burned one he found in the archive room. Spotting his leather jacket, the young detective grabbed it and crept out of the room quietly.

"Where am I?" he whispered to himself.

The door led into a hallway with a few dozen framed photos of kids Jack had never seen before. He was engulfed by the smell of worn leather that seemed to be everywhere. More candles lit his way as he crossed another empty room. The ominous glow was a strange reminder of how he'd met Luminista at the Holiday Hotel. He expected her to beckon him forward at any moment.

"You're late," a woman's voice called out.

Jack realized she was talking to him. "Late? Late for what?"

"Everything…" the woman said again. "You're late to arrive, late for what's coming. Lately, you've been late in life. Put your life on pause a long time ago, didn't you? You need to move forward already. Time keeps ticking, no matter where you stand."

He stood away from the door, wrestling with the idea of who the woman was. The sound of objects scraping wood as they were pushed around a table made Jack cringe.

She gave the table an impatient tap. "Well, come in here already. I am too old, and we ain't got all day since that froad and spib nearly drowned you."

Jack continued gingerly, peeking around the corner to see who was inside. He blinked several times, not expecting to see the old woman from the arena sitting at a table, displaying his flashlight, broken totem, the enhanced cog, and a long box. Surprisingly, the young boy from the arena with the emerald necklace stood at her side, playing with a puzzle box, while two chairs remained empty. He grinned at Jack's shocked look.

"Who are you two?" Jack asked. "Why am I here? How am I here?"

"Have a seat, and we'll get to your questions," the tiny old woman offered. "Did you bring the letter from Shadow?"

Jack hesitantly presented the letter and took a seat, eyeing his flashlight and totem. He took in the room, searching for a way to get out just in case. The walls stretched up much higher, and a ring of candles hung above. A door to the woman's left held a full-length mirror but didn't seem to be attached to anything. It merely leaned against the wall, reflecting the rest of the room. The kid remained silent, playing with the box.

"This is Paper." She gestured to the boy. "He is my last remaining son. He protects me from those who I'd prefer not to be found by."

"Paper?" Jack asked. "Kind of young for protection duty, isn't he?"

"The boy's eleven now, but he has some talent, just as you do. Don't let his size fool you. I've had several children. Pencil was my oldest, then there was Pen, Glue, and Scissor. Quill was my first girl, then the twins Chalk and Marker. Staple, Eraser, and quite a few others, but Paper is the last."

Paper sat the puzzle box down, completely solved. Jack studied the emerald amulet dangling from the boy's neck. Then Paper took out a yo-yo from his pocket.

"There was a really big guy that saved you from the hanging cages in the arena with that same emerald necklace." Jack focused on the frail woman. "That was this kid all along, wasn't it? Some science or magic he has? But who are you?"

"For your purpose, I am someone to help you for a mutual friend. I'm a messenger, mostly. I can accept and send things across different realities and planes, like my son's amulet that grants him strength and size. Here, I'm known as a conjurer of the swamp. Those who make it this far have called me Mist. Not sure if it's for the misty swamp or the mysterious way I work, but no matter. Use it if you'd like."

Jack looked between the two of them, wondering if he'd fallen for another trap. "What kind of magic can you do, then?" Jack asked, prepared to make his totem and flashlight vanish, then run.

"Are you really questioning me after seeing what my son can do?" Mist asked with a soft smirk. She balled her wrinkled hand into a fist and tossed a pink powder at Jack. Before he could react, he felt his body tense. His nose suddenly smelled the leather stronger than ever, and he had the urge to roll in the mud outside. His hands morphed into hooves, and his skin became a pale pink. He attempted to speak, and a loud squeal projected out, followed by short snorting oinks.

In the mirror attached to the leaning door, he could see he'd turned into a small pig. Paper looked at him with hungry eyes.

With a wave of Mist's hand, Jack's curly mop of hair reappeared, dangling in his face, along with his regular hands and tan skin. Paper returned to his hardened look of disappointment.

Jack, fully clothed, gasped with his hands on the table. "Why does everything smell like bacon now?" he asked woozily.

"Would you prefer the smell of hamburgers next?"

Jack shook his head.

"Good, then let's continue."

She had the same smug superiority Mr. Shadow held, wrapped in a small woman's body. Jack decided it was probably better to be on her good side. So he listened to her intently, desperate to find out where her story would lead.

"Your advisor sent me something to help you while you are in the challenge," she told him. "Do you have the letter he sent you?"

Jack rummaged before producing the letters, and she took them both hastily. "What is this one?"

"I found it in the kingdom's archive room, but most of it is covered in smoke damage. Not sure why I kept it. Just seemed like someone didn't want it to read, so it might be important."

"Have you tried your flashlight?" she asked, brushing it with a finger before pausing. "The things it can shine light onto extend past normal darkness, you know. Ancient magic has brought the flashlight to life. It is a very special totem, Jackson. Wonderfully more powerful than you realize."

Jack watched as she admired his flashlight. He hoped Rocho was all right and wondered how she'd been able to get him back into flashlight form. She pressed Mr. Shadow's letter against a box lying on the table. Made of old black wood and as wide as the table itself, the box was rectangular and had a locked metal clasp. A shadowy wisp escaped the box as it unlocked itself.

Inside lay the remaining pumpkin handle and blade tip of Trick's sword, still blunted and chipped from Trick's last attempt to escape the hotel.

"What am I supposed to do with this?" Jack asked. "It's not even half a weapon."

"Boy, hush up and listen." Mist held out her hand. "The magic in it is locked, but before I can release it for you, I need payment and something to power it. Everything has a cost, and this one is gonna need one of your totems and the cog."

Jack looked down at the flashlight and shook his head. "No way. It took too much to get Rocho back. And I need Nucalibur and the enchanted cog to get back to Cloud City. Besides, Nucalibur is broken."

She held up the enhanced cog between her bony fingers. "This is not the enchanted cog. That thing around your neck is."

Jack lifted the gold sun-cog dangling over his shirt. "This? This is what I needed?"

She examined the broken pieces of Nucalibur. "Of course the King would never admit the mold was found in the swamps when the kingdom was first built. But trust me, that's the cog. The machines that create the so-called advanced machines are powered by that thing. I should know, I transported the mold here. And it appears a small amount of magic still remains in your fishing rod. With it, you may be able to return to the capital."

Delaying an instant, he chose to sacrifice the broken parts of the fishing rod. She placed the parts of the handle next to the rod. Paper handed her the red enhanced cog, which she pressed between the two weapons with her palm.

"Power from the cog should be more than enough," she said. "Same power from the vines. Magic is powerful here in the swamp because of the roots leading from the source. That is what makes the swamp so dangerous, and that is what allows me to conjure and manipulate items here. I was curious to see what changes the pup will go through. His lightning radiates fire like I've never seen since he chewed the root. "

"Is that why you stay here in the swamp?" he asked, fixated on the glimmering pieces.

"It is one reason." She brushed the remaining dust from her hands. "There we are."

Both the sword and the fishing rod totem lay on the table, fixed and whole. They gleamed with a fresh new vitality. One notch on Nucalibur remained illuminated. The heart lit in pink but quickly faded, while transferring a pink aurora to the sword. Then it was completely lifeless. The sword radiated with shadowy black wisps, and a heart-shaped peg formed in the pumpkin handle.

The handle remained the same, but the blade had been curved and wide like a pirate's saber when Trick owned it. This new creation was thinner like a katana but a few inches shorter. It was just the right length for Jack to wield it with ease.

"I will keep what remains of your broken fishing rod."

Jack found it curious that she would want to keep it now that it was ordinary and powerless. "Why do you want it?"

"The line is strong and the rod sturdy." She waved him away. "I believe there will be a party who will find this particular fishing rod useful. Now you may take your weapon and go."

Jack stood, reaching out to take his flashlight and the sword, but paused. "Wait, there's something else I need."

A frustrated scowl struck her face. "Oh, is there? And what would that be, junior?"

"Can you tell me where I can find the Medicine Man?"

Mist and Paper looked at each other.

"What do you know about the Medicine Man?" Her voice became stern.

Jack removed the contract from his sneaker. "You do know him? I need him to create a cure for the illness from the king's smoke. If I can get it from him, I can stop the war between the kingdom and the village. He's the last piece I need, and I was told he was last seen here. Please, tell me where I can find him."

She pressed her fingers together, staring at Jack until her eyes rested on his hand. "The smog is not a simple thing to cure. It will cost quite a bit to make it."

"What would I have to pay?" Jack asked, placing his flashlight securely in his pocket.

"Hmmm… your watch looks pretty old, too." She pointed. "Magic is nearly as old as the one used to change your flashlight."

Jack sighed. "It was a gift from Phoenix, but I can't give it up. I can't even take it off."

"Who said anything about taking it off?" She smiled.

Jack began stepping back. "Lady, you're not cutting my hand off! I need both my hands. They came as a set!"

"No, you simple boy. I can separate the magic from your watch without removing it. The ancient sand inside is magic, not the watch. I can bottle the sand pretty easily, but it's nearly used up. I'm sure I can make use of what's left if you'd like to trade?"

Jack grabbed his wrist, rubbing his hand against the band. "I guess I can't use it much anymore anyway. Ages me too fast now when I slow down time."

She inclined her head. "You haven't discovered its other use? Slowing time will hurt ya more and more, but have you not thought about peeking into the future?"

Jack had never thought about what else the watch could do. The first time he'd used it was an accident, and every attempt since just caused more pain. He almost didn't want to know what turning time forward would do to him.

"Lucky for you, I am fair with my transactions." She withdrew her hand from Jack's wrist as nearly a spoonful of white sand dripped into a vial she had prepared. "I'll let you keep enough for one more use. All right, follow me. The Medicine Man is resting at the moment, but we don't get many new faces. Might not mind being woken up."

She stood, gesturing for Jack to follow her to the mirrored door. Paper moved the mirrored door to the other side of the room, placing it firmly against the wall, where it stuck. He then moved away. Mist stepped in front of the mirror and stared at her reflection until there was a small click from the door's handle. It swung open. Paper stayed in his spot, playing with his yo-yo again, as Mist led Jack down a spiraling staircase. He followed the frail woman into a new area of murky stone walls and dripping ceilings poorly lit by torches.

The dank room had tall ceilings. Several parts of broken, rusted, or melted machined parts lay about the floor. More vials were in this room than the rest of the house. The room itself was much bigger than the rest of the home. Tools sat on different tables, along with medical instruments and surgical pieces.

Mist continued to a pantry on the side. Shelves nearly reaching the ceiling lined the walls, which seemed to go on for an impressive stretch before turning a corner and stretching farther. Thousands of jars and vials containing plants, dusts, and unmoving creatures rested on the shelves like library books. After pushing a rolling ladder down a few sections, the conjurer climbed and placed the vial of sand on display.

As Mist climbed down, Jack's curiosity got the better of him. "What is all of this for?"

"Transactions…" She pointed to a metal chair that resembled a mechanical throne intertwined with wires. "Fortune-tellers can send their minds to different planes, interact with people for a short time, and see trending paths with special tools. Oracles are stronger; they can see interlinking paths far beyond fortune-tellers and live in other planes for long periods. I, however, trade what people give me for what people need from one plane to another and am the only one capable of transferring items not made for one world or the other. That's my job as a conjurer, to deposit and withdraw items. How do you think your flashlight got to your father?"

His mouth fell open, then he held the flashlight out to the elderly woman. "Wait, you sent this to my dad? Why? Who told you to?"

"I've just told you why," Mist advised. "I make withdrawals and deposits from world to world. As far as who, well, that would be my business, wouldn't it? I'm sure you'll hear from them one day if they want you to. I suppose you could call me a banker of sorts, really. Yes, I quite like that. Mist, the Great, the Conjurer, the Banker."

Jack heard gears spinning, steam expelling, and water bubbling. "No one told me about a banker."

"Why would they?" a new voice bellowed, deep and rough like grinding metal, projecting from the chair. "Very few people even know I still exist. And nearly no one knows she does."

It rose from the chair, yanking the wires off, sending red sparks flying and casting a monstrous shadow. Tubes fell from its joints, dripping onto the floor. Metal plates made up its arms and legs, and a red energy coursed throughout the body, putting off a bright glow. However, its head surprised Jack the most. From a forged-metal face with bolts and gears, wires connected an enclosed glass casing protecting a human brain.

"Remember, Jack, light will always shine brighter in the darkest places." Mist pointed. "This is the Medicine Man."

Jack remained frozen in place, unsure if he was fascinated or merely terrified. "You're a machine…"

"No." He stepped into the light. "My mind is just as organic as it always has been. Only my body has changed. It has evolved as I have evolved. In my exploration through science and magic, I finally discovered a way to live forever. I am just as human as long as my mind is intact. I have simply discovered immortality."

Jack looked over at Mist then back at the Medicine Man. "Well, that's new."

"The enchanted cog." The Medicine Man stepped closer to Jack. "Has it been that long since I've witnessed those horrible Gem Arena games? I have not seen that golden symbol in many years."

"Took a lot to get it," Jack admitted. "I was lucky a few times to get as far as I did. Lucky I made it through the swamp, too."

"This place is much older than you know," Mist said. "The red vines you've seen in the water travel from the mountain source to here—and create the impossible. I found the bandages when I discovered your body in the water. That is what healed your shoulder, and that is what keeps the Medicine Man immortal. It also happens to be one of the ingredients that will cure smog sickness."

"Is that what the boy is here for?" The Medicine Man waved off the issue as something simple and went over to a lab table. "I assume Mist has already received her fee, or else you would not be here, but first, I must tell you something. When King Aurum came to me about this illness, it had only started to spread to the kingdom. All of the work using these red roots and veins to extend life is what caused the air to change. The smog clouded the skies. The people it afflicted first, however, were those of the Middletown."

He mixed a few substances together, including a tiny red particle from his chest cavity. "Many of them were far past the curing stage, but once we developed a proper medical aid, they were the first ones we applied it to. Some of my associates believed it was pointless and that we should let time take them, but I proceeded. I refused to accept failure. The side effects changed them drastically, some even into horrific monsters, but thanks to me, they lived. It's unfortunate that the smallest sun fell soon after."

He heated the substance and bottled it promptly. "The reason I've told you this is to let you know you cannot always choose the right answer, but making no choice is still a choice."

He handed Jack the bottle. "You may not understand now, but I can feel it in these wires: sometime in your journey to deliver this bottle, you will be stuck with a difficult decision. All I can say is think about if everything is better with it or without it. I will live more lives now than ever before, but I am now more machine than man. What is life worth if it's not lived?"

With that, he returned to his chair and rested. Mist guided Jack back upstairs, where Paper continued playing with his yo-yo. Jack placed the archive letter in his pocket, along with the flashlight and vial. The sword slid behind Jack's belt smoothly. To be cautious, he set the agreement back into his shoe before reaching the front door.

"Paper will guide you out of the swamp, but a final warning, Mr. Taylor: not everything is as it seems. Perhaps both science and magic can exist together. Maybe the ground lives, and maybe it does not. The better question is, if there is no compromise and no deal to be made, can you live with that final decision, and do you have a choice?"

With that, she shut the door softly. Jack stood in front of the house, looking out at the swamp, surprised at how close he was to getting back home. Paper rolled a heavy metal ball a third his size attached to a long chain over to a pile of shrubs and leaves. He moved the shrubs out of the way, uncovering a three-wheeled vehicle like the general's, with beefy tires.

"Why don't you change into the big guy?" Jack asked, following the straining boy's movement. "You can barely push that ball over in this size."

"My amulet only lasts awhile before it has to be recharged." Paper shoved the ball onto the vehicle's lift and clasped it to his arm. "This ball and chain is my burden. It powers the amulet when I'm chained to it, but I'm still plenty dangerous without it. You ever had a paper cut? Mamma's only got me left to take care of her. Not that she really needs my help often, but when the arena games begin, we get things we can't anywhere else."

Jack glanced at his watch, which ticked away normally. His pocket warmed, and he knew Rocho was itching to get out. As he removed the flashlight, letting the pup stretch his legs, Jack turned to get a last look at the home and was taken aback by the shape. The house he'd been in was in the shape of a giant shoe. The holes and rope he'd noticed earlier were actually laces, and the top was sealed by a regular roof.

Before he was capable of fully understanding why a large boot would be turned into a house, Rocho began barking. The water of the swamp bounced like raindrops on a drum. The ground shook softly at first but quickly escalated into a shudder.

Before long, trees began to sway then fell, as the earth itself started to separate. Rocho rapidly became bear-sized, beckoning Jack to climb on. Paper pushed the ball and chain onto his roadster before turning to Jack.

"Something's wrong," he yelled. "We better get moving." A moment later, he was off, and Rocho followed as Jack clung tightly.

Even in his bear size, Rocho was swift following Paper. The terrain continued to shudder as he evaded the splitting swamp and tipping trees. The roadster handled well, gripping the swampland with its tread. Waters swelled as they rode by a split in the path that held an actual three-pronged large fork in the center. The veil of brown fog that turned people into trees was nowhere to be seen. Millions of leaves, however, had been shaken loose. Massive piles blanketed the ground, and the trees were nearly bare.

They were nearly out of the twisted swamp when Jack spotted the open sunny field. Without warning, the jolting ground calmed. They stood just outside the line of mossy trees on a new jagged edge protruding from the soil overlooking the empty green field. It appeared safe, but the damage had been done. Cracks were spread out among the land, and it was strangely quiet. The animals that normally grazed near the kingdom's farms had run away, and the people were gone from the mines in the distance. It left Jack unsure if everyone was hiding or if they'd fallen into the massive gaps.

He looked toward Middletown a few dozen miles away and then at the kingdom. "I can't tell if that was Old Man Winter or just an earthquake." He squinted, still atop Rocho's back, searching for anyone yelling for help out of broken houses and the crumbling rock of the kingdom's stone walls. His chest felt warmer as he browsed the field. Looking down, he realized the enchanted cog was heating with a soft red glow.

He spotted Paper, who'd circled the area, coming to a stop and looking into the darkening sky, pointing. "Looks like more bad news."

Jack's mouth fell open. "Oh no…" he muttered, looking up from his medallion and grasping why the sky had gotten dark so quickly. "It's a solar eclipse. The villagers… the war is starting now."

Chapter 10
A Giant Problem

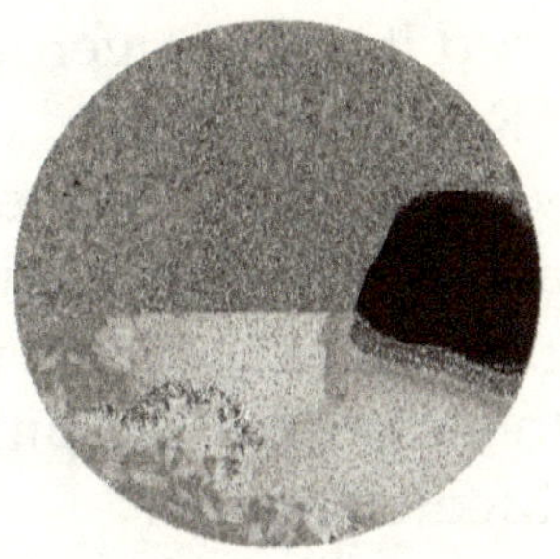

"Gather the soldiers!" the general called. "Get them to these walls now! We need protection around every crack. I want them all battle ready now."

Jack rode in on Rocho just moments after those in the kingdom's city had recovered. Most of the stone walls were broken or completely obliterated. Layers of the crumbling wall continued crashing to the ground. The king's soldiers arrived to protect the walls armed with spears, swords, and shields. Through the wall's gaps, Jack watched dozens of mechanized suits of armor being lifted from the labs and brought to the borders. He instantly knew what that meant.

"Where's the king?" he asked one of the wall guards. They stood their ground, not moving to let Jack through or answer any of his questions. "Let me speak to Prince Orblanc, or at least tell me what's going on. We have an agreement."

"Look who has returned so soon." The general stepped up to the walls, and the soldiers stepped aside. "One of the few contenders to win the arena gallops off into the swamps for more thrills? How far did you make it before you turned around? You were warned it was dangerous."

Jack climbed off Rocho and pulled the agreement from his shoe. "I need to have this signed by the king."

The general scratched his chin, reading it over. "Is that so? Aren't you missing some crucial parts to that agreement?"

Jack reached into his pocket and pulled out the Medicine Man's vial. "From the Medicine Man."

The soldiers looked at the vial, and many of them exchanged looks. Prince Orblanc had just arrived at the gate.

The general gave the slightest hint of shock himself before recovering. "You either have a lot of luck or a lot of heart. I don't know if you've realized it, but we've had an attack recently. It is now priority number one for a call to action."

"But I have the vial and the agreement," Jack said. "I can get the agreement signed by Chief Mizzi and have him decode the map!"

"Your actions are admirable, but it's no longer needed." The general placed his helmet on and backed away into one of his machine armors. "You couldn't deliver it before this war started, and now we have orders from the king to advance to the mountain, find the source, and pull it out ourselves. We'll destroy that mountain if we have to and destroy anyone who tries to stop us. With the sun blocked by the moon and the walls down, the natives can attack us at any time. We only have half our gargoyles functional. Believe it or not, I like you, kid. You have the making of a good soldier, if you could follow orders. Best you leave before we have to treat you as an enemy."

The machine armor lifted its massive blasters and took aim at Jack before the general stomped off. The other soldiers raised their swords and shields, blocking Jack from interfering. The prince continued into the city.

Rocho's fur sizzled with static, but Jack patted his head. "It's okay, Rocho. We got somewhere else to be." Climbing atop the bear-sized pup, Jack turned quickly. As Jack rode off toward the village, Paper scowled at the soldiers and followed.

Riding on Rocho made traveling much more manageable. He was surprised to see Paper still riding beside him. "I'm coming with you until we figure out what this eclipse is all about."

"I don't think it'll be anything good," Jack yelled back. "The village's shaman warned me about the sun and that a war would happen. I'm just afraid it's too late for me to stop it."

The distance that had taken days to walk took only hours while riding the pup. Before long, they'd come upon Middletown, which had been destroyed by the earthquake. The wooden shacks and houses were in shambles, and the wreckage was all that remained. Rocho raced through it and toward the lake, where the bridge had sunk into the water. Only a few broken pieces floated atop, so Jack and Paper were forced to take the long way around.

By the time they reached the sandpit, the transparent drilling birds had gone. The pit appeared whole, but Jack could still see parts of the metal pumas scattered about from his first day falling in the sand. He yawned simply thinking of that day and the overwhelming feeling of wanting to go to sleep. The dreamer stopped Rocho just outside the brim of the pit before heading into the forest. Removing the sword from his belt, he dipped the blade into the sand.

Paper pulled up behind him. "What are you doing?"

"Insurance," Jack said, looking into the sandpit's center. The sword swirled with the shadowy black mist and shimmered with a red portion of sand. "No telling what's waiting on the mountain. For now, you should stay here. I don't know if you'll be able to come into the forest with me, and I need someone watching for the king's soldiers. If I'm not back in an hour, ride around the forest."

Paper grew excited. "Think you'll need me in a fight?"

"Or a getaway driver. Either or."

After a quick dash around the sandpit and past the cliffs, Jack arrived at the border of the Usiku Forest. Looking into the dark woods, he heard those same growls he was sure Prince Orblanc had heard when he was near. Climbing off Rocho, who was panting, Jack kneeled, and as if reading his thoughts, the pup instantly shrank to the flashlight size and rolled into his palm. Switching the light on pierced the dense blackness of the forest, allowing him a decent amount of visibility inside. He removed the moonleaf stone from his pocket. Glancing at the sun peeking around the edges of the moon blocking it, he took a breath and stepped in.

His moonleaf stone ignited with a pale-bluish light. The forest seemed to accept him. Either the wind or some sort of magic bent a few leaves and branches out of his way as he went farther in. Before long, he was setting a swift pace through the woods. As he had in the mines of the arena, he felt a pull from the stone guiding him in the right directions. The light between the branches cast shadows on the ground that looked like arrows pointing. It took no time at all before he understood how the chief's daughter was able to find her way so comfortably through the Usiku forest. Before long, he was sprinting through the woods, maneuvering like Celeste.

It didn't seem to take nearly as long before the warriors positioned in the trees had arrows pointing at him, and Jack babbled. "I need to speak to Chief Mizzi. He knows I'm coming."

Some warriors glared at Jack's chest. He realized the gold enchanted cog around his neck was still radiating. He held up the unsigned agreement, sure that the warriors would not understand it. "Umm… a villager I met in the kingdom told me to tell you the shaman's whispers are true? If that means anything."

A few of the warriors nodded and pointed their arrows forward. Jack went ahead, running into an unexpected matter. It appeared the entire village had gathered for a celebration and feast that Jack had forgotten all about. He moved around the natives before locating Chief Mizzi at the head of the table.

"Ah, the Sky Boy has returned to honor the moon over the sun!" the chief announced, sloshing a drink. "Were you successful in rescuing your friend?"

"Yes." Jack held out his flashlight, which Chief Mizzi looked upon strangely, but Jack chose not to explain Rocho's transformation. "But I have to tell you what I found out before it's too late."

The chief laughed joyfully. "What could be wrong on this day? Did you make it to the king?"

"Yes, but—"

"And were you able to convince him of my terms of peace?" the chief interrupted.

"Yeah, but I—"

"And were you able to gather the antidote for my daughter?"

"I have it here, but—"

"Well, this is great news to celebrate," Chief Mizzi proclaimed. "I will decode the map. My daughter will be healed. You will eat with us and fill your belly, as you have helped us bring peace in this great land and—"

"War is coming right now!" Jack finally broke in. Most of the villagers within earshot stopped eating, including the chief.

"What nonsense is this?" The chief waved him off.

"The earthquake destroyed their wall and…" Jack paused, noticing how perfect the structure of the village was. "I guess it didn't hit here, but the general is heading up to the mountains right now and preparing to fight anyone who gets in their way. They're ignoring the unfinished agreement. They found a way to decode the map themselves. You have to tell them you had nothing to do with it."

Chief Mizzi looked around at his people staring back at him. "The time has come. War has been forced on us with the coming attack of the earth. We must protect it. We must protect ourselves. Gather the warriors and the shaman. He will bless our armor. We must arm ourselves against the sun walkers and the suns themselves."

"Wait! It doesn't have to be this way!" Jack argued. "There has to be another way before this goes further."

"This is the only way." Chief Mizzi stood from the table. "If they storm past our borders, they will not turn back unless they get their power. My people expect their leader to protect them and fight for the land we've been blessed with. Only one group will survive this. It has been predicted. The king is no closer to allowing peace, and we can no longer wait. We have no time left. War is here. You should go, Sky Boy, before it comes for you."

With that, the chief began preparing the warriors and had the shaman provide magic Jack hadn't seen before to change their weapons. They each had throwing axes that multiplied after being thrown. Their warriors seemed to increase as the shaman coated their armor with a magic substance. He appeared confident, blessing each warrior, and nearly too happy for the war to begin, Jack thought.

Jack skimmed the village for Celeste but didn't see her. He felt helpless watching the villagers, and his eyes drifted to his sword. The young detective couldn't help but feel its weight in his belt drag him down, useless to stop the fight from happening and unable to help Celeste or Prince Orblanc. Just as he'd decided to head back through the woods, Jack felt a tap on his shoulder.

"Is it true?" Celeste approached him. "Is the war happening?"

Jack nodded.

"And the prince?" she asked.

"On his way to the mountain, I guess." Jack shrugged.

She checked to see if anyone was watching. "We must go to the prince now."

"We do?" Jack was yanked to the side by his wrist.

She hid behind one of the huts near a cleared narrow path. "I cannot let him get hurt. I must find him. Will you help me?"

She looked into Jack's eyes, and he felt fear from her from the first time, although he could tell it was for the prince. He took a deep breath. "This is the kind of thing I'd usually avoid, but he's probably headed to the mountain with the general and the king. I'll go there with you. I have a friend who might come with us."

She kissed Jack on the cheek before ushering him through the side clearing. "This way will be much faster."

Jack clutched his flashlight tightly in his pocket, making sure it didn't fall out. "Well, if I die here and come back as a spirit, just know I'm haunting you first."

They dashed out of the forest and headed toward the mountains in the northeast. He'd never seen this part of the woods before. They could see the top of the Great Tree protruding out of the forest as they exited, finally within view of dimmed daylight. The woods opened up to a mile of new green field with sparse trees and wild deerbras romping about. The grass led to gravelly ground sloping up into a gray mountain with white peaks.

Jack's mind was set on what he would find on the mountain. The natives and king's soldiers would be confronting each other soon. He couldn't understand how close he'd come to getting home just hours ago, and now it might be for nothing. He was fumbling with the flashlight in his pocket when he found something else crumpled near it. The roar of an engine took his attention.

Prince Orblanc arrived on one of the three-wheeled roadsters. Steam billowed from the vehicle as he came to a stop. He promptly hopped off and embraced Celeste.

"What are you doing here?" she asked him.

"Coming to get you out," the prince answered. "I can't have you anywhere near this war. I just found you. I am not losing you now."

Jack felt awkward being around the intimate moment. Luckily, Prince Orblanc acknowledged him. "Nice sword. Did our scientists make that? Wait… I thought you'd be headed home now. What are you doing here?"

"No, actually it's a crazy story." Jack brandished the sword, and a trail of shadowy black wisps wavered in the air. "Traveled to the swamps, fought a giant red frog with hands, and this huge spib, think I got turned into a pig 'cause I keep smelling bacon—"

"We came to find you," Celeste interjected. "We have to get to the mountain before our people meet."

The prince shook his head. "That won't work. You've heard the stories of what's up there. Beasts made of rock, giants larger than life. I'm not even convinced our army will survive, and they are armored with mecha suits."

"If we don't try, our fathers will die killing each other, and so will our people."

Celeste and Prince Orblanc continued talking as Jack admired the vehicle and the deerbras. He didn't like the idea of trying to tame or ride one of the strange horses. So instead, the dreamer reached into his pocket for Rocho. Along with it, he withdrew the smoky crumpled letter, and he remembered what Mist had told him.

He shined the light's beam through the smudged paper until he could finally read the written words.

To my king and golden prince,

This is the hardest thing I will ever have to do in my life. The fighting between us has become so horrible, I no longer see the man I married. You continue to search for a cure for my illness, but the Medicine Man has gotten no closer. Ever since you found me hiding beneath the floorboards of Middletown, I have loved you, cared for you, and bore you a child. He is the reason I've stayed. He is the reason I will find a cure where you won't look and return.

Jack read the letter, barely hearing what Prince Orblanc
and Celeste were discussing. "Wait—white hair?"

The roar of an engine came around the forest's side to
where they stood. The prince drew his pistols, but it was a
single roadster Jack recognized.

"Soldiers on the other side," Paper said, coming to a stop.
"A lot of them in mecha suits."

The striped white-and-purple tiger Celeste kept as a pet
came sprinting to her. "Drums…" She pointed back at the forest.
"Warriors are coming. We have to go to the mountain before my
village finds you. We must get to the source before the others
do."

The prince climbed onto his vehicle while Celeste stroked
the back of the striped tiger. It dissolved into a light-purple mist,
and the chief's daughter absorbed the cub's essence. Her
features changed into that of a grown tiger. Rocho leaped from

Jack's hand and grew to his large size. Jack climbed on just as the villagers left the forest. Their shoulders, chests, and necks were all wrapped in moonleaves taken from the Great Tree. Even though Jack couldn't explain it, he could feel magic radiating from each one of the warriors as he followed Celeste and the others to the mountain.

They had a good start ahead of the warriors, who'd continued to spread out and walk to the mountain instead of riding the wild deerbras. They seemed to shuffle out endlessly, and Jack assumed there were too many warriors and not enough deerbras. Wave after wave of natives left the woods, with no end in sight. A few thousand or more warriors had left before Jack gave up watching.

Celeste was faster than them all in her primal form as each of the boys struggled to keep up on their vehicles and Jack on Rocho. The base of the mountain was ominous, overgrown with black roses. Paper dismounted his roadster and rubbed his amulet before yanking on the chain attached to the heavy metal ball. The boy suddenly lifted it out, changing into the large man who'd rescued Mist from the spiked pit. He shouldered the weighted ball by the chain and continued on as if nothing strange had happened.

Jack walked beside Celeste, while Paper brought up the rear. Prince Orblanc led, his tri-barreled pistols drawn. Celeste re-formed into herself, with her pet beside her. She walked fearlessly and was ready with her daggers. The terrain was rough and rocky, but nothing seemed out of the ordinary.

"Do either of you know where we're going?" Jack asked as Rocho darted beside him.

"I know where my father is leading the soldiers," Prince Orblanc said. "From what they deciphered of the map, it shouldn't be too hard to navigate."

Jack glanced at Celeste. "But don't you know where it is?"

"My father knows the code to decipher the map. He was taught by his father, who was taught by the mystics so no one else would go near it. He has not yet given the information to me. All that I know are stories of what is inside."

Jack jumped over a significant dip in the ground. "So we could be going in the wrong direction completely and end up back in the valley or the swamp? Great…"

As they climbed, the sun traveled farther away from the eclipsing moon. A breeze picked up across the mountain, and Jack shivered. Trails split off into different directions, but the prince didn't hesitate. Rocks tumbled down from above, forcing them to dive out of the way.

"Do you think they're up there already?" Jack called up.

"Unlikely. I left well before the general and went around the forest to find you two. The army will be close but not—"

A loud screech tore through the air. Jack could see only more rocks falling along the trail in the distance, but the sound definitely seemed like a warning. The closer they climbed, the more the rocks reminded Jack of the trees in the swamps—as if someone had formed a few out of people or animals.

"Anyone wanna tell me what that sound was?" he asked.

"Must be the wind whistling through the mountain," the prince answered.

Jack paused. "This place might be different than I'm used to, but since when did a mountain get lips to whistle?"

The prince continued on cautiously. Rocho followed, sniffing the air. Then his barking stopped the group. The mountain shuddered suddenly as if the earth were beginning to quake again. It rose and fell very slowly beneath their feet, as if it were deciding whether or not to erupt.

"Do you feel that?" Jack asked as Rocho backed away, barking more urgently.

Celeste placed her hand on the surface of the mountain. "The earth, I can feel it… breathing."

A loud screech wailed through the air. Shadows flashed by overhead. Jack heard rocks and the flutter of wings. More pebbles fell to the ground, and something ferocious swooped in from the sky. Jack couldn't believe what he was seeing. The creatures were just like the ones guarding the outside of his father's hotel: six pairs of long talons, small shields, and reptilian bodies with beaks all made of stone.

"Gargoyles?" Jack pointed.

Celeste placed a hand on her tiger's head, and purple striped fur sprouted over her body, whiskers grew on her catlike face, and her arms and legs enlarged with muscle. She began throwing daggers as the gargoyles swooped in. The prince aimed his tri-barrel pistols, but Paper stepped between them, dropping his metal ball from his impressively large fists. "Let's see if I can hit these two birds with one stone."

The three of them were impressive. Celeste was agile like the tiger she'd fused with, leaping through the air as she jumped and pivoted from different rocks. Prince Orblanc was able to shoot the wings off the stone creatures, causing them to crash into the mountainside. Paper knocked one gargoyle into another with a single massive swing of his ball and chain. However, the gargoyles were learning quickly — and something worse was coming.

Two came after Jack, and he hesitated. They circled him, clawing madly, then lifted him by his jacket, leaving him kicking through the air. They were ferocious and stubborn. Rocho tried jumping after them, but they were already too high.

Jack couldn't reach his sword, so he continued to flail as he was taken higher up the mountain.

Jack spotted villagers swarming the mountain's base. Other tall figures were coming down from higher up the mountain. Two shots echoed off the mountainside, and one of the gargoyles dropped his shoulder. Jack grabbed his sword. With a blind stab up, he pierced the other gargoyle's chest, and it instantly released him.

He fell like a skydiver without a parachute. The rocky ground was coming in fast. He gripped the sword tightly, watching Celeste and Paper fight off the remaining swarm while Rocho circled beneath him.

"Get out of the way!" he yelled down to the pup. He felt the sword get cooler in his hand. Black swirls engulfed his arm and began to glow. Just before he hit the mountain, he felt his body hover for a moment. A dark figure appeared and took the shoulders of his shadow just before impact. Its shape was the same as Mr. Shadow's, and he guessed the dark figure was the shadow always following the Halloween spirit. Just after setting him down, it vanished. Unfortunately, two more gargoyles remained, and the tall figures descending the mountain were getting closer.

"Guys, rock giants!" Jack yelled.

Celeste had just stabbed one of the flying gargoyles in its back using a pair of curved daggers, basically surfing atop it before it came crashing down. Nearly the height of the Great Tree, a few stone giants had already begun hurling pieces of the mountain at them. Their footsteps shook the ground, and massive gray arms swung in unison, though their rough rocky faces never changed.

"We have to get out of their range," the prince said. He fired his blasters, but they seemed to only chip the giants.

Celeste pointed at a low cliff. "There!"

They ran and took cover from the boulders being thrown in their direction, smashing just beyond them.

"They're still headed this way."

Rocho darted around the rocks in his tiny lightning-fast form until reaching Jack. He tried to shelter them both from the thrown mountain pieces.

"We need something to make a bigger dent in them."

Celeste closed her eyes and repeated an incantation even Jack couldn't understand. While the prince reached into his pocket for new ammo in his pistols, she kept going until her knives shimmered in green. Paper's amulet began glowing, and his muscles grew larger. The moment there was a break in the boulders falling, they ran out. Weapons aimed and ready to stop their targets, they attacked together.

Celeste's daggers struck the mountain just at the giant's feet. Green bolts of magic produced more blades all around them, firing into at least five of the giants at once. Prince Orblanc's bullets were fiery red. They seemed to find six separate targets before blasting a hole in each one of them. Paper cracked a small portion of the mountain itself, swinging the metal ball around on its chain like his yo-yo before slamming it down. Two giants fell into the crack and were stuck like whack-a-moles. Jack was more impressed by Rocho, who'd become stronger than Jack had realized he could. He pounced up the mountain, changing into his bear size just before crashing into a rock giant, then he sprung into another as a small bolt. He continued the tactic until he'd collided into nearly a dozen. But the giants kept coming.

Several crumpled like the creations from the Sandman. Still, more shuffled down the mountain in droves that never seemed to end. The more Jack and his companions destroyed, the sooner the giants were replaced. Filing out like blood cells protecting the body from a virus, they marched on. Some had reached Jack. Fear swelled inside him. His worst fears seem to enter his mind for no reason.

"Not the clowns again…" Distracted by his own imagination, he shook his head. The giants swung their arms to grab him as more dropped down. Jack could hear his friends getting more tangled in their own battles as Celeste's magic wore off. Before long, Jack was cornered by four menacing giants staring down at him. His fears were growing stronger as he worried about his parents and Sonny, monster clowns attacking him in his sleep, and the Sandman.

As he backed away from the giants, he could see images of his fears all swelling into the sword. As hard as he tried, he couldn't drop the blade. He tried to project those thoughts out while swinging his sword, keeping the giants at bay. He felt a release as a small pumpkin rolled from his hand. It sparked from its green stem as the giants stood near. Fearing he knew what it was, he kicked it in the giant's direction before scrambling up the cliff. The pumpkin exploded, blasting the stone giants near the mountain's base.

Debris showered him. He rolled over to see the others still fighting their way up but being overtaken by the army coming down. Jack could finally see the opening where the giants were pouring from. A cave entrance sat on the mountain nearly halfway to the top. Jack was able to pull three more pumpkins from the handle, and each ignited instantly.

"Guys, get away!" He tossed the bombs at the giants while the prince and Celeste dove out of the way. Paper was able to handle his own, but his amulet was flickering. Rocho wriggled free from the two giants that had caught him, only narrowly escaped the falling wreckage. Jack could see it singed his fur badly. He ran up as fast as he could to protect the pup.

"You'll be okay, buddy." Jack patted him as he changed into the flashlight, then directed the others. "We have to get up to the cave. I think the source is there." Jack pointed.

Fighting together, they bombed, cut, smashed, and shot their way through the rock formations. For a while, it seemed to be working, but the overwhelming numbers refused to slow. Jack panted, struggling to swing his sword a final time, glaring at the would-be destroyers.

Below them, he heard something cutting through the air. Something sailed over his head, whooshing air by his ear. The bit of sun still peeking around the moon had gone entirely black as arrows crawled through the air like ants. They fell sharply, piercing the rock giants, while others whizzed by him like red flurries striking the flying monsters and shredding them down like paper.

The villager warriors were still a reasonable distance below, but they seemed capable of matching the giants' increasing numbers. The rock giants emptied out of the opening with persistence as the warriors climbed the mountain.

"It is our time now." Prince Orblanc led the four of them, both tri-barrel pistols drawn and firing at the remaining giants left by the striking arrows.

Before long, they'd climbed to the hidden entrance where boulders fell from the cavern opening like large muddy raindrops. Landing in a puddle at their feet, a boulder formed into a rock giant. Prince Orblanc was quick to shoot it down, beginning at its knees, but another boulder dropped and began to develop a giant behind it.

"We need to stop it here!" Jack yelled, stabbing the newest giant mold with his sword.

Raising her dagger, Celeste chanted again then hurled it at the next falling boulder. It soon stopped forming. A blue light sealed it completely, freezing it all in place.

"Magic from the village," Celeste said. "I will need to use more daggers for it to last, but it won't be long before I am out."

"Hopefully, we won't be long then." Jack snuck beneath Celeste's blue seal of the forming boulders and into the mountain's entrance. The walls were pegged with red crystals that led deeper and rose higher into the mountain's center, where gems were arranged in a circle. Powerful red light brighter than anything he'd witnessed before beamed from them, like neon exit signs that only made him want to escape more. He paused before continuing, wondering if the crystals were a warning.

He heard shouting, the footsteps of an army, and several gears winding down, all the way back at the entrance. Celeste stuck another dagger into the formation, freezing it again. "My village should not have arrived here yet!"

"But my father could," the prince said.

Sure enough, Jack heard the king loudly giving orders to the general, to guard the mountain's entrance as they arrived. Ducking down, he could see them at a distance from the encircled crystals, approaching the entrance. The king gleamed in his armored suit adorned with several gears as he withdrew a mighty sword with his bulky arms and gave Celeste a look of distaste. She maintained her gaze on the formation, preparing another freezing dagger. Jack remained still, wanting to continue uphill to the crystal formation but afraid to move. The gears of the king's suit were similar to those on the prince's guns, making Jack fairly sure his armor was a weapon too.

"Son, what are you doing here with her and the traitor?" the king asked, entering the cavern.

"She is not our enemy." Prince Orblanc pointed. "You don't understand. She is important to me. We share a connection."

"I don't care what *connection* you think you have with these savage people." King Aurum spat, pointing his sword to threaten Celeste. "This war began long ago, when her people started it, and now we are too close to our rightful empowerment. I will not be stopped now!"

Jack heard more shouting behind them. Angry yells followed thousands of footsteps. The king lowered his sword slightly as he heard his general rallying the soldiers into a defensive line. Jack knew it was too late. The war would begin any moment once the natives had made it up. Just then, Jack caught the prince and Celeste exchanging looks, and what came next he hadn't expected at all.

"Lower your sword, Father." Prince Orblanc, his eyes sorrowful, aimed both of his pistols at his father.

"You would dare threaten your father? *Your king?* Have you lost all honor since your mother was taken?"

"I cannot be part of a kingdom formed by a tyrant," the prince responded.

Jack's heart leaped as a shot was fired. Celeste turned quickly; Jack assumed she feared the king or his son had been hurt. Prince Orblanc stared down at his tri-barreled pistols in confusion, and the king checked his armor with his free hand. The shot hadn't come from inside the cavern.

The king left first, followed by his son. Just outside the cavern entrance and farther down the mountainside, the groups were at a standstill as the two factions remained opposite each other. A sea of village warriors at least thirty thousand strong had advanced up the mountain, their magic axes, spears, or crossbows pointed. The warriors easily outnumbered the king's soldiers, who had merely a third of the natives' numbers. But the mechanized armored suits gave them an advantage. Twice the size of the warriors, the suits were armed with heavy guns and hundreds of ammo rounds. Behind them were steam-powered robotic soldiers with enhanced golden cogs. They seemed to follow orders much like drones.

The general stood from his vehicle. He wore lighter armor, a sword strapped to his back, and mechanized gauntlets that wafted smoke in the air. A massive robotic machine more menacing than any other stood beside him like a guard. Jack recognized it as the general's mecha suit, which was able to move on its own, as well, apparently.

Unexpectedly, the shaman from the village stood beside him. His arm was smoking beneath a cloak partially covering his outstretched arms. Jack nearly missed the shaman's new arm, which had been replaced by a gold mechanical limb radiating in the same magic he'd blessed the warriors' armor with. Both the natives and the king's soldiers remained motionless. A strange aura surrounded the warriors' armor and the collars of all the mechanized soldiers. The soldiers inside the mechanized suits struggled to move the levers. Finally, Jack spotted Chief Mizzi. Swollen with lean muscle and a long ax strapped to his back, he kneeled, wounded at the knee from a gunshot. It didn't take long for Jack to figure out what was happening.

"If you refuse to follow my clear instructions again, sir, I will shoot again," the general warned.

The king stepped up to the scene, clearly confused but brimming with pride. "My excellent soldier, how did you manage this?"

"Careful planning and the will to do what is necessary," he replied, pressing a button on his remote. His roadster turned toward the king, who urgently took guard as the guns aimed at his chest.

The king paused. "What is the meaning of this?"

"A new era, my former king," the general said confidently. "With the kingdom moving forward into a new revolution of power, it needs a proper leader. Someone willing to put aside the past to embrace the future, and that means learning as much about the source as possible to harness it. We need the natives for that. And under my control, we will work together instead of destroying what could be valuable laborers and citizens for the rest of this land. A kingdom is simply not large enough for my thoughts. I will have an empire."

"No!" the king shouted. "I will not allow you to take what I've built. They stole my queen from me! I will not let you take my kingdom." His armor expanded, revealing two blasters from his arms, but before he could shoot, it powered down.

"Both the kingdom and natives are now under my control." The general held up his remote. "My ally and I have been working together, sending items through the tradesman, sharing our strengths, spells, and science that brought you both together, making each other stronger than ever. And now both sides will be united under a proper ruler. Their magic is what has powered our control over the machines, and our science has rebuilt his missing limbs." The general prepared to shoot the king, who, like his soldiers, struggled to move. The prince seemed ready to stop him in a moment's notice as his fingers grazed the grip of his pistols.

"It already has proper rulers to unite them," Jack interrupted, dropping his flashlight behind him. "Prince

Orblanc and Celeste can unite both sides. They were born for
it."

"What are you doing?" the prince asked.

"What I think I was sent here to do." Jack returned his
attention to the people around him. "I found a letter from the
kingdom someone tried to have burned. A letter meant for the
king, written by the Queen before she left him. She chose to
leave after she became sick. She came to the village on her own
shortly after the prince was born and was rescued by Chief
Mizzi. She fell in love and had a daughter before dying. This
explains what happened to her. And it explains why they are
the only two people with white hair like those who lived in
Middletown. Just like their mother, because they're brother and
sister."

"My wife would not leave me," the king argued. "She
would not leave my son and me alone!"

Jack stepped forward, producing the burned letter. "This
is her handwriting, isn't it? They both carry identical bracelets.
They are brother and sister. They knew they were connected. I
just don't think they knew how." Jack could see Celeste
listening from the cave, staring at the prince as if she'd known
all along. Their matching bracelets dangled from their wrists.

The chief attempted to stand, and Jack thought he could
see resentful understanding before he spoke. "I believe the
words you say. I believe they are both her children. I can feel
her presence in them both. And I still believe it is his fault she
died." He stood firm, even with his wounded leg, glaring at his
enemy.

"You don't have to do this anymore." Jack held out his
hands. "You both loved her. Destroying each other would mean
destroying part of your children. They are your legacy, aren't
they?"

The chief looked at his daughter struggling to keep any more rock monsters from forming. "If I fall, you must lead your people, my moonlight. You must lead them all, understand?"

Understanding flushed over Celeste's face as she nodded mournfully.

Jack felt his arms and legs stiffen and sword slip from his fingers as pain surged through his body.

"We should not be listening to this outsider who serves us no purpose," the shaman proclaimed.

"You are a traitor to your people," the chief said, refusing to look at the shaman. "By the power of the night and moon, I will make sure those new limbs will be cut from your body."

"I believe I agree with the boy," the general stated gruffly, arming his vehicle. "Their legacy is not mine. My empire must be ruled by me, as I have no personal vendettas to stop progress. I can't have anyone stop that from happening. I should have burned the archived letters myself."

It happened quickly. The general used his free hand, gripping the broad sword on his back. With one downward hack, he cut the shaman's magic arm clean off. The shaman wailed in pain as the general picked up the golden limb still controlling the warriors.

"I don't believe my new land will have a need for you any longer. Animal laws always win. Survival of the fittest, and you have always been dependent on those much stronger than you." The general kicked the kneeling shaman, who fell down the mountain as so many watched, paralyzed.

He turned to the king and Chief Mizzi next, with the controller and magic arm pointed. "As for our former leaders, I will give you both exactly what you've wanted."

Onlookers watched as their leaders were forced to present their weapons. Against his will, the king aimed the guns on his armor at Chief Mizzi, who'd withdrawn his double-edged ax, gripping them with both hands. Jack didn't want to see what was about to happen. The leaders of the two groups stepped closer to each other until they were within arm's length. The chief held his ax held over his head with both arms. The king's blaster was ready to fire at the chief's heart. Jack closed his eyes as the general proceeded.

A loud whack followed muffled shrieks as the king was struck down and a dozen shots were fired into the chief's chest. Two loud thumps confirmed they'd each fallen onto the mountainside. Neither side spoke, but when Jack's eyes opened, he could see the resonating guilt and sadness of both armies turn to hatred for the general. In his anger and fear, Jack produced another pumpkin bomb from the sword. He hastily concealed it using the technique from the forest natives before anyone noticed.

"And now to rid us of the queen's past mistakes." The general prepared his vehicle's weapons. "There's no need to be sad for your parents. Your miserable excuse of a family will be whole again soon enough."

A large metal ball soared through the air and smashed into the vehicle. It rolled over a few times before the weapon discharged, hitting the general.

Paper emerged from the crowd. "Sorry, not much for politics. Too much mudslinging."

The shaman scrambled for the gold limb controlling the native warriors. Rocho changed from the flashlight to the bear-sized dog and ran into the shaman hard. At his feet, a pumpkin bomb appeared, rolling in his direction. Jack grinned and immediately took cover as it exploded. Wires, bolts, tubes, and the mechanical arm flew apart as the shaman was blasted down the mountain.

Everyone was instantly freed from their holds, but the general's mecha guard was sparking from its collar. The red gem changed to blue, and it was suddenly moving on its own. The machine-suited soldiers were ejected from their mecha suits, and a moment later, the drones' gems also glowed blue. Jack discovered the reason when he found the remote crushed a few yards away from the general's body.

The machines attacked everyone, firing from their blasters at the king's soldiers, the native warriors, and anyone else alive. Chief Mizzi lay on the ground, lifeless. The king appeared to share that fate, with the ax buried in his shoulder, but the village warriors leaped into action while the soldiers were still recovering.

Flying arrows and axes pelted the machines, changing them in ways Jack hadn't seen before. Some shrank into toy-sized figures; others caught fire, and at least two began attacking each other wildly. The machines' metal exteriors were easy to defend, though. They efficiently scattered the warriors with their guns, blasting hundreds of holes into the mountain and stunning several natives who were protected by the moonleaf armor. The soldiers finally regrouped, attacking the machines like insects on spoiled fruit. They ripped apart essential gears, apparently knowing just where to find them, but the mecha drones continued batting them away. The general's suit did the most damage with its bigger arms, using the general's fallen sword to strike down several people.

It was too early to tell who had the advantage. The native warriors and soldiers of the kingdom fought their new mechanical enemy with everything they had. Jack watched red glowing weapons slash through the air, bullets flying from soldiers, deafening explosions, magic arrows, and steam spewing out, but the machines had no emotion or pain to slow them. Jack felt as if he were in the center of a war game. Gripping his sword tightly, he didn't know what he could do.

An arrow nearly hit Jack before Rocho pushed him out of the way. A robotic soldier was struck in the leg, and it spun until it flew apart. Jack dropped and rolled to avoid being fallen on, and he nearly toppled off the mountain's jagged cliff.

Another explosion rippled the mountain's surface. All sound went away except for a distant ringing. Everything moved in a hazy slow motion as he held his ears to stop the painful ringing noise. The muffled sound of someone calling his name eventually broke him out of the trance.

"Jaaaack!" Celeste yelled, clearly weakened. The tiger cub's mist poured out of her, re-forming into her pet. "I don't have any more daggers. They'll rebuild soon."

Rocho barked at him to stand up, and he spotted a hand reaching out to him.

"You've got to get to the source before they tear you apart!" Paper had lost all of the power from his amulet and returned to the child size as he helped Jack to his feet. The chain had disconnected from the ball and was wrapped around his waist. He rushed Jack back to the cave entrance. "Magic's all used up for now. The metal ball is out there somewhere. Can't recharge my amulet."

"What about you two?" Jack insisted, pointing at the war raging on. "What about all of the people? What can we do against the machines?"

"There isn't time," Prince Orblanc said. "There's a chance you striking the source will give them nothing to fight over and remove power from the machines. The scientists have them linked together. They may be linked to the source, too. Go to the cave. Do what you came to do before it's too late."

Jack hated hearing that. Time was always against him. He imagined the mountain using the machines to defend itself through the power taken from the veins. The possibility of the world being conscious made him uneasy, as if it felt them all like a virus. As the formation above them began to break from its frozen state, Celeste rushed to his side with her tiger cub.

"It is time." She pointed to the rocky center up the trail from the cavern entrance. "My brother won't be able to hold the rock monsters for long."

"I'll help him," Paper said, grabbing what remained of his ball-less chain.

"Wait—your necklace," Jack said. "You're out of magic. You can't grow. You won't be strong enough."

Paper shook his head, wrapping the chain around his small arms. "They'll get me either way. At least I can do something."

"Why?" Jack took the boy's shoulder, similarly remembering Opal. "You'll just walk into a fight you can't win. You don't even look afraid. What's wrong with the kids in this place?"

"Fear is contagious, but so is being brave." Paper twirled the chain like a whip. "So I'm gonna see if paper beats rock."

Jack stared at Paper until Celeste stepped up to him. He looked at his sword made from the totem then at Rocho before reluctantly moving forward.

Everything until now had already been a brutal journey. Celeste accompanied him up the incline of the cavern entrance to the ring of red crystals. Jack had trouble believing he'd survived long enough to make it to the mountain's center even as he approached it. Before he was near enough to see it, he could feel the heat radiating from it.

The source in the center of the crystal ring was much bigger than he'd expected. Apple shaped but as large as a garbage truck. The cause was surrounded by the red rocky enclave and trapped beneath those glowing crystals in a large X. The protective gems over the source resembled the chains in the courtroom of Cloud City, confining the elemental rock. Strangely, the rocky ring around the source and the red glow inside reminded Jack of a volcano exactly. He cautiously stood over it, hoping it wouldn't erupt. Thicker red veins arched out around the ground and walls like thick roots. Rocks crumbled behind him near the entrance as he read writings scribbled onto the rocky walls.

It is at rest. Life or death, it will test. Power is an illusion judged by nature and created from fear. At the heart of the mountain, balance keeps us here. If given full life or full death, we will die, and the world will forever be changed from earth to sky.

Jack stood over the ring of crystal blocking the rock. "What is that supposed to mean?"

Shots were fired behind him at the cavern entrance. Jack was sure it was Prince Orblanc and Paper doing their best to keep the rock formations from attacking Celeste and him.

"The mystics…" Celeste said, reading the words above the source. "It is their carvings."

Standing over the source, Jack could hear the prince struggling at the entrance. He looked into the radiating red glow, uncertain after reading the writings.

Celeste gripped his shoulder tightly. "Jack, you have to do something."

Rocho growled loudly, sparking up his fur. Jack found two empty spaces at the lip of the source. One was oval and the other the same shape of a spiked cog. He removed the enchanted cog from his neck and the moonleaf from his pocket then placed them gently into the empty spaces. They each began to shimmer, one blue and one gold.

The cavern shook violently. The crystals in front of Jack shattered like glass, leaving the source accessible. A hole in its center became visible. Everything suddenly went silent. He turned, fearing the rock formations had gotten Paper and the prince, but they stood behind Jack, noticing the quiet, as well.

The rock formations froze, crumbling into piles on the ground. Even the battle outside seemed eerily quiet. What came next scared Jack to his core. The source pulsed.

The entire mountain shuddered. The source pulse happened again and again, becoming harder and more rhythmic as it continued. Before long, Jack could feel the whole mountain rise slowly then fall while wind blew all around the interior of the cave. Celeste ran to the entrance, followed by the prince, and soon Jack, Paper, and Rocho were watching from the cavern entrance together. Outside, several bodies lay on the ground, but even more were still prepared to fight, yet frozen in confusion. The combined efforts of the warriors and soldiers had nearly destroyed the mechanized drones, but they were suddenly powering down on their own. As the ground continued to rise and fall, the chief's daughter put her hand to the mountain.

"The earth is waking," she stated grimly.

The prince looked worried. "Our scientists predicted something like this would happen. Our technology was supposed to stop any more quakes from happening by removing the source safely."

"I don't think it's an earthquake." Jack felt himself rise again from the surface, barely hearing either leader. "I think it's breathing."

The ground shook more violently than ever. He picked up Rocho, changing him into the flashlight, and secured him in his pocket. Suddenly, everyone was forced to cling to the mountain as the ground continued to heave. The mountain's surface proceeded to tilt, rising and sailing through the air. Then the entire world was suddenly moving. Animals and people screeched through the air as they went from standing flat to dangling from the mountain's side. The atmosphere grew even darker as something new in the sky blocked the sun from view. It was humongous and made of stone—Jack realized it was a hand. The ground continued to shift until a pair of eyes rose from beyond the mountain, along with twisting vines framing what looked like a face.

Jack struggled to hang from the sloping cave entrance. "Big… like big, big. Really, really big. Big!" was all he could mutter.

It was a giant, but only for lack of a better word. Jack was part dangling, part standing in the presence of something so gargantuan that it dwarfed the term *colossal. Titanic? Immeasurable? Gargantuan..?* They all fumbled in his mind but were far too puny. The truth was the ground itself had lifted from the world and was looking at Jack as if he were a gnat on its skin. Everything they'd been traveling and fighting on, from the kingdom and mines, to the forest, sandpit, and mysterious swamp—the earth was indeed alive.

Chapter 11
Winter's Bane

The sounds that left the earth giant's mouth were unintelligible, but Jack could tell it clearly was not pleased with the people clinging to his body. It was loud and rough. His mighty hands sailed through the air and smashed onto part of the mountain. Several natives and soldiers were crushed or fell from the mountain's sloping surface. The mountainous feature shifted, and hundreds of birds flew away.

Jack couldn't see Celeste anywhere, but the prince, unconscious, swung from his holster, which had snagged on a jagged rock. The giant sat up straighter and yawned, causing a wailing wind that rippled the water below its massive legs. Jack held on for his life, and once the movement paused, he made the decision to climb up before it got worse.

He struggled to pull himself up the steep slope as if he were on a tilt-a-whirl ride. Every inch higher, he hoped the giant wouldn't notice him, as the horrific shrieks of warriors and soldiers falling through the air made his skin crawl. Jack clung tightly to the mountain's side as a warrior fell past him after toppling from the giant's wavering head. Just after, the prince's eyes fluttered, and Jack could see him slipping as he panicked within arm's reach.

"Try not to move," Jack whispered, but it was useless. The moment the prince realized how high he was dangling, he began scrabbling for something to hold onto. Jack searched for a way to grab onto him, but he was barely able to hang on himself. Grappling at the walls, the prince attracted the giant's notice, and Jack spotted the hand coming down. It was like watching a movie he'd already seen. He knew the prince had seen the hand block the light and his only options were being crushed or to fall. So Jack made a decision.

With his sword out, he dove toward the prince, anticipating the hand colliding. They fell for a few yards before Jack was able to drive his sword into the mountain, but it only slowed them down before he nearly lost his grip and found a crack to stick it in. The giant shook its head—Jack assumed the sword had felt like a tiny prick. The motion nearly made him lose his footing as he held the prince with one hand. His grip was slipping from every finger, and the dreamer realized quickly he wouldn't be able to hold them both. Gravel hit his face, and he looked up to discover things were growing less in their favor.

"This may be the last thing I do, but I will make sure your father's poor leadership ends with you." The general emerged from a crack in the mountain's surface a short distance above them with a blaster from the king's armor pointed at their faces. He hung from a grappling hook attached to his gauntlet just inches from the king's body. It'd been pegged between the mountain's jagged surfaces. The giant's hand rose again, threatening to crush them all.

The general grinned. "We are all subject to how nature decides who is strong enough."

Jack and the prince were stuck as the giant hand prepared to collide and the general was ready to shoot. Before the palm could crush him, the general attempted to swing away, but something was gripping his ankle. Jack glanced down to see the king's spreading smile as he held tightly to the general's foot. The general's expression turned to horror as the hand cast a shadow over his eyes.

Jack pulled his sword out just as the hand plowed down again. Both the prince and Jack fell a short distance before tumbling onto mountain peaks, barely able to hold on. A look of dread flashed across the prince's face, as if he'd admitted defeat, just before a flush of relief.

Vines, long and leafy, whipped through the air and unraveled near them like ropes. They were stringy like hair, dangling all around them. Jack quickly swung the prince over to one, where he was able to support himself. Several of the other soldiers and warriors around them began doing the same. Looking up and over the rough mountain edges, Jack found Celeste, her eyes blank and her hair flowing in the air, and other villagers holding their hands to the mountain, causing the vines to sprout. Several soldiers stood beside them, pulling up a bushel of vines or using their grappling hooks, each side helping to bring people up. Jack was glad to see Paper, using his chain, pulling with everyone else.

Jack couldn't believe Celeste had found a way for them to work together — but she had. The prince nodded his thanks to

Jack while being hoisted. Jack reached out to grab a vine for himself when his sword loosened, and he held onto it with both hands. It suddenly grew darker than ever as both of the giant's hands blocked out all the light. Together, they came toward the mountain as if the giant were preparing to wipe away a crumb. Jack closed his eyes tightly as the hands came closer and closer, stirring a cold breeze, and crushed him completely into the surface.

Jack felt his body turn from solid to something like a liquid, yet somehow, he was still conscious. He wondered if this was what dying felt like. Everything was dark just before the hands lifted. He could feel the rocky hands move through his body. Both of his hands continued to grip the pumpkin-handled sword, but something had changed. Jack's hands were much darker, nearly black, but he could see right through them. A dark-plum-colored mist swirled around the handle. His entire body had melded into his shadow.

His body felt weightless as he attempted to remove the sword from where it was wedged into the mountain. He pried it out fairly quickly, ready to grab on to the ledge, but there was no need. He hovered in the air, watching others above him being pulled to safety.

"I don't know what I did, but please don't stop," he said to the sword. He struggled to move up through the air, floating in place, attempting to make it to the heart of the mountain. He only managed to wave his arms a few times and kick his legs before he simply moved backward. "How am I supposed to get back up to the heart?"

Jack was far enough away from the giant to see the upper portion of its massive body. He traced the giant's head with his eyes, outlining the mountain as the nose attached to its face. The forest appeared to be its beard, which fell just a few miles short of the sandpit, and miles farther away was the lake, large and circular like a belly button. Jack tried to follow it farther and realized the heart of the mountain was the wrong place for the giant's heart.

"If the mountain's heart is in his head… that would mean the brain should be in his chest."

Searching the remainder of the titanic giant's body, he spotted the mine where the king's men were searching for veins. Several miles north of the mines, the polymoos were rolling toward the sandpit then digging into them. He remembered what Peddlin' Pete had said about them being lucky, always heading for safety. Jack was curious why they stayed so close to the pit.

The mirrored birds still circled over the sand, reflecting an upside-down view of the mountain whenever they flapped their wings. The sand seemed to ripple more than ever. Waves pounded from deep beneath the dream sand.

"The mountain's reflection…" Jack said to himself. "And the sand—that must be what's kept it asleep all this time."

As he gripped his sword, his newly discovered shadowy form changed things. After some struggling, he was eventually able to will himself to move in the right direction. It was draining and took all of his focus, but he'd finally drifted down toward the sandpit. It was the same method he'd used to make Nucalibur and Pete's sack of money vanish. He felt guilty for leaving the villagers and the citizens of the kingdom's capital on their own, but he knew it was his best option.

The closer he got to the pit, the more he strained to keep his form. The clouds shifted as the wind picked up, and it seemed to assist him. The sun became visible again, and he could suddenly feel the rays like never before. It burned his shadowy form, stinging him like wasps, pricking his skin with heated tips, and causing him to drift around randomly. He could feel his entire existence ready to extinguish like the flickering of a candle's flame. Following the reflective birds and worms sticking their heads above ground level, he focused on the center and dove down like a dagger, into the upside-down mountain of sand.

It was getting harder to catch his breath the farther he went. The pace of his flickering became faster and faster, but he kept at it. Everything felt heavier and hurt more, and deeper down, the sand's waves were even stronger.

His eyes drooped, and he could taste sand in his mouth. Seconds later, he had to help himself along with his hands, pushing the sand away from him, but he was determined. Blue waves sailed by him, and he knew he was close. His sword hand became stiff, and he knew the magic had worn off. It was only a matter of time before he ran out of air, unless he could push through.

Sand stuck to his sweaty face as he struggled to stay awake. His arms were exhausted, and his legs had kicked so much, they'd grown numb. His heart raced toward the blue wave, but it was more from being afraid than tired. Afraid of letting Sonny down. Afraid of losing his father again. Of failing everyone. Of being lost forever in the strange world. Never seeing his mom again.

His pockets were being weighted down too, and he felt the slightest pull coming from inside, but he kept swimming down. The flashlight was slipping out, and he was stuck between leaving it behind and drowning in the sand.

"Rocho… lightning." His fingertips grazed the handle. He couldn't accept losing it. He wouldn't accept it. He allowed his eyelids to become heavy, until he was swallowed by the sandpit.

Jack could hear a spark ignite near him. Above him, the birds screeched. Jack could smell fur burning. Static engulfed his body, and sizzling sand clung to his hair and skin. Yellowish-red sparks lit up the sand, then a green blur whizzed by him like a racecar given the green light. In a flash, Rocho was off.

The sparking light darted all around the pit. Bolts popped through the sand like an overcharged battery. The sand around Jack began to harden into crystal. The pieces were bonding together like the ones in the mines and mountain. Before long, the sand surrounding Jack was solid and gleaming like glass. Unable to move in the crystal prison, he spotted Rocho shattering the glass as he bolted through. Finally, the pup took a last charge toward the funnel end of the pit.

Rocho broke through the crystals with a sharp blast out, causing it to shatter. It rained down onto the new area's ground with a gentle sound like wind chimes. Jack's face and hands were covered in cuts, and his jacket and jeans were ripped. Some solid pieces of glass formed around him, cuffing his ankle and leg so he couldn't move. Rocho whimpered, then his ears perked up.

Jack gasped, filling his lungs with air and coughing up sand. He clawed forward with one hand, his lungs begging for air, as he used the sword in his other to pry pieces of glass off that still latched on. Above him, the sand crystallized into a peak, like a glass mountain hanging over him. He could feel it weighing down on him, but at last, his head shot up from the floor he'd landed on. He smelled beach and bone. He repeatedly blinked, rubbing his eyes to remove the sand from his face. Jack was embraced by a chamber of more rock and crystals, except these crystals held a blue shimmer down a tunnel on his right side, slowly turning red farther down. Jack assumed that was where the miners were leading up from the south. A blue moonleaf and gold cog symbol were inlaid on the floor. A rocky door had already retracted in the circled opening like a heart valve.

"You are definitely the smartest dog I've met, Rocho." He petted the pup. "When we get out of here, I am getting you so many rubber balls to fetch."

The pup seemed delighted for a moment, but that was short-lived.

Farther into the chamber, Jack could see the blue object causing waves through the crystals. "Brain activity?" Jack searched the area. He stepped inside, brushing the sand away from his clothes. Each wave from the blue mind seemed to push his progress back. Suddenly, all he wanted to do was curl into a ball on the floor. Dreamy images began blending in with reality.

"That bed is so close." He imagined a soft bed in the chamber, followed by blue walls, and eventually his entire room. He thought of how easy it would be to stop and just accept it, stay in the dream and let it be real.

Then he realized that would be too much like accepting death, drifting off into nothing. He was far too stubborn to let that happen to him or his father after how far he'd come.

"Just another step," Jack told himself repeatedly. "Just another one." His knee finally hit the outer wall protecting the brain.

His mind felt ready to burst as rushes of headaches took his concentration and replaced it with sharp pains behind his eyes. Fighting the waves and that bright-blue glow, he fought to raise his sword. He struggled not to grab his skull or beat himself over the head. Tears streamed down his face—then, with a grunting yell, he plunged the sword into the titan-sized brain. The waves slowed. The blue glow faded, and the chamber grew dark. Only the pink light of the heart symbol on the pumpkin-handled sword grew brighter and brighter, pulsing in rhythm as if it were beating.

The giant's movement halted, and moments later, Jack felt the most significant shake of the ground he'd felt since entering the place, as if the earth giant had fallen. It rocked the world itself in every direction. Jack clung to his sword. It stuck to his hands as if it were attached to him. He knew the giant had fallen, but a new fear crept into his mind now that he was able to think clearly.

Jack dropped to his knees. "What if I was wrong?"

The chamber was quiet and still. Sweat framed Jack's face. Then he heard gears moving beneath him. Something was powering up below the brain, and it flickered purple light like an old bulb turned on after several years.

Confused, Jack stood. "It's part machine?"

The chamber rumbled, shaking the sand. The purple flicker became a solid beam. Jack yelled as it burned his hands and face, engulfing his body. The pink glowing heart went dim. A moment later, black silence filled the chamber.

Wind rushed over his body. It was a familiar rush that he hadn't felt in days. He was traveling somewhere. Images flew by him: The village. The kingdom. Celeste and Prince Orblanc sharing a funeral for their fathers. A peace treaty being formed. Using both science and magic, the brother and sister sealed the mountain.

He traveled toward a yellow dot in the distance. As he glided closer, he could make out several people inside a portal standing in a tall room. And they all seemed to be arguing.

"That kid should've never been left in your care." Redd Rocket pointed at a cloaked figure. "I trained him in basic combat myself. I'm thinking it's strange you come along volunteering for a dreamer. You don't even like the kid. I don't think you like *anyone*."

"Maybe you should leave the thinking to those capable of using the proper equipment," Mr. Shadow responded coolly. "And, no, I'm not very fond of him, but I'm not fond of most people. Yet I don't seem to have a checklist of people to send to the well of lost souls, either, do I?"

"Did you just call me dumb?" Redd asked, clearly infuriated.

Mr. Shadow snickered. "If I had to pick two words that should never be associated with each other after meeting you, soldier, they would be *military intelligence*."

Redd Rocket prepared to leap onto Mr. Shadow, who stood his ground, but the Spirits of Father's Day and Mother's Day intervened. Besides the holiday spirits who'd entered, the courtroom appeared empty. Jack spotted a few J.A.C.K.s watching the commotion but remaining still on opposite sides of the portal. One seemed focused on his guard duties, yet the other seemed to be daydreaming about lunch.

"What is going on in here?" Father asked.

"As I recall, you were in the navy, weren't you, Shadow?" Redd yelled. "Did you get booted out? Didn't have the heart to deal with war? Don't have much heart in your past life or your afterlife, do you?"

The room became fearfully darker for a moment. Redd Rocket had obviously struck a nerve with Mr. Shadow. Mother was already doing what she could to calm the spirits down, but the room became frightfully cold. Then a judge entered from one of the alcoves.

"What is going on in my courtroom?" Old Man Winter demanded. Snowflakes fluttered in with his bitter-cold wind and waving white beard. "What nonsense are you spirits dragging in while a challenge is being held?"

"I requested your presence, Judge Winter," Mr. Shadow said. "Something has happened within the challenge. I believe someone has been affecting it from the outside."

"Yeah, and we all know who it is," Redd said.

"Why would I bother doing something like this only to turn myself in?" Mr. Shadow spat without a single glance in Redd's direction. "I do have a thought on who actually is responsible."

"How is this possible?" Father asked. No one seemed to have noticed Jack's return, and he began to wonder if he was witnessing what happened when someone failed a challenge. Was Jack stuck in a world between realms, or would he be sent back into the challenge repeatedly until he got it right—fighting off that titanic earth giant until he was beaten? He wanted to stand, but his body had been through so much, it refused to move.

The city's investigative detective entered the courtroom, accompanied by four cloud keepers. "I would like to know, as well. Cloud keepers have been around the portal nonstop."

"I don't know how it's happened, but there have been strange occurrences," Mr. Shadow explained. "Attacks on the dreamer that could only be caused by a powerful source, and I would like to know how it happened."

Winter's cold, frosty eyes darted around the courtroom before finally settling on Mr. Shadow. "And you've witnessed this for yourself as his advisor? Then, please tell us how someone was able to attack him beyond the portal."

"That is the very issue I wish to address." Shadow stepped closer to the podium. His eyes were dark beneath the cloak as he peered up fearlessly at Old Man Winter, whose mouth fell open to argue as the other judges arrived.

Autumn entered with her usual fair yet serious appearance. Spring's rainbow eyes were flushed with worry, while Summer looked as if he'd just rolled out of bed, still yawning, stretching his arms, and sporting a case of bedhead.

"What is this all about?" Autumn demanded, looking over to where Jack lay. "Has the dreamer reached the mountain and made a decision?"

"It appears there have been some adjustments to this challenge," Mr. Shadow announced to Autumn after a glance in Jack's direction. "As his advisor, I have watched over his journey and have witnessed several disadvantages that may have altered the way he performed in the challenge."

"Is that what this is about?" Winter shouted. "Another dreamer cheated? Another loophole to avoid the lesson to be learned, I suppose. If so, there will be no mercy this time, and swift action must be taken. Avoid any mistakes this round—we should send him directly to the island's prison!"

"Winter, we cannot simply make judgments without all of the facts," Autumn said. "But these accusations are grave. *Has the dreamer manipulated my challenge?*"

Mr. Shadow never hesitated. "I, more than most, would sympathize with the judges' reasons to be harsh on the dreamer and believe his actions should be dealt with accordingly for the greater good of this world."

Jack couldn't believe what he was hearing. He continued to struggle but was still unable to move his body. He could barely move his head, as it felt stiff yet light. His flashlight was next to him, and the totem-turned-sword Nucalibur was still clutched in his hand. Strangely, he noticed the handle was glowing.

Jack suddenly realized why everyone was ignoring him. The moment he'd returned from the portal, the Halloween Spirit had covered him in a blanket of shadow that made it impossible for him to move. It seemed Shadow had a plan Jack wasn't aware of. Whatever it was, it would stop Jack from having a chance to show himself or argue.

Was this what he'd planned all along? Jack thought to himself. *Help me just enough through the challenge so it would seem he'd been trying to help me, just for me to be banished like Teddy?*

"If it appears that the dreamer has discovered a way around the choices he was meant to make, and no one has affected his challenge, then I would agree with your judgment," Mr. Shadow continued. "However… I have seen frost chase his steps throughout the forest, twisting and turning with every move he made, as if sent to hunt him. That is not something I would call natural in the challenge." He looked at each of the seasons.

"That is impossible," Autumn stated, holding her usual tone. "No one other than a judge has the power to manipulate the challenges."

Winter's cold smile and cruel laugh jolted Jack. "I must be mistaken, but it's beginning to sound as if you may actually be suggesting one of *us* has been attacking the boy?" Winter said. His grin faded, and his fingers froze over. "But I know you would not be either this bold or this stupid."

His eyes were wide as he looked down at the courtroom, but once again, Mr. Shadow kept his composure. "Of course I would never suggest something so obviously outrageous. Yet, unless I'm mistaken and this was all a natural part of the challenge, something unusual has happened. What will happen to the people he intends to rescue, if it is discovered the challenge was manipulated?" There was a small tremor in the spirit's voice as he glanced over at Sonny, who was beginning to stir, though she remained chained to the wall. Jack's father, however, was nowhere to be seen, and that worried him. He heard chains moving, but as his body was still paralyzed, he couldn't see if Sonny had woken up or not.

The four judges exchanged looks between themselves, silently questioning one another.

"And to think I was gonna stay in bed today!" Summer folded his arms. "This is not cool, dude."

Winter looked at the other judges, who were all glaring at him. "You can't possibly believe these accusations from this spirit! It wasn't long ago that he was accused of several crimes. All due to the actions of his symbols! This could all be his plan for revenge!"

Autumn shook her head softly. "No one is judging you, Winter."

"I am!"

Autumn ignored Summer's objection as she finished. "But we do need to explore every possibility."

Spring remained quiet as if afraid to speak up against the season who had grown increasingly furious with every eye on him.

"I have been a judge for longer than any of you. Who are you to accuse me of anything? Especially you!" He pointed at Mr. Shadow, who remained unmoved. His face was still hidden beneath his hooded cloak, but Jack was sure it had somehow darkened. He hadn't felt it in a while, but he was convinced that bone-rattling chill had just surged through him again. Jack heard a chain jerk again, but no one seemed to pay Sonny any attention.

"I only look to do what I can in aiding the dreamer, as I volunteered to do," Mr. Shadow said. "I would suggest that we all watch what has happened throughout the challenge and judge for yourselves."

Winter began to argue once again, yet he seemed to have second thoughts after witnessing the expressions on the holiday spirits', the cloud keepers,' and the other judges' faces.

The four seasons turned into raindrops, fall leaves, rays of heat, and snowflakes then transported themselves to the lower level with everyone else. There, they replayed the challenge for everyone to see, using the portal like a television. None of them noticed Jack was just on the other side.

They replayed Jack's entrance into the challenge, fighting off the strange birds. Next, they watched Celeste rescuing him then the metal pumas chasing them. When the portal showed the freezing ground, Autumn turned toward Mr. Shadow. "So, it is true."

Spring continued watching while Summer shook his head, disappointed.

Winter was already prepared to argue. "This is outrageous! I have done nothing to alter this challenge. Someone is plotting against me. We as judges all have made enemies from those we have rightfully judged. Someone is attempting to divide us. I've heard the whispers. Someone is coming for us. You think I'm too ancient to be a judge now? I've grown past my prime and need to be replaced? I still have plenty of fight in me!"

The others simply stared at him as he shouted wildly about conspiracies. Frost began covering the ground just as it had in the challenge. They all watched it spread along the ground, stretching out to the walls and doors.

"Now, Winter," Autumn said patiently, "we are only looking for the truth. There's no need for you to lose yourself."

"I have been fighting the good fight for centuries, and you all think it's time for me to step down now?" Icicles with glassy points had formed across the ceiling. "I am as strong as ever. I am as sharp as ever. And anything I do is for the good of us all."

Everyone had taken a few steps back.

Staring at Old Man Winter, Spring said softly in Jack's direction, "Was it just the frost?" An uncharacteristic smirk appeared on her face as if she were hinting something.

Jack began to shiver violently from the cold frost scaling the walls around the courtroom. Something dark flowed toward him, along with a drafty wind. His body was weakened, but he continued to fight the shadow holding him down, struggling to get the judges' attention. Winter continued to rage on as he watched the images in the portal. A ghostly white arctic wolf developed from a patch of ice just behind him, with cold blue eyes and a growl like the beasts Jack had faced in the challenge's zoo.

"Where is the boy now? In hiding, like the last dreamer? Are they working together? Did you help them escape?" Winter pointed again at Mr. Shadow.

"No." Shadow waved his hands, and Jack felt his body rising from the ground. "To my surprise, he has actually survived his challenge."

There was a silent shock from everyone as the black mass holding Jack down released him. A rush of pain hit him as he was finally freed, struggling to cough up the right words he'd meant them all to hear. A noise rustled behind him—he assumed it must be Sonny stirring.

Jack could only wonder how he must look to them after what he'd been through—bruised, broken, crushed, transported through portals, burned, imprisoned, and at one point turned into both a pig and a monkey. His clothes had been ripped, patched, and mixed with tribal cloths and leather armor from the kingdom. But he was back to the city, able to move—and that was enough.

"Why have you hidden him?" Autumn asked.

"To make sure what I had to say to you would be heard." Mr. Shadow glared at Winter as his shadow crawled along the floor and attached itself to him once again. "And to be sure who was behind all of this before he was discovered. I sent my ex-symbol's sword into the challenge with my shadow attached to watch over his progress. It seems my shadow has discovered quite a bit."

"No, I will not be remembered this way." Winter held out a hand, clutching the air as if an invisible ball rested in his palm. "I am not the enemy."

"Don't lose your cool, bro," Summer warned. "We all know how you feel about the dreamers."

"I have a sense of discipline, unlike you."

Autumn nodded. "It is true you have always enjoyed making the challenges more adventurous, Summer. And you find all of ours boring in comparison. It may have been you, after all."

"Me? What about you? It was your challenge, dude, and you always said these things were a waste of your time. Besides, if anyone is suspicious, it's the quiet ones like Spring."

Spring turned to them, particularly furious. "What have I done now?"

"You totally run around the city where you know you shouldn't be. You're the oldest of anyone else here, although you look like a third grader, and I don't trust how fake you come off," Summer answered. "You come off so innocent, but what were you doing at Phoenix's party this year? Were you a part of the Sandman's escape? No one would ever see you coming, would they, little dude?"

More eyes were on Spring than anyone else. "I do represent the season of spring. Don't you think I'd rather be outside than guarded like a princess in a castle surrounded by dragons?"

They continued to argue until, eventually, no one could be found with more motive and evidence than Winter. He now seemed to care less and less about talking and more focused on preparing to fight.

"Stop!" Jack finally yelled, shaking from the bitter cold and his weak words. "It was all of you…"

There was a clatter of footsteps from those in the courtroom talking as a few more spirits who'd helped Jack train arrived, including Valentine's Day and Thanksgiving, along with Cassandra, Jack's lawyer sent from Lucky.

"You'll be weak for a few moments as your body adjusts to what it's been through in the challenge," Mr. Shadow explained. "But it will pass. Just be still, boy."

Summer scratched his head after waving away a ball of heat he'd created, Jack assumed to repel Winter. "What do you mean, dude? You think it was all of us? Who else can make frost chase you? Torturing dreamers isn't part of my journey. That is *not* how Max Heat gets down, bro."

"No, it was all… of your powers." Jack struggled to explain. "You've been manipulated… everything that happened in the challenge… the frost was just the first. There was a storming rain coming from nowhere that flooded the ground. It all seemed so unusual, as it was the only time rain fell. Then there was a thick fog when the weather turned extremely hot. It must have evaporated all that water. And just after I came back from the swamps, there was a crazy earthquake where all the leaves of the trees fell. All of the seasons' powers… were used."

Jack eyed the hourglass containing the Sandman before that horrible feeling of déjà vu that always seemed to follow him crept into his mind. "I remember when the Sandman used Sonny and she didn't know what she was doing. I think you may have had something similar happen to you all."

"But the Sandman is still locked away in the shuttle pod, prepared to serve his sentence on the island," the investigative detective stated. "And the magic required to rebuild his body now would be nearly impossible to obtain. But that doesn't explain how the four judges' powers were manipulated."

"No one else can affect the challenge without power from the Four Seasons." The Spirit of Father's Day spoke to Jack as the judges continued to argue. "Winter is the only one it could be, and he needs to be stopped. You know this. I know this is a lot to ask of you, Jack, but he is more powerful than all of us. The four seasons demand a sacrifice to keep the elemental rock powered. You, as a dreamer, cannot be sensed like a spirit. If you can pierce his cold heart, we can end this before anyone gets hurt. You and your father can return home, if that is still what you want. Be brave, son—do what you think is right."

Jack stared into the sunken eyes of the Father's Day Spirit, who was smiling kindly. Sometimes it took only a look from his own father to make him realize what the right thing to do was. Taking the sword with him, he stepped quickly up to Old Man Winter, who'd been surrounded by the other judges. His cold aura chilled the area as he prepared to attack everyone at once. Jack crouched down as he'd been trained, stepping behind the judge. He drew the pumpkin-handled sword back, ready to drive it through the heart of Winter, and he paused.

Jack noticed his reflection in the blade's metal. Months appeared to have gone by in just a few days. He was bruised and beaten, but it was his own eyes he didn't recognize. They were dull and gray. In his hesitation, he realized Father had that same dry glaze over his eyes. The three judges facing Winter seemed to be waiting for something to happen, but it was Jack they were watching. If he didn't know better, Jack would've sworn time had stopped. Winter hadn't turned, but he waited all the same. Deep in the reflection, his pupils were glittering with sand, as something Father said jolted him.

"Take my father home…" Jack whispered. "You told me that was impossible. I've researched it for months, and you've always said there was no way. It's like you want me to destroy Winter, but what benefit would that give you? The only one who would really want that is—"

Jack lowered his sword, and only then did Winter turn to him. "Do what you were meant to, boy. After what I've put you through, I know you want to. It would be so easy. So simple. You and your father are so much alike. Always afraid to do what's necessary. Stop being like him. Stop being a coward!" Winter yelled.

The other seasons were advancing on Jack, their images shifting and changing in front of him.

"No—no way that's possible." Jack backed away, raising his sword. He ran to the hourglass in the opened shuttle. Every spirit, season, and cloud keeper watched him like lifeless drones. They each raised an arm to grab him as they chased after Jack.

Winter's cold voice washed over him like a chill. "You know you'd rather remain blind to the outside world and live blissfully here. You still have a chance. Do what you were meant to. Be the hero and rescue your friends and family."

Jack turned to see a small army at his back as the courtroom filled with more dazed-looking spirits. But when he turned back toward the hourglass, his father appeared in front of it.

"You will never have me any other way, son. What is real and what is not is all a state of mind. You decide what you want to believe, and you now have the gift to choose. Sleep for eternity and be happy, with me."

"I'm sorry." Jack pulled his sword back like a pinball lever but couldn't move. He was unable to control himself as he turned and faced Winter, stepping closer to him with his blade ready. With each step, he begged himself to stop, but his body persisted.

Come on, Jack, wake up! Wake up, wake up, wake up!

Just before he drew the sword back farther, he felt the floor firm and cold beneath him. His eyes stung more than they ever had, as if he'd forgotten how to use them. His hearing seemed unaffected as he turned toward the hurried footsteps. His arms were weighty, holding the pumpkin-handled sword at Winter's back. He wasn't sure what was happening until he heard a voice call out to him.

"Calm yourself, stupid boy. You're safe now," Mr. Shadow said quietly. His voice was not what Jack had ever expected to consider calming, but for the moment, he was glad for it. He remained rigid, still unsure if he was where he should be.

Winter turned to him in the flash of a cold snap. "What do you think you are doing?"

"What… happened?" He dropped the sword onto the floor. His voice burned his throat as he coughed up words like phlegm.

"You must have just returned." The Halloween spirit looked down at Jack beneath his hood, handing him a dream catcher. "Wave this over your head quickly."

"Why was I about to… the sword?" Jack swallowed. "It's happened again."

"Use the dream catcher, boy," he demanded. "We have to be sure."

Jack did what he was asked, waving the dream catcher above him. "How long… how long has it been going on?"

Mr. Shadow took the dream catcher from Jack as the Four Seasons and a few other holiday spirits looked on. "You've been sleepwalking, for weeks now."

Jack remained on the ground, struggling to stand as Mr. Shadow offered no help. He was still in the courtroom. Cloud keepers stood guard, making sure none of the other holiday spirits came near him. He was surprised to see the Four Seasons begin arguing with each other again over him.

"Weeks?" Jack asked, panting.

"Someone poisoned you with dust from the Sandman days before you went into the challenge. It's amazing you survived a single day, but according to the witch doctor, you've been fighting it the entire time, shifting in and out of the dream. The remaining particles of the Sandman were unable to consume you fully. Most of what happened to you was real, but other aspects… sleepwalking can be a powerful hypnosis. If I wasn't personally aware of your past stupidity and failures, I might be impressed. I'm confident it was just luck."

He found his way to stand but wavered. "How do I know I'm not dreaming now?"

The spirit simply pointed up. "Nina. She has developed a powerful dream catcher over the courtroom. The room is clean of any more escapes from the hourglass, and it is safely in the capsule. It will not, however, help anyone who is already affected by the sand. Until we discover who was behind your attack, I am the only one allowed near you, as your advisor for the challenge."

"They still trust you to help me?" Jack backed away a few steps.

"You may have forgotten this fact, but I was once accused of a crime I didn't commit for nearly thirteen years." Mr. Shadow sneered. "I have no reasons to be suspected any longer. As such, since I am the only one allowed near you besides the judges, it would be far too easy to be caught, would it not? No, whoever is behind this would need proper motivation and be smart enough to use others to do their work for them."

Feeling finally returned to Jack's limbs, along with a prickling on his neck and ear as though someone were calling out to him from a distance. "So why did you volunteer to help me?"

Even beneath the dark hood, the spirit was clearly not pleased by the question. "I have my reasons, and that is more than you need to know. You should be more concerned with who has been trying to ruin your efforts of winning the challenge. What you have experienced in and out of your dreams is done. Someone has been tampering with your challenge, and only the four judges have that ability, which is why this argument continues. So stay here while we figure out who has been manipulating you in there."

Jack was still groggy, but his understanding began catching up to him. "So the fog, the rain, the frost… the arena, the swamp, and the mountain battle between the kingdom and natives… everything that happened in the challenge while I was sleepwalking actually happened?"

"It can't just be me who believes speaking to you is like speaking to a child who continues to lose brain cells, can it?" Mr. Shadow stopped with his arms folded behind his back. "The events that happened still happened. It seems obvious to me, someone has manipulated you to attack Winter as well. Your actions may not have all been your own, but that is a matter you can debate with the mirror another time. Let me know who wins."

He walked over to where Detective Young was speaking to a cloud keeper as they watched Jack's challenge replay, while two others guarded either Sonny or the door. The four seasons continued to argue among themselves, occasionally looking at Jack.

Something in the challenge stuck out to Jack. "What if there was another source?"

"It has finally happened." Mr. Shadow shook his head. "Your ignorance has traveled into your ears and made you hard of hearing… I've just told you, only the four seasons' power could cause snow and massive heat and rain, as it did in your challenge."

"But they have to get their power from a source," Jack tried to explain. "In the challenge, there were two sources. The giant's heart and mind were in two different places, but they were both there."

"Do you believe there is a fifth season we don't know about?" Mr. Shadow's annoyance grew. "The Sandman tried that twice now and has failed. Now, are there any other theories, or do you mind if I take care of other matters?" He stepped away, demanding a cloud keeper release Sonny, leaving Jack to stand alone.

But for reasons he couldn't explain, Jack didn't feel alone. Dots danced in his vision as he attempted to focus on the room.

The young detective could see the shuttle in the distance, ready to be sent to the island prison. He leaned on the table of evidence as he regained his composure. Chains rattled, and he turned, expecting to see Sonny dangling above him. But it was another voice below him that he heard.

Jack stared mindlessly at the gaping hole in the center of the floor. Raspy whispers funneled out. He continued to feel that prickling sensation on his neck as he realized something was missing over the hole. It was completely exposed, revealing the sky below and chains wavering around it. *The Sandman's sand… what if it was used to give power to something. In the challenge, I stabbed what I thought was the heart of the mountain, waking the giant. The sand kept the mind alive. That's what powered the giant. What if it powered the —*

Across the room, Jack noticed the detective remove his badge, which unraveled into a long whip as the room suddenly became darker, and he spotted the sky hole on the ground. "It's gone. The elemental rock is gone. Cloud keepers, be on your guard!"

All of the cloud keepers, except the one who'd continued to hold a blank expression, made a move to get the seasons and Mr. Shadow out of the courtroom, but the door had become frozen solid by a block of ice. Frost had lined and covered the doors and walls with icicles, and the ground looked like a skating rink. Everyone began questioning Winter as Jack took in the room, realizing the strange prickling on his neck and the sound of his name had come from the hollow area below him. Jack scooped up the sword, guarding himself. He could hear the haunting whispers all over again.

"The Valley of Lost Souls?" Jack looked over the edge of the hole that revealed a sky view of the valley on the first cloud, along with the black swirling vapors of dead spirits trying to claw out. He found himself looking down directly over the well. "This is where the courtroom is hidden? Crammed between the first and second clouds above the well of dead spirits!"

"Jack… why am I chained up here?" Sonny had woken up. Her curiosity ablaze, she shook the chains that held her up, staring at all of the frightened faces nearby. "I didn't sleepwalk again, did I? Or are aliens experimenting on us? Blink once if I'm missing any limbs. I can handle it—just tell me. I'll be fine…" She sniffed. "Is someone making bacon?"

Jack rushed over, thrilled Sonny was awake. "It's a pretty long story. I was in the challenge, and someone tried to stop me from winning using magic from the Four Seasons. While I was inside, I was attacked by robotic pumas tiger sharks, survived an arena tournament, rescued Rocho, turned into a monkey and a pig. I stopped a huge giant the size of a small state then landed here only to find out *I* was in and out of sleepwalking from dream sand. When I finally did come out of both the challenge and the sleepwalking, you were supposed to be freed."

Nodding, Jack took in a deep breath, thinking just how unbelievable it all must sound even to someone like Sonny. "I just realized how many rock monsters I fought in there between the mountain and the giant. Strange pattern now that I think of it."

Sonny simply nodded slowly. "You blinked. So… yes on the aliens, and I am missing a leg?"

"No." Jack slammed the sword he'd forgotten he was still holding against the evidence table. "Didn't you hear what I told you?"

"Yes, and it sounds both absolutely incredible and exhausting, but it doesn't explain whatever that thing is." She tried to point with her cuffed hands.

Behind Jack, a low grumble rolled across the courtroom. It was an earsplitting noise like a chainsaw chipping away on something too hard to cut through and the growl of some terrible jungle creature. It seemed to come from all around them. A loud crash interrupted them as a blast of water shot from the ceiling. Spring watched it as it jetted toward her like a hundred fire hoses.

The water blasted with enough power to drown her, even in this afterlife. At the final moment, Old Man Winter leapt in front of her with his arms wide, pushing her away from the blast. He was pelted against the wall, then a shot of the coldest wind Jack had ever felt froze the judge instantly, crawling up his arms and over his neck, engulfing his face until his body was frozen solid.

His final look was at Spring. "My sun…" he whispered.

She stared back at him until the cracks formed around the frozen season. The cracks splintered over his limbs, head, and even his white hair, until all of the cracks reached his chest. He shattered, and the pieces fell to the ground like broken glass. Only a frozen blue orb remained hovering in his place.

Everyone looked up, with either their hands or a weapon raised. Jack's sword trembled in his fingers, but he couldn't tell if it was from cold or fear. Another crash through the table behind him, and the beast landed. Jack stumbled backward, away from the monster that had been in front of them all along. Sand swirled in its core, charging the four colorful stones in its chest. "It was a warning. That same nagging thought of so many rock monsters. It was the Elemental Rock all along."

Chapter 12
Uncloaked

A rock mound landed like a meteor, splitting the table in two. Jack was propelled to the benches. He dropped his sword as Sonny was flung back against the wall, dazed and hanging from her chains. A tail the length of Jack's body with small jagged pillars uncurled, falling to the ground with enough weight to dent the floor. Its legs and arms were like tree trunks. Its torso held the four colorful stones, and sand glittered around them with each powerful breath. Its face was like gravel mixed in cement that continued to change its expression.

"That scent… I haven't inhaled it in centuries." The rock spoke in a horrific beastly low growl, slowly raising himself like a fallen warlord. "Fear…"

He looked out at the cloud keepers, dreamers, and holiday spirits staring up at the monster, still struggling to understand that Old Man Winter was gone. "You… should all be running away now."

His massive arms swung forward, casting fire out in arching waves. It ignited the courtroom in an orange glow before everyone scattered in a panic. The heat melted part of the ice that covered the doors, and Jack heard banging. Recovering, he ran back to Sonny when the cloud keepers fired at the Emperor. The detective tried his best to get to Jack, using his badge to shield himself from the fire and charge forward.

"You are no ruler, Onyx!" Autumn yelled before swirling leaves around to form a pile that erupted into a magnificent bear. It pounced toward the Elemental Rock with a trail of fall leaves followed by several blasts of orange and brown razor leaves from the judge herself.

Summer's robes fluttered as he created then hopped on a wave of heat. He was barefooted, his arms outstretched as if surfing and riding the tide around the rock. A shark made of sand and fire dove in and out behind him. Autumn's bear had grown bigger than Rocho, and she climbed atop it, riding it like a knight into a battle.

Spring was obviously scared. Several moments passed before she could look away from the remaining pieces of Winter evaporating from the ground. The ball of ice still hovered in his place like the final piece of his spirit. Her hands trembled as she caused rain to drop around her. The mist and water vapor came together to form a dragonfly as big as she was.

At once, the remaining three judges attacked and repelled the demon rock as it rolled and shielded itself. Changing its body into water, the creature slipped away from the attack. It then turned to a pillar of fire, blasting cloud keepers to the ceiling. Two had been launched over the hole that swirled with echoes. Jack noticed the emperor never moved too far away from this sky hole. Just as a block of ice crashed toward him, the detective shoved Jack out of the way.

"We've got to get you somewhere safe," he yelled over the fighting.

The young detective clung to the sword, watching Mr. Shadow scurry out of the way — determined to hide, Jack assumed. "He's such a coward… why is this happening?"

Detective Young bent over, covering Jack. "That monster held on to power for far too long and only wanted to watch the world drown, burn, and be crushed so he could conquer. The Emperor wanted to unite all of the cities and rule over them all, with his children leading his armies. The beings stopped his children, but he absorbed their essence, making it impossible to fully destroy him without turning the world to chaos. He is all that remains of the four elements."

"That's why he was kept nearly alive?" Jack asked.

The Cloud City detective nodded. "We depend on the elements for survival, but he has to be stopped. So the question was how to make something less dangerous without destroying it."

Jack instantly thought of the challenge he'd just escaped. "Destroy the mind and keep the elements alive."

"But someone has found a way to reanimate his mind using the Sandman as a source. Those chains are powerful. He can't escape them no matter how he moves or what he changes into — as long as he doesn't get the key. For now, my only concern is getting you out of here before something — " His body stiffened, and his legs buckled. Then he collapsed, unconscious.

"Oh no, you can't be leaving already. This welcome-back party is just getting going." Teddy stood behind the motionless body of Detective Young, holding an upgraded version of his remote. It contained more buttons and a chrome casing. Its new antenna had a sharp pointed end that was sparking. Teddy's eyes were exhausted, his skin nearly snow white, and he was sickly thin, wearing a cloud keeper's uniform.

"What are you doing here?" Jack demanded.

Teddy mockingly patted Sonny's chains while leaning on the motionless cloud keeper guarding her. "We dreamers have to look out for one another, don't we, dork?"

Jack was ready to reach for Trick's sword, but Teddy stopped him, holding his self-made remote control. "I wouldn't suggest you make any more complications than you already have. My new remote has been controlling this cloud keeper, and who knows what I may have him do to your girlfriend here."

"So it was you all over again?" Jack asked, ignoring the comment.

"Well, obviously I had a hand in it," Teddy whispered. "The Elemental Rock did all the manipulating for me. But believe it or not, I'm actually here to help you. I've even brought dear old Dad back to you, hidden inside the shuttle over there. Might as well hand him over to you since I'll be going back home soon."

Jack checked his pocket for the flashlight. "You need your totem to get back home."

"Wrong. I don't need that mutated mutt of a flashlight to leave this place. Can't trust it, but I also can't have you using it against me. Besides, there's no telling if it would work properly now. And the judges make the new totems deactivate the moment you return… if we return, that is. So your sword is useless to me, too. Luckily for me, I found another totem no one has thought to deactivate."

The battle raged on beyond them, occupying everyone in the room. No one but Jack had even noticed Teddy was there as they fought back the Emperor.

"What totem are you talking about?" Jack asked.

"The original one." Teddy stepped over to the array of items on the evidence table. "The first totem is here. It is evolved, but still more powerful than any other. It can allow passage to and from any world I need."

"The original totem? You mean the quill?" Jack remembered the story he'd heard of the red-and-silver quill totem before he was thrown into the challenge. "You'll never find it."

Teddy laughed a little. "I've had the totem since you returned and already put part two of my plan in motion. After hiding for so long, my employer will be very proud of me for getting this for the portal."

Jack wanted to keep Teddy talking while he figured out how to stop him from whatever he was planning to do next. "So what do you plan on doing? Putting everyone to sleep all because you cheated your challenge? I had to go through the challenge, too. It was tough, but I made it. What makes you so different from what I had?"

"You weren't there!" Teddy was on the verge of yelling. "The time you spent in the challenge, alone in the dark, headed to the Great Tree? That was every day for me, for months. But you weren't alone. You had the Sandman with you, even if you didn't know it. There was someone always whispering back to you. But not me. Did you ever black out and not remember how you saved yourself? Or speak to someone no one but you ever saw?"

It was like a switch being turned on in his mind. No one else ever saw Opal. Looking back, he was sure he'd been manipulated by the sand.

"The only ones who heard me were the monsters from my nightmares. The ones always hunting for me," Teddy continued. "But there was no sleep. Never fall asleep, never stop moving… never fall apart. It was just an endless dark mall, and I had to depend on myself in the challenge. No, not a challenge. It was just a very cruel test created by a very bored old man. And I was his entertainment."

"Is that why you tried to have me stab Winter in the back?" Jack asked, reaching his sword with his foot finally. "Was that your failed revenge on both him and me?"

A new smirk edged onto Teddy's face as he circled around to the enclave. "It would have made a small victory… but there is something much bigger at play. You were just my distraction, dork."

Cloud keepers were flung against the wall and knocked unconscious. Jack turned quickly to see Autumn summoning a mound of leaves around her. "Why tell me any of this? What are you planning on doing? Destroying everyone?"

Teddy bent down so that his nose was near Jack's.

Jack struggled to regain his footing.

"I'm only doing what I've had to every step of the way, spaz. Dream dust on that stupid cloud keeper. Using my remote to control the sand that powers the Four Seasons. My employer will finally send me home once the totem is back. And Emperor Onyx's doing just what I need. Causing a major distraction and getting rid of everyone who's sacrificed kids like us. Now none of us will be used like that again."

The three seasons continued to fight the former emperor as he changed his body into molten rock, burning a ring into the floor with every step. Lifting her arms into the air, Spring produced an army of water warriors from a puddle on the ground. They bombarded Emperor Onyx with shots from water cannons, but he turned every blast into vapor.

Summer surfed around on his heat wave, taunting and distracting the rock, while Spring tried to form storm clouds in her tiny trembling hands. A few clouds appeared and sparked, but nothing powerful enough to do more than slow down the demon rock with a few blinding lightning strikes.

Autumn's bear rammed into him, knocking him closer to the hole overlooking the well. A flurry of leaves circled the courtroom and cut into the rock like a thousand chisels. The emperor was resourceful, though. For his large size, he had no trouble moving from one element to another. He quickly hardened his body into stone, followed by a cyclone of wind that slammed everyone in the courtroom.

"Now, about my old totem." Teddy recovered, standing Jack up. "Where did you hide the flashlight, spaz?" His eyes were wide and wild. The remote was out, and the antenna was sparking in bright blue.

Jack didn't like how close he was to Sonny as he waved the remote threateningly.

"I don't know where the flashlight is," Jack said calmly as pieces of the ceiling fell around him.

"Don't lie!" The remote sparked, and Sonny swung herself away. " Where is it?"

Jack surveyed the room, not knowing where his flashlight was, but he swiped the sword at Teddy wildly. Teddy dodged and slashed his remote back, blocking the next attack and kicking Jack away. The room sizzled as the two metal pieces clanged together.

"I've been here for fifty years, dummy! Do you think I haven't been training? You can't save yourself, and you can't save your friend, either." He waved his remote again, ready to hit Sonny.

A shadow loomed over Jack, snatching his sword from him. The sword instantly began surging with magic as Mr. Shadow pointed it and his shadow tackled Teddy. "Sonny," he whispered to her.

Jack stared at the hooded holiday spirit, who continued looking at Sonny. Before he could form a question, he felt Old Man Winter's bitter cold resurface.

"Argh!" The fingertips of the dazed cloud keeper Teddy was controlling were barely touching the frozen orb left behind by the winter judge. An ice patch appeared on the ground, turning the water soldiers into snowmen fighting the elemental rock. The cloud keeper cracked instantly before shattering, just as Winter had.

The snowmen soldiers continued fighting, but the emperor melted and cut them with every strike. The remaining judges used their abilities to push the emperor toward the well. Leaves fluttered from the bear Autumn had created. Sand littered the ground around Summer, and puddles were left from the melting snowy soldiers.

"You are not strong enough!" The emperor seemed to become every element at once. He blended into a smoking whirlwind with dark-red eyes, repelling the judges. Smoky limbs threw cloud keepers into the ceiling. The whirlwind deflected the judges' attacks, nearly hitting Jack. Mr. Shadow sailed through the air, knocking Sonny's chained body repeatedly into the wall.

"There is no season, no being, and no monster more powerful or more frightening than me!" the emperor roared, still held in by the chains.

Mr. Shadow watched Sonny's head dip. He reached out to her, but she only stirred slightly. He turned and drove his sword into the ground. "The true horror and strength of a monster is the moment just after it leaves the shadow." The hood flew from his head, and his cloak came off his shoulders. It fluttered to the ground just as the pumpkin handle rolled off the sword.

The small pumpkin grew limbs and a body made of straw like a scarecrow's, and the cloak on the ground filled with crawling worms and bugs until it was stuffed and self-stitched with arms, legs, and a head. The frail-looking old man beneath Mr. Shadow's hood was finally exposed. Pale and bald, he had a sharp nose. His eyes were dark, and he had no smile, but an aura of shadowy purple magic surrounded him, making him appear much more powerful than before.

His body changed into pure shadow as he attacked the demon element. His two new monsters followed as he yelled to Jack. "My Pumpkin King and Boogie Man will only hold them off so long. Get Sonny to safety—now!"

Jack was shocked back into reality as he realized every cloud keeper was lying on the ground helplessly, the three seasons were fighting off their own powers, and Jack had no weapon. He searched for a key or Rocho to help him free her. Finally, he spotted the flashlight buried in broken floor pieces in a corner near the prepared shuttle pod. Jack rushed to it, shielding himself from falling parts of ceiling, before noticing Teddy was already there. He waved Sonny's pen, taunting Jack while standing next to the shuttle pod. Something was moving inside it, and Teddy had a truly smug look on his face.

"I have what I need to go home now, Jack." He held open the clear shuttle door. "But I need to make sure no one can follow me, and it won't transform on me. So give me the flashlight, and I'll let you have what you've really been searching for. It's a fair trade."

"What I've been searching for?" Jack's eyes suddenly widened. "Dad?"

"You really are not as smart as you think you are, dork." Teddy shook his head. "Tell me where the flashlight is, and everything goes back to the way it should have been. I just wanna go home to my own parents. Well, at least back to my mother. What would you risk to get back to your parents? It's too late to—"

The monster element pulled on the pillars surrounding him. Jack registered that it was to escape those unique chains by destroying what they were connected to. The pillars tumbled down, crashing behind Teddy and propelling him over to the hole above the well. He managed to grab onto the ledge before falling in. Jack could hear the whispers begging for him to drop. "New… life," he thought he heard the well repeat. At the same moment, the door slammed on the shuttle his father was locked in, and it was preparing to take off. He could see Teddy losing his grip on the lip of the opening. Jack felt the same hesitation he had over Peddlin' Pete.

Jack was already stepping toward his father before he heard Teddy yell out, grunting to climb back up. He watched the shuttle powering up on one side and Teddy on the other. *Why do I even care about Teddy?* he debated with himself. *Why should I care what happens to him? He'll just keep coming after me. After my dad… whoever he works for won't ever—* He paused. None of it would stop unless he figured out who Teddy worked for, and that would mean saving him. The awareness came in a flash—he didn't have time to rescue them both.

A fresh breeze rushed in from the open sky revealed by the caved-in ceiling. It chilled the metal band on his wrist, and Jack remembered he might have time after all. The watch on his wrist continued to tick away. The magic to turn it back was gone, but if he moved the hand forward…

He adjusted the dials, and everything around him continued on its current pace. The remaining seasons fought the demon emperor, with the help of Mr. Shadow and his two monsters. Green fire radiated from the Pumpkin King, while rotten candy and insects swarmed around the Boogie Man when they attacked.

But Jack also found two blurry images of himself moving into view, like fuzzy ghost versions. One ran to his father's shuttle, picking up his flashlight. He and Rocho both struggled to open the shuttle door. The other him ran to the hole, where he grabbed Teddy's hand before the boy could fall into the well. Then both images faded. It only lasted a few seconds, but it was enough. He sprinted to the edge of the well, sliding face-first with his arms outstretched. Just as Teddy lost his grip and began falling, Jack caught his arm.

"I've got you." Jack pulled. "Don't let go."

The look Teddy gave Jack was so unexpected, Jack nearly slipped.

"Why are *you* helping me?" Teddy spat, disgusted.

"I wanna go home just as badly as you do," Jack said. "I need to get into that shuttle and help my dad first. I might as well be pushing you in myself if I didn't help you. Let me help you get home, and you can help me save him."

Teddy gave him the same smirk he always did when he was about to do something unexpected or cruel. "That totem your *girlfriend's* been writing with was created from the ancient totem, dork. It was the very first one from the first challenge. Has power no other totem does. I could come and go from either plane anytime I want, and I dropped it in the shuttle. Nobody will get to it now."

"We can if you stop being stubborn and let me get you up."

The dark dead spirits with their grim and decaying withered faces suddenly began clawing for Teddy to be dropped.

"Maybe you could empty your pockets or something? Make it a little easier for me to help you."

"I don't need you!" he yelled, yanking his arm away with each pull. "I don't need any of you. You and these holiday spirits and those judges are the reason I'm here. My job is done, and now, I will be rewarded."

"What job?" Jack only had him by a few fingers, as Teddy wasn't helping at all. "Tell me what this is all about!"

The ground shook, and the flashlight rolled toward him. Teddy grinned bigger than ever with a deranged look in his eyes. "I just needed to set the pieces in motion. The emperor has done his job, and so have I." He pulled himself farther on Jack's arm so he felt much heavier. He was slowly dragging them both into the hole. Teddy pulled himself closer and whispered in Jack's ear, "Father will save me."

With a quick jerk of his arm, Teddy released himself from Jack's fingers. "Father will save me… Father will save me…" He continued falling, wearing that broad evil grin as those echoes grew louder than Jack had ever experienced. The black wisps of dead spirits completely swallowed Teddy's body.

Behind Jack, an alarm sounded and an engine powered on. Smoke filled the courtroom. As Jack watched helplessly, the shuttle pod blasted off. The seasons attempted to fight off the emperor, but it was strangely quiet, as if the dead spirits in the well had finally gotten a much-needed meal. He wasn't sure how much time had passed when he heard a loud crash, followed by Mr. Shadow calling his name.

He snapped out of it and ran toward the empty shuttle port, scooping up his flashlight. It instantly changed into the pup, and Rocho seemed ready and eager. He blazed through the courtroom with lighting speed and morphed into his bear size just before smashing into the emperor. Rocho seemed more powerful than ever. If possible, he was bigger than Jack remembered—and radiating static. His fur was spiked down the middle, and the electricity was brighter. Instead of a golden yellow, it was nearly white, singeing his fur like the gradual burn of paper and sparking in every direction.

The emperor only laughed at this challenge, changing his arms into sharpened stone as the pup rallied Summer's swimming sand shark, Autumn's feral leafy bear, and Spring's misty multiplying dragonfly with just a few barks. Each judge's animal protector floated in a line behind Rocho.

"Spirit animals?" The emperor laughed. "Your loyalty will be rewarded. A new cemetery will be built in your honor."

During a flash of claws, rock pillars, spilled candy, and straw, Jack finally ran toward Sonny as Mr. Shadow had instructed. He pulled on the chains that held her, but they wouldn't budge. She was still barely conscious, dangling from the wall. "Sonny, you gotta wake up."

The Spirit of Halloween continued looking back at Jack and Sonny as the elemental emperor destroyed Summer's sand shark and chased Autumn. Onyx turned his body to pure ice, stomping his massive foot onto the floor. The ground instantly turned to glossy ice, covering the hole before he could fall in.

Jack carried on looking for a key, searching the pockets of fallen cloud keepers as Autumn, covered in a suit of armored leaves, was nearly drowned. Jack ducked Summer taunting Onyx as he searched another pocket. The only things Jack found were items he'd picked up since the Holiday Hotel: the defective mask, Holly's bottomless sack, the hand buzzer ring, a skeleton keycard, and his nearly silver coin from Lucky.

"I don't see a key anywhere," Jack called up to Sonny. Her eyes flickered open, and she seemed to be following the battle as a section of the wall was smashed through. The open air of the hovering room flowed through from every new hole. Jack was forced to crouch as a pillar crumbled from above.

He looked up, trying to reassure her. "I'll find something to break the cuffs off, and we can get you down."

"Jack!" Her eyes never left the fight as she called after him. "I think I recognize Mr. Shadow."

Jack began to turn around when he heard Rocho growling from a corner. The emperor had broken through Summer's mound of beach sand and was now being pelted by volleyballs."

Rocho leaped from one broken pillar to the next, shocking the air, making it impossible for the emperor to change into water without suffering.

"Max Heat is on fire, bro," Summer said, using long whips of seaweed to lash at Onyx until he fell to a knee. The emperor was continuously shocked by every movement Rocho made. "I've got a sandcastle prison waiting for you when I'm done. You've just been beaten by the hottest season around, dude."

The emperor roared loudly, morphing into a mix of water and earth that allowed him to resist Rocho's bolts. He caught Summer by the leg.

"Fire." The fallen emperor took Summer in two massive rocky fists before setting himself ablaze. "With fire."

The ice around the arena melted, and even Jack began to feel faint as he tried to avoid being seen still searching for something to help Sonny. Steam swelled through the courtroom as the flames evaporated the melting ice. The straw of the Pumpkin King caught fire instantly, as did the sack holding the Boogie Man together. The air coming from outside fanned the flames, and Summer began to wail in pain.

A shadow raced across the room with the pumpkin-handled sword in hand, followed by a dozen more with shadowy daggers. One by one, they each struck Onyx's shadow. The shadow weapons sliced through his body until he released Summer, who fell next to Autumn, unmoving.

"Shadow?" Onyx searched the broken room that seemed to tilt in his weight. "Where have you been hiding? Still playing the opportune chess move. I wonder what you will do when there are no more shadows to hide behind…"

He turned up his fire, erupting in flames and filling the room with light. The shadows tried to hold the emperor by dragging his shadow down, but the light was warping them all. Mr. Shadow dove toward the emperor, but Onyx swatted him away like a fly. Mr. Shadow's sword sailed over the sky hole. Jack ran to catch it just before it fell over the ledge.

The emperor stared down at the final judge who remained standing. Trembling, Spring backed into a corner. Rocho ran to her aid, barking wildly. Jack struck Sonny's cuffs with the sword, hacking, stabbing, and prying up with everything he could muster, but the clasp wouldn't budge. He finally stopped when he heard a loud whimper.

Rocho lay in the corner in front of Spring, soaked in water and sizzling. He was panting hard as Spring stroked his matted wet fur. "You're a bully! I'm not afraid of you."

"Oh no, Spring," Onyx responded, raising his rocky fists in the air. "I am no bully. I am simply taking what rightfully belongs to me. I know they would only trust you with the key to free me. And now you'll learn what they all have learned. The world should only be ruled by one."

He brought his hands down like hammers but stopped suddenly with an uncontrollable jerk. He fought forward, but he wasn't able to attack. The chains seemed to be tightening the more he struggled. He turned to see Jack standing behind him.

Jack was holding Teddy's remote. "I've got your key right here, matchstick." Jack pushed and twisted random knobs, trying to control Onyx. His rocky limbs slammed to his sides, but his head was free. He blew Jack back, and the remote skidded across the broken floor. Jack scurried back for it, but the antenna was snapped off, and the buttons ceased working.

"Foolish boy." The emperor snarled. "You should've run away."

"Jack, just go!" Sonny yelled. "Go… why are you still here?"

He moved back as Emperor Onyx advanced. Jack remembered what he'd gone through in the challenge—how hard it was to stand up to mechanical hybrids, walk away from hallucinations, watch people being sacrificed in an arena, journey through a cursed swamp, and fight a colossal giant. He didn't know how much of it was him and how much was sleepwalking, but it all felt real enough to him.

Looking over at Sonny, he knew exactly why he stayed. "You… you gave me a reason to be."

"You could've escaped." The emperor rounded on Jack. More monstrous than ever, he towered over the bodies that littered the ground, bringing a clawed hand over his chest. "You could have lived, boy. I pitied you dreamers. Mere children forced into these challenges, suffering as my children had by these false rulers, but you still choose them… whispers of your story have flooded the courtroom for months now. You wish to be with your dead father? You wish your family to be whole again? I will happily arrange it. I will end your mother's life and drag her body across the planes myself, so she can watch you and your weak father beg for my mercy, because there is no one left to stand in the way of my freedom."

"I am." Jack gritted his teeth in anger as he brought the pumpkin-handled sword out of the shadows, using the wall to get him to his feet. "I might be standing between a rock and a hard place, but I'm still standing. If it's the last thing I do, I will drive this blade so far into you that pumpkin spice will be a new element."

He swung his sword but was caught by the emperor lifting Jack with a single rocky fist. He blew Jack back at the wall with a bitter wind, pinning him against the icy door. Jack crashed onto the floor. He felt his chest tighten and something in his shoulder crack.

A large flame formed in Onyx's fist. "Look at you, pathetic child. What could you have done to the rightful leader of the world? You will both be gone soon enough. Why would you bother to continue? So she may watch you die? What makes her so important to you? What is she to you?"

Jack took a shaky breath, barely able to lift his head. With his eyes focused not on the monster in front of him, but on Sonny, he said, "She's… the only friend I have."

The ball of fire raged in the demon emperor's fist before he hurled it at Jack. He stood ready with the sword in his hands, embracing what was coming next. But he wasn't ready. Burning fur engulfed his senses, followed by the sound of a sharp whimper. Jack opened his eyes to see Rocho in his bear size, trembling just a few feet away, a large burning gash in his side. His glowing eyes drifted to Jack before drooping closed. Jack dropped the sword, shaking his faithful dog in disbelief, but Rocho didn't stir and remained un-breathing.

"At last… freedom." The emperor picked up the remaining piece of Teddy's remote. His chains unraveled to the ground. He turned to Spring, stretching his arms with renewed power. "The last season left standing. For my own children's sacrifice as the seasons attempted to do to you, I show mercy to you, boy. This will be your final warning. Stay here, and you will die."

"I already have." Tears swelled in Jack's eyes, and his vision was blurry as a small bit of sun came through the clouds of the destroyed ceiling. A calming hatred expanding in his chest, he glared at Onyx, who turned toward Spring. "Do you know what it felt like?"

Before Emperor Onyx was able to get close to Spring, he lurched back. Something sharp stuck out of his chest just below the center of the core where his heart should have been. The pumpkin-handled sword had been impaled through him, and Jack stood hunched behind him, one arm lifeless, barely able to breathe or stand, and tears streaming down his stern face. The heart symbol transferred from his totem illuminated as shadow magic swirled out. It was black and tar-like swarming around the emperor's back, shoulders, legs, and soon most of its body. Only the elemental core shining brightly kept the shadow away. The sunlight began burning the shadow-covered parts, and his body steamed, but the sun's rays soon faded, covered in more clouds. Onyx shook his head, disappointed. He appeared barely fazed by the shadowy sword or Jack.

"Leave him alone," Sonny pleaded.

Hunger in his eyes, Onyx loosed a savage growl.

Jack looked down at Rocho sprawled helplessly on the ground. He stood in front of the pup, ready to take the final blow, defending the last connection to his father, just as his companion had for him. Onyx held a magnificent grin, staring down at Jack, charging across the courtroom ignited in every form.

Shaking her chains, Sonny called out, "Stop, leave him alone!"

Jack raised his chin with a final look at Sonny, who continued yelling the last thing he knew he'd hear from her. Panic struck her face, and her arms flailed wildly as she continued to shout. "Leave him alone. Leave him alone! Leave him *alone!*"

Onyx raised his arms into the air. The air sizzled with energy ready to rain down on Jack.

A blinding-white light flickered behind the emperor, who stopped charging, casting a large shadow over Jack. A deafening crash followed as the remainder of the building began peeling away as if an explosion had occurred. Jack covered his ears, only able to focus on the emperor standing over him. The structure surrounding them crumbled until only the floor was left.

Jack felt the sun had somehow left the sky, come down into the courtroom, and exploded. As he felt the temperature rise, the light became too blinding to look at directly. A moment later, the dishonored emperor was petrified. His arms, legs, and head turned black like burning wood, beams of light burning holes into his body and shining through the other side. He crumbled away like ash until the un-living core of elements were the only pieces left.

Jack was still covering his eyes but could make out a figure appearing behind Onyx. An aura of golden-white light surrounded a girl with fiery blond hair. A pair of barely visible wings expanded as she drifted toward Jack. Tears twinkled on her face as she floated with a furious gaze he'd never seen, like a mother lion protecting her cub. Her clothes had gone completely white, but those green eyes were unmistakable.

Sonny floated toward Jack, her face sharp and determined. Her yell still reverberated in every direction, although her mouth was closed. She inched closer, her hands out. Jack timidly stretched his hand to her's as if she were a savior. She drew closer, until they were only a foot or so apart. Then, suddenly, the light dimmed, the wings vanished, and she collapsed to the floor like a doll.

"Sonny?" Jack crawled over. "Sonny… Sonny!"

He cradled her in his arms and shook her, but she didn't move, and her breathing was shallow. He continued calling her name, begging her to wake up.

"Give her to me." Mr. Shadow, nursing a nasty head wound, shook Jack's shoulder, startling him.

Jack refused to let go.

"It's all right, boy. Let me see her."

Jack stared at her closed eyes before finally letting Mr. Shadow take a look at her.

"She's still breathing. We need to get her the right kind of help. The Sisters of the Sun will know what to do with her."

"Why?" Jack asked finally. "What made you help me now?"

Mr. Shadow gripped his chest. "It became personal… once I remembered."

"How do you forget your own granddaughter?" Jack blurted out to Mr. Shadow's mild surprise. "Yeah, I figured it out. You used the same type of yellow notepad paper Sonny does. And there's a picture that was shipped here in the iPlane when we sailed to Cloud City. I saw the same picture later on your mantel. You had other pictures, too."

"My wife." Mr. Shadow nodded, still looking at Sonny. "Some spirits have a harder time letting go of their past lives. I had Dr. de Luca remove my heart so I wouldn't remember my family anymore until I was ready to move on. But seeing my granddaughter in this world triggered something. I knew I should remember her."

"So you really were heartless?" Jack said. "The heart in the jar was yours. That doesn't make any sense. I don't understand how removing your heart would make you forget her."

"We don't have time for this."

"*Tell me!*" Jack insisted, grabbing the spirit's arm.

"Memories are held in the mind, boy, but loved ones… they are always kept in the heart." The Halloween Spirit gently put a hand on Sonny's forehead. "I'd forgotten my granddaughter, forgotten my daughter who left us all, and even my lovely wife. The pictures in my home were hidden from the doctor so I could keep a piece of them. They were all I had left. It just hurt too much to keep those memories and not have them."

"I guess that included my neighbor," Jack said.

Cloud keepers, Autumn, and Summer began to wake. There was a loud knocking on the icy door, but Jack ignored it.

"That's why she was in that picture. It was her and Sonny. What are the odds you would be married to my widowed neighbor, Mrs. Johnson?"

"Those odds would be impossible. This is something else." Before Mr. Shadow could finish, Redd Rocket crashed through the door, carrying a shoulder-mounted rocket launcher, but was instantly disappointed when he realized the fight was already over. Cloud keepers and other spirits flowed in behind him. Detective Young was still twitching from the shock Teddy had given him, but he ordered his officers to begin working at once and to check everyone who might've been sleepwalking on Teddy's command. There was a close moment when one of them nearly touched the floating ball of glowing ice.

"Stop!" the detective yelled. "Nobody touches the essence of Winter."

A cloud keeper backed away from the blue orb. "What happened in here? We saw the light shining through the clouds like a bomb had erupted."

"It was her." Spring stepped in from a corner, pointing at Sonny. "She stopped the emperor. She's a guardian. She projected pure sunlight."

Autumn and Summer gasped as more cloud keepers rushed in through the portal. They carefully lifted Sonny onto a floating carpet. The Sisters of the Sun were waiting just outside the entrance, praying silently. The holiday spirits, however, appeared just as confused as Jack felt.

He continued watching Sonny. "What's a guardian?"

"A very old and rare breed of spirits," Autumn answered. "They are ancient spirits originally chosen by the two beings to cross over into the living world and live among you. They have no knowledge of who they are when they are born into your world, but often find worthy people and help them in times of need."

Jack stared at her. "I don't understand. Are you saying she's a spirit? That she's dead?"

Summer shook his head. "No, bro, not at all. Her spirit is no different than yours, except it's totally older. Like one thousand years old, reincarnation style. It just gets recycled every new life, kinda like Phoenix, but regular life, not *after*life. Her spirit has gifts she would never know about. At least until she came here and had to protect whoever she's clinging to. Which looks like might be you, dude." Summer smiled.

"Like a guardian angel?" Jack said to himself. He watched as the J.A.C.K.s attended to the injured and worked to contain the elemental core. The room had been nearly destroyed, and he suddenly felt the weight of it sticking to his heart as he sat up and walked over to Rocho. "I'm so proud of you, Rocho. I'm sorry I wasn't as strong as you." Jack stroked his fur, and the pup instantly changed to the flashlight. Jack was surprised that any magic still worked in it.

The Spirit of Father's Day stepped through the portal and went directly to Jack. "I felt it the moment it happened — your father and Rocho. I'm sorry, son."

The flashlight looked worn but capable as Jack held it carefully in his hand. "He sacrificed himself for me."

"The next season will be chosen," Autumn announced. "The essence of winter will be carried on. When it is time, a worthy successor will take their place among us. It must remain here. If anyone touches the orb and is deemed unworthy, their fate will be judged just as coldly."

"Is that understood?" the lead investigator asked. "No one goes near it. We will tape it off but allow the judges to take care of this matter."

Jack stared at the port where his father had been moments ago. The Spirit of Father's Day put a hand on his shoulder, but Jack stepped away from him. He wasn't sure if he was just upset or if it had something to do with Teddy's last words as the dreamer fell, but Jack didn't care at the moment.

"After everything I went through, I still couldn't save them." Jack sighed. "My dad… Sonny… Rocho… even Teddy. Winter sacrificed himself to save Spring, but what could I do?"

"You did everything you could do, son," Father assured him. "What happened, you had no way of controlling, or slowing down. It was going to happen the way it did. The Sisters of the Sun will know how to help Sonny. As for the pup, he may never be the same, but that doesn't mean he's gone. I created the totem, and something may be possible."

"And my dad?" Jack turned. "I don't even know where he is, and Sonny's pen is with him. Where was that shuttle going?"

Father hesitated, but Autumn was nearby. "They were sent where we intended to send the container imprisoning the Sandman. Oracle Island is the prison for dangerous entities like the Sandman. Your father will, unfortunately, be sent there and assumed a prisoner, just as the essence of the Sandman will be."

"*What?* We have to get him back."

Autumn shook her head with that same unmoving expression. "That is not possible. The shuttles are sent in from the prison, but no one knows where to find it. We are only able to send messages once the shuttle returns. However, that could take months, as they are sent randomly. There is no way to track it or find the island. Unless you have been to the island, it is impossible to locate. And no one who has ever been to the island has ever escaped it to tell where it is located. I am sorry."

Father shook his head. "See? You couldn't possibly venture out there alone. You would never survive. I'm sorry, but I can't allow you to do that. You're only a boy."

Jack looked depressed, but someone else had been listening to him, as well.

"He is not just a boy," Detective Young said. "He is a detective. Or he will be when I am through with him."

Jack turned slowly. "What do you mean?"

"In my position, I cannot interfere with the system in place on the island," the investigator continued. "It is protected by J.I.L.L.s, which is an entirely different division. Jurisdiction Island Law Limiters are among the most elite officers. You have been trained to fight, hunt, and survive, but I will teach you to be a real detective."

"Why would you help me?" Jack asked.

"Innocent people shouldn't be punished, and I have seen you suffer enough for one lifetime." His badge gleamed in the dying embers. "This will not be like fighting in an arena, training for the challenge with holiday spirits, or hiding from a city of sleepwalkers. I only care about results, as breaking into this prison will be the hardest thing you've ever done, and breaking out will be nearly impossible. It won't just test you; it will break you by doing everything it can to keep the prisoners in—and you out."

The detective leaned in closer to Jack. "I will train you the way you should be trained. I will teach you the skills you've dreamed of having. I will train you in the art of seeing what others miss, detecting the missing connections, and glimpsing into a person's mind."

"He's only thirteen," the Father's Day Spirit argued. "Jack, this man is very good at what he does, but he is dangerous. He reimagined the officers who protect us today and trained the J.I.L.L.s used on the island. His training methods are less than traditional. We can find another way to rescue your father."

"There is an art to everything. A thin line separates brilliance and insanity, and that is where art really survives," Detective Young said. "If you agree, I will teach you that art. Are you prepared to remove all fear and doubt? Be broken down to be rebuilt stronger?"

Jack looked back at the empty space where the shuttle had been, then at the chipped lens of his burned flashlight. A bitter disappointment swelled in his chest. "I have nothing left of me to lose."

Detective Young removed his black sunglasses from his eyes, glaring at Jack intently. "You'll need time to recover, but once you do, we will find out just how true that is."

The next two days were a blur of hospital lights and faces on Cloud Nine. Jack was focused entirely on getting back on his course to find his father. The news buzzing around the city mostly involved his lawyer Cassandra declaring his case won and the essence of Winter being guarded after his sacrifice to save the city. Neither Jack's nor Sonny's involvement in stopping Emperor Onyx from escaping was mentioned, and the cloud keepers told Jack that was for their protection, to keep Sonny's light show from becoming public. Jack was a few days behind locating his father, and it was the longest period he'd gone without seeing Sonny since he'd met her. It was also the longest he'd gone without his flashlight.

As Jack prepared to leave, his doctors visited once again.

"It seems some good rest has made you as strong as ever." The witch doctor Jack had met his first day in Cloud City, with a partial skull mask covering his face, checked over Jack.

"Heart seems strong, breathing regular, and your wounds seem to be healing quickly. Looks like you are still alive. That is good news for you. I've asked Dr. de Luca to see if you are mentally prepared to leave."

"You're worried about my mental state?" Jack asked the Valentine's Day Spirit, offended. "I thought they cleared me of all the sand."

"We have," Dr. de Luca assured Jack. "The entire city has been cleansed of the Sandman—we are absolutely sure of it now. The remainder is safely sealed and on its course, but there are things we must discuss with you."

Jack sat up. "Is something wrong with Sonny?"

"No, no. I've been told the Sisters of the Sun have been caring for her, and she is recovering nearly as quickly as you."

"But… they still won't let me see her?" Jack sighed.

"Not for the moment. The Sisters say she is a very special girl and want to make sure she understands what she needs to about her episode in the courtroom. I wouldn't worry about her too much. As you know, every cloud has a silver lining."

"Yeah, I've been told." Jack rolled his eyes. "And I've known she was special for months. She believes in aliens, clones, conspiracies, and just happens to be a guardian angel. Explains why she's constantly upbeat when I thought someone had been giving her Island Fiz."

"Chances are she won't remember everything that happened," the doctor said. "Her spirit is old, but she has no knowledge of it. Keep that in mind."

Jack was curious about another dreamer, but that feeling of guilt was creeping into his stomach. "What about Teddy? And Winter, for that matter? He saved Spring. Is he really gone?"

"Winter's essence is all that remains, but fate will choose another when it is time, as it was meant to." Despite the hovering white mask, Jack saw the grim expression that flashed over the Valentine's Day Spirit's face. "As for the hole the dreamer fell into, it funnels directly into the well. You are familiar with that particular well, I believe?"

"You could say that." Jack nodded, remembering the whispers and the grim, lifeless looks on so many decaying gray souls.

"It has never happened before, but I can only say that when a dreamer like Theodore enters the well, those lost souls there will latch on to any form of life they can, and the well will swallow him just like any other energy. There is no returning from it—it is death for those in the afterlife. He is forever lost there. I'm sorry, Jack, but death itself would have to reject him to bring him back now."

More confused than before, Jack gazed around the small hospital room. "I don't understand. Why is there a well? How do spirits die if they're already spirits? Why do you even have a hospital?"

"The afterlife isn't much different from the life we had before. We still eat, sleep, laugh, cry. Both good and bad things happen to us, but here, the afterlife can last much longer, spirits don't age, and the ability of magical beings is obviously much more visible. Not everyone is like the holiday spirits in Cloud City. There are more cities and areas filled with spirits enjoying their afterlife who do not have the abilities we holiday spirits do. Like your father, who created the hotel, which I believe has much to do with you."

"There's no way my dad would end up in that well, is there?"

The Valentine's Day Spirit sighed before answering. "Like most deaths, it isn't something any of us like discussing. It would take a large amount of force to destroy someone's spirit. Bad spirits are weakened the moment they cross over, which makes them much easier to be taken by the force inside it. The well takes the most violent souls. I wouldn't worry about your father. He was a good man in both his life and afterlife. His spirit is strong."

Jack looked away.

"Do not blame yourself, Jack. Mr. Shadow told me what you tried to do. You could not save Teddy if he didn't want to be saved."

"Actually, he was sure he was going to be saved," Jack said. "Just by someone else."

"That is another matter I must discuss with you before you take leave." Dr. de Luca handed Jack an object wrapped in a thin cloth. "Your flashlight was mended as well as could be."

Jack removed the wrappings carefully, exposing his green flashlight. It had been buffed to a shine, and the magnifying glass had been mended. Only an internal chip remained in the inlaid glass, but the gold writing glittered brilliantly. Jack touched his flashlight as if it were a fragile glass egg. It changed slowly into the loyal pup. Large gold eyes stared up at Jack as if the fight had never happened. Jack lifted the puppy and hugged him tightly as Rocho licked his cheek happily.

"I was asked to warn you that he won't ever be the same," the doctor said. "He will never be strong enough to grow into his larger size again."

"He's the strongest little pup I've ever met," Jack said, staring into those large, excited eyes. "I don't care what anyone else says."

"Well, Father just wanted to warn you after spending the last two days fixing it, especially if you are still thinking of going to the island." The doctor stepped closer to Jack's bedside. "And training with the city's detective."

"I definitely don't care what *he* has to say about it all." Jack remembered Teddy's final words of being saved by Father and the warnings from before. He couldn't ignore the signs any longer.

"Well, be that as it may, he is not the only one who is against the idea of you rushing off," the doctor said sternly. "It is a journey I, as well as Redd, Holly, Lucky, and even Mr. Shadow believe you should avoid taking. We all understand how important it is to find your father, but this would simply force you into a situation you cannot win. No one has ever escaped the island, so you have no way of finding it. I am sorry, Jack, but it can't be done."

Jack felt defeated. That was until a thought dawned on him like the sun's morning rays chasing away the night. "No, that's not entirely true. No one has ever escaped, but there is one spirit. The only one who has ever been to the island prison and returned. And fortunately for me, that spirit owes me a favor."

About the Author

Christian N. Wynn was born in California, and his father's military service took the family all over the United States. For over twenty years he has called Delaware home. The personal experiences of his friends and family are often his most important inspiration for the characters and stories he creates, including the middle-grade fiction series, *The Jack Taylor Cases*. This series has been described as *The Hardy Boys Mysteries* meets *The Nightmare Before Christmas*.

Along with the *Jack Taylor Cases*, Mr. Wynn's future writing plans include a book series about strange summer vacations, a trilogy of children's books featuring warrior teddy bears, and a book of fables based on characters in the *Jack Taylor Cases* with the profits from the publication being donated to charity. When he isn't writing, Christian enjoys slipping obscure movie lines into conversations, collecting refrigerator magnets from his travels, and reading written works by Rick Riordan, Suzanne Collins, and Daniel Handler. He's also a Hufflepuff and a Los Angeles Chargers fan.

You can find more about Christian Wynn and the Jack Taylor Cases at www.jacktaylorcases.com.

www.jacktaylorcases.com
facebook.com/jacktaylorcases
twitter.com/jacktaylorcases